Selected praise fo— ... **by bes—**

"A first-class thrill ride from a top-notch talent.
Cameron Cruise is going to be around for a long time."
—John Lescroart

"Ms. Cruise delves deep into these two characters and
comes up with pay dirt. Seven and Erika are phenomenal.
Complex and edgy, *The Collector* is a wild, twisty ride into
a dark, creepy terror. As a post note, [it] will have a sequel—
maybe even become a series. I hope so. I am not ready
to leave Ms. Cruise's wonderful characters just yet."
—*Romance Reader at Heart*

"Cameron Cruise is a phenomenal new talent.
The Collector is compulsive reading! The details are rich
and meaty, the pace brisk and the edge razor sharp."
—*New York Times* bestselling author Suzanne Forster

"*The Collector* is an extraordinary multi-faceted novel…
Intriguing…a story you cannot forget."
—*The Mystery Reader*

"Cruise's debut has a serpentine, impossible-to-adequately-
summarize plot and a wealth of interesting characters.
But what really makes an impression is the story's sense of
time, place and culture."
—*Romantic Times BOOKreviews*

"A check-under-the-bed read from Cameron Cruise! Talent
and dramatic instinct conspire in this powerful novel."
—Bestselling author Stella Cameron

DARK MATTER

CAMERON CRUISE

MIRA®

If you purchased this book without a cover you should be aware that this book is stolen property. It was reported as "unsold and destroyed" to the publisher, and neither the author nor the publisher has received any payment for this "stripped book."

MIRA

ISBN-13: 978-0-7783-2503-1
ISBN-10:   0-7783-2503-2

DARK MATTER

Copyright © 2008 by Olga Gonzalez-Bicos.

All rights reserved. Except for use in any review, the reproduction or utilization of this work in whole or in part in any form by any electronic, mechanical or other means, now known or hereafter invented, including xerography, photocopying and recording, or in any information storage or retrieval system, is forbidden without the written permission of the publisher, MIRA Books, 225 Duncan Mill Road, Don Mills, Ontario, Canada M3B 3K9.

This is a work of fiction. Names, characters, places and incidents are either the product of the author's imagination or are used fictitiously, and any resemblance to actual persons, living or dead, business establishments, events or locales is entirely coincidental.

MIRA and the Star Colophon are trademarks used under license and registered in Australia, New Zealand, Philippines, United States Patent and Trademark Office and in other countries.

www.MIRABooks.com

Printed in U.S.A.

For Jonathan.

1

The first thing Jack heard was the *drip-drip* of water. The first thing he felt was metal biting into his wrist.

Handcuffs?

He felt groggy, like maybe he was dreaming, stuck in those magic moments right before his eyelids fluttered open and he woke up. He tried hard to hang on. Sometimes, he could do it…fall back into the story in his head.

Jack didn't like to wake up. Waking up meant being cold and hungry.

He felt cold, but not hungry. That was different.

"Jack?"

The voice sounded far away. Jack looked around the room, squinting in the dim light. He shivered. Someone there? Standing over him?

He tugged at his hand and heard metal rattling. Handcuffs—the real kind. A rush of adrenaline hit.

Not a dream.

He felt sick. He was going to throw up. *Shit!* What had he gotten himself into?

He hadn't done a lot of drugs. Sure, there was always the occasional john who wanted to get him a little loose, giving him a few drinks. Men didn't like to think they could hurt a kid. Jack always assured them he was seventeen, but could pass for a lot younger. He'd never tell them his real age, fourteen.

He yanked the hand strung up by the handcuff, trying not to freak out.

"You're awake."

The voice sounded familiar. Jack blinked up at the blurry image hovering over him and tried to focus. He remembered going to dinner last night, some fancy Italian place where he'd eaten his fill. But he'd only drunk a soda. So why did he feel so weird?

"You know what they used to call it in the old days? You'll get a kick out of this. They called it a Mickey Finn. I slipped you a Mickey, Jack."

Jack reached up to rub his eyes, only to have his hand stop dead, his wrist tethered to something solid and heavy. He realized he was propped up against some piece of furniture, a desk maybe.

The guy, the john from last night, leaned closer. His breath smelled minty fresh with Altoids.

"These days, they call it a roofie. You know what that is, don't you, Jack?"

The guy said *roofie* like he was having fun with it. His lips wrapped around the word, giving it a slight whistle. Through the haze in his head, Jack remembered that smile. Last night, he'd thought it was nice.

They were in some kind of basement. There was a musty, earthy smell and a naked lightbulb hung in the middle of the room, giving off a bleary glow. The guy was close enough that Jack could see his even, white teeth.

A roofie was a well-known date-rape drug. Basically, it knocked you out. Eventually, when you woke up, you never knew what hit you.

"How do you feel?" the man asked.

"Like an ice pick is having a go at my head," Jack answered.

"An ice pike? Yikes."

The fuzzy image gelled into longish red hair that feathered around the man's face, vivid blue eyes and a strong nose. And dimples; Jack remembered those from last night, too.

The guy was young, maybe in his early twenties. Even though he had red hair, he didn't have a freckle on him. Jack remembered thinking he could be one of those models on the billboards; he was that good-looking. And tall, like maybe six feet five or something. Nothing like his usual john.

The sights and sounds from the night before flooded Jack's brain. The guy standing over him—last night he'd told Jack his name was Adam—had picked Jack up at his usual corner at Hollywood and Vine. He'd taken him to dinner. A *real* dinner, like Jack was someone who deserved a menu and a waiter with a tie.

They'd both ordered sodas. Adam had asked for a root beer, Jack, a Pepsi.

In the old days, they called it a Mickey Finn.

"You slipped me a roofie?" Jack said, his tongue thick and tired around the words.

"Had to." The guy stroked the side of Jack's face.

Jack pulled again on the handcuffs. He was having trouble catching his breath.

"What are you gonna do to me?"

Immediately, he regretted the question. When he'd first hit the street six months ago, the more experienced kids had let him know what was what. To get out of a mess like this, he had to act all cool, like he was in the know. The worst thing he could do was get all scared. The bad ones liked you scared.

Only, he felt so funky. Woozy and like he'd been sucking on a stick of chalk. With a hammer having a go at his
head. He had to concentrate—raise your right *hand*—but
still there was this time delay.

"It's the drug," Adam explained. "It makes you feel…
disjointed. Try not to worry, Jack. I promise. It won't hurt
too much."

Jack knew he'd landed in some serious shit. Here this
guy was smiling at him, looking like nothing was up. Sure,
Jack was handcuffed in some dark, damp cellar and this
weirdo was talking about pain. *So what,* that smile seemed
to ask? Nothing wrong here—not with such a beautiful
face shining down on him.

But then Jack saw that Adam was holding a needle, the
kind doctors used to give flu shots, only bigger. He plunged
the tip into a glass medicine bottle. The syringe filled with
a milky-white liquid. Jack blinked, forcing his eyes to
work, focusing on the handsome redhead and his smile.

"What are you doing?" he asked, the words slurring.

"Something very special. I'm going to make you a
superhero, Jack. Give you special powers. You'd like that,
wouldn't you? No more cold nights on the street, pimping
yourself out. I'm going to make you *someone.*"

The man named Adam winked, then leaned in close and
whispered in Jack's ear, "Trust me, Jack. It will be worth
it."

Jack didn't even see the needle coming when the guy
jabbed the syringe into his neck and sunk the plunger.

2

Gia Moon woke to the sound of screaming.

It took her a moment to understand she was actually awake. Screaming was a normal part of Gia's sleep; her dreams were often filled with the hideous imagery of bloodied body parts and faces contorted in pain. It didn't necessarily mean anything. It didn't *have* to be real, portents of things to come.

Only, tonight was different. Tonight the screams weren't Gia's.

She glanced at the digital clock on the nightstand: 3:07 a.m.

More screams. This time, she registered the source. The sounds clearly emanated from her daughter's room.

"Stella," she said, throwing back the covers.

Gia raced for the door and careened into the hall. She stumbled across the living room, bumping into the coffee table with her knee and sending last night's board game crashing to the floor.

Not so long ago, her daughter slept right alongside Gia in her king-size bed. Only recently had Stella started to flex her newly minted teen muscle, choosing to sleep in her own room. After a lifetime curled up next to her mother,

her daughter had proclaimed her independence shortly after her thirteenth birthday.

"Stella?" Gia cried, pushing open the bedroom door.

She found Stella sitting upright in bed. She looked like a puppet, her arms stiff at her sides and her legs sticking out like two planks of wood. In the dim glow of the night-light, Gia could see the sheets and quilt bunched at Stella's feet. She imagined her daughter kicking the covers aside as she swam up to the surface of her dreams.

Even with her eyes wide open, Stella kept screaming.

Gia swept her daughter up in her arms and held her tight. She made soft soothing sounds intended to help Stella transition out of her nightmare. Stella eventually quieted down, but her eyes remained fixed on something across the room.

Gia followed her daughter's gaze. She was staring at the stool in front of the Queen Anne vanity as if someone were sitting there.

"What is it, baby?" Gia whispered. "What do you see?"

But instead of answering, Stella buried her face in her mother's neck.

In a normal family, waking up screaming in the middle of the night might be explained as a simple night terror. No big deal. Any cause for concern would be temporary, nothing a kiss or a cup of hot cocoa couldn't fix. But normal didn't describe the lives of Gia and Stella Moon.

Gia felt her daughter trembling against her. Stella was small for her age, her tiny size a contrast to her great spirit. Stella had been born an old soul, not prone to hysterics. Waking up in the middle of the night, that would be Gia, the woman haunted by her gifts.

"I'm okay," Stella told her, all too soon pushing Gia away. "It was just a nightmare—a *real* nightmare," she assured her mother. "The normal kind."

The normal kind.

Not a vision, Gia thought with some relief.

Her daughter crawled back under the covers, pulling the quilt up to her chin. Tucked in her bed, her inky curls and vibrant blue eyes contrasted dramatically with her flawless white skin. Lying there, Stella presented a virtual Renaissance painting. Gia's artistic sensibilities appended the dewy full lips and cheeks, heightened in color from the nightmare. The antique sleigh bed with its starburst-pattern quilt in shades of blue was a fitting background. It wasn't quite chiaroscuro in the glow of the nightlight, but close.

Gia brushed back a curl from Stella's face. There was this perceived resemblance between mother and daughter. *Goodness, Gia, she's a mirror image. A clone.*

But Gia knew better. The dramatic coloring—black hair, blue eyes, translucent skin—deceived. Those curls, that delicate nose and dimpled chin, these were all Stella… Stella and Gia's mother, Estelle.

"Geez, Mom, you're freaking out for no reason, okay?" Stella added.

Gia hesitated, knowing when she was being dismissed. Suspicious of just that.

Sealing it, Stella closed her eyes and turned onto her side, giving her mother her back. "Don't be weird. I'm fine."

Which meant she was hiding something.

It happened more and more often these days: Stella shutting her out. Gia knew it was a normal part of growing up. She'd read all the books; teenagers needed space.

But tonight felt different. Secretive. And not in a good way.

She glanced back at the empty stool in front of the vanity. Only Gia and her daughter atop the sleigh bed reflected back in the mirror.

There wasn't even a glimmer of a presence.

Gia nodded toward the opened door and the hallway beyond. "Sure you don't want to crawl into bed with me? I could use the company."

Stella rolled her eyes, giving her a mental *puhleeze!* She settled deeper under the covers. "I just want to go back to sleep, okay?"

Once again, Stella gave her mother her back, but not before Gia caught her daughter's nervous glance toward the vanity and the empty stool.

Gia took a breath and held it. But in the end, she rose to her feet and stepped away from the bed. "All right, sweetie."

Out in the hall, Gia felt torn between her desire to run back into Stella's room or allow her daughter to set the pace for her revelations.

She knew Stella was lying. The question was *why?*

She froze at the entrance to the living room, her hand on the light switch, trying to shake off her fears. That look Stella had given the empty stool…there'd been a presence there. A presence Gia couldn't see.

Gia Moon, psychic artist and mother to one very precocious teenager, hadn't seen a damn thing.

She hit the light switch. The floor lamp glowed to life, spotlighting the Scrabble tiles scattered across the Navajo rug under the coffee table and the oak floor boards beyond.

The living room showcased her eclectic tastes. The top of the coffee table, a mosaic of broken pieces of china, served as a foil to the green papier-mâché leaves sprouting from the arms of the burgundy cloth sofa. The leaves crept up the wall behind as if some wayward philodendron had managed to take root and thrive in the darkened room.

Opposite the sofa stood a love seat covered in Mexican

serape cloth. There was quite a bit of religious art—a hand-painted crucifix with the bleeding heart, a Greek icon of the virgin, a statue of the elephant-headed Ganesha, the wise and gentle Hindu god known for removing obstacles.

But to Gia's eye, the focus as always was on her daughter. There were drawings, from stick figures to watercolors, matted and framed like great works of art. And photographs, each documenting cherished moments, snapshots of the tiny miracle that was Stella.

On her hands and knees, Gia picked up the lettered tiles and tossed them back into their box. She told herself she'd talk to Stella first thing in the morning. She'd learned the dangers of keeping secrets and she'd remind her daughter of just that. Gia suspected she knew what was bothering her daughter—Stella was just the right age. Gia needed to convince her that whatever changes Stella faced, they'd face them together.

That's what she'd been thinking—*tomorrow, I'll lay down the law, no secrets*—when she stopped herself in the act of scooping up the game pieces.

On the rug under the coffee table she saw five tiles from the Scrabble set. The game pieces formed a perfect half circle. She stared, realizing the letters spelled a word.

Seven. Just like the number.

Gia frowned. She reached for the *S*.

As her hand reached for the tiles, a static charge like the snap of a rubber band shocked her fingers. She sat back on her heels, stunned.

Seven.

"Don't," she told herself, grabbing the Scrabble pieces in a sweep of her hand and throwing them into the game box with the others.

Back in her room, she dropped onto the bed and stared

at the phone on the nightstand. The last two months, the desire to call him had been a dull ache inside her. Like a toothache, she'd learned to ignore the pain—part and parcel of a past that had trained her well to deal with regrets.

But now, that desire burned in her chest. She rubbed her hand, recalling the shock of static electricity.

She glanced at the clock: 3:17 a.m.

When she'd first heard Stella screaming, she'd checked the hour, as well. The time had been 3:07.

Seven, Seven, Seven.

She shut her eyes. "No," she said out loud.

She shoved aside the covers and massaged her pillow into a ball before settling in. She told herself her gift didn't work like that, cute little signs that could easily be mistaken for coincidence. That's how the heart worked; it looked for meaning where there was none.

She'd had a scare tonight. Of course, she'd think of the man who had once saved her life.

Gia woke up three more times that night. Each and every time—by coincidence—the digital clock showed the number seven.

When the door shut behind her mother, Stella threw back her bedcovers and sat up in bed.

"Go away," she hissed at the boy sitting on the vanity stool.

She recognized him from her dream. She'd seen him so clearly during that horrible nightmare that waking up had been this weird business: the image in her head seemed to crash into her dimly lit bedroom.

The whole thing reminded her of one of those overhead projection sheets her geometry teacher sometimes flashed on the wall. You had to stare at it awhile before anything made sense.

The dream had been a bad one, like nothing she'd ever had before. The kid sitting on the vanity: she was pretty sure that, in her dream, someone was torturing him.

She could still remember the cold bite of the handcuffs on her wrist. She'd even caught the scent of shadow-man's cologne as he'd bent over the boy.

When the guy stuck the needle in the boy's neck, she'd felt that, too.

The pain of that needle, she'd felt it as if it were happening to her. Not the boy, but *her.* That's why she'd woken up screaming, bringing her mother running.

Only now, the kid—she guessed he was about her age, tall, maybe as tall as five feet eleven, with gray eyes and dark blond hair—was sitting on her vanity stool, the nightlight shining at his feet. To Stella, he looked completely real, the living breathing version of the boy in her dream.

Of course, she knew he wasn't *really* there. He couldn't be. No live kid was sitting in her room, creepy eyes watching her.

He was a ghost.

And Mom hadn't seen him.

Mom—the lady who talked to ghosts, who painted portraits in order to pass along messages to loved ones left behind—hadn't even known he was there.

In Stella's life, it was Mom who did the woo-woo thing. Her mother had these dreams. Visions. A lot of times, the awful stuff her mother saw came true.

"Go away!" she said, louder this time.

The ghost just stared back at her.

She told herself she wasn't like her mother. Sure, she'd

get a weird vibe every once in a while, mostly about her mother's paintings. But the really scary stuff, like waking up in the middle of the night and seeing someone who wasn't there, that was Mom's gig.

"Please," she whispered. "I can't help you. Just leave me alone, okay?"

Stella slipped back under the covers, tucking the sheets and quilt under her chin, using them like a protective shield. She concentrated on a giant sunflower painted on the wall across from her, part of a mural her mother had painted in Stella's room, turning it into a kind of English garden. She tried to forget that awful basement and the sound of the boy's screams.

When looking at the flower didn't work, she squeezed her eyes shut. What did people do to fall asleep? Count sheep?

Suddenly, she felt a cold touch on her neck. She opened her eyes.

The kid, he was right there, standing next to the bed.

"Get out!" she said.

She pulled the covers over her head, breathing hard. How many times had her mom told Stella how to banish a bad spirit? Why hadn't she paid attention?

Get a grip, Stella! She tried to even her breathing, telling herself that if she'd had anything to do with bringing him here—some weakness a loose spirit might glom onto—she should have the strength to make him disappear.

After a few minutes, she lifted the sheet, scared of what she'd find.

He was gone.

She let out the breath she'd been holding. She knew her mother could get in touch with some pretty gnarly things. She'd heard Mom explain it once, how the really bad spirits were drawn to powerful psychics. And that's what her mother was. A superpsychic. Last year, she'd even helped the police catch two serial killers, a woman and her son who'd targeted other psychics.

Her mom had a very powerful gift—the kind of gift Stella didn't need.

The only thing Stella wanted was to be normal.

She glanced back at the stool in front of the vanity. It was still empty.

He was really gone.

Stella lay back on her pillow, staring at the ceiling. Funny how that fact didn't make her feel better.

3

There was blood everywhere—on the mats, on the cage itself, in the men's hair and dripping down their bared skin. And the noise...the sounds of violence washed over Evie, drugging her.

The Junoesque redhead with striking blue eyes sat near the front row of the MGM Grand's Garden Arena. Tonight, the stadium housed a near-record crowd, each and every fan mesmerized by the battle on the raised platform, center stage. The caged enclosure called The Octagon housed two fighters locked in a human cockfight.

Suddenly, the champ, Curtis "The Native" Santos, felled his opponent with a double-leg takedown. The crowd went insane as Santos scissored his legs around the challenger's midsection. There were two minutes left in the final round.

Sweat mixed with blood as the two warriors remained locked against the cage's vinyl-coated fencing. Wearing only shorts and light gloves with the fingers cut off to allow for grabbing, both gladiators heaved for breath. The challenger, Teri "The Greek" Dupas, defended against the champ's relentless attack, now pinned in a rear choke. The men's muscles clenched and gleamed under the white-hot lights.

That's exactly what she wanted, Evie thought. Those hands on her. That battle for life embracing her.

With just under a minute left in the match, the crowd began to get antsy, screaming for a standup. The referee complied, bringing both fighters to their feet. Santos didn't waste any time, nailing Dupas to the canvas with a killer left hook.

The crowd went ballistic as more blood sprayed from the challenger's nose. The round before, Santos had hammered Dupas to the mat with a straight right, opening the floodgates.

Men and women chanted "San-tos!" jumping to their feet as the champ landed punch after punch. Santos maneuvered Dupas into a mount and scored yet another takedown. The crowd began counting down the last seconds of the fight as if it were New Year's Eve in Times Square. When the bell sounded, marking the end of the fight, Santos, bald and tattooed, paraded around the ring, pumping a fist in the air.

Ten minutes later, the redhead's long-legged stride took her out to the casino floor. Popping gum and listening to "Fergieliscious" on her iPod nano, she pushed past the minions working the slots and video poker machines.

As she walked past, each and every slot hit.

The clatter of falling coins accompanied by the bells and whistles of the machines was almost deafening. Chaos ensued as men and women jumped to their feet in disbelief. The redhead kept walking, unfazed, a faint smile on her lips.

She stepped out the entrance made famous by a forty-five-foot bronze statue of the MGM lion. She'd been playing hooky coming here, blowing off the VIP ticket Zag had given her to see the new Lance Burton wannabe at

Mandalay Bay. The magician's final act featured the band Do It To Julia vanishing off the stage after performing their new hit single.

Zag had masterminded the gig for his charity du jour. He'd be pissed that she'd missed it. Still, she was in Vegas, the land of don't-ask/don't-tell.

She was showgirl tall and wore black leather pants and Gucci boots. Her cherry wraparound silk blouse displayed a nice amount of midriff—Evie worked out. But it wasn't just her looks that turned heads. There was an air about her, as if here was trouble, but not the kind most people wanted to avoid.

She caught the eye of the doorman and signaled for him to hail a cab. The instant she stepped off the curb, a gray Bentley swerved to a stop, blocking her path. The tinted window rolled down.

She took out her ear buds and leaned down to the window. "Hello, Zag," she said with a smile.

He lowered his leopard print Dolce & Gabanna shades. He looked absolutely furious.

"You missed the show."

"Did I?" She glanced back at MGM's entrance. "And here I thought I caught the main event."

The door opened. "Get in."

It wasn't a request.

"Someone's feeling grouchy," she said.

She slipped inside the Bentley next to him, throwing her Prada bag and iPod on the floor. Zag pushed her up against the white leather seats. Evie knew he'd been onstage with the band as a guest guitarist. He still wore stage makeup and was dressed in an electric-blue suit with tails but no shirt. She ran her hand through his spiked, bleached hair, staring into his eyes.

There were many unique things about Gonzague de Rozières, not the least of which was his name. Like a rock star, he went by the moniker Zag. He had the wiry frame of a long-distance runner but managed to appear imposing despite being a good two inches shorter than Evie's six feet one. He had more money than God and just as many secrets. But to Evie, the most unique thing about him was his eyes.

The pupils appeared always enlarged, as if he lived on some perpetual high even though he didn't do drugs. There was almost no pigment to the iris, either. The color changed depending on the light and his mood. At the moment, they appeared a steely-gray.

"You want a show?" he asked.

She leaned against the door of the Bentley. With the grace of a ballerina, she raised a Gucci-clad foot and pressed the stiletto against his bare chest, pushing just enough to know she'd leave a mark.

"What do you think?" she asked.

He took her boot by the ankle. He shook his head, smiling. "I told you to stay away from the cage."

She pouted. "Why? Don't you enjoy the effect?"

She kissed him, hard, and then bit his lip, almost drawing blood. He returned the favor by grabbing her arm and pulling it tight up her back.

"Now, now," he whispered in her ear. "No fair biting."

Evie was twenty-six. She'd been with a lot of men. But there'd never been anyone like Zag. He could take everything she handed him. And then some.

By the time they reached his suite at the Wynn, she knew she'd have bruises. It's what she wanted. Seeing those men in the cage, drawing that energy to her, she needed the release.

Afterward, they lay naked on the Egyptian-cotton sheets of the California King Wynn "Dream Bed," one of the hotel's most talked about attributes. Like everything about the Wynn, the suite was opulence itself. At two thousand square feet, it was larger than some New York apartments and featured wall-to-wall, floor-to-ceiling windows with a gorgeous view of the Strip…which was why Zag preferred the salon suites to the more exclusive villas on the hotel's golf course.

Zag covered her body with his, making that connection with his eyes that she only had with him. Despite a broken nose—a memento from a mountain-climbing expedition in the Himalayas—he possessed an almost striking beauty. He had a thick head of bleached white hair, but absolutely no body hair. A genetic condition, he'd told her.

He reached for the bottle of Cristal nestled in the bedside ice bucket. He took a drink from the bottle then offered her a sip, holding the bottle up to her mouth. Only, champagne wasn't what Evie wanted.

She dropped the bottle on the carpeted floor. She heard it roll away as she pressed her lips to his with enough force that his head sunk into the down pillow.

She continued their kiss, forcing the issue when he tried to push her away. She didn't stop to catch her breath, felt herself getting light-headed. She visualized the men in the cage—the blood—the idea of death making her feel so alive.

She felt her head yanked back by a fistful of her hair.

Zag stared at her, his eyes almost colorless now. Catching his breath, he said, "Be careful, Evie."

She smiled, breathing just as hard as Zag. He kept his grip on her hair, but she didn't care.

She brushed her thumb over his swollen bottom lip where she'd bitten him earlier. "Fuck that."

Evie locked her legs around his hips and bit his lip again, this time drawing blood.

The next thing she knew, he rolled them both off the bed. He pinned her to the carpeted floor, straddling her.

"I said, be careful!" This time, he meant it.

That was another thing she enjoyed about Zag. He was one of only two men who could best her physically.

She turned her head and looked at the Cristal bottle and the champagne soaking into the confetti design of the carpet next to her face.

"Oops," she said, smiling coyly.

"Gracious, was that almost an apology?" he asked, nibbling her earlobe, his anger easily forgotten.

He stood and held out his hand. Pulling her to her feet, he clucked his tongue at the empty ice bucket.

"Cristal." He made a soft sound of disappointment deep in his throat. "What a waste."

But Evie was already heading out of the bedroom toward the wet bar in the living room. The marble floor, in a deep shade of cocoa, felt deliciously cold under her bare feet. She passed the room's most touted feature: a fifty-inch plasma screen set dead center against the wall of curtained windows. Anyone watching the high-def television would have the Vegas strip as background courtesy of the floor-to-ceiling windows.

The furnishings were chic and contemporary, the color scheme soothing. The russet grasscloth wallpaper served as the perfect foil for the cherry-toned furnishings. Two sofas bracketed the marble-topped coffee table and Andy Warhol prints graced the walls. Steve Wynn had spent two-point-seven billion on his namesake casino hotel. The opening had featured an exclusive with *Vanity Fair* magazine and a commercial during the Super Bowl. Zag prided himself in knowing all the right people, people like Steve Wynn.

In the living room, she took in the flotsam and jetsam of Zag's other life. A curious array of scientific papers, business journals and scholarly tomes covered most every surface. Tucked among such lofty subjects as "string theory" and "dark matter" were the pseudosciences that so fascinated him—several copies of the *Journal of Parapsychology,* printed articles examining sundry paranormal phenomenon, a report on remote perception put out by PEAR, the Princeton Engineering Anomalies Research program. One title in particular caught her eye: *The Atlantis Generation.*

She almost laughed. Apparently, Zag wouldn't be satisfied until he reached his goal of becoming both man and myth. Evie knew she was an important part of his quest for the latter.

She picked up a bound copy of proceedings from the coffee table and weighed the heavy tome in her hand. She'd turned down his offer of the company jet, choosing to drive into Vegas the day before, presumably so they might spend some time together. But Zag had been in town for days attending one of his precious paranormal conferences.

She turned back toward the bedroom where Zag now stood in the doorway, his hands braced against the door-jamb. She took a moment to appreciate his naked body. The combination of alabaster skin and lack of body hair made him look like a Greek statue: his muscles were as clearly defined as sculpted marble. Even the broken nose served to give the refined, almost feminine features more gravitas.

She dropped the proceedings back on the coffee table, where it landed with a heavy thud. "Always mixing work with pleasure."

"Always mixing pain with pleasure," he countered.

"True. But my mix is ever so more fascinating, don't you think?"

"Have I ever told you what a goddess you are?" he asked.

She preened in her naked glory, completely aware of her beauty. Despite her waist-length red hair, she didn't have a freckle on her body. Any mark came from grueling practice fights in one of several martial-art disciplines she'd mastered.

As she turned away, Zag came up behind her. He cupped her breasts in his hands and kissed the nape of her neck. She reached back and dug her fingers into the hard muscles of his thighs, pressing back against his awaking erection.

"Not to mention all those boring charity events," she continued. She pretended to snore loudly as she turned in his arms. "I forget. What was it this time?" She bit her lip in mock concentration. "The fur and diamond deprived of Beverly Hills?"

"Autism," he answered. "And it was a fabulous success— which you'd know firsthand if you'd bothered to show."

She gave him a quick kiss, then danced out of his reach when he tried to spank her. She headed for the bar where she did indeed find another bottle of Cristal in the refrigerator.

"And have my picture splashed all over the tabloids as your new mystery woman?"

She turned the champagne's wire cage handle the requisite six half turns. The cork flew across the room with a satisfying pop. Champagne foamed over her hand, spilling to the marble floor.

"I can think of worse things," he said.

"Pass," she said, drinking from the bottle.

Innovator, playboy, bazillionaire philanthropist, Zag, Evie knew, liked the headlines, and not just on the ho-hum pages in *Barron's*. Playing guitar onstage at Mandalay Bay was the sort of thing that guaranteed Zag a mention in

People, a magazine that had already proclaimed him one of the sexiest men of the year, dubbing him the Mad Magician.

She took another drink from the bottle, letting the tiny bubbles fill her mouth. She walked back to Zag and pressed the bottle to his lips.

As far as Evie was concerned, Zag, the self-proclaimed Bill Gates of the psychic community, didn't have anything to worry about when it came to making good press. His company, Halo Industries, provided paranormal services in sundry forms—employee evaluations, intuitive counseling to Fortune 500 companies, forecasting future trends for Wall Street firms. It was even said he'd been hired by certain sectors of the government, though Zag always pleaded "no comment" when asked.

Then there were those pesky rumors about his strange lineage—rumors he denied and cultivated with equal effort.

While the man could be a jack-of-all-trades, Evie knew his true passion. The bound proceedings she'd dropped back on the coffee table were as thick as the yellow pages. Playfully, she pretended to pour champagne on *Indigo Children and the Evolving Brain.* Zag grabbed the bottle away, shaking a scolding finger.

Indigo Children referred to a rare breed of kids singled out in the last ten years. Presumably, they were more highly evolved than the general population, many possessing psychic abilities. Some claimed they even used a higher percentage of their brain. The term had been published by Lee Carroll and his wife. Carroll channeled the entity, Kryon, who sent information through Carroll to help mankind ascend to a higher level of consciousness. But there were other theories about the origins of the Indigo phenomenon.

Synesthesia was a neurological condition that could cause a person to experience two physical senses simultaneously. A synesthetic might hear with their eyes or get a specific taste in their mouth whenever they heard a particular sound. A psychic by the name of Nancy Ann Tappe, who had the condition, had claimed to see auras—a New Age concept that argued the body was surrounded by a luminous field of color.

This same psychic began seeing an indigo aura surrounding these more highly evolved children. Eventually, the term became linked with certain conditions such as ADHD and autism.

She pushed Zag onto the couch and straddled him. "You know what they say. All work and no play."

"I'm hardly that."

She filled her mouth with champagne and kissed him, sharing the taste of the Cristal with their kiss.

Zag had his own theory about the Indigo experience, going so far as to claim the existence of "Halo-effect" children, a smaller, more select group of children who had "evolved." Halo Industries now had schools where parents could send their special offspring to fine-tune their gifts. Their unique curriculum presumably helped hone psychic abilities. That's where Evie came in.

On the couch, Evie rose up on her knees. Her hair fell like a curtain over her and Zag. But as she lowered her face for another penetrating kiss, she heard her cell phone in the bedroom, its ring tone, Handel's "Water Music."

Hearing the distinctive ring, she broke off their kiss, handed Zag the Cristal and rose to her feet.

There was only one reason he'd call her at this hour.

Back in the bedroom, she grabbed the cell phone and stepped over to the floor-to-ceiling windows. She stared at the phone, allowing it to continue ringing in her hand.

"Aren't you going to answer?" Zag asked from the door.

She glanced down at the street below. "Isn't it funny how, here in Vegas, it doesn't matter if it's day or night? The lights are always on."

Of course, Zag would recognize the ring tone.

She was trying to decide if she should take the call here with Zag listening in or risk his censure by asking for privacy.

"Let him leave a message then," Zag said, his voice in dulcet tones as he lay back on the Dream Bed. "Come back to bed, *cherie*."

Only, they both knew she wouldn't.

Evie flipped open the phone. She whispered into the cell, "Hello, lover. How's our boy doing?"

4

Detective Stephen "Seven" Bushard stared at the body lying in the mud. The girl appeared nestled in the cordgrass, her legs and arms disappearing into the knee-high vegetation. She wore jeans and a Roxy T-shirt, the surfing brand, a favorite with young girls here at the beach.

The officer on the scene, one of Huntington Beach's finest, had told Seven's partner some Iron Man stud training for his next triathlon had found the body. This section of the wetlands, the Bolsa Chica Ecological Reserve, featured a one-and-a-half mile loop around a water inlet, the walking trail was part of a three-hundred-acre coastal sanctuary for wildlife and migratory birds. After thirty years of litigation, the restoration project had been the compromise between environmentalists and developers. Already minimansions with multimillion-dollar views had sprouted where Shoshone Indians had once hunted on the mesa. People still found cogged stones in the area, artifacts from an eight-thousand-year-old burial site soon to be paved over. Progress, Seven thought. Go figure.

Seven crouched down for a closer look. He had almost sixteen years on the force, eight of them in homicide, but he would never get used to this.

The way the girl was curled up in her bed of grass, she

appeared to be sleeping. Her head was turned toward him, but three-quarters of her face was buried in the mud. Still, he could make out her youthful features.

Jesus, she's just a kid.

He had to give the cop in him a mental kickstart. The wetlands might not be his jurisdiction, but if someone thought it was important for him to be here, he'd damn sure get the job done.

He took off his sunglasses to better examine the body. Most likely, the tide had dragged the victim here via the channel that cut through the Pacific Coast Highway. The waterway refreshed the wetlands with ocean water. To the tide, she'd be so much trash floating like the detritus left behind by the beachgoers every summer.

Seven took out his pen from inside his jacket and used it to gently push aside the cordgrass, exposing the girl's left hand. There was obvious bruising around the wrist.

She'd been tied up.

He tried not to imagine the worst. Rape. Torture.

He pocketed his pen, searching for that objective observer inside. He'd given himself the pep talk on the ride over; he'd get it back, that ability to compartmentalize. The last year hadn't tainted him forever. Any second now, he'd be able to hover over the dead girl's body and search for clues like a good cop.

Only, the details that popped for him had nothing to do with murder. The glitter nail polish…her thick blond hair coiled in ringlets. When she was alive, those curls would circle her face like a crown.

He turned away, acting as if he was giving the crime scene investigator free rein to snap more stills. He stared up, focusing on the cloud cover overhead. The haze made for a steely morning sky. The same dull color reflected off the water trapped in the low marsh. The tide differentials would be at their highest this time of year—probably why the body was beached here.

Just last week, Seven had brought his eleven-year-old nephew to the Bolsa Chica. They'd been fishing down by Warner and the PCH. Posted signs told visitors of the Belding's Savannah Sparrow, an endangered species that bred and nested here. Shore crabs grazed on algae and snowy egret high-stepped through the pickleweed. But Nick, he'd been all about the brown pelicans, watching them dive-bombing into the water for fish.

Really, the place was idyllic…if you didn't count the dead body.

His partner, Erika Cabral, came to stand next to him. Her sunglasses looked huge on her face—designer, no doubt, the kind celebrities wore. Erika always said there wasn't much she couldn't fix with a little retail therapy.

"So why'd we get the call?" he asked. "Last time I checked, this is some sort of jurisdictional no-man's land for the sheriff and Huntington Beach PD to sift through."

She nodded. "An interesting question, no doubt."

He gave it a minute. It was never good when Erika tried to hide something from him.

"That's all you got?" he asked. "An interesting question?"

"A woman of mystery, that's me."

The Latina had always been a girly girl, one who regularly kicked his butt on the firing range. She was all of five feet two inches tall and had the classic good looks of a Penelope Cruz—dark hair, dark eyes, and lots of curves.

Only lately, Seven noticed she'd stepped it up a bit. Nice sweaters worn under fitted jackets, lip gloss that made her mouth look shiny and wet…as if the sexiest detective in Orange County needed any help in that area. The other day, she'd even mentioned that four letter word: diet.

And her hair. No more messy French twists or ponytails. Last week, he'd made the mistake of lobbing some weak compliment. The next thing he knew, he was listening to how she'd straightened her hair *then* used some big-barreled curling iron to get just the right wave, like she'd been possessed by the spirit of Revlon.

He figured there was a man involved. He hoped to hell it wasn't that dick of a reporter he'd punched out last year. But then, Erika did like a challenge.

"So now we're playing twenty questions?" he asked, still wondering what business two detectives from Westminster had in the Bolsa Chica.

"You say it like it's a bad thing. Look, don't stress, Seven. Why don't you try taking a couple of breaths? Like this." She demonstrated. "In through the nose, out through the mouth. It's yoga. Good for whatever ails you."

He gave her a look from beneath his aviator glasses. "You do yoga?"

"You think I keep this figure sitting behind a desk?"

He was thinking more like Krav Maga. Despite her petite size, his partner could kick some serious ass.

"You should come to a class with me sometimes." She made an elaborate gesture with her hands around his head and shoulders. "Your aura. It could use some work."

He didn't let her see him smile. If there was anyone on this planet who didn't believe in auras, it was his partner. Her Cuban mother had seen to that, spending a small fortune on *espiritistas* and *santeros* who promised cures…for the right price.

She nodded toward the body. "What do you see?"

"Ligature marks on the wrists."

"The ankles, too." She took a minute. "She hasn't spent too much time in the water."

He nodded. "Maybe she was dumped. She's not a floater."

A submerged body, a floater, decomposed at an accelerated rate. Within a day, or even hours depending on the temperature, anaerobic bacteria trapped in the intestines produced gases that distended the stomach cavity and bloated the body beyond recognition. Other than a little mud, the victim before him looked pristine.

"Not a drowning?" Erika ventured.

"Or a crime of passion." He indicated the ligature marks. "Whoever killed her took his time."

"Poor baby." She seemed to be talking to the girl as if she could hear her. "We're going to find the piece of shit that did this to you."

Watching Erika there beside the girl, Seven got a flash of a different, even more disturbing image. His nephew, Nick, lying there in the mud.

Jesus, the girl was only a few years older than Nick.

He looked away, obliterating the image and getting back to business. "So who are we waiting for?" he asked, deducing that someone of authority had made the call to put them on the case. He glanced around at the milling law enforcement. "Or are we just supposed to stand around? Maybe twiddle our thumbs?"

She turned to look at him. "What? You want to go fishing? Maybe take a jog around the loop?"

"I was thinking more like roust a couple of budding ornithologists." He nodded toward the wooden footbridge with its viewing platform. He could just make out the bird watchers and their telephoto lenses trained on the crime scene. "Maybe even before our victim shows up on the front page of the paper."

"They're birders," Erika said, turning to look in their direction.

"Ornithologists, birders, same difference."

"Actually, ornithology is the scientific study of birds." She nodded toward the guys wearing camouflage and standing next to binoculars so big they required tripods. "The birders?" She lowered her voice suggestively. "They just like to watch."

This time, he gave her the satisfaction of seeing him smile.

The word game had started last month after a night spent watching a rerun of the Scripps National Spelling Bee. A couple of beers and several artery-clogging bowls of buttered popcorn later, they both claimed the superior vocabulary. Seven was pretty sure Erika kept score…and that she was ahead.

Having done her duty and sicced a uniform on the birders, Erika knelt next to the body. "Come look at this."

Erika took out a pen from her jacket and carefully separated the strands of hair covering the girl's neck.

"See that?" she asked.

There was a red mark on the neck, like a prick of some kind. The skin around it appeared discolored.

He crouched down alongside the girl and frowned. "What the hell is that? An injection site?"

"She has another one here," Erika said pushing aside the cordgrass with her pen to indicate the top of the girl's hand.

"Doesn't look like track marks. Could it be some sort of bug bite, or a crab or a fish having had a go at the body?"

Erika shook her head. "Too uniform."

His cell went off. Without taking his gaze off the strange mark, he reached for the phone on his hip. But it rang only once, stopping before he could answer.

"How's Beth doing?" Erika asked, not even trying to disguise her distaste.

He ignored her and focused on the body and the curious marks. Erika assumed the call was from Beth, his sister-in-law, par for the course the last two years. That's when Seven's older brother, Ricky—the happily married man and Nick's father, the perfect son to Seven's prodigal—had pleaded guilty to second degree murder. Ricky, a plastic surgeon, had killed a male nurse, the man who'd been his lover.

Beth, Ricky's wife, hadn't exactly taken her husband's betrayal in stride. She'd fallen into the bottle. It had been up to Seven and his family to keep the pieces together for Nick.

But now Beth was in AA. She was studying for her broker's license. Sure, she'd lost the waterfront home and the fifty-five-foot yacht, the condo in Big Bear. She and Nick lived in a small house that Seven owned with his father…and she seemed happier than ever.

Only, Erika wasn't the forgiving type. She hadn't bought into Beth's new lease on life, or the fact that she'd given up on her game of musical chairs with the Bushard brothers. According to Erika, Beth was only waiting for the ink to dry on her divorce papers before she made her move on him.

Out of the corner of his eye, Seven caught sight of a familiar movement. A strange prickling heated the back of his neck. Standing, he could feel his heart pumping hard as his body acknowledged the threat long before his brain could put the pieces together.

"Fuck," he said under his breath.

Someone of authority had just arrived, all right.

The woman marching toward them was blond and tall

with the lanky build of an Olympic high jumper. Her long-legged stride forced the tech beside her to give a little skip just to keep up. She wore black slacks and a blazer with a simple white blouse, and accessorized with the requisite dark aviator glasses. But the thing that stood out—what made him instantly recognize her—was that damn Black-Berry in her hand.

She was headed straight for Seven and Erika, instructing the crime-scene tech jogging alongside, while no doubt browsing the Web on her BlackBerry. Special Agent Carin Barnes liked to multitask.

"Getting back to those twenty questions," he said to Erika. "Why exactly did two Westminster detectives get called in here?"

Erika stood, training her gaze on the blonde. "I think you skipped the part about it being bigger than a bread box."

"A hell of a lot taller, anyway," he said.

Bright and early, Erika had given him a call. A DB—a dead body—in the wetlands. Female. Very young. He'd gone into automatic; his partner was calling him to the scene of a crime. Why ask questions?

He frowned. The fucking FBI.

"Since when do you have an in with the feds?" he asked Erika.

She lowered her sunglasses for his benefit. "Honey, I have an *in* just about everywhere."

She popped the glasses back on the bridge of her nose and stepped toward the approaching agent. Since he'd last seen Special Agent Carin Barnes, she'd clipped her hair boy-short. It was a valiant attempt at looking the part of tough federal agent but there was too much of willowy blonde there to achieve the proper effect.

The women shook hands. Seven and Carin Barnes were of a height, just under six feet. Standing next to Erika, the two made a curious picture: A Viking warrioress looming over a Pictish princess. He couldn't hear what they were saying, but he knew those two wouldn't waste time on pleasantries.

"Special Agent Barnes," he said, bracing himself as the FBI agent came to a stop before him. "Fancy meeting you here."

"I assume that's your attempt at levity," Barnes said, pocketing the BlackBerry, "which we both know is wasted on me. This isn't the killer's only victim. Megan Tobin of Henderson, Nevada. We found her last month, dumped just like this. She'd been cutting school. According to her best friend, she was meeting someone, an older man. Possibly a love interest. Megan was the second vic. We found Mark Dair three months before her, same MO."

"Anything on Megan's computer?" Seven asked.

A lot of times, these kids were lured into meeting some stranger after prolonged discussion over the Internet.

"Nothing," Barnes responded.

"You're sure they're connected to our vic?" Seven asked.

"All three had these stones in their hands."

She held up a plastic evidence bag. Inside was a flat, rounded stone, the kind used by kids to skip on the water. The surface had been carved with curious markings that reminded Seven of Egyptian hieroglyphs.

"An artifact?" Erika asked, not bothering to hide the surprise in her voice.

The fact was, Barnes wasn't your ordinary FBI agent. She worked for NISA, the National Institute for Strategic Artifacts. The agency always reminded Seven of that last scene in that Indiana Jones flick, where a forklift takes the crated Ark of the Covenant and stores it in some enormous warehouse, giving the idea that the thousands of crates lining the aisles were filled with similar treasures never again to see the light of day.

Erika and Seven had first met Special Agent Carin Barnes ten months ago, while working on the fortune-teller murders. NISA stepped in when it turned out a local business tycoon, David Gospel, had managed to amass a sizable collection of mystical artifacts—all through the black market in antiquities. Unfortunately, the collection cost the man his life.

The story went that one of the artifacts was possessed by some evil spirit, having a kind of Hope Diamond curse. The spirit could attach itself to anyone who messed with the artifact—a crystal about the size of a man's fist, called the Eye of Athena—turning them into rabid killers. Gospel's wife ended up shooting him, but not before she and her son amassed some serious carnage.

Of course, Seven didn't buy into the hocus pocus. One of the victims had been Gospel's mistress. Seven liked the old-fashioned motive: Her man had done her wrong and Mrs. Gospel flipped her lid.

After they'd wrapped up the case, Seven had done a little research on NISA, but he hadn't come up with much. It appeared that anything on the mysterious branch of the FBI was buried so deep, there was no sign of it on paper. Not even the conspiracy buffs on the Net had gotten wind of it.

"How many victims are we talking about?" Erika asked.

"This is our third. I think we'll find our vic was drowned. That she's fourteen years old. She would be missing exactly three weeks."

"Jesus Christ," Erika whispered. "A serial killer?"

"Toxicology?" Seven asked.

Barnes gave him a sharp look.

"Detective Cabral found what looks like injection sites at the jugular and on the back of her hand," he said by way of explanation.

Barnes nodded. "We're still sorting that out."

Which was FBI-speak for he was on a need-to-know basis. *Damn feds.*

She turned with the precision of someone who hadn't wasted her time during those drills at the academy. He'd give odds Special Agent Barnes had been at the top of her class at Quantico.

Just then, Barnes stopped and pivoted back, almost as if she'd forgotten something. She frowned, completely focused on Seven.

She took off her sunglasses. Her normally gray-blue eyes looked the color of gunmetal.

"Has Gia Moon contacted you?" she asked.

The question brought on a strange tingling sensation straight up his spine. He didn't know why—there really wasn't a connection—but he thought immediately about his cell phone and that single ring, almost as if whoever had called had changed their mind.

Gia.

"The psychic?" Erika asked, for the first time not looking so pleased with her buddy, Special Agent Barnes. "She called you?" she asked Seven, the question, almost an accusation.

"I haven't heard from Gia in months," he answered.

A genuine smile changed the agent's normally guarded expression. For an instant, Barnes looked years younger than her thirty-five. He wasn't sure why, but he found the expression disturbing.

She cocked one brow. "Interesting." To Seven, she added, "You'll let me know when she calls."

Erika and Seven watched the agent stride off to meet with the local hoi polloi. Seven recognized investigation teams from both the city and the county. But then murder in the marshlands was heady stuff for the normally quiet beach community.

"I notice she didn't say *if* she calls you," Erika said.

Seven took out his cell. He had one missed call. He stared at the LCD screen, and punched up the number.

A name popped up: *Gia.*

That's how he'd programmed her number into his cell, by her name.

"Why would Barnes bring up Gia Moon now?" Erika asked.

"The usual reason," he told his partner, putting the phone away before she could see the screen. "To mess with our heads."

5

Gia stared at her daughter as Stella dug into her cereal. Stella liked Cap'n Crunch, the kind with Crunch Berries. The sugar content was probably through the roof but at least it was vitamin fortified…not to mention the only way Gia could get her growing daughter to drink milk.

Spooning cereal into her mouth, Stella looked just like any other teenager. She'd tortured her black curls under one of those driving caps that were all the rage with the celebrities in the magazines. She wore layered T-shirts and low-rise jeans that made Gia wince every time her daughter sat down. For all intents and purposes, Stella had nothing weighing on her mind other than how to keep her mother off her back.

Of course, she didn't fool Gia. Her daughter was working mighty hard to achieve that air of nonchalance.

Something was up.

Gia glanced at the kitchen clock, a kitsch black cat with a swinging tail and shifting eyes that ticked off the seconds. By Gia's calculations, Stella had been reading the same passage in the newspaper for the last fifteen minutes.

"More orange juice?" Gia asked, holding up the carton.

Stella glanced up, her mouth full of cereal. She chewed and swallowed. "I'm fine."

Gia poured herself a glass, asking, "I'm fine as in, I

don't want any more juice—" she put down the carton and folded her arms on the table, "*or* I'm fine because I don't want to talk about what happened last night?"

Stella pushed away the paper and rolled her eyes. "Why do you have to make such a big deal about everything?"

"I could think of several *really* good reasons."

"Yeah, okay." Stella stood abruptly. "So we're a bunch of weirdos and sometimes you get visions and there's death and mayhem. But last night, I had a nightmare. A *dream.* It doesn't have to mean anything."

Gia grabbed Stella's hand before she could walk past. "Stella, please. Talk to me."

"You're trying to make this into some stupid psychic thing we can bond over—"

"Is that what you think?"

"And I am completely over it." She pushed her mother's hands away and grabbed her backpack from the floor. "I'm going to Mindy's after school to work on our history project. I'll probably have dinner there."

"You have your cell phone?"

"Yeah."

She dutifully kissed her mother's cheek. But before she could step away, Gia whispered, "Are you sure, sweetie?"

It was a loaded question. *Are you sure you want to hide things from me? Dangerous things.*

For an instant, her daughter's blue eyes, so much like Gia's, held a faint cloud of indecision. Stella's gaze darted to her side.

Whatever she saw there seemed to galvanize her. "Positive," she said stepping away.

Stella didn't so much as pause as she headed for the door. Gia frowned. *Oh, baby.*

When she heard the front door slam shut, she stood. She

carefully stepped around a particular spot on the floor as she walked over to the kitchen window. She pulled back the blinds and stared out at the front yard. Stella practically sprinted down the rose-lined walkway leading to the front gate.

So we're a bunch of weirdos….

And her daughter didn't want any part of it.

"Who can blame you, sweetie?" she said.

She grabbed a dishrag off the counter near the sink and walked back to the spot on the floor she'd avoided earlier. She knelt down to wipe the tiles where there was a circle of muddy water.

Gia hadn't seen the spirit, but she knew her daughter had. Stella had tried to hide her nervous glance here, but Gia had caught it.

Suddenly, she felt a tingle at the back of her neck. She glanced up at the clock.

It was 7:27 a.m.

Seven.

The image came, unbidden and unwanted: hazel eyes more green than gold, barely tamed chestnut curls and broad shoulders. And his smile. The memory of it brought a warmth that reached all the way to her toes.

She stood, wadding up the dripping rag. "All right, all right. I give."

She dropped the rag in the sink and wiped her hands before reaching for the phone. She didn't know why or how Seven was involved, but clearly someone or something wanted her to contact him. Her daughter might not accept who she was but Gia didn't have that luxury. She was too familiar with her gift to ignore the signs.

Just before breakfast, she'd dialed his number. But she'd panicked, ending the call before he could pick up.

This time, she let it ring.

* * *

Stella waited until she was sure her mother couldn't see her before she dropped her backpack and stopped to catch her breath.

The boy had been standing right *there,* next to her mother. His clothes were wet and dripping this dirty water on the floor. He was covered in some sort of mud or slime.

He'd looked dead. His lips were blue and there were these dark circles under his eyes. His skin—it was all white and puffy and bloodless. He looked like he'd drowned.

He'd kept those wet, gray eyes right on her, almost daring her to acknowledge him standing in the kitchen. Stella kept thinking that, any minute now, Mom would turn to the stupid ghost and start asking him questions.

Only, she hadn't.

Mom can't see him. She really can't.

More than anything else, that scared the crap out of Stella.

She picked up her backpack and headed for the bus stop. She was in eighth grade, her last year of middle school. Her life was supposed to be about silly things like whether she should start shaving her legs or wearing makeup.

Only she had ghost boy here to remind her that she wasn't normal. That she never would be.

Right now, he was walking alongside her like they were buddies, dripping water and mud with every step.

Stella whipped around and screamed, "Leave me alone, you freak!"

He didn't respond. He stood in place, just staring at her.

"Great. Just great. I have psycho ghost attached to me."

She started walking again, faster this time, but the ghost

dogged her every step. Just a couple of months ago, she'd made peace with the fact that sometimes, she had this ability. She'd tried ignoring it, having read somewhere that, if you didn't use a muscle, it would grow weak. Well, this muscle wasn't getting any weaker.

She hated it. She didn't want to see things that weren't there or have some dead soul hanging around, making her life all about their problems. She had her own stuff to deal with.

Last year, she'd learned a bunch of things…secrets, bad secrets, about the past. Things her mother had hidden from her, trying to protect her.

Some of it wasn't so bad. Like the fact that Stella had a grandfather, Morgan Tyrell. He was filthy rich and ran a clinic that studied the brain and psychic stuff in San Diego. Morgan was way cool. And she could tell that he liked her. Lots of times, he'd send his limo and she and her mom would end up going someplace amazing for dinner with him. Or she'd spend the weekend at the Institute and he'd let her help with the research and everything.

But the other stuff, the really weird stuff about her past, still freaked her out.

Like the fact that her mother had changed her name, that they were living *in hiding*. All these years, Morgan had been a few hours away and her mom had been too afraid to contact him, her own father.

And her grandmother was supposed to be this famous psychic archaeologist who got kicked out of Harvard for being just a little *too* psychic. She'd been obsessed with finding this artifact, the Eye of Athena. It finally killed her. Now she had a cult following with blogs and Web sites that treated her like she was the freaking Dalai Lama or something. All Stella had to do was type in "Estelle Fegaris" and she'd get, like, a bazillion hits.

Then there was her father. Stella had grown up believing he was dead. All along, he'd been the reason she and her mom were hiding. He turned out to be some psycho who'd killed Stella's grandmother because he'd wanted the crystal—the Eye of Athena. It was supposedly worth a fortune *and* it was haunted. After he stole it, he went nuts.

The whole time, her mother had been living this double life, acting like everything was cool. Like they were just regular folk and the only things they needed to worry about were her mom's weird visions.

Only her mother knew the truth. That one day Stella's dad would end up on their doorstep and try to kill them both. Preparing for just that day—trying to keep Stella safe.

In the end, it happened just like her mother had seen it in her vision. The cops killed her father before he could shoot her mother.

Well, not the cops. Seven, the detective her mom liked so much. He's the one who'd saved the day.

Yeah, all that stuff from the past was kind of heavy. She didn't blame Seven for disappearing once he learned the truth about them. She knew he liked her mother—he'd even told her he did. He'd said he cared about them *both*.

So here was this really cool guy who made Mom happy…he'd even saved her life, like some knight in shining armor. But her mom's life was complicated. And a guy like Seven, he wouldn't want anything to do with the ghosts-and-goblins gig. Who could blame him?

Stella walked faster, ignoring ghost boy.

And she was supposed to be okay with it? Embrace her gift? Just give in and accept that she could never be normal? Could never have a *normal* life with *normal* friends. Couldn't have a cool guy like Seven hanging around because people like him wanted *normal*.

Well, forget it. She wasn't about to tell her mother about ghost boy, even if he showed up all muddy looking like a zombie, trying to scare her into some stupid reaction. Spirits attached themselves, and the way Stella saw it, if she ignored him long enough, he'd get good and unattached.

Stella kept her head down, ignoring the spirit walking alongside her. She didn't want any part of the kid and his problems.

Sooner or later, she'd figure a way to get rid of him.

Whatever it took.

6

Jack could hear the ocean inside his head. He loved the beach. Sometimes, when things got really rough with a john, he'd just think about the waves crashing on the sand. Santa Monica pier was the first place he'd gone when he'd gotten off the bus from Indiana. If he closed his eyes, the cars on the freeway even sounded like the waves. He could almost smell the salt in the air.

There were two of them now, a man and a woman.

Funny, but they looked alike—a lot alike, actually, like maybe the guy from last night cloned himself. They were both really tall, way taller than Jack. And they had this pale skin with red, red hair. The girl's hair was straight and down to her waist; the guy wore his layered so that the ends just brushed his broad shoulders. They had really dark blue eyes, almost black. Even their voices sounded the same.

He noticed that sometimes one would start a sentence and the other would finish it. Other times, they didn't talk at all but he could see they were communicating somehow. Like maybe they could read each other's minds.

The guy, Adam, told him the girl's name was Evie.

At first, Jack thought they were kidding him. Adam and Evie? Come *on*. Then Adam stuck another needle in him and everything just sort of went away.

It didn't hurt as much the second time. The first time, the stuff burned going in. And his body started to spasm like he had no control. He thought he was having a seizure. Then everything just went dark.

He woke up completely covered in sweat. Every muscle hurt. He'd never felt so strange. Tired and exhilarated at the same time.

Adam said he'd get used to it.

The woman, she was really pretty. She had this soft mouth and her voice was like music. She would sit on the cold cement floor and stroke his face. Her smile reminded Jack of his mom.

Adam reminded Jack of Uncle Pete. The johns always reminded Jack of Uncle Pete.

Pete wasn't really Jack's uncle. He was his mother's boyfriend. Mom really liked him because he had lots of money. Pete owned a dealership in town. He bought Mom stuff all the time. He'd buy Jack things, too. And take them to expensive dinners.

Right away, Jack noticed how Pete and his money brought a real smile to his mother's face, not that tired, fake smile he remembered. It was the first time they'd really had anything. His mother told him Jack's dad had taken off the minute he found out she was pregnant.

Jack couldn't remember when he'd figured out she was lying. He just knew that, whenever he'd asked about his father, his mom would look away really fast and change the subject. So he stopped asking.

He had a feeling that, before Pete, Mom had made the kind of choices Jack had the last months living on the streets. She probably didn't even know who his father was.

Jack looked just like his mom. *Like looking in a mirror, baby boy.* How many times had she said that to him? She loved the fact that they looked alike. He knew his mom was proud of him. He didn't need to get good grades or be smart, she just thought he was special because he was all hers.

That's why, when Uncle Pete started touching Jack, he let him. He kept thinking about his mom and how happy she was. How much better her life was with Uncle Pete's money.

It always happened in the basement, one just like this. The musty smell, the sound of dripping water in the sink, it was all too familiar. Jack remembered he'd focus on that sound, pretending that someday it would be the ocean he'd be listening to and not Pete's heavy breathing.

He'd always thought his mother didn't know. I mean, if she knew, she'd put a stop to it, right? His mom loved him, no matter what.

Then six months ago, she took Jack aside and gave him a sweaty wad of money. She said she'd been saving a little bit every time Pete gave her some cash. She thought it would be enough.

She told him he had to go away. *I need you to be a man now, okay, sweetie?* She'd been crying the whole time, kissing him all over his face, holding him so tight.

She kept saying how sorry she was.

Jack remembered feeling numb. He hadn't cried. He hadn't even hugged her back. All he could think was: *She knows. She knows everything.*

He didn't know what hurt more. The horror he felt knowing that anyone—let alone his mother—knew his horrible secret. Or the fact that she'd let it happen.

Now, sitting in another cold basement, handcuffed to an old metal desk, he wished he'd told Mom that it was okay. That he understood how maybe she'd convinced herself nothing was wrong, how Uncle Pete couldn't be this dirty old man—until the truth hit her so hard in the face she had to admit what was going on.

He didn't blame his mom. After some of the things he'd done since coming here, he understood what it meant to fight to survive.

"Jack, you need to pay attention."

Right, he thought, realizing he'd let himself drift. Evie wanted him to focus. She needed him to think about the past. Only, she wasn't talking about Uncle Pete or his mother. She wanted something else.

"Open your eyes to what's possible, Jack."

He wasn't really sure what she meant when she said stuff like that, but he knew he wanted to please Evie. She called him things like *baby* and *sweetie.* And she'd stroke his hair, just like his mother used to.

"That's it, baby," she whispered. "That's very good."

She sounded so happy. And that voice of hers, the way she'd say things like *very good* and *I'm so proud,* it felt like a wave of heat warming him in that cold basement. He actually smiled even though his head hurt like someone was taking a pen and jamming it in his ear.

He loved the way she touched him. *Just like Mom.*

"You did well, sweetie."

She unlocked the handcuffs and folded him into her arms as a reward, again repeating how well he'd done and how special he was.

Adam had said the same thing. *You're special.* He'd told him he could turn Jack into a superhero.

Jack didn't know what that meant exactly, except that it wasn't all good. Not if it meant handcuffs and that huge needle.

Only now, Evie was rocking him in her arms. And

Adam, he knelt down beside them and put his arms around them both. The way he looked at Jack. *He's proud of me, too.*

They were both smiling at him, Adam and Evie. And he could hear them talking inside his head. Even though their lips didn't move, the message was so clear. *We're a family.*

Family. That's the only word that described the emotions he felt coming from Adam and Evie. They cared about him. They loved him.

He wanted to reach out and hug them back, but he couldn't move. He realized he was paralyzed or something.

But he could listen. So that's what he did. He just lay there, in Evie's arms, and listened to the sound of their voices inside his head.

7

The great city of San Diego did not claim to be paradise on earth, but it came damn close. An average temperature of seventy degrees Fahrenheit, less than twelve inches of precipitation annually, a slice of blue sky and seventy miles of beach pretty much clinched it. After Morgan Tyrell weathered one too many Boston winters, the city was also the site of the Institute for Dynamic Studies of Parapsychology and the Brain.

The Institute, as it was known, commanded a nice piece of real estate on the Point Loma peninsula. With the pounding surf below, the compound's architectural design—a central galleria ringed by labs and offices—assisted its multidisciplinary collaboration. Hard science worked alongside soft, some might even say pseudoscience, the Institute being home to a phalanx of psychics.

Morgan had long ago adapted the scientific method to the study of paranormal phenomena, a feat for which he had been equally revered and ridiculed. Over the years, the Institute had a finger in extrasensory perception, psychokinesis and remote viewing, as well as sundry other psi disciplines. There'd even been a case involving a poltergeist that had, unfortunately, received quite a bit of publicity.

In the early years, Morgan hadn't minded making headlines. The opposite, in fact. Morgan Tyrell had been accused of being quite the publicity whore. His motto: Create a scandal! That's how a man made his mark on the world.

These days he had more than his reputation to think about. After living his life with his work as a singular focus, he'd somehow managed the coup of having a family.

The one thing his daughter didn't want was publicity.

So Morgan had brought it down a notch—several, in fact—enjoying a more subdued lifestyle. On weeknights, he would send his limo for an evening out with Gia and Stella. Sometimes he even had his granddaughter, Stella, up for the weekend. There wasn't anything Morgan enjoyed more than watching her peek in on the laboratories to discuss ongoing research conducted under the Institute's many grants.

For the sake of his daughter and granddaughter, the only scandal Morgan created these days happened in a laboratory. Morgan and his minions at the Institute had handily managed to alienate both the scientific and paranormal communities, a fact that often brought a smile to the face of its fearless leader.

The Institute bragged state-of-the-art facilities that included a Cray Supercomputer and a NMR spectrometer. It housed ten laboratories in over three hundred thousand square feet overlooking the Pacific Ocean. At any one time, its offices supported a minimum of eight hundred professors, postdoctoral fellows and graduate students in research that spanned from conventional to downright weird, anything that demonstrated how human consciousness interacted with the physical world.

While nonprofit, it was a well-known fact that Morgan's millions floated the Institute's continued existence—which seemed only fair considering many believed he'd been un-usually lucky in the stock market. Again, that rumored army of psychics.

When asked if he employed some paranormal tech-nique in choosing his investments, Morgan always winked and answered it never hurt to bet on a good hunch.

At the moment, the Institute's crowning gem, its self-proclaimed Brain Trust—a secret circle within what was already a circumspect community—held court in one of several glass-enclosed conference rooms. A teak sideboard from the Jaipur region of India lay loaded down with pastries and gourmet coffee. An ornate tapestry of a White Tara, the female Buddha worshipped in Tibet, added to the room's tranquil atmosphere. Around an antique oval table carved in the traditional Tibetan style sat five famous, as well as infamous, academic figures.

At the head of the table, Morgan sat with steepled fin-gers pressed against his mouth as he leaned back in the soft leather chair. He wore a perfectly tailored Armani suit in a shade of gray that complimented his silver hair and pale blue eyes. As always, he played moderator for today's topic of choice: Does God play dice with the universe?

The question, originally asked and answered by Einstein in the negative, had inspired one member, Gonzague de Rozières, or Zag as he was called, to publish a provocative article entitled *Dark Matter and Free Will* in the most recent issue of *Journal of Parapsychology*. Morgan had signed on to the article, bringing on the ire of one particular member of their sacred circle.

"Dark matter, dark energy, I don't care what you want to call it, the concept has nothing to do with free will, the soul, the color of your aura or any other mumbo jumbo that you, Zag, want to legitimize with some slight-of-hand quantum equations."

The challenge came from the cosmologist of the group, Dr. Theodore Fields. Theodore—never Ted or Teddy—was the group's resident skeptic. At the moment, the man's receding hairline did a nice job of displaying his furrowed brow. Zag never brought out the best in the man.

Theodore's penchant for colorful bow ties—today's was a splashy red-and-yellow-striped number—seemed to magnify rather than update his age. Despite Theodore's valiant attempt, there was nothing cool or modern about the dumpy figure tossing verbal grenades from across the table, which made absolutely no difference to those who coveted his company. The man was a certified genius in physics.

"Once again, Theodore, you seemed to have missed the point."

The challenge came from the article's author and the group's more colorful personality. Zag, the youngest member of the Brain Trust, never tired of waving the psi flag before Theodore's nose.

"Really?" Theodore replied, acid in his voice. "And here I was certain you didn't make a point, at all. Not a valid one, in any case."

"Oh, come now. I was quite clever in citing your own take on the uncertainty principle to validate my thesis," Zag replied silkily.

Morgan held back a smile. In the world of quantum physics, the location of a particle can never be discussed with a hundred percent certainty. Rather it can be discussed only in terms of probabilities. And while a Google search of the Heisenberg Uncertainty Principle and free will would yield over a hundred thousand hits, it was the mathematical dexterity Zag used, manipulating Field's own equations, that made his take truly unique, worthy of publication in a peer-reviewed journal and bearing the Institute's name with Morgan as a coauthor.

The younger man reminded Morgan of himself during his early years: self-made, fearless in establishing his dominance in the field of parapsychology. There was even a slight physical resemblance. Both men possessed a shock of white hair; Morgan's the product of age, Zag's, a credit to his stylist.

Morgan had never seen hair so white-blond it was almost translucent. And the fashion eccentricities didn't stop at his hair color or the occasional eyeliner. Last week, Zag had shown up wearing a leather kilt.

But then, given the company he kept, rock stars and Oscar winners, the choice in wardrobe was hardly surprising. His suit today was a patchwork of suede dyed in shades of brown, making the man's near-colorless eyes appear almost beige. Like Morgan, he was popular with the ladies. Only his broken nose prevented his delicate features from being too pretty.

Morgan always claimed it was Zag's seminal work in auras that had granted him the keys to the Brain Trust. But there was also the matter of money. Zag's corporation, Halo Industries, made even Morgan's vast fortune appear modest. Even now, work was being done on a new underground laboratory, courtesy of Halo Industries, one to rival any used by the government for its supersecret black projects.

"If all the laws of physics are set," Zag continued, "then from the moment of the big bang, everything is predetermined. How you act, how you think, even if you should want spaghetti for dinner, these are just atomic interactions—in your brain, in your body. At a fundamental level, even people interacting are just atoms interacting."

"But even as you yourself point out in the article, the

laws of physics are not set. Under quantum physics, the world is full of uncertainties."

This soft lob came from Martha Ozbek, considered by many as Theodore Fields's opposite number in academia. An anthropologist by training, she had developed an expertise in psychic artifacts and the paranormal. Her recent book, *How To Find Self,* a tome discussing man's unique relationship with the paranormal over the centuries, had remained on the *New York Times* bestseller list for half a dozen weeks.

While cagey in revealing her own beliefs, she was a fervent advocate for the paranormal, often coming to Zag's defense in these clashes. She'd had the privilege to work with the likes of Thelma Moss, a parapsychologist known for her work in Kirlian photography, photographs that purportedly supplied tangible proof of supernatural auras. To Martha, the belief in the paranormal dated as far back as the cave drawings in France, and therefore, was a legitimate area of study for an anthropologist.

Martha herself was worthy of a little study. At almost sixty, she could still catch a man's eyes. She favored flowing caftans in colors that accented her bright blue eyes and short platinum hair. Recently, there'd been rumors of a talk show.

Zag held up his hands and smiled. "That's right, Martha. The world is full of uncertainties. Anything is possible. In quantum physics, all outcomes are merely a matter of probability, which opens the door for free will. Come on, Theodore, you can't tell me it's not at least worth discussing?"

"It's worth discussing about as much as it is worth pondering the question *do pigs fly?*" Theodore scoffed. "You're trying to use quantum mechanics as the scientific basis for free will. And there is no scientific basis for free will. You can't observe it, you can't measure it, you can't study it."

Martha placed a calming hand on Theodore's. "And yet, before Galileo, we didn't know the equation for the relationship between velocity and acceleration. Perhaps, Theodore, we merely do not yet know the equation to study free will."

Theodore grimaced. "Don't you see what he's trying to do? If you buy his argument, you can use quantum mechanics to legitimize anything—even his kiddie camps for pseudopsychics."

Zag leaned back in his chair, enjoying the moment—the great Theodore Fields losing his cool. It seemed to happen more and more these days. And Zag was just getting started.

"Is that how you see the Halo-effect schools? Kiddie camps for pseudopsychic ability?"

"Or worse," Theodore said.

Zag grinned. "Oh, please, Theodore. Don't hold back."

"I can understand bamboozling some rich asshole who wants to cultivate some fantasy that his child is *special*. But this recent addition of working with autistic children at these schools—really, Zag, it's too much. You tell their poor, desperate parents that their children are unique rather than disabled, that you can help them develop their unusual gifts, milking them with that hope."

"But they *are* unique, Theodore," Zag continued coolly. "I've been working with autistic children since graduate school. I've seen these children do incredible things. You want to put them in a box and drug them, I see them as an evolutionary next step in brain development. My work is to try and use psychic tools to access their potential."

"Psychic tools? *What* is a psychic tool? Oh, wait!" Theodore reached for an empty space on the table and held up his hand as if holding something. "Here it is! My psychic tool!"

Morgan held up a hand. "Enough, gentlemen. While I enjoy your verbal sparring, I believe we were discussing Zag's unorthodox use of the uncertainty principle. Lionel?" Morgan asked, reaching out to the group's resident mathematician and referee, who was sitting between Theodore and Zag. "Do you want to chime in here?"

Dr. Lionel Cable had recently been recognized for his seminal work in algebraic topology. A compact man of African American descent, he had a prominent scar in the middle of his forehead caused by a childhood accident. He was the most recent recipient of the Fields Medal, the equivalent of the Nobel Prize for mathematics and the only cool head in the room.

He didn't hesitate to step in. "It is true that the uncertainty principle can be misused. Since Einstein, we've been trying to apply quantum physics on the cosmic scale. We have no idea if these principles are even relevant at the macro level."

"We *don't* know being the salient point, Lionel," Martha argued. "So why run from the discussion? During the eighteenth century, the French Academy of Science denied the existence of meteorites. Museum curators all over Europe threw out their collections of meteorites for fear of appearing backward. Stones falling from the sky? It smacked too much of religion—the hand of God and all that. Once it was the church persecuting theorists, now it's science? Well, I for one refuse to be bullied from discussing the topic at hand."

Morgan turned to Lionel. "Isn't the macro level merely the summation of what happens on the molecular level?"

"Wonderful," Theodore said. "You make up a law and then find a way to apply it broadly. That's great science. Did we read the same article, people?" He looked around the table, sounding almost desperate. "The man quoted Edgar Cayce and Madam Blavatsky!"

Edgar Cayce, the sleeping prophet, was possibly the best-known American psychic. He was also responsible for some of the more controversial theories about the lost city of Atlantis—a favorite topic of Zag's and another one of Theodore's pet peeves.

"Cayce believed that the Atlanteans had a great crystal that allowed its people to focus their extraordinary abilities to achieve fantastical things. Helena Blavatsky claimed that Atlanteans invented airplanes and grew extraterrestrial wheat," Theodore continued, his face growing ever more florid. "Atlantis is fodder for Disney, for God's sake, not science. Is this the kind of hogwash you want to sign your name to, Morgan? I can't believe it was published in a peer review journal."

"Both Cayce and Blavatsky were mentioned as historical context only," Zag said.

"Or to keep the tabloids interested," Theodore countered. "The man feeds these ridiculous rumors that he is some kind of descendant from Atlanteans who escaped in aircrafts before their own big bang."

"I actually found Zag's discussion on Atlantis quite fascinating," Lionel said, again acting as mediator. "I don't believe anyone has ever postulated the possibility that it was in attempting to isolate dark matter that the Atlanteans caused their destruction."

"Well, then, perhaps you don't read enough science fiction," Theodore added.

"Then there's the idea of the Atlantean crystal," Lionel

continued. "It's somewhat reminiscent of Morgan's psychic artifact, the Eye of Athena. I believe it was your point to connect the two, Zag?"

But before Zag could answer, Theodore threw up his hands. "Now it's back to psychic artifacts? More mumbo jumbo!"

The crystal, the Eye of Athena, had been an ongoing topic of conversation with the Brain Trust. Ten months ago, it had made the headlines as part of a collection of psychic artifacts confiscated after the murder of David Gospel. The man, a local real-estate mogul, had accumulated quite the collection—most of it obtained on the black market, of course. And while many of the artifacts had been authenticated by their own Martha and colleagues, the Eye of Athena had turned out to be a fraud.

Soon thereafter, Morgan began discussing the crystal, artfully dangling the possibility that he'd gotten his hands on the real deal. Thus far, Morgan had refused to produce it, talking about the Eye of Athena only in the theoretical, claiming his interest in the artifact had been brought on by the recent headlines and his own history with the stone.

It was a facile explanation. Morgan's lover, Estelle Fegaris, the mother of his only child, had been obsessed with the Eye. Some said the crystal had even cost her her life.

"The comparison seems more than plausible," Martha mused. "The theory is that the Eye works on the brain, helping to enhance certain psychic abilities…facilitating what Zag refers to as brain evolution. I believe Cayce made similar claims for the Atlantean crystal." She turned her attention back to Zag. "You suggest, of course, that the artifacts are related. But do you also believe that the crystals actually *are* dark matter?"

Again, Theodore answered. "If this object—a theoretical object that Morgan refuses to even admit he possesses—*were* dark matter, our humble building would be weighted down by what was essentially over a ton of gravitational pull. Tell us, Morgan. Do you have a miniature atom bomb hidden somewhere?"

"I know how much you enjoy sounding important, Theodore," Martha said with a wink, "but for those of us in the room who speak English and not techno nerd, please elaborate."

But it was Lionel who answered this time. "As I explained last week, the existence of dark matter was first theorized to explain the rotational speeds of galaxies. An answer to the missing mass problem," Lionel explained. "Dark matter reconciles observable phenomenon with the big bang theory. It, along with the more nebulous concept, dark energy, allows for a sort of fudge factor. Theodore is right. If the crystal were dark matter, it would be significantly heavier than plutonium."

"Couldn't the crystal possess a femtogram of dark matter?" Martha insisted.

"Add a pinch of spice and make everything nice?" Theodore scoffed. "That's about as brilliant as Zag's concepts about these crystals focusing psychic energy like some idiotic lens. Oh wait, I get it. That's one of your psychic tools, isn't it, Zag? Do tell! And what would a parapsychologist of your training, Morgan, title such an artifact? A magic wand?"

"A magic wand?" Morgan grinned. "Now I rather like that, Theodore—and not just because I'll enjoy watching you eat those words someday when it comes to the Eye. Unfortunately—" Morgan glanced at the conference room clock "—the topic will have to wait for another day."

Morgan was the self-appointed timekeeper of the group. Discussions like these, while extremely valuable to the Institute, could get out of hand, lasting for hours. But that wasn't why Morgan cut short today's debate at what was surely its most interesting juncture.

Later, when he found Zag fast on his heels, Morgan knew his timing had been perfect.

"Morgan." Zag continued hurrying down the hall toward him, the excitement in his eyes unmistakable. He was almost breathless when he stopped and asked, "How long are you going to keep us guessing? Do you have the Eye or not?"

"Wouldn't it be wild if I did?" Morgan answered.

"So you haven't authenticated it?"

Morgan paused, meeting the man's curious eyes. At the moment, the pupils appeared impossibly large, showing only a rim of ice-water blue.

Morgan lowered his voice, dropping his final crumb of bait. "I've run some tests."

The Eye of Athena was the oldest psychic relic ever found. It could be traced back to the Oracle at Delphi—even to Athena, the Greek goddess. Presumably, the Eye, or the central crystal on the ancient necklace, had been worn by the goddess herself. While he'd never explicitly stated he had the crystal, the last months Morgan had carefully hinted to having it ensconced in his vault, hoping for just this interest from the enigmatic Zag.

"I can help. You know I can," the younger man said, reaching up to grip Morgan's arm.

Jesus, he was practically salivating.

"If you're suggesting some sort of collaboration?" Morgan asked. "I might be interested."

Suddenly, the man's curious eyes widened. A smile

crossed his lips as he dropped his grip on Morgan and took a step back. "Why do I suddenly feel so easy?"

"I haven't the slightest idea what you could mean by that," Morgan said with a faint smile of his own.

Morgan hadn't wanted to be the one to come, hat in hand, asking for help. Rather, he'd fanned Zag's enthusiasm for the stone, knowing that eventually it would be Zag begging him for a chance to play.

"Well done," Zag acknowledged. "Of course, you need my resources."

"As I said," Morgan answered carefully, "I am open to a collaboration between us. Here, at the Institute, and with my people in charge."

The younger man acknowledged Morgan's conditions with a quick nod. "You won't be disappointed."

Fifteen minutes later, Morgan was almost to his office, marveling at today's success. For years now, he'd worked to capture the interest of Gonzague de Rozières and Halo Industries. Zag was exactly what the Institute needed: young blood and powerful ambition. At just thirty-four, Zag had done the impossible: he'd made the paranormal a bankable industry. And while his public-relations machine didn't exactly publicize the true goings-on at Halo, Morgan had his sources.

Remote-viewers working for homeland security, research on artificial limbs—computers, even video games, operated by conscious thought. And then there was his pet project, his Halo-effect schools.

When Morgan alluded to having the crystal, he'd expected Zag to fall in with his plans.

What Morgan hadn't anticipated was finding Carin

Barnes waiting in his office, those stormy gray eyes cocked and ready to fire as he entered the room.

"You have *got* to be kidding," she said, all Sturm und Drang as she jumped to her feet. "You are not going to give *him* the crystal."

She made an imposing sight. Tall, just shy of Morgan's six feet some, she had the slim figure of an athlete. She wore what Morgan had come to call her uniform: a dark suit with a cuffed white shirt underneath, looking every bit the FBI agent. She'd recently shorn her hair to within an inch of its life. The boy cut only made her gray eyes look larger on her refined face.

"Why would you even think such a thing, Carin?"

"Do not bullshit me, Morgan," she said, stabbing the air with her finger. "Ten months after I hand you the Eye, Zag writes a check big enough to buy even your filthy-rich ass and I'm supposed to believe it's not connected? I did not risk my career so that you could trade it in for some easy capital."

Carin Barnes worked for NISA, the National Institute for Strategic Artifacts. Ten months ago, when David Gospel's collection of artifacts surfaced—presumably purchased from black-market dealers—the FBI had been on the case. Carin's job: bring back the stolen goods and deliver them to their country of origin.

Only, like Morgan, Carin and the Eye had a history, the kind that was difficult to ignore. She might be a dedicated agent, but her desire for the Eye went beyond even her duty to God and country. The last thing she wanted was to have such a powerful artifact end up filed away like some X-file project at the Bureau.

Carin had been the special agent in charge when the police confiscated Gospel's collection of rare artifacts.

With Morgan's help, she'd been able to switch out the crystal for a clever fake.

"I know what you did for us," Morgan said, stepping in to take both her hands in his. "I won't throw it away. But Zag might be just what we need. Think about it. Halo Industries and all its resources at our disposal."

She brushed off his hands. "You're not thinking. Jesus Christ, Morgan, three weeks after I hand you the Eye, Zag suddenly takes an interest in the Institute? You don't find that a tad convenient? You didn't have to bring Zag into your confidence, signing him up for your damn Brain Trust. He knew you had the Eye—he came here just for that."

"Don't let your history with the man cloud your judgment."

Carin's cheeks flamed red. "Is that what you think?"

"He broke your heart and ruined your academic career. I wouldn't blame you for carrying a grudge. But a man can change, Carin. It wasn't so long ago that I committed similar damage to someone I loved."

"My *history* with Zag taught me one simple fact. Something you ignore at your peril. You can't trust him."

But Morgan pushed on. "Okay. You're right. You know him better than I ever will. But we've had the crystal for ten months and we are no closer to finding out how to harness its unique powers than the day you handed it to me. We need Halo."

"It's a bad move, Morgan."

"But a necessary one."

She slammed her fist on his desk in frustration. "Do you really think you're in control here? Do you know how desperately Zag wants the Eye? He tried to buy it off Gospel just months before the man died!"

"Which only means he's made a careful study of our

prize and most certainly has valuable information—information from which we stand to greatly benefit." He came in close, grabbing her shoulders. "Estelle gave her life for that crystal. What good is it doing sitting in my vault?"

"Estelle?" She shot him a look, her eyes the color of a summer storm. "That would be the woman whose heart you broke and whose career you ruined?"

He had the audacity to smile. "As if she cared about such things. Like you, Estelle had grander ambitions. And what about Markie?" he asked, stepping back. "Isn't this exactly what you wanted for your brother? Why you entrusted his care to me and what we could offer him here? Imagine it, Carin—a crystal that can enhance human brain functions. Let me do my job. Let me find out how the damn thing works. Let me use it to help people like Markie."

"How dare you?"

Morgan knew he'd overstepped, opening deep wounds. Carin's brother was a twenty-three-year-old autistic man living at the Institute. Twelve years her junior, Markie was the agent's raison d'être…and it had been her work on autism—research meant to help her brother—that Zag had sabotaged.

Still, he pressed his point. "Do you remember the day when you brought Markie to Estelle? You'd never even heard the sound of his voice before then. She gave you that, Carin," he continued, reminding her that it was Estelle's gift as a psychic that had allowed Markie to utter his first and only words: *I love you.*

"Let's finish the job she started," he said. "It's what Estelle would have wanted. It should be what we all want."

She shook her head, looking away. "You're a son of bitch, Morgan. You know that?"

Carin glanced down at his desk. Suddenly, she reached for one of several photographs and turned it to face Morgan.

The photo showed Morgan's daughter, Gia, holding his granddaughter, Stella, in her arms.

"You said it yourself, Morgan. You ruined Estelle's career and broke her heart. Be careful who you sell out this time."

She put the photo back and walked out, slamming the door behind her.

Theodore Fields hobbled through the parking area toward the front door of his waterfront condo. Damn Achilles tendon. Every morning he woke up barely able to walk, it felt so tight. Now the damn thing was giving him problems even after a long drive in the car.

Seriously, he was beginning to feel ancient.

He switched the bag of Chinese food—it was probably already cold—to his left hand and took out his house keys.

Fucking Zag.

Theodore didn't consider himself a violent man. But more and more he wanted to shove his fist into that pompous face.

The fact was, Zag de Rozières had everything. Money, prestige, good looks.

And youth. The bastard had years ahead of him to accomplish whatever he wanted in life.

Not Theodore. He had a bitter ex-wife who'd taken him to the cleaners and was still bleeding him for alimony, and a daughter who'd come out of the closet. Last week, she'd brought her butch lover to their lunch together, parading her around for anyone to see.

Fuck. What a bunch of losers.

Theodore hated losers. All his life, he'd been a winner. He'd won the fucking Nobel, for God's sake. And he was still the man when it came to membrane theory.

But there was Zag, sitting smugly across that ridiculous table and its Tibetan carvings, talking about bullshit like magic crystals and Atlantis. He could publish his silly theories in legitimate journals solely because he had more money than God…as if anything that man came up with could forward real science.

He should never have agreed to associate with Morgan and the Institute. He'd never have done it if it weren't for Lionel's involvement. Now there was a *real* scientist. And for a while, the work had been interesting. They'd been able to achieve statistically significant samples of tele-kinesis at the molecular level. That's why Morgan had brought him on, to keep them on the straight and narrow.

Only now, Morgan was obsessed with this artifact, this Eye of Athena. And he'd signed on as coauthor to Zag's embarrassing article. Theodore couldn't help but fear that his current association with the Institute was putting his reputation on the line. It had been too long since he'd pub-lished anything significant. And now, he was involved in this bullshit. He was in danger of becoming the laughing-stock of physics.

Shit, he could already feel his acid reflux kicking in. Forget the Chinese. He wouldn't get through the night.

"Theodore?"

The sound of her voice startled him. Theodore turned, his heart hitting his throat, making it difficult to catch his breath. He searched the shadows and found her standing near the bougainvillea.

Her bright red hair was severely pulled back and she wore a black vinyl trench coat tied tightly around her slim waist and ruby-red spiked heels, the same color as her lipstick.

Immediately, he cleared his throat—a nervous habit. He

walked to her and grabbed her arm, steering her deeper into the shadows.

He looked around nervously. "I told you never to come here!" he whispered harshly.

But he could already feel his growing erection. *Jesus.*

She stepped back. In clear view of his neighbors, she opened her trench coat to expose her beautiful naked body.

Her bright red pubic hair had been shaved in the shape of a heart.

"Should I go home, baby?" she asked sweetly.

His hands shaking, Theodore couldn't get the front door opened fast enough.

8

Seven balanced two bags of groceries as he walked up the path to the house. "Dinner has arrived!" he called out loudly.

Nick, his eleven-year-old nephew, burst out the door, an enormous smile on his face. That smile made Seven's heart just stop right there in his chest.

Jesus, Ricky. What you're missing….

He handed one of the bags to Nick and tousled his blond curls. "I'm cooking."

"No, you're not."

Beth was already standing at the door, holding it open. She was wearing jeans and a lacy white blouse, her blond hair loose around her face. As he passed, he gave her a peck on the cheek. "I'm cooking," he said again.

She shut the door and followed him into the kitchen. "No, you're not."

The three of them stood in the modest kitchen, unloading groceries. Just a year ago, Beth had been an upscale harbour wife, involved in all the right charities, taking classes in interior decorating. The kitchen of their waterfront home in Huntington Harbour had been her masterpiece: granite counters, two built-in Subzero refrigerators, top-of-the-line Viking equipment. Now she stood in a kitchen not much bigger than the galley of what had once been Ricky's fifty-five-foot yacht.

He remembered the day Beth finally looked at him, her brown eyes tired and flat. Her words chardonnay-slurred, she'd told him, "Let them have it. I can't make up for what Ricky did, killing their son. If this is what they want," she said, signaling to the house and beyond, "they can have it. They can have every penny."

She'd been talking about Scott's family. After Ricky had pleaded guilty to the murder of his lover, Scott's family had filed an unlawful-death suit.

She'd been drunk at the time; Seven had no idea if she'd meant what she'd said. But the next day, she'd called her attorney and made the arrangements. A week later, Beth started AA.

The last ten months had brought on more changes. The five-hundred-dollar cut and color in Beverly Hills had given way to Lady Clairol and a local salon in Seal Beach. Sweater sets and slacks worn with ballet flats from Neiman's and Bloomie's were downgraded to jeans and dresses from Target.

The funny thing—she looked younger. Hipper. More alive. She'd been working at a friend's real-estate firm. Next month, she was going for her broker's license.

"Look at this." He held up some filet mignons and portabella mushrooms. He had a bag of prewashed mescaline greens and three potatoes, each practically the size of Nick's miniature Nerf football.

"I'm telling you guys. Even I can't blow this," he said with a grin.

Mother and son gave each other a look.

"What?" he asked.

Beth picked up the steaks and the mushrooms. She

gave Seven a pat on the cheek. "There's beer in the refrigerator."

Nick headed for the sink with the potatoes. "Mom, can you preheat the oven?"

"What?" Seven asked again. "Hey, that thing with the pot pies, that was a fluke. I swear, I think the thermostat was broken or something. No way those things would have gone up in flames otherwise."

Forty minutes later, they were seated around a small glass table in the kitchen, the steaks perfect, the mushrooms divine, the potatoes slathered with sour cream and butter. A delicate vinaigrette had been tossed into the salad.

They'd let him wash the "prewashed" salad.

Still, it felt good, looking around the table. Nick was starting middle school in the fall and was excited as all get-out. He'd tested into the higher math classes, although English wasn't looking so good. Hearing the enthusiasm in his voice, Seven felt a hard knot in his throat. Ricky had always been the brains of the family.

Like father, like son.

But Seven could only see the good things in Ricky's son. His brother's blond hair and green eyes—the athletic build that soon would bring the attention of too many girls. Already, Beth complained about the phone calls.

"Nicky," she said, scrunching her nose in distaste. "They call him Nicky. *Is Nicky there?*" she mimicked in a breathy, nervous voice of a preteen girl.

"Mom!"

They were having a good old time teasing poor Nick. It was the kind of evening Seven hated to end.

So he'd offered to drive them down to Main Street. On Tuesday nights, the area was closed off to traffic. Street musicians and booths selling anything from jewelry to produce made for a loud and colorful walk ending at Cold Stone Creamery.

Nick hooked up with friends from school. Beth and Seven had taken a table in the corner, giving the kid some space.

Beth looked down at her cherries and chocolate chopped into French vanilla ice cream. "I am truly going to regret this come morning."

"Nah," Seven said, digging into his Heath-Bar-Crunch-studded chocolate.

"Seven, I have gained almost ten pounds."

He shrugged. "It suits you."

And it did. Those years playing the perfect wife, with perfect hair and nails, perfect body and perfect tan, she'd looked almost plastic. A Barbie doll his brother kept on display.

She shook her spoon at him. "Thanks, but no thanks. I need to lose at least five of those."

They settled into comfortable silence, every once in a while, glancing over at Nick. His nephew looked damn happy, laughing and playfully punching one of the other boys in the arm. Here at last was a boy who wasn't thinking about his father the murderer.

He'd been watching Nick, smiling to himself, when Beth caught him off guard, asking, "Bad day?"

Seven used his napkin to wipe his mouth, giving himself some time. "Yeah."

"You want to talk about it?"

He pushed away his empty ice cream cup. "Not particularly."

He focused again on the bits and pieces of other people's lives. There was a young couple at the next table with a crying baby. Both parents huddled over their offspring, the father shaking plastic keys, the mother offering a pacifier, acting as if world peace hung in the balance. A couple in their late sixties fed each other spoonfuls of ice cream. Sitting here with Beth and Nick, he could almost believe it was still possible. Marriage, kids. That happily ever after. The world was a good place and people didn't snatch kids like Nick and dump their bodies in the marsh.

"Erika and I have this bet," he said, changing the subject. "Who has the better vocabulary? Just the other day she hit me with *'Sounds like ursprache.'*"

Beth frowned. "Ursprache?"

He leaned forward. "The general translation she gave was something like: 'Sounds like bullshit.' I looked it up in the dictionary. It means a protolanguage or something."

Beth nodded as what he'd just said made perfect sense. "Well, that clears it up."

They both laughed.

She played around with her ice cream in a way that made him think she had something more to say. He gave it a minute.

She switched ice cream cups, giving him her half-filled one for his empty cup. He didn't hesitate, picking up the spoon and digging in.

She said, "Laurin called."

Laurin, Seven's ex-wife, now mother of twins with a doting accountant husband.

"Really," he said carefully.

"She wanted to know how I was doing. It was…awkward."

"I'll talk to her."

Beth put her hand on his. "That's not necessary. It's just that…" she sighed, "she should have stuck by you."

Seven glanced down at the ice cream. Of course, Beth

wouldn't get it. To her, he was some kind of knight in shining armor.

That wouldn't be his ex-wife's take on things.

"She was a cop's wife, Beth. It's not an easy life. The work, it starts to take over. Suddenly, you don't have anything in common with normal people. You start cutting them off. There's stuff you can't talk about. Pretty soon, your only friends are fellow officers."

"Gee, I wonder if that's anything like being married to a prominent surgeon and finding out he killed his gay lover."

Their eyes met. Yeah, Beth was no stranger to his kind of alienation.

"Laurin didn't give up on me. I gave up on us."

But Beth shook her head. "You are a good man, Seven. I know there was a time when I asked for too much. I was devastated and lonely and you were my great big shoulder to cry on."

"Beth—"

She squeezed his hand. "No, let me say it. You were gentle in your rejection. And now, you are my dearest friend and possibly the closest thing to a father my son will ever have. I guess I just need you to be happy. I don't want you to give up, you know? I see how you are with me and Nick. You deserve your own family. A wife, a couple of kids." She sat back, smiling. "And then there's the fact that you're not getting any younger."

Again, they both laughed.

"If only it could be that easy," he said. "Swear to God, I look in the mirror and I see a big red *D* for divorce right there on my forehead." He picked up his spoonful of ice cream and winked. "I think it scares the babes away."

But Beth didn't laugh. "I might be joining you there. Adding that big red *D* on my forehead."

Seven stopped eating, the spoon halfway to his mouth. He knew she'd been thinking about it. "Really."

"It's twenty to life, Seven." Her brown eyes looked serious. "And the whole Scott thing." She shook her head. "I have to think about Nick. I have to think about my own happiness."

He put the spoon down. He asked, "Is there someone else?"

She shook her head. She smiled and looked over at her son. "I'm not alone," she said. "And I have time."

Seven watched her, thinking about the accusations Erika still slung in Beth's direction and how wrong she was. Beth wasn't that woman anymore. She was over the whole *I need you, Seven, please love me, Seven.*

The weird part? He wasn't sure *he* was. Beth had been only too right when she'd said he'd gently let her know he could never go there—Nick was screwed up enough. How would he handle his uncle moving in if he and Beth became involved?

But it had been nice, someone needing him. Loving him.

His cell phone sounded.

"That's the third time tonight," Beth said. "Someone's avoiding his calls." She cocked an eyebrow. "I'm guessing it's a woman."

"It's just work," he said.

She shook her head. "It's a woman. If it were work, you wouldn't hesitate to answer, Mr. Cop."

"Wow," he said, finishing the ice cream. "I'm impressed."

Thankfully, Nick came bouncing over just then. Beth immediately took her son's hand and headed for the door.

Seven could only sigh in relief as he followed them out.

* * *

Half an hour later, he sat reclined in the Barcalounger he'd inherited from his dad, his cell phone unopened in his hand. His mother had remodeled recently and dissed his dad's favorite chair. His father had begged him to save the closest thing to a family heirloom that he possessed. Seven had taken the chair gladly.

Seven was still mulling over Beth's message: Don't give up.

Immediately, an image of Gia came to mind. He'd always had this thing about Jennifer Connelly, so maybe he saw a resemblance that wasn't really there. Still, at the moment, he wasn't thinking about the actress. He was thinking about the Brothers Grimm.

Skin as white as snow, lips as red as blood, hair as black as ebony.

And then there were her eyes, a deep fathomless blue.

Beth wanted him to be happy, to marry and have children of his own. But what if the woman he wanted was off-limits?

Just then, the phone in the kitchen sounded off like an alarm. *Time's up!*

"Shit."

He rocked forward in the Barcalounger and stood. This time he didn't hesitate, heading for the kitchen. Beth was right; he'd avoided Gia's calls long enough.

Without glancing at the caller ID, he picked up. "Bushard."

"You're not answering your cell now?" Erika asked in an irritated voice. "I've left you five messages. Jesus, Seven. It's not like we have a dead body or anything."

A little of that tension eased from around his chest.

"Sorry," he said. "I must have turned it off by accident."

He heard a grunt of disbelief on the other end. "Right. Because that's so easy to do. Listen, do you have dinner plans tomorrow?"

"I don't think so."

"Good. House of Brews after work. Your treat."

She hung up.

He stared at the handset. "Sure, Erika. No problem. And by the way, isn't it always my treat?"

Not that he cared. The last year, Erika had been his touchstone—the one person who could slap him across the face and tell him to snap out of it…even as she covered for him at work.

He grabbed a beer from the refrigerator and headed back into the front room. He might not have ESP, but he knew what his partner wanted: a nice little chat about the FBI and a certain psychic.

Well, he had a couple of questions of his own. Like why in hell his partner hadn't given him the heads-up about Special Agent Carin Barnes.

He dropped back into the Barcalounger. It still smelled like cigars, his father's hidden vice. Seven didn't smoke, but he was far from free of vice.

Gia.

It had been ten months, five days and nineteen hours since he'd last seen her.

For a moment, he let his mind drift to all those months ago. Without Gia, they never would have broken open the fortune-teller murders. The fly in the ointment: her help came with a price. Seven had shot the murdering whack job Gia had been hiding from the last twelve years, fearing for her life and the life of her child.

Seven took a long sip from the beer. No matter how many times he told himself he didn't believe in her "psychic" abilities, there'd been something truly bizarre about how the whole thing had gone down. Like she'd known exactly what was going to happen. That it would be Seven who'd pull the trigger and save the day. The thing was, she hadn't bothered to share any of it, letting him walk in blind.

Of course, she wouldn't see it that way. There was probably some secret code for psychics: Don't let the minions in on the details. Just pull the strings and let the puppet show go on.

Unfortunately, she'd been sleeping with this particular puppet. Apparently, she could trust him for sex but that was about it. When he'd nailed her with the truth—that she'd used him—she hadn't even bothered to deny it. She'd just let him walk away.

With a sigh, he took out his cell phone. He checked to see that indeed, he had several messages from his partner.

And one from Gia.

Somehow, he didn't think she was calling about unrequited love.

There was this anecdote about Enrique Fermi, a physicist for the Manhattan Project, the first guy to create a nuclear chain reaction in the 1930s. The story went that Fermi would be meeting a great general. Being the scientific type, Fermi asked what made the man great. The reply came that, if the guy won five consecutive battles he was one fine general.

Only, Fermi quickly figured out that statistically a significant number of *all* generals win five battles consecutively just by pure chance. Using math, Fermi flushed down the toilet the man's definition of greatness.

So here Seven was thinking, throw in a little statistics and just about anything, even a call from Gia, could be coincidence.

It was a good argument, Fermi's. But Seven didn't buy it. Not this time.

A fourteen-year-old girl lay dead in the wetlands. She'd been bound and most likely drugged. And she wasn't alone. Two other vics had been found just the same way.

And here they were again. Erika and him, Special Agent Barnes and Gia, playing the serial-killer merry-go-round.

Her number highlighted on the LCD screen, he punched Send.

She picked up on the first ring, almost as if she were waiting right there next to the phone. He couldn't help but smile. That impeccable timing of hers. Uncanny, that was another word he'd used on Erika: suggesting the operation of supernatural influences.

"Gia," he said, trying to sound imperturbable, another word he'd just learned. "You called?"

9

Ghost boy came back with a vengeance.

Stella was at Mindy's house working on their history paper on ancient Rome. She'd calmed down enough to believe it was safe—there'd been no sign of the boy all through school or here at Mindy's. She'd had a nice quiet dinner with Mindy's family; the meal had been completely spook free.

After dinner, she and Mindy had been seated around the marble-and-glass coffee table in Mindy's family room, both focused on their paper. It was due Monday, but Stella had plans to spend the weekend in San Diego with Morgan, her grandfather.

That's when ghost boy walked into the den right behind Mindy's mom, who'd brought them a bowl of popcorn and a couple of juice boxes claiming neither girl had eaten enough for dinner.

Stella did her best to ignore him. She flipped through the pages of her history book, pretending to read. That was her new tactic. If she just believed hard enough that he wasn't *there*, he *wouldn't* be.

But her heart pounded hard in her chest. She thought for sure Mindy could hear, it sounded so loud in her ears.

The more she ignored ghost boy, the more difficult it became to breathe.

She watched him out of the corner of her eye. She told herself he was just a sad, puppy-eyed kid. She didn't need to be scared.

So why was her heart racing?

"Stella?"

Startled, Stella glanced up at Mindy's mom. Stella liked Mindy's family a lot. They were so…well, normal. They lived in a normal house, painted a normal color. Nothing artsy or weird hung on the walls; there were no papier-mâché leaves sprouting out of the furniture or odd crystals hanging from the light fixtures like at Stella's house. They ate meatloaf with ketchup on top. Mindy's dad had his own business fixing boats. Mindy had a cute older brother who played lacrosse. She went to Supper Club and the National Charity League.

Only now Mindy's really normal mother was looking at Stella like something was wrong.

"Do you feel all right, Stella?"

"Yeah," Mindy said. "What's the deal? You've been reading that same page, like, forever."

Stella knew she had this funny frozen smile on her face. "You know," she said. "I do feel sort of weird. Just give me a minute, okay?"

Stella stood, making her way to the bathroom down the hall, the ghost walking right behind her.

She wondered when it had first happened to her mother, that stray spirit tagging along. She'd never even asked, avoiding the conversation altogether.

She'd thought it couldn't happen to her.

Kids her age didn't worry about attached spirits. They

thought about homework and boys. Stella suddenly giggled, realizing that the only boy in her life was dead.

Once inside the bathroom, she locked the door and turned to face the kid. At the moment, he didn't look so weird. There was no mud, or clothes dripping with water, no ghastly white skin. He had dark blond hair cut in a bowl shape around his head and nondescript gray eyes. He was wearing the same clothes as before, a short-sleeved plaid shirt and jean shorts hemmed just below his knees.

"Okay. I get it. You're not leaving until I deal with you. I'm not sure how this works," she said, pacing nervously. She stopped and demanded, "So what do you want?"

The only thing she knew about the spirit thing was what she'd overheard between her mom and her clients. Men and women would come scratching at the back door, their eyes full of pleading. They wanted to know if Sam was okay or if Lois had forgiven them.

Stella called them the people-with-holes-in-their-hearts. They came to her mom with the hope that she could patch them up with her paintings. That's what her mother did— patch up the broken people, give them answers. She'd take a photograph or a memento and she'd paint, using her talent like an Ouija board.

It wasn't something her mom advertised. Stella figured she didn't make much money at it, either. If your father was some bazillionaire, like Morgan, you could afford to ignore the bottom line. By word of mouth, they found her mother, hoping that her paintings could somehow connect them with lost loved ones. Her mother was really good at it, too, communicating with the dead through her art.

Now Stella wished she'd asked more questions.

"Can't you talk?" she asked.

Ghost boy just stared back at her, completely silent.

"Well, that's just stupid," she said, frustrated. "You're the one following me! So what am I supposed to do now?"

Ghost boy stepped forward. He raised his hand so that his palm faced her.

Stella frowned. Her heart thumped in her chest like it might just pop right out. She licked her lips and raised her hand.

Slowly, she lined up their fingers and pressed her palm to his.

Instantly, her legs gave way. Her knees hit the bathroom tile. Ghost boy hovered over, their hands still linked.

"No. No, please," she whispered.

She felt anchored to the floor by a thousand pounds pressing on her chest.

She was in a cold, wet room, like a basement. She could hear water dripping. A woman and a man were holding her, rocking her in their arms.

The pain. There was so much pain.

"Stella!"

She woke up to find herself on the floor of Mindy's guest bathroom. The shower was going full blast. So was the water in the sink.

Mindy's mom was on the floor next to her, holding her up while Mindy watched from the hallway. Mindy looked pretty scared. Her brother was there, too, both of them crowding around the doorway, staring.

Because I'm a freak.

"I'm okay," she said, pushing Mrs. Poder away, trying to stand.

"You were screaming," Mindy said in a sharp, scared voice. "You wouldn't open the door. Mom had to pick the lock."

She had no idea how much time had passed. How long

had she been lying on the floor in the bathroom? She could imagine what they were thinking. Why had she turned on both faucets? Was she having some kind of fit?

"I'm okay," she repeated.

But Mindy's mom seemed to understand. All business, she quickly turned off the faucet in the shower and then the sink. "Of course you are," she said. "Come on, everyone. Show's over." To Stella, she whispered, "Let me take you home. You guys are almost done, right? I'll help Mindy finish up."

She slipped her hand into Stella's and walked her down the hall. Stella fought back tears, knowing what came next: Mrs. Poder would take her home and report to Stella's mom.

But it wasn't the meeting ahead that bothered Stella. What concerned her most was the fact that Stella could hear the woman's thoughts like whispers inside her head.

She brushed back her tears, already trying to figure out what she'd tell Mrs. Poder on the way home. How to explain?

She glanced back. There, standing in the doorway to the bathroom, ghost boy stood smiling.

10

Gia stared at the paintbrush in her hand. She'd loaded the tip with ochre, the color of the noon sun.

It had been a bright, shiny day and she'd spent it trapped in her garage studio painting death.

Death wasn't always a bad thing. Sometimes, her paintings brought solace: a voice from beyond to forgive or grant release…a final goodbye or a message of love.

But not today. At the moment, the images in her head had nothing to do with the sunny shade of yellow on her brush. And now she'd gone and lost her place in the puzzle of it all.

Putting the pieces together, that's how she'd come to see her process. Clients would approach her with a photograph or a cherished memento from a lost loved one. In time, Gia would gather up the bits that came to her and arrange them into an image. Sometimes, the ideas erupted full force in a vision. Other times, she couldn't even remember the act of painting itself. It felt as if she were sleepwalking. She'd wake up and find herself standing in front of a canvas full of color.

Those were usually the worst. Gia had come to understand that when it came to her gift, strong emotions never boded well.

Like now. A trusted client had commissioned this particular painting. She'd given Gia a photograph, a faded three-and-a-half inch square glossy of a man smiling on the pier just off Main Street in Huntington Beach. The clothes of the passersby and the man's own swimsuit and long hair dated the photograph somewhere in the sixties. She could see whitecaps and a strip of beach in the background. The man was holding a fishing pole, a fish dangled from the line.

After Stella left for school, Gia had gone to her studio intending to begin work on the painting. But the moment she touched the photograph, she'd been bombarded by images from a completely different direction.

She'd painted until she'd been drenched in sweat and her back ached. She'd taken very few breaks. Now she stood before a canvas covered with gruesome images that held absolutely no relationship to a photograph of a smiling man on the pier.

She sighed, trying to make sense of it all. She'd come to her garage studio hoping to find a distraction. Difficult as it was, her work could shut out the world, taking her to a different time and place.

But not today. Today, she stared at the four-by-five-foot canvas and felt only confusion. Worse yet, she kept replaying her conversation with Seven in her head like an endless loop.

"Gia, what's up?"

"I've been thinking about you. A lot."

"Why does that sound ominous?"

"Because it is."

"And?"

"I don't know. It's still early."

"You'll call me, then?"

"I wasn't the one who hesitated, Seven."

"Right."

She'd hung up, having made her point. Her gift was urging her to reconnect with Seven—no easy thing given how they'd left it between them. But she'd swallowed her pride and called just the same. If he needed her help on a case, it would be up to him to take the next step.

She stared back at the painting. She'd mixed her pigments like magic potions and set out her brushes and palette. The ritual was a launching point for her process. But nothing on that canvas illuminated the fate of the man in the photograph.

"So why am I here?" she asked herself.

She heard a gasp behind her. She turned to see Stella standing at the entrance to the studio. With her backpack at her feet, Stella's blue eyes focused on the painting.

Gia could understand her daughter's reaction. The macabre painting appeared like a surreal landscape of doom and gloom.

Just like the man in the photograph, the boy in the painting stood holding a fishing pole. But that's where any similarities ended. Despite the boy's smile and bright brown eyes, his face, arms and legs showed clear signs of decomposition. His clothes hung from his body in wet, muddy tatters.

The boy waited at the side of a nondescript road with a ditch of murky water just beyond. Syringes stuck out of the ground at the water's edge like darts on a board, arranged in the shape of one of those crime-scene chalk outlines. At the water's edge, daffodils captured the light, their bright yellow still loaded on the paintbrush in Gia's hand.

Suspended in the blue sky above the boy's head hung

several smooth rocks, the kind kids used for skipping on water. Scratched on the surface of each stone were strange lines that looked like a form of ancient writing.

Stella walked forward, transfixed. Without touching the painted surface, her finger traced the boy's fishing pole and stopped where, at the end of the line, a small empty birdcage hung like a fish.

"What do you see?" she asked quietly, recognizing her daughter's expression.

It happened like that sometimes. Stella would stare at one of her mother's paintings, captivated. She would start to see things, revealing an understanding that eluded anyone else, including Gia.

Gia had always thought that was part of her daughter's gift: to be able to see and interpret what others couldn't.

"Who is he?" Stella asked, a breathy quality to her voice.

"I don't know." Gia turned back to the canvas. "Carol brought me a photograph of a man fishing off the pier," she said. "This is what I saw."

"The boy." Stella took a couple of steps back. "He's dead."

It wasn't a question.

"I think so, too," Gia answered.

Stella shut her eyes and shook off the effects of the image. Gia watched her daughter physically catch her breath before opening her eyes.

Her gaze locked on her mother's, those dark blue eyes wide and unflinching. "Mindy's mom said to call her. She wants to talk to you about something. Probably sooner rather than later."

"What's going on?" Gia asked, instantly alert.

But her daughter didn't answer. Instead, she grabbed her backpack off the floor and disappeared into the house.

Mindy's mom said to call her...

Gia dropped the paintbrush on the palette and wiped her hands on a cloth hanging off a small table. She pushed her bangs from her face and headed inside the house.

She found Stella in the kitchen talking to a wall. Arguing with it, actually. Only, her daughter wouldn't be talking to the wall. She would be talking to someone— someone Gia couldn't see.

"Stella?"

Suddenly, the kitchen faucet turned on, blasting water down the sink.

Stella whipped around. Her blue eyes opened wider as she stared at Gia.

"Who is it, Stella?" she asked. "Who's here? Is it the boy in the painting?"

Stella stared at the water running down the sink. She said, "You really should call Mindy's mom."

Gia walked over and turned off the faucet. "Strangely enough, I think I already know what she's going to say." Gia took a couple of deep breaths. "When did it start?"

Mother and daughter stared at each other. There was a space between them, a few feet of emptiness neither seemed willing to breach.

Only Gia knew it wasn't empty. There was someone there. A spirit, most likely. A spirit only her daughter could see.

Slowly, miragelike, a puddle of water appeared on the floor between them.

Before her mother could stop her, Stella turned and ran out of the kitchen.

As Gia watched, the pool of water trickled ever so slightly after her daughter and toward the door.

11

Carin raced down the hall, her beeper wailing at her side.
Markie!

She couldn't catch her breath. The years she'd trained with the FBI, the marathons she'd run, none of it seemed to matter. When that beeper went off, her heart rushed into her throat and panic pushed out her breath.

She kept an office at the Institute courtesy of Morgan. She'd been in the middle of an important conference call, describing what had been found at the crime scene and how it compared to the prior victims.

When she'd gotten the call yesterday about the body in the marsh, she'd known what to expect. The victim would be around fourteen years old. There would be ligature marks around the wrists and ankles. And an injection site. Whatever the bastard was doing to these kids, he was off the charts.

The bodies were always dumped in or near water. But that's not where he killed them.

When her beeper went off, she'd had no less than four criminal agencies, local, county and federal, on a conference call. Without explanation, she'd announced Detective Erika Cabral as the local FBI liaison officer would, along with her partner, coordinate their efforts on the Huntington

Beach case. She'd hung up and raced to her brother's location.

Now she flung open the door to find a white-coated technician sitting on the floor, holding her brother in a safety hold. As well as the technicians, there were five other patients in the room, a special kind of laboratory set up to test physical, mental and occupational faculties. The subjects ranged in age from nine to their early twenties. Like Markie, they suffered from varying levels of autism. Following protocol, they were shuffled out of the room just as Carin dropped down beside her brother.

Markie's eyes had rolled back into his head, showing only the whites. His legs and arms trembled in spasms. She could hear a gurgling sound coming from deep in the back of his throat.

The female technician carefully transferred Markie into Carin's arms. As always, her touch soothed her brother. She felt the tension ease as his body folded into her.

She kissed his forehead and his hair, catching her first clear breath. "We're okay," she whispered. "We're both okay."

She didn't expect a response. She hadn't heard her brother speak in a dozen years. Still she continued whispering, "We're okay, Markie. We're okay."

She kept her brother cradled in her arms, rocking him gently now that he'd quieted down. She tried hard not to think about her meeting with Morgan the day before, the fact that she'd risked everything to bring her brother here.

Ten months later, Markie seemed only worse. These fits, as she'd come to think of them, were coming closer together.

Autism presented in varying degrees. Unfortunately, Markie was "full spectrum," experiencing what was considered profound autism. Nearly dysfunctional, he even had a label: low-functioning autism, LFA.

But Carin refused to buy it. Holding her brother in her arms, she remembered a time when he did communicate…and the woman who had brought him out of his silence, if only for a moment.

Estelle.

Carin's brother was a miracle child, born to aging parents who'd long since given up on the possibility of a second child. But soon enough it became clear something wasn't quite right. Carin had been fifteen years old when he'd been diagnosed: autism, a brain disorder that left children unable to speak and often performing compulsive, repetitive motions.

These days, autism was headline news. A mysterious increase in the condition baffled scientists, many calling it an epidemic. But twelve years ago, her brother's condition wasn't even on the radar.

Carin's parents had died when she'd been in college. With their death came the responsibility of caring for her younger brother. But it was after she'd entered graduate school that her guardianship had taken on a whole new dimension. More than ever, her research focused in areas that could change the lives of kids like Markie.

That's when she'd met Zag de Rozières.

She'd been doing postdoctoral work at Caltech when he'd walked into her lab. He'd already made quite a name for himself as the up-and-coming prince of the paranormal. When she'd found out he was joining the lab as a postdoc, she'd been prepared to see him as just another parlor trick. The man could basically buy his way into the university of his choice. She figured he had some time on his hands. Why not get a degree or two to try and add legitimacy?

But that's not what she saw when he stepped into the lab that first day. He wasn't a large man, and yet, there was something about him that made him seem bigger than life. That spiked, near-white hair, those colorless eyes, the almost feminine features and broken nose. It all gelled together in a way that made the women in the lab swoon.

And then there was his intellect. Zag was a genius. It had been a heady thing, working alongside him, sharing ideas.

It wasn't long before they'd started sleeping together.

The bastard hadn't been satisfied with getting in her bed; he'd needed to get inside her head. Soon enough, she confided all her secrets, telling him about Markie and that—in a complete breach of ethics—she'd included her brother as a subject in her research.

Carin was a neurobiologist. Over the years, she'd focused on neuroplasticity, changes in the brain that occur as a result of experience. Decades past, scientific dogma was that connections among brain nerve cells were fixed early in life and did not change in adulthood. But with the advent of new technology such as positronic emission tomography, PET scans, studies now showed that the brain was capable of being trained and physically modified.

Richard Davidson of the University of Wisconsin took the theory of neuroplasticity one step further. By studying the brain activity of Tibetan monks, Davidson showed that, through meditation, the monks were able to change the actual circuitry of their brain, much in the same way that golf or tennis practice can enhance performance.

But it was Davidson's results on gamma waves that captured Carin's interest. Electrodes showed a greater activation of unusually powerful gamma waves in the monks who meditated. On a hunch, she tested her brother during a focused activity and found that, when measuring the electrical impulses in his brain, his gamma-wave activation was far below average. She began to wonder if there was a connection. Could the reduced gamma-wave frequency be a key to her brother's autism?

When she shared her theories with Zag, he'd directed her to Morgan Tyrell and his work at Harvard on the "evolving brain." Morgan had found a correlation between high levels of gamma-wave activation and an increase in psychic ability. But his research had no breadth, focusing on only one psychic, an archaeologist at Harvard named Estelle Fegaris.

Morgan's theories had been criticized as crazy insane. But here was Carin making some of the same connections.

She'd contacted Morgan directly, asking if it was possible to stimulate similar brain activity in the brain of an autistic. Morgan invited her to his lab; he'd introduced her and her brother to Estelle.

With Morgan beside her, Carin had watched Estelle use her psychic ability to reach inside her brother's mind. With Markie in Estelle's arms, Carin heard him say the words she'd longed to hear: *I love you.*

Only, that's where it stopped. Estelle and Markie finished the session drained. What's more, what she'd accomplished with Markie was a rare thing; there would be no repeat performance. Estelle's only hope to help someone like Markie was the Eye—a crystal that would enable her to focus and perhaps even to enhance her psychic skills. With the Eye to aid her, Estelle truly believed she could change Markie forever.

Carin hugged her brother, taking in the smell of him, a combination of cinnamon and cloves that always reminded her of family holidays. She'd never forget that meeting with Estelle or the sound of her brother's voice. She'd always wondered if Estelle was right. In the right hands, could the Eye alter the circuitry of her brother's brain?

From that day forward, the entire course of her life changed. Zag, of course, played a pivotal role in those changes, and not in a good way.

When she'd returned to Caltech, her advisor informed her that she was no longer welcome in his lab. She'd included her brother in her research without discussing his participation first. She'd turned what was once a scientific study into a personal quest. She was no longer the detached observer. He couldn't justify the use of grant money to support research tainted by personal gain or prejudice.

The only other person who'd known she'd included her brother in her work was Zag.

Five months later, her theories and data were published in an extremely well-received paper. The paper's author was Zag de Rozières.

The pain of that betrayal had been excruciating. And still, it had served as a valuable lesson. What she wanted—what she needed—was to help Markie. No more distractions.

Yesterday, Morgan had compared her to Estelle. Well, in that sense, they were the same: two women driven by their desire to help their families.

All Estelle had ever wanted was to bring psychic ability into the light of day. Her goal was to make certain that her daughter and others like her would no longer be marginalized by a society that feared psychic abilities. When Estelle was murdered, it had been left to Carin and others like her to carry on her quest.

Forced out of academia, Carin had joined the FBI,

knowing that NISA would be her best chance at locating the Eye. It was only a year after she'd moved into NISA's basement headquarters in a nondescript building in D.C. that the Eye surfaced.

The crystal had been part of an investigation on the fortune-teller murders. A serial killer had apparently targeted Vietnamese psychics in Little Saigon, a suburb in Southern California. A bead from the Eye's necklace setting had been found in the mouth of the first victim.

NISA was the FBI's version of the X-files—its manpower was anemic at best. Not a lot of agents jockeying for position from their basement headquarters. Once she'd discovered that the Eye was connected to the case, she hadn't hesitated to get herself assigned as special agent in charge.

Of course, she'd put her career—and most likely her freedom—at risk by switching out the real crystal for a fake. And she'd do it again. If NISA had the Eye, they'd bury it. And then there was the very real possibility that the artifact would disappear into some secret military laboratory.

She'd stolen what was one of the most important artifacts of her time. She'd brought it here, to Morgan. She'd thought that, at the Institute, she could at last tap the crystal's unique properties to help Markie. Yet ten months later, she was no closer to finding a cure for her brother.

"Do you want me to take him now?"

Carin nodded and handed Markie's limp body to the tech, who would take him to the clinic where he would be medicated. Markie had the best care available. That had been part of Carin's arrangement with Morgan. She'd given him the Eye; he, in turn, took care of Markie.

So why are his seizures getting worse?

Just then, the door flew open. A tall, elegant redhead

briskly walked past, heading straight for Markie. Without a word, the woman took him from the technician's arms.

Carin turned. *What the hell?*

She was just about to intervene when the woman spoke softly to her brother. He looked up, appearing by that slight gesture to acknowledge the woman.

Carin stopped. That look on Markie's face, she'd seen it before. With Estelle.

Carin stood frozen, her eyes on the woman. She wore a white lab coat over a dark blue pantsuit, her red hair pulled back in a severe French twist. As Carin watched, she cupped his face in her hands and smiled at Markie. Carin couldn't quite figure out what just happened, but her brother seemed different somehow.

The woman took his hand in hers. Together, they walked toward the door. There, the woman handed Markie to the tech again.

"He'll be fine now," she said. "Just take him back to his room."

Carin frowned as the tech guided Markie, now walking on his own, into the hall and beyond. The woman, the redhead in the white doctor's coat, stepped toward Carin, her hand outstretched in greeting.

"You must be Markie's sister. Morgan told me all about you. I'm sorry to meet you under these conditions."

She shook Carin's hand firmly, giving a confident smile. For the first time, Carin felt something ease inside her.

"My name is Dr. Slade," the woman said with shining blue eyes. "Evie. I've been working with your brother. I'm his therapist."

12

Erika Cabral didn't believe in love. But like most single women in their thirties, she did dabble in it.

She stared down at the Cosmopolitan the waitress set before her and sighed. Greg, however, wasn't much of a dabbler. He plunged in, headfirst.

Erika glanced over at the bar where Greg was doing his best to appear completely disinterested. She was seated at a booth waiting for Seven. During dinner, she and her partner, now officially FBI lackeys, would be discussing murder and mayhem. Having her boyfriend stalking her wasn't part of the night's entertainment.

With a sigh, she picked up her drink and headed for the bar.

A year ago, she would have said men like Greg weren't her thing. He sported a receding hairline and thick glasses. The faded jeans and neon Hawaiian shirt didn't do much for a complexion that screamed I-work-indoors. Erika clocked him at five-nine, maybe one hundred and ninety pounds. And still she could feel her heart skip a beat as she sat on the barstool next to him.

"Do I need a restraining order?" she asked him, raising the Cosmo he'd sent over for her.

"Wow." He shook his head. "And here I thought things went pretty well last night."

Erika hid her smile as she took another sip. "No comment," she said.

"Clever girl."

Greg Smith, the man who had shared Erika's bed for the last ten months, was a damn good reporter. As it happened, he wasn't bad in the sack, either.

He tapped his bottle to her glass. She grinned when she saw he was drinking a low-carb beer. Erika was in top shape—her job and her vanity required it. Greg joked that she loved him for his big giant brain—and other parts. No need for him to lose weight or work out… Only, the other day she'd peeked in his briefcase and found a bunch of books on the South Beach diet.

"A restraining order?" he asked, nodding his head. "And here you're the one with the handcuffs."

"And a gun," she added. "Don't forget the gun."

"As if I could?"

A gun she'd actually threatened him with, although it hadn't been loaded at the time. Not that she'd let Greg know.

He'd deserved it, of course. He'd picked her up at this very bar, acting as if all he had in mind was some great, casual sex. In reality, he'd been targeting her for weeks.

He'd even slipped the bartender money to find out her name. A couple of Google searches later, one of *The Register's* finest—as well as most ambitious—reporters had the lead detective on the fortune-teller murders in his sites. The grisly, ritual killings had been the biggest story to hit the paper in years.

Even now, she knew he was putting together a book deal about the murders committed by a socialite and her son…although Greg was smart enough not to rub salt in the wound by pumping her for information.

That hadn't been the case when they'd first met. At the time, he would have lied, cheated and stolen for that byline, the biggest of his career. He'd used every trick in the book—including sleeping with her—to get what he needed.

That should have been the end of them. But like everything else in her life, her relationship with Greg Smith was complicated.

Ten months later, the man had his own drawer and twelve inches of coveted space on the rod in her closet.

"Keeping that gun in mind," she asked. "Why are you here?"

He held up his beer bottle. "A man can't just show up for a drink?"

She took his hand in hers and gave it a squeeze. She met his gaze. "Go home, Greg. This is business." And when he didn't respond, she added, "Business that better not end up on the front page of *The Register.*"

He frowned. "You still don't trust me."

She took her hand away. "If the story were good enough?" She rolled her eyes at him. "Come on, Greg. You couldn't help yourself."

He flashed that cute smile she loved. "You're selling yourself short."

Again, that strange skip of her heart.

She nodded, in on the joke. "You're right. For a guy like you, a byline is everyday stuff. But great sex?" She took another sip of the Cosmo and threw in a mournful shake of her head. "God knows when that's coming your way again."

She took any sting away with a quick kiss, pushing him away playfully when he tried to deepen the contact.

"You're just lucky I'm not the jealous type," he said, keeping his lighthearted tone. "What? Not enough hours in a day? You need to meet Seven after hours? And, may I point out, at an atmospheric watering hole used by many for purposes of hooking up?"

"Or just to order a damn fine steak."

She hadn't told him who she was meeting. She could smell his tactics a mile away, throwing out the question to see what might come.

The problem was, she couldn't figure what interested him more: her relationship with her partner or the case they might be working on so diligently after hours.

She stroked his chin and smiled. "Go home, baby."

"Oh, you mean before Seven gets here and sees us together?" he asked, huddling down as if trying to make himself less visible in case Seven should be stepping through the door. "What's the matter? Afraid he won't approve?"

She tapped the tip of her finger on his chin. "Wasn't it just about here that Seven's fist connected with your face?"

"A lucky shot. So what if he's six feet and all lean mean cop muscle. I can take him."

"Greg?"

"Yeah, okay." He took her hand and kissed the inside of her wrist. He finished a final swig from the bottle. "Home to my cold and lonely bed, it is."

"But cold and lonely for only an hour or two."

He gave a wistful sigh. "Promises, promises."

Watching him walk out, she couldn't hold back a girlie smile. He reminded her of a great big teddy bear.

It was her turn to give a thoughtful sigh. He was right. She didn't want to explain Greg to her partner—but not for the reasons he'd given.

She kept thinking Greg would wear off. She'd wake up

one day and they'd be over it. Why parade him around Seven if it wasn't going to stick?

Erika knew she was hot—a Latina who could make just about any man's top ten. And it wouldn't be with just guys like Greg. Her type usually ended up in the tall, dark and handsome category.

But here she was, all head over heels.

Greg Smith, go figure.

"Jealous my ass," she said under her breath.

The man knew he had her. Why else would she still be sleeping with him after he'd tried to lie, cheat and steal a story out of her—a story that might have very well ended her career?

She was still mulling it over, the complete contradiction of a homicide detective in love with an ambitious reporter, when the other man in her life walked into the restaurant.

Now Seven, he was any girl's type. Just a skosh— couldn't wait to use that one!—under six feet, to-die-for hazel eyes and brown curly hair cut short but barely tamed. His grandfather had been French Canadian and Erika thought he had a bit of the French thing going on in that chiseled jaw and aquiline nose. Really, the man was hot enough to turn even her head.

They'd slept together only the one time. But for a while there, she'd carried the memory around like some lovesick puppy.

Of course, it had been a mistake. He'd just found out his brother had killed a man. Wasn't every day someone you loved and trusted turned out to be a murderer, a weak point for anyone for sure. And like a good partner, she'd been there with a shoulder to cry on while she poured another shot of tequila.

Next thing she knew, they were naked in bed together.

Somehow, they'd managed to keep it from ruining their partnership, but only just. Erika took credit for holding it together; she was damn good at hiding her feelings. Most attractive women in law enforcement were. They got a lot of practice.

She hated to admit she'd been just a tad bitter watching Seven buy into Beth's cry-me-a-river routine. The poor woman wasn't used to carrying the load, sure, but buck up, babe, because shit happens.

At the very least, Beth should have kept it together for her son's sake. But Seven's sister-in-law couldn't manage without him, calling him day and night.

All those years, Beth focused on charity events and keeping her hair the right shade of blond. When her world fell apart, why wouldn't she look to replace her doctor-gone-wrong with bachelor number two…even if it was her husband's younger brother?

Then, as if Beth weren't bad enough, Gia Moon strut into the picture.

That had been quite the slap in the face. Beth, she could understand. Nothing brought people together faster than death and scandal. They'd mourned Ricky's transgressions together. And God knows Seven *loved* his nephew.

But there was Gia waiting in the interview room one hot summer's day, long black hair and vibrant blue eyes and movie-star good looks—practically every man's dream come true. Sure enough, Seven had fallen. Hard.

Erika picked up her drink and motioned for Seven to follow her back to the booth. She hadn't thought about the damn psychic for months. But yesterday the woman she called "Sherlock," Carin Barnes—the FBI's X-file super-agent—had dropped the name like a stink bomb.

Seven ordered a beer from the waitress and folded his

hands on the polished wood table, leaning forward. Yesterday, he and Erika had been assigned by the chief as liaisons for the FBI. Erika figured Carin Barnes must know people in high places, or maybe their past success together in the fortune-teller murders had greased the wheels. Who knew?

Seven had been taking care of their open cases while Erika got up to speed with the feds. Greg wouldn't know it, but this was her first chance today to catch up with her partner.

"Does a pay raise come with your new gig? Because if it does, you're picking up the check."

"Ha, ha," she said. Of course, she'd told him about the awkward handoff from Sherlock during the conference call.

"What *was* that?" she asked. "I mean, here we are in the middle of a white-hot murder case and she bails?"

"Looks like you need to get your agent in line, Erika," he said with a wink.

But Erika shook her head. "It doesn't gel. She's the special agent in charge. Why would she rush off in a cloud of mystery? Sherlock never struck me as sloppy."

"Girl crush gone wrong?"

"Isn't it always the case with the feds?" she quipped.

As the lead agent for the FBI, Carin Barnes had scheduled the conference call to coordinate efforts with the local law enforcement. She'd had the sheriff's department, the mayor's office and Huntington Beach PD all lined up, ready to take their piece of the pie when she'd made the handoff to Erika.

There'd been quite a bit of carping from the others on the phone. The Bolsa Chica was outside Westminster's jurisdiction, after all. Erika had been quick to point out that

Special Agent Barnes had recently worked with both Erika and Seven. It made sense that she'd seek their help.

Only it didn't. Which meant something else was going on, something that left Erika with a bad feeling about the days ahead.

Seven took the beer from the waitress, waving off the glass. "So why the ambush yesterday?"

Erika shrugged. "It's not like I had any big heads-up. Besides, I knew you could handle it. And that look on your face when you spotted Sherlock? Priceless."

"I'm happy to be so entertaining, but when exactly did Barnes contact you?"

"Right before I called about the DB in the Bolsa Chica." She gave it a few seconds. "It's a big case, Seven."

He nodded. "How many?"

"Three that we know of. All on the West Coast. Somebody is killing children."

"But why call us in?"

"Isn't that the million-dollar question? I *thought* it was our fabulous work on the fortune-teller murders."

"And now?"

Erika finished the Cosmo and slid the glass away, at last getting to the point of tonight's get-together. She turned to look at her partner. "She mentioned Gia Moon."

Immediately, he looked away, taking a long pull from the beer bottle.

"Shit," she said. "Sherlock was right. Gia called you, didn't she? No, don't bother to deny it. You have that look where your eyes go all glassy and you ignore the beautiful woman at your side. That would be me. Your partner. Give."

He shook his head. "One day, you're going to teach me that trick of yours. The mind-reading thing."

"Still waiting."

"Yeah," he said. "She called."

She let it sink in. So it was true. Gia Moon was back in the picture.

There was something dangerous about that woman, something Erika couldn't ignore—even if everyone around her thought Gia was the real deal. From the first day she'd come to the department to report her vision about the fortune-teller case, Gia had honed in on Seven with unnerving interest.

He'd ended up sleeping with her…and killing for her.

Sure, it had been a righteous shoot. The man Seven killed was the bad guy, complete with gun in hand. But the thing had come off a little too conveniently, making Erika wonder if they all hadn't been manipulated into doing exactly what Gia wanted: rid the world of the man who had once vowed to kill her and her daughter.

"So, what did the lovely Ms. Moon have to say?" She snapped her fingers. "Wait, let me guess. The connection between you is so strong, she's figured out we're involved in another murder. She's had a vision!"

He put down the beer. "We didn't exactly get into it."

"Hmm."

He was saved from answering by the waitress handing over menus. Erika took another drink of the Cosmo as she watched Seven pretend to study a menu he surely had memorized, they ate here so often.

Still, she knew it was no use pushing. She'd have to do the whole walking-on-eggshells thing, carefully ignoring the pink elephant in the room: Gia Moon.

Whatever, Erika thought. She knew that if she had to, she'd take care of Gia herself.

"We have an ID on our vic," she said, pulling out the file from her bag. "Her prints were in the system. Katie

Sweeny, a foster kid from the Valley. Just like the others, she was reported missing three weeks ago. A runaway."

"Let me guess," he said. "Katie was all of fourteen years old."

"Matching the profile."

"Megan Tobin had a mystery older man. Do we know how the others were lured away?"

She flipped through the file. "The first vic, Mark Dair, from Alpine, California—that's a spit's throw from the border. An online predator the feds can't trace. Our perp isn't stupid."

"What's Alice got to say about the time of death?"

Alice Tang was the county coroner. Any cases involving suspicious deaths would go through her office.

"She's doing the autopsy tomorrow."

Seven nodded and shut the menu. "So, are you thinking what I'm thinking about our fearless leader?"

She leaned back, away from the table. She realized Seven was right. They definitely had the mind-reading thing between partners going on.

"Sherlock," she said, using her pet name for Special Agent Barnes. "She lied about the stone with the weird writing."

"And the lady gets the prize."

Barnes had told them a similar stone had been found with each victim. She also claimed it wasn't an artifact.

"Last time I checked," Seven said, "NISA has jurisdiction over cases involving stolen artifacts."

"Exactly."

"So she's hiding something and we're flying half-blind, working with limited information."

"Exactly."

He shook his head and grabbed his beer. The expression on his face spoke eloquently, but he said it just the same. "Damn feds."

She signaled the waitress, thinking she'd order another Cosmo with dinner. "Exactly."

13

Stella stood in her mother's garage studio in bare feet and a long T-shirt, examining her mother's painting. It was just past midnight. In six hours, her mother would expect her to wake up and shuffle off to school.

Just another day....

Stella walked slowly around to the other side of the painting, then turned and paced back. She kept her eyes on the dark-haired boy standing next to the fishing pole, a birdcage eerily hanging from its hook.

When she'd first seen the painting, it had been ghost boy holding the fishing pole.

The sight of him in her mother's painting had brought back that same suffocating panic she'd felt in Mindy's guest bath. Instantly, that familiar weight came crushing down on her chest, making it impossible to breathe.

She remembered taking a step back and closing her eyes. When she'd opened them, she realized ghost boy wasn't at all the kid in the painting. The boy in the painting had dark hair and eyes.

But for just those few seconds, it had been ghost boy she'd seen wearing the tattered clothes and dripping with slime.

She hadn't returned to the garage after that, afraid of the

painting and what she'd see. Even now, she felt really weird, like maybe if she closed her eyes and opened them really fast, she'd catch him back on that canvas.

She shivered and wrapped her arms around her stomach.

After her mom had found her arguing with ghost boy in the kitchen and all the freaky stuff started with the water, Stella had gone to her room and slammed the door shut. She'd ducked under the covers with all her clothes on and prayed for sleep.

Two hours later, her mother had slipped inside her room. Without saying a word, she'd crawled into bed and put her arms around Stella.

After what seemed like just a few minutes, Stella had fallen fast asleep.

Tonight, she hadn't waited for her mother's rescue. She'd gone straight to her mother's bedroom to sleep beside her in the king-size bed.

Her mother never said anything; she didn't need to. Gia wasn't like other mothers. She'd use her "higher power" to feel out the situation.

Now, staring at the painting, Stella sighed. What she *wanted* was for her mother to use that power to get rid of ghost boy.

But Stella would never ask her. Never.

She couldn't take that risk.

For as long as she could remember, Stella had been the one to sleep in her mother's bed, alert to Gia's nightmare visions. It didn't seem like a big deal at the time. She'd wake up and find her mother screaming. She'd shake her awake, let her mother hold her tight as if her mother were comforting Stella and not the other way around.

Then, last year, something changed. Instead of screams

to wake her, Stella found her mother lying beside her in the bed. She had her eyes wide open, but she wasn't breathing.

Stella remembered how scared she'd been, trying to shake her mother awake, praying that, once Gia disconnected from her vision, her mother would be okay.

Ten months ago, her mother's horrible visions came true. Stella's dad, the guy who tried to kill her grandmother—who'd stolen the Eye and gone whacko—was dead.

Stella thought the nightmare was over. That they'd gotten through all the bad stuff.

Until now.

Stella licked her lips. She wondered if the same thing that happened to her mother would start happening to her now. In the Poder's bathroom, she'd stopped breathing, too.

"Can't sleep?"

Stella turned to find her mother standing in the doorway. She stepped into the garage studio as Stella looked back at the painting. She placed her hands on Stella's shoulders and kissed the top of her head. Her mother wasn't all that tall, but she towered over Stella's four feet, eleven inches.

"I remember my first vision," her mother said. "I was living with your grandmother then. I tried to hide it, but she knew right away what was happening. She called it my gift, but I saw the whole thing as a curse. The curse of the Fegaris women."

Stella didn't respond. *Now, I'm part of that curse,* she thought dismally.

"The first time it happened to me," her mother continued gently, "I was so scared. All I could think was, I don't want to be like her."

Stella shut her eyes. When she opened them again, she heard her mother ask quietly, "The spirit, is he the boy in the painting?"

Stella shook her head, feeling her heart skip a beat with the admission. "The first time I looked at the painting, it was him, ghost boy." She glanced back at her mom. "That's what I call him." She stared back at the painting. "But it was just a trick. The boy in the painting is someone else."

"Do you know what the spirit wants?"

"He won't say. He just stares at me like I'm supposed to know. Only, I don't." She frowned at the painting. "One time, he showed up looking just like this. All wet and gnarly. It was…weird."

Her mother took her hand. For the first time in her life, Stella could find no comfort in the touch.

"What am I supposed to do?" she whispered.

"You mean, we. What are *we* supposed to do?" she said, turning Stella to look at her. "You're not alone in this. You'll never be alone."

Stella nodded. "Yeah. I guess."

Her mother smiled, trying to look reassuring. "Can you see him now?"

"No. I haven't seen him all day. The last time was after I came home from Mindy's."

But she'd felt his presence. It gave her a creepy feeling of being followed. Like, maybe if she turned around really quickly, he'd be there again, dogging her steps.

"I'm tired," she said.

Without another word, her mother took her hand and led her back into the house. She tucked Stella in bed, just like she used to when she was little.

Her mother sat down on the bed next to Stella and brushed her dark curls from her face.

"I'll join you in a bit," her mother said. "I'm going to lock up the studio." She kissed her forehead. "Rest you gentle."

"Sleep you sound," Stella responded in their familiar ritual.

When her mother closed the bedroom door, Stella sighed and turned on her side. When she'd asked her mother what she was supposed to do, she'd corrected Stella, giving that *we* a special emphasis. *What are we supposed to do?*

Stella tucked her knees up and curled into a ball. She clasped her hands around her stomach. Her mother was a powerful psychic. But the fact that she couldn't see ghost boy? Well, it just didn't have a lot of *we* to it.

14

The doctor watched the room's sole occupant cry out and then drop his voice to soft whimpers in French. The change wasn't the least remarkable. She knew this particular patient well enough, having heard the man ranting before. The leather cuffs strapping him to the bed attested to his advanced psychotic condition—the man believed he was Frederic Joliot-Curie. If the doctor understood correctly, "Frederic" was reliving the German occupation of France during the Second World War.

Along with his wife, Irene—the daughter of Pierre and Marie Curie—the real Frederic Joliot-Curie had received the Nobel Prize in Chemistry for developing new radioactive isotopes. Husband and wife had recorded the principle of nuclear reaction as early as 1939, though the knowledge had been hidden away for fear that it could result in a terrible weapon of mass destruction for the Germans. Frederic Joliot-Curie was long dead, which didn't matter the least to the man in the bed. For him, the barrier of time didn't exist.

Absently, the doctor patted the lapel of her lab coat, her hand stopping when she found the badge. She knew Dr. Polly Hughes would be scripted across the plastic, her photograph laminated directly beneath. Reassured, she drummed her fingers on the clipboard balanced across her knees, watching as a thin stream of spittle oozed from the corner of the patient's mouth. The room smelled of Lysol and urine; it went nicely with the peeling paint and the yellowed tape x-ed across the cracked and barred window. Next door, another patient in similar restraints fantasized the life of Jose Marti, the Cuban patriot.

Soon enough, Dr. Polly Hughes stood to check the clinic's hall, something she'd been doing for nearly an hour. Her patience was rewarded. The nurse who'd been hunched over the glossy pages of an issue of *Match* had disappeared with her magazine. Back inside, Polly withdrew a syringe from her coat pocket and uncapped the needle. A glass IV bottle hung upside down at his bedside, its metal cap held in place with white medical tape. It was a simple thing to plunge the needle into the saline line feeding the patient's vein.

She wanted to put the poor bastard out of his misery before she left.

She waited another count of ten before slipping into the hall.

Breathing hard, the excitement catching up with her, Polly took another five minutes to reach the service entrance to the cafeteria where the clinic received deliveries each morning. Like a dance, the steps came to her. Pocket the badge. Ditch the lab coat in the trash bin. Dump those potatoes from the crate and hide the clipboard and syringe inside. She tucked her long brown curls into a hat. Hefting the crate of potatoes onto her shoulder, she walked out, wearing the worn trousers and shirt of a day laborer. She whistled through her teeth, doing her best manly strut.

Blinking against the pink horizon, she ducked into the back of a waiting truck, the side emblazoned with three-foot-tall letters spelling Metro Fruit. The boxes of produce had been piled high; she managed to crawl behind several large crates.

She could smell the sweetness of overripe cantaloupe, the fragrance so sharp, it made her mouth water. After a few minutes, a soporific weight slipped into her veins, making her blood heavy. The drugs again. The drugs always made her so tired.

She didn't know how long she'd slept before the engine trembled to life beneath her. The truck rocked forward. Minutes later, she heard the driver salute the guard at the security gate.

Blood pumped in her temples, drowning out the men's words. Sleep had left her disoriented, unprepared. She thought of the patients at the clinic strapped to their soiled beds. Any minute now, she'd be found out and spirited back to that room where she could drool right alongside Frederic. *Let's have a look in the back.* Had she imagined that voice? She listened harder, trying to make out the men's whispers—*never know what the inmates here are up to…maybe there's someone hiding…someone we'll drag back to the clinic, screaming like an animal.*

But the words filtered through her fears, transforming into the mundane. She translated quickly. Something about lottery tickets.

A few seconds later, the truck once again lurched forward.

After a while, Polly Hughes started to laugh, the sheer joy of escape rushing in.

Adam watched Polly Hughes writhing on the bed, her wrists and ankles secured by leather cuffs. From her arm, IV tubing snaked up the metal pole beside the bed where several plastic bags of differing sizes hung like bats.

"Did she make it out this time?"

The question came from Nathaniel Slade, who stood next to Adam.

He glanced down at his father. Unlike Adam and his twin sister, his father was short and compact with an enormous head and caterpillar brows. Despite his near sixty-five years, his hair remained dark brown, showing very little gray. It was the only youthful thing about him. His eyes had long ago turned a milky blue and his clean-shaven face gave way to a sallow complexion. Like his head, Nathaniel's hands were monstrously large.

Adam always wondered how his mother—a beautiful woman, a mirror image of her twin children—could have fallen in love with such a gnome of a man.

He turned back to Polly strapped to the hospital bed. Her head thrashing from side to side on the pillow, she was lost in her nightmare vision, living a past that didn't belong to her. He didn't have to read his father's mind to know what Nathaniel was thinking. *Another failure.*

He wasn't sure what reality this host had tapped into. It was different for everyone. But the girl seemed fixated on escaping some dilapidated insane asylum in the French Caribbean.

"Yes," Adam said, answering Nathaniel's question. "She made it through the security check this time."

Adam found a strange solace in the fact. Why shouldn't the poor thing at least achieve some kind of freedom, even if it was just in her mind?

She'd been brought into the program three weeks ago. Adam had found her at a bus stop. She'd been a skinny little thing wearing clothes much too provocative for her age. She carried only a backpack and had that frightened look he'd come to understand so well.

And still, that light surrounding her—what others termed her aura—had the brilliance of an aurora borealis, swirling and flowing around her.

When he'd offered her a free meal, she'd been happy to follow along like a lost puppy. That's how women usually reacted to Adam. Like his sister, he had an irresistible charm.

After her first session, she'd spoken only in French. He suspected that, in real life, she didn't speak a word of it.

That wouldn't matter, of course. Just like the escape, the memories belonged to someone else—another woman in a different time and place. The sad fact was that the girl strapped to the hospital bed hadn't escaped, at all.

As he watched, a thin stream of drool slipped from the corner of Polly's mouth. There was a slight pink tint to the spittle.

Not much longer now, Adam thought sadly.

"When it's time," Adam said. "I'll take care of the body."

"No," Nathaniel answered sharply. "Evie will do it."

Adam kept his eyes on the girl. "You're pushing Evie too hard."

"Let me worry about your sister," his father said tonelessly.

Adam didn't bother to respond. Nathaniel had his own ideas and he clung to them stubbornly. Long ago, he'd determined the order of his children's lives. Adam was the human divining rod. It was his talent to find the hosts. Evie was able to manipulate their minds and take them to places they dare not go otherwise.

His father explained everything in life required a careful balance. Yin and yang. Adam was the Finder; Evie, the Destroyer.

The lights in the room had been dimmed. The last year, they'd learned the cycle of things. The first week, after the drugs began to take effect, the hosts complained about the painful brightness.

The room itself had been converted into a laboratory of sorts. Medical equipment warred with antique furnishings original to the Victorian house Nathaniel leased just six months ago. He'd moved his operation here once he'd read about the unusual collection belonging to the murdered tycoon, David Gospel.

Adam gave a deep sigh. He was thinking about Jack, the boy still handcuffed in the basement. How much longer before it was Jack spouting his nightmares?

"You'll call your sister?" Nathaniel asked. "You'll let her know when it's time?"

To put the host down, Adam supplied silently. Euthanize her like a suffering animal.

He nodded. "Of course."

He waited until Nathaniel left before he approached the girl strapped to the bed. Gently, he stroked the brown curls from her face. She was fourteen, just like the others. It was the age he and Evie found easiest to work with. Any younger and their fear just burned up their minds; any older and their minds were too protected from this kind of intrusion.

The girl began struggling on the bed again. He sighed and reached for the syringe on the metal tray bedside.

"Sweet dreams, Polly," he whispered, driving the needle into her IV.

15

Nathaniel Slade was a forgotten man. Twenty-six years ago, he'd made damn sure of it. That's when Nathaniel had officially pronounced himself dead.

He'd left evidence, of course. In the days before DNA testing, it was ridiculously easy, particularly given his training in U.S. Army intelligence. Distraught over the sudden death of his beloved wife, Celeste, he'd perished in a car accident, his body incinerated beyond recognition.

He'd left a will, of course, as well as an extremely generous life insurance policy that paid out millions. There'd been detailed instructions on the care of his beloved twin son and daughter. At his tragic death, Nathaniel's dear friend—and the children's godfather—became the twin's guardian.

The "friend," of course, was Nathaniel himself, resurrected with the help of a forged birth certificate.

He'd needed the liberty of a fresh identity. The CIA would never have let him live if they'd known his intentions. He was much too important, his knowledge, far too dangerous.

When the first inklings of government-sponsored research into the paranormal leaked to the press, powerful forces within the government moved swiftly to snuff out the truth. Detailed studies by the CIA, the American Institutes for Research and the National Research Council discredited any possibility of psychic phenomenon. The press moved in like rabid dogs over a bone with headlines proclaiming the government's findings—no ESP had ever been used during intelligence operations.

Those clowns had no idea that the powers-that-be had only declassified the dross for the press. The truly amazing results remained top secret.

The cover-up had been successful beyond any possible expectations. Ask the man on the street about Star Gate and you'd get some nonsense about a sci-fi series on cable television.

No one ever stopped to wonder why the CIA—after twenty-four years and twenty million taxpayer dollars—wanted the world to believe their research was an utter failure.

Nathaniel knew better. He'd been there, an experimenter who'd seen firsthand the mind-blowing results of Star Gate, the government-funded program to study the phenomenon of remote viewing.

Nathaniel's introduction into the phenomenon began in the 1970s at the Stanford Research Institute, a think tank in Northern California. Back then, there'd been plenty of money and interest coming from the CIA and the Defense Intelligence Agency, especially after Dr. Harold Puthoff, a theoretical and experimental physicist working at SRI, circulated among his peers some observations he'd written up on the psychic Ingo Swann.

Apparently, Swann had drawn with impressive detail the interior workings of a magnetometer, an extremely sophisticated scientific instrument used to measure magnetic fields, and something Swann had never seen. The magnetometer, whose design had yet to be published, was located in a vault beneath the SRI. But Swann, a New York artist, could somehow "see" the instrument—even describe the machine's working parts—as clearly as if he were standing in front of it.

That's when the CIA came a-knocking. It seemed that the Soviet Union's security services had shown a great deal of interest in parapsychology. In a kind of psychic-arms race, the CIA set out to find and study more people like Swann who could "remote view," or see objects that were separated from the viewer by time or space.

Nathaniel had been recruited by the CIA to work as a facilitator. He would monitor a remote viewer as he or she attempted to study their target. He'd been assigned to supervise Remote Viewer 008. Her name was Celeste Montgomery.

From the moment he'd first seen Celeste, Nathaniel knew she was different. She had an ethereal beauty—slim with flowing red hair and translucent skin—as well as a calm strength. But it was her eerie abilities at remote viewing that truly mesmerized him.

At first, Celeste's findings fell along the lines of military intelligence. She'd write pages and pages, reporting secret Soviet plans for a nuclear submarine or verifying the location of a high-security military site in Siberia.

He remembered how much he'd loved to watch her hands during those sessions. She would use them when she talked, the fluid motion reminding him of a Polynesian dancer. Her gestures told part of the story.

They fell in love, secretly married and planned a future together. But when she became pregnant, everything changed.

Overnight, the ability of Remote Viewer 008 to scan for

military secrets wasn't limited to observations made in present time. With her pregnancy, Celeste's amazing sight could just as easily travel through time, discovering futuristic technology that, up until then, had been unimaginable.

Soon thereafter, Remote Viewer 008 became herself a secret military mission: Remote Viewer A-001 the Atlantis Project.

Celeste, of course, hadn't realized the danger her ability would bring. But Nathaniel had. He'd been in military intelligence long enough to know what the CIA could do to someone like her.

So he'd taken his pregnant wife and escaped to a cabin in the mountains of Virginia. Those months had been some of the most memorable in his life. Celeste grew more beautiful with each passing day. And it wasn't just the pregnancy that transformed her. It was her work remote viewing. She appeared to evolve with each session as she traveled with her mind through time and space.

Her joy at her findings became addictive. Each and every morning, he'd wake to find her in his arms and think: What about today? What will she see today?

He'd thought they'd have a lifetime together. He suspected that, with her ability, Celeste had known the horrible truth all along.

She began calling herself the host. She told Nathaniel the children growing inside her somehow magnified her abilities. And despite his protests that she was doing too much, Celeste continued to push herself. In hindsight, her desperation was of course part of her special knowledge—the one secret she never shared with him, the secret of her death.

Today, Nathaniel had a room filled with documents recording the images she'd been able to remote view those last critical months. And a plan.

Walking down the parquet floors of the Victorian house, Nathaniel understood Adam's disquiet and the implications of the young woman's sacrifice back in that sad room with its hospital bed. Hadn't his beloved Celeste made a similar choice?

The fact was that their work was worth every sacrifice. Celeste had given up her life so that humanity could discover the truth. And despite the pity he'd seen so clearly on his son's face, Nathaniel knew Adam would do what was necessary. They all would.

Nathaniel entered his office. The entire room was an ocean of documents. Ancient texts, scrolls, maps and, of course, transcripts of Celeste's final months of remote viewing covered his desk, as well as several tables. The room was originally a kind of gallery with high ceilings and windows. There was also an enormous fireplace. Nathaniel preferred to work through the night. He required very little sleep.

On the mantle above the fireplace was a painting, a self-portrait of his wife just before she died giving birth to the twins. Celeste's image was large enough to be seen from every corner of the room, her youth and beauty frozen forever in time.

For the last twenty-six years, he'd worked hard to fulfill her legacy. He'd raised their children, paying special care to enhance the abilities they'd inherited from their mother. Adam and Evie were his final hope at realizing Celeste's dream.

He rested his fingertips on the frame of the painting. He understood his son's regrets. They were all sorry for any loss of life. But the work they did here was fundamental, something that would change the world forever.

Some things were worth any sacrifice. He'd learned that much when he'd lost Celeste.

He sat down before the file he'd been reading when Adam had called him in to check on the girl. The desk was overflowing with historical documents. Many were copies, but some were valuable originals he'd purchased on the black market.

He pulled forward a map of Atlantis attributed to the great poet, Dante Alighieri. It appeared as concentric circles, belts of canals and islands. A single road connected the inner city to its outer rings like the radius of a circle, much like the Atlantis originally described by Plato in his dialogues, *Timeaus* and *Critias*.

He carefully stroked the parchment surface. There was almost human warmth to the sheepskin. Had the document been part of a museum collection, he wouldn't be allowed this luxury. His only access would come locked in a vault, temperature and humidity carefully controlled, with gloves on his hands.

Nathaniel had long ago realized the true value of the treasures that surrounded him now. Celeste had taught him that much. She alone had uncovered the amazing truths the government kept hidden.

Now, it was just a matter of time before he could prove it to the world.

16

Living in Southern California, Seven thought, you had to love sitting in a car. He heard a good joke on the radio the other day: If you needed to find a parking spot—another thorn in the side of any native—there were plenty to be had on the 405.

Which is exactly where he and Erika found themselves. Parked on the 405 freeway on their way out to the Valley.

"Traffic today seems particularly *onerous*," Erika said, keeping one hand on the steering wheel as she reached over to bump up the air conditioning.

In the passenger seat beside her, Seven put some thought into his response. He'd bought one of those vocabulary-builder books students used to study for college entry exams.

"*Operose,* even," he said.

"It's a *Brobdingnagian* problem, all right," she shot back.

Seven gave her a look. "You made that up."

She grinned. "Ten bucks says I didn't."

Erika merged the Crown Vic into the neighboring lane on the off chance that it would continue crawling forward at its snail's pace. No such luck. The car came to another dead stop.

"Fuck," she said.

Seven leaned back and closed his eyes. "I think I'll let you have the last word on that one."

Forty-five grueling minutes later, Erika exited at Ventura Boulevard and rolled through the streets of Glendale to one of its less manicured neighborhoods. She parked on the street where Katie Sweeny once lived. Seven and Erika made their way toward the house, passing a lawn loaded with kids, who were keeping it to a dull roar.

The stuccoed single-story house was typical of the working-class homes in the area. Only the kids scrambling around its makeshift playground of a plastic seesaw, slide and sandbox, added color. Erika punched the doorbell.

A woman answered the door in jeans and the kind of shirt worn by nurses, this one printed with teddy bears. She looked to be in her early fifties, but dyed her hair dark black. She wore her mood even blacker.

"Patricia Nichols?" Seven flipped open his badge.

Ms. Nichols stood almost eye-to-eye with Seven. He figured she outweighed him by a good twenty pounds. She leaned into the doorjamb. "Is this about Katie?"

"May we come in?" Erika asked. "We'd like to ask a few questions."

Instead of showing them in, the woman stepped onto the porch and shut the door behind her. "I can answer any questions right here."

It wasn't the first time Seven had played bull's-eye to such a glare. The system didn't exactly make life a cakewalk for foster parents.

He glanced around the yard where the kids had stopped playing. They ranged in age from kindergarten to their early teens and were all the colors of the rainbow. He counted six; each and every one of them looked clean and well-cared for.

"You reported Katie missing three weeks ago?" Erika asked.

"Look, I already gave a statement when I went down to identify her body."

Erika pulled out her notepad. "You said Katie had been here only a few months? That you thought she was having some problems adjusting?"

"Yeah," the woman answered, not bothering to elaborate.

Seven took off his sunglasses. "Ms. Nichols, we're trying to find out who murdered Katie. She may not have been the killer's only victim."

For a moment, he saw a flicker of emotion on that steely face. But she quickly shut it off. "I already told you people everything I know. Anything else, I want my lawyer present."

She stepped back inside and shut the door.

"How do you like that?" Erika said, shoving the notepad back into her purse.

Seven put on his sunglasses. "I don't."

But he knew enough about the case to realize this wasn't about a foster parent abusing her charge. He glanced around the yard as the kids made their way back to their toys, the excitement over.

There.

He turned to Erika. "You want to give me a second here?"

She followed his gaze. On the sidewalk, the oldest—a girl in jeans and a T-shirt hawking the newest boy band—watched them with a heavy dose of suspicion.

"Going to use that French-Canadian charm?"

"It's a bit rusty, I admit," he said, "but I thought I'd give it a go."

"My advice? Work the boyish smile."

As Erika made her way back to the car, Seven headed over to the girl.

"Hey," he said, holding out his hand. "The name's Seven. You are?"

The girl reluctantly took his hand and gave it a weak shake. "Tanya. Seven, like the number? That's a weird name."

He paraded out the smile just as instructed. "I prefer the term unique." He nodded back toward the house. "She always got an edge like that?"

"Patty's okay," Tanya said.

"So why the attitude?"

Tanya had her hair in cornrows with multicolored beads at the bottom of the braids. They made a soft clinking sound as she shrugged and shifted her weight.

Seven gave it a minute. She looked all of thirteen, but her expression said older—and that she was itching to give him a piece of her mind.

"Why don't you guys leave Patty alone?"

He made a show of looking around. "Is someone giving her a hard time?"

"Patty's really good to us. She doesn't deserve getting crap about Katie. That girl was weird."

"Weird, huh?" He took off his sunglasses. "You didn't like her?"

Again the shrug. "Whatever."

But he could see she was holding back.

"Did she have a boyfriend?" The victim in Nevada had been skipping class to meet with an older man. The boy in Alpine had been lured by an online relationship.

"Katie? No way."

The strength of her denial brought out his detective radar. "Because she was weird? Maybe you just didn't like how she dressed or something?"

Tanya's eyes narrowed, reacting to a tone that implied she was being unfair—exactly what he'd intended.

"Look, I know Katie's dead and everything. And I'm sorry about that. But she went around telling everybody she was *psychic*."

"Psychic?" Seven repeated in a flat voice.

She nailed him with another look. "Where I come from, that's damn weird."

Gia Moon was thinking about her mother.

The memories weren't easy ones. Forget June Cleaver, her mother had never been what television had taught Gia to expect. Estelle didn't bake cookies or supervise sleepovers. The few times Gia actually *had* a friend to invite over, her mother left it up to the girls, never getting involved.

She'd been too busy. Estelle Fegaris—renowned archaeologist and professor at Harvard—had to focus on what really mattered. When your goal in life was to change the world, you didn't exactly have the time to help your daughter build a California mission out of flour-and-salt paste.

It had taken Gia almost a lifetime to forgive her. It wasn't a question of neglect. If anything, her mother's attentions were almost too much to take. The whirling dervish of her mother's life could consume anyone. They traveled—a lot—living for months at a time at dig sites around the world run by her mother.

And then there was her mother's gift. Estelle Fegaris

was openly psychic, her discipline, psychic archaeology: the use of paranormal abilities to locate archaeological sites of significance. Her mother used retrocognition—she would look into the past to see artifacts or events of particular relevance to her work.

Certainly, she'd been a colorful figure at Harvard. But her uncanny success at finding important artifacts and dig sites gave her a measure of respectability—until Estelle strayed off the professional path to achieve full-blown cult status. It was the final straw for the university. Her mother set off on her own, following her psychic agenda, while Gia wished for nothing more than a normal life.

Last night, Gia began to wonder: Despite all her efforts to be different from her mother, did her own daughter feel just as betrayed?

There were parallels. Like Stella, Gia hadn't known her father…and Gia's work wasn't the sort of thing you talked about at career day. Judging from last year's headlines—Psychic Aids Police In Fortune-Teller Murder—her attempts at subterfuge had failed miserably.

Gia knew her daughter longed for the staid and ordinary life that had eluded them too long. The last few months, Gia had allowed herself to believe that might be possible.

And now this.

Last night, she'd gone back to the kitchen to check the studio, a ploy to give Stella time to settle in. But when she'd come to bed, she'd found Stella staring up at the ceiling, completely awake.

She'd tried to comfort her, whispering the story of the Fegaris women as Stella turned in bed to play possum and pretend sleep. She'd told her daughter that the women in her family didn't live in fear. The gift they had was an ancient one, borne by many generations.

Stella would learn to manage the intrusions. It didn't have to be something horrible. She just needed a little faith.

But even as she delivered the speech, Gia knew it was pabulum. There was nothing manageable about the spirit world.

The best she could do was sleep alongside her daughter and feel her small body tense at every creak of the house. This morning, she'd sent Stella off to school with a warm breakfast and dark circles under her eyes.

And a spirit. That much, Gia knew when the puddle again appeared on the kitchen floor right before Stella ran out to catch her bus.

Her daughter would want to stick her head in the sand, a tactic that was certain to fail. But Stella wasn't alone in her denial.

Gia had known this day was coming. And still, she hadn't prepared Stella, allowing her daughter to turn away every time Gia broached the topic, giving her space. She'd thought she'd have more time.

She'd been thinking about just that—a mother's blindness—when the doorbell sounded. Gia glanced at the kitchen's black-cat clock and frowned. It was 12:45. She was seated at the bistro table in the tiny kitchen, staring at a cup of coffee she'd poured a good half hour before.

The doorbell rang again.

She dumped the coffee into the sink and rinsed the cup, then made her way to the front door where her impatient visitor had again rung the bell.

When she opened the door, she couldn't hide her surprise. "Detective Cabral?"

Erika Cabral was a beautiful woman. Petite in size, she was a study in creamy shades of chocolate—tanned skin,

dark eyes and hair she wore in waves around her face. She
didn't seem like the type to carry a gun or tackle criminals…until she opened her mouth.

"Why, Ms. Moon. You look surprised to see me. I guess
you weren't expecting me." Erika frowned. "Isn't that considered bad form for a psychic?" She flipped open her
badge. "It's official police business. May I come in?"

"Yes, of course. And please, call me Gia," she said,
gesturing Erika inside.

Gia took a couple of deep breaths. At least Erika wasn't
here about Stella—which had been her fear when she'd
first opened the door. If her presence had anything to do
with Gia's daughter, Erika Cabral wasn't the type to beat
about the bush, her voice dripping with sarcasm.

She watched Erika walk around the living room. Everything about the woman's behavior, how she casually
checked out the room's decor, acting as if she had all the
time in the world, smelled of a fishing expedition. She
imagined Detective Cabral was on her lunch hour. She
wouldn't want Seven tagging along to visit Erika's version
of the psychic black widow. Detective Cabral believed her
partner much too susceptible to Gia's wiles.

Erika picked up a charm from a pottery bowl on the
coffee table. "Now this is more like it," she said.

The charm was made from a brown seed about an inch
in diameter that had been strung with red string. There was
a red wool tassel on the end and the image of the Virgin
Mary lacquered on the face of the seed.

"You collect these things? Charms and amulets?"
Erika asked.

"It was a gift from a client."

"Ojo de Venado," she said, recognizing the charm.
"Deer's Eye charm. It's Mexican. Used for magical pro-

tection." She put the charm back in the pottery bowl. "I must admit, when I first drove up, the whole gingerbread house and English garden seemed a little out of character."

"Am I missing my neon sign flashing Psychic?"

"The one with the palm?" Erika laughed. "I forgot you have a sense of humor."

"How can I help you with your official police business, Detective?"

Erika clucked her tongue. "Oh, come on. Don't you at least want to take a stab at reading my mind?"

"Seven," Gia said succinctly. "He told you I called."

Erika tapped her nose, the universal gesture meaning she'd given a correct answer.

"So this is about Seven?" Gia asked. "Are you here to warn me off, Detective?"

Erika laughed. "Hardly. Seven's a big boy. He doesn't need me to hold his hand…even when it comes to your ample charms, Ms. Moon."

"Something's happened," Gia said, getting that prickling at the back of her neck. "Something, you believe, might involve my…abilities."

"Getting warmer." Erika tilted her head. "Been painting anything interesting lately?"

Gia thought about the painting of the boy…and the fact that she'd been guided to contact Seven. Now a spirit had suddenly attached itself to Stella.

She sighed. "This way, Detective."

She took Erika out to her garage studio. Detective Cabral had been there before, during the fortune-teller murders. She was familiar with Gia's talent—even as she denied the legitimacy of her visions.

"I find it strange that you'd seek me out, Detective. Last time I checked, I'm a fraud."

"Let's just say a very important little birdie whispered your name in my ear. Can't blame a girl for being curious."

"And that's all I'm going to get," Gia said, feeling Erika's hostility like a laser beam.

"Oh, come on. I think I'm being quite the Chatty Cathy."

The studio walls were covered by enormous canvases, some finished, others still only half-formed. Gia led Erika to the one of the boy. Seven's partner stopped before the canvas. Her expression gave nothing away.

Gia found that the people who feared her gift always kept themselves in check around her. It was as if Gia might be watching for a hint, something she could use to "read" them like a charlatan.

In Erika's case, Gia suspected she'd had some practice at hiding her emotions. The strength of her feelings against Gia's gift suggested a woman who'd had experience with a charlatan or two.

"Why exactly are you here, Detective?" Gia asked. Whatever was going on, Gia needed as much information as possible if she was going to help her daughter.

Erika didn't even acknowledge Gia as she flipped open her phone and punched in the number.

Into the cell, she said, "Seven? It's Erika. I'm at Gia's. Get your ass here, pronto."

17

Evie's visions began like a Wagner opera. At first, there was no distinction between aria and recitative. Rather, she heard only an endless melody—the dialogue, difficult to understand; the emotions, overwhelming. It would be an easy thing to lose herself in the maelstrom.

And so, she would struggle to turn down the volume. If she kept still, quieted her mind, she could unravel the threads of the opus streaming through her head.

The experience felt a lot like those hidden picture puzzles. She must unfocus, relax her mind until the static vanished and the haze gelled into an image.

There, she thought, closing her eyes and rocking Markie gently in her arms. The trick was not to *try.*

Evie smiled. She'd been brought here to help this man. Markie was sick, suffering from a condition that cut him off from the world. He was treated like a child, someone who needed others to care for him. But Evie saw the gift of his condition rather than the curse.

To Evie, he was a mystic. His state allowed him to achieve something others could not. Markie could shut off the noise. He *lived* in a continual ganzfeld state.

Not everyone knew about the ganzfeld experiments. Developed in the 1930s, the ganzfeld protocol required creating an unchanging sensory state—*ganz,* being the German word for total, and *feld,* the word for field.

In the late 1970s and early 1980s, the ganzfeld technique again became popular. The subject was seated in a soundproof room. Headphones piped in white noise, ping-pong ball halves were taped over their eyes and a red light created an undifferentiated visual field. In this manner, researchers attempted to suppress any sensory stimuli, much like a sensory-deprivation tank.

Research at the time theorized that psychic ability could be drowned out by the noise of everyday life, going unnoticed. Studies into parapsychology searched for a way to shut off the distractions, resurrecting the procedures used in ganzfeld. Once a subject achieved a ganzfeld state, the nervous system became receptive to perceptions that were normally drowned out by the constant stimulation of life, facilitating psi powers.

Evie smiled, holding the man in her arms. Here was her ganzfeld experiment. In Markie's head, she could reach beyond even what she and her brother had achieved together.

It had been Zag's idea to channel into Markie's stillness. Autism was a central area of research at Halo Industries.

It was a common belief among the New Age crowd that Indigo Children—those with a purple aura—possessed psychic abilities. The claim became even more controversial when believers linked the Indigo condition with autism.

Was autism really a weakness, they asked? Or could it be a misunderstood evolutionary process?

Believers pointed to the sudden rise in autism. What others termed an epidemic, true believers called a wake-up call. It was time to renovate the educational system and medical institutions. These were highly gifted and intelligent children; ignorance and drug therapy would only deaden their gifts.

But Zag had gone well beyond even current New Age thinking with what he termed his Halo-effect kids. While Indigo Children heralded the New Earth, the utopian society many longed for, the Halo-effect children recalled the secrets of the past.

It was those secrets Evie searched for within Markie. He was her host. Blanketed in his beautiful silence, she could travel using only her mind, searching for the place her mother had found with such ease when she'd been pregnant with Evie and her brother.

The others, the children her brother found, they felt like dried husks in her arms when compared to her experience with Markie. In those sad sessions, she could feel their fragile life force thinning into gossamer threads she simply sliced through. Still, her father insisted they continue their work on both fronts.

Think of them as practice, he'd told her.

And he was right. With growing excitement, she could sense her abilities progressing. In Markie's mind, she didn't feel lost or clumsy, pushing aside the cobwebs to search for what she wanted. Here, she had the precision of a scalpel.

He's so strong.

Not like the children Adam brought to the house. Even from the first, when she held them handcuffed in the basement, she knew they would die.

But with Markie in her arms, she could feel herself reaching for her mother's secret place.

Her father had a room filled with transcripts, each and every one proving the impossible. That the human mind could travel through time and space. That there existed other dimensions from which important knowledge could be gained. Mankind had been denied its legacy too long. She and Adam were part of that legacy.

It's what she'd been trained to do from birth. Even before birth, when her mother carried her and Adam in her womb. Then it had been Celeste who had used her abilities to remote view the secrets others had failed to find. Now, it was up to her and Adam to show the world what was possible.

Evie smiled, stroking Markie's hair as she focused ahead.

At last, she thought.

At last....

18

Seven stared at the painting, allowing himself the indulgence of admiring her talent. The brush strokes, the choice of colors. She made everything look so *real*.

But Gia's paintings didn't really allow for such musing. Like the Daliesque image before him, they were filled with too much death.

"His name is Mark Dair," he told her. "He was killed four months ago."

He'd seen the boy's photograph in the file sent over by Special Agent Barnes. Mark Dair was from Alpine, California. He liked waterskiing and fishing. He'd just been cast in his high-school musical. It was a small part, but he was just a freshman. He had a bright future...until they found his body dumped in the Morena Reservoir in San Diego County. The first victim.

Using the camera on her cell phone, Erika snapped a photograph of the painting. "These designs scratched on the surface of the stones. Do they mean anything to you?"

Gia shook her head. "Not really. They appear to be pictographs or some sort of paleography." When Erika gave her a sharp look, she explained, "My mother was an archaeologist, Detective. You have no idea how many of these things I've seen around the world."

"Paleography," Erika said. "A kind of ancient writing. So these stones may very well be artifacts?"

"I couldn't say," Gia answered truthfully.

Erika turned to look at Seven. He knew what she was thinking. *If it walks like a duck and quacks like a duck...*

"What is it?" Gia asked. "What aren't you telling me?"

"It's part of an ongoing investigation—"

"Of which I'm well aware, Detective," Gia said, interrupting Erika. "I didn't need what you term my *pseudo*psychic powers to deduce that your visit wasn't a social call. You came to me," she reminded Erika. "You thought I could help. *Let* me help."

Erika's only response was an enigmatic stare. Gia's visions may have helped break open the fortune-teller murders, but it would be a cold day in hell before she'd get the thumbs-up from Erika.

Gia turned to face Seven, her arms wrapped around her stomach, her expression fierce. She wore jeans and an embroidered cotton blouse. She'd pulled her shiny black hair into a ponytail, making her look years younger than her thirty-two.

I wasn't the one who hesitated, Seven. That's what she'd told him over the phone when he finally returned her call.

Of course, she hadn't hesitated. She wasn't the type who would. Not Gia. She'd jump in, buoyed by her faith.

Well, Seven couldn't imagine that kind of belief. He'd been trained to question everyone and everything...which was why he'd kept his distance these last ten months. It was all well and good to imagine he could keep his sanity around Gia, to pretend he could hang tight to cool logic. *At best, she lied to me; at worst, she used me.*

But reality was another thing. Even now, just standing

here looking at her, it was like a physical pain to keep his distance. To just watch her and play the detached cop.

He told her, "Three days ago, we found a body. A girl in the Bolsa Chica. Your favorite FBI agent and mine contacted us for help."

"Carin?"

She spoke the woman's name with clear familiarity. No *Agent* Barnes or even Carin Barnes. She said simply, *Carin.* But then Seven was well aware of Gia's history with Barnes, an agent with special expertise in the paranormal.

It was Erika, not Seven, who pounced. "Agent Barnes seemed to think you would be contacting us."

"Ah," Gia said, nodding knowingly. "This would be your little birdie, I presume?"

Erika crossed her arms. "As a matter of fact."

Gia looked away. Her eyes grew unfocused in thought. "Yes," she said. "Carin would know."

Erika looked eager to push on, but Seven spoke up. "Erika, how about you go to the station and start writing up some theories on the case? Let me handle things here."

He'd expected the Cabral glare, right between the eyes. But his partner surprised him, giving only a nod. "I'm on it," she said and headed out.

"Thank you," Gia said. "She can be a bit…intense."

"And then some."

But Gia wouldn't be talking about his partner's personality. Nothing was ever that simple with Gia.

She pinched the bridge of her nose as if dealing with a severe headache. "All that resistance I feel coming from her, it's exhausting."

"Yeah, well, it's a tough case. Can't blame her for being strung a bit tight," he said, purposely misunderstanding. "Come on. I'll make us some tea."

It was a gesture, an attempt to let her know he wanted the barriers down. But she didn't fall in. She stepped away from the painting, watching him with an expression that asked: Are we ready for this?

He thought, *Do we have a choice?*

As if she could hear the words, she sighed and walked around him, brushing past. He felt gooseflesh on his arms, the good kind.

Once in the kitchen, he sat her down at the bistro table in the corner, taking over. The room had a kooky color scheme—yellow and orange tiles accented with red grout—that somehow worked. Every niche had some special knickknack, a tea tin in the shape of an elephant, an interesting piece of bark in a blown-glass bowl. He found the teakettle and filled it with water. The other things, cups and spoons, tea and sugar, he knew where to find them all, which drawer and what cupboard. Oh, yeah. He was fucking at home here.

"I miss you," she said, watching him work.

He turned and looked at her. "You know what I miss? I miss the sex. The sex—" he shook his head as if in disbelief "—it was…hot. Sizzling, even."

She smiled. "I deserved that."

"What?" he deadpanned. "It wasn't a compliment?"

She tilted her head, giving him that look that always put him on guard. It was a strange thing to date a woman who just might read your mind.

"It was a diversion," she said. "You're not here to talk about what happened between us. Point taken."

In a way, meeting Gia had come—to paraphrase Dickens—at the worst of times and the best. He'd been numb from his brother's confession of murder, a zombie at work with his partner constantly covering for him.

Whatever energy he had went to keeping Beth from losing it and to helping Nick, letting them know they were family and that this brother wouldn't let them down.

Gia had read about the fortune-teller murder in the paper. She'd come in to the station claiming to have had a vision that could help the police. As always, she'd painted an enormous canvas reflecting key details in the case… details that had never been released to the press.

Even then, she'd been a shock to the system—literally. The first time they shook hands, he'd felt a jolt, as if all the static electricity in the room had built up for that one touch.

Funny enough, she was still a shock. That black hair, those blue eyes, her flawless complexion. She was, in fact, stunningly beautiful. But not in any fancy way. Hers was all natural, like she should advertise face cream or hiking gear.

He sat down with the tea in the chair opposite her at the small table. "Chamomile okay?"

She smiled. "My favorite."

"Not to mention the only choice in the cupboard."

She gave him a mischievous glance. "Not to belabor the point, but the sex was great."

He sighed dramatically. "I know. I get *lots* of compliments."

The irony of the situation was that he'd been practically celibate. Other than that one mistake with Erika involving a hell of a lot of tequila, Gia had been the only woman in his life since his divorce.

"So what's going on?" he asked.

She played with the cup, turning it on the glass table. "It's Stella. She has a spirit attached to her. I'm pretty sure it's related to your case."

She said it like it was nothing…and in the world according to Gia Moon, such statements were everyday stuff.

He'd already heard the spiel—an entity attached itself to its human host. Often, these attached spirits could cause the person affected to change overnight. Suddenly, Dr. Jekyll became Mr. Hyde.

Unfortunately, dark spirits had become a kind of specialty for Gia. She claimed a powerful gift—the kind that attracted some pretty gnarly stuff in the spirit world.

He remembered the first time he'd taken her out, breaking the cardinal rule of getting involved with "a person of interest" in a case. She'd proposed that possession could explain even his brother's crime. According to Gia, there were cases of mental illness that didn't fit any other category. How else could you explain a perfectly normal doctor—a happily married man—turning to murder? As if killing Scott was something out of Ricky's control.

It was heady stuff, what she proposed…and oh so tempting to believe as an explanation for his brother's crimes. How great to think that he could somehow fix Ricky by getting a spirit to follow the light and float on home?

But in the end, he couldn't see it Gia's way. For him, his brother's case was only too typical. Ricky needed to be that perfect son…the successful surgeon. He wanted the pretty society wife and the mansion on the water. Scott exposed him in a way his brother couldn't accept.

Ricky wanted out. Scott made that impossible, threatening everything his brother held dear—his family and his reputation. So Ricky killed him…and lost it all, just the same.

No, Seven didn't believe his brother was possessed. But that didn't mean he didn't regard Gia's gift as deadly serious. Whatever it was that made her tick, she was crazy accurate when it came to this kind of thing.

"You've seen this spirit?" he asked. "The one attached to Stella?"

"No," she said.

There was a look of real fear in her eyes.

"Last time I checked," he said slowly, "it was you seeing the spooky stuff, not Stella."

"Not this time." She scrubbed her face with her hands. "I've tried talking to her. I even tried summoning the spirit myself but it's not me he wants. And Stella, she's completely shut me out."

"What is she now? Thirteen? Right around the time a kid is supposed to think her parents are the enemy. That way, when she has to jump ship in a few years and make it on her own in the big bad world, it's not so scary."

She shook her head. "This goes beyond teenage rebellion. When she looked at the painting, she almost passed out. But I don't see a damn thing. Only, I know it's here." She stood and walked to the sink. "There's water everywhere this spirit goes. The faucet turns on by itself. Or a puddle forms on the floor."

He took a moment. *Shit.*

But there was no way he could hold back. Not if his silence could hurt Stella or Gia.

He stood. "Mark Dair and the girl in the Bolsa Chica weren't the only victims. There was a third. Another girl. All were found near a large body of water. Cause of death for all three appears to be drowning."

She took a step back, almost staggering. There it was. The tortured expression of a mother frightened for her child. Stella was an old soul, but no one her age deserved to see the things that were happening to these kids.

He walked over to stand in front of her. The urge to take her into his arms and comfort her was almost overwhelming.

Seven had married young. The day Laurin asked for a divorce had cut almost as deep as his brother's betrayal. And still, the connection he'd found with Gia—and the split that followed—hit him at a whole new level. It was almost as if, after all he'd been through, he never would have taken the risk, getting involved with her, if what he'd felt wasn't so deep.

He shoved his hands into his pockets. "Do you think she'll talk to me?" he asked.

"As a cop?"

"As a friend."

She gave him a desperate look. "She trusted you before."

"Then let me help," he urged her.

She nodded. "Okay." She kept nodding, as if trying to convince herself. "But do it soon. The timing on all this," she said. "Well, there's too much synchronicity."

"Synchronicity?" It was a good word for Erika. "I don't understand."

She leaned back against the kitchen counter. "Meaningful coincidence. It's a theory introduced by Carl Jung."

"Meaning," he said, playing with the words, "there is no coincidence."

She gave him a wan smile. "At least, that's what I believe."

He nodded, wondering how to breach the next topic—one he'd steadily avoided.

In the end, he jumped right in.

"So…what are you *not* telling me?" he asked.

Her head jerked up. The look in her eyes; she hadn't expected it, the distrust.

"Come on," he said with a grin that said *no big deal*. "It's not like we haven't taken a turn around this dance floor."

It was the shadow that hung between them. Never once had she talked about her vision to him...the one in which Seven pulled the trigger and killed her attacker. But she'd known. She'd known before they'd started sleeping together. She'd known from the first day they met.

"No," she said softly. "I'm not hiding anything."

She stood and walked out of the kitchen, letting him know their meeting was at an end. And why wouldn't she? He'd trotted out the ugly past, making sure they both remembered the pain.

Following her out to the front room, he wondered when it would stop being so fucked up in his head, this thing between them. The anger warring with the attraction. But he pushed away the question, knowing it was a trap.

At the door, he told her, "Try not to worry."

"That's me. Little Miss Sunshine. Not a worry in the world."

They both stood at the door as if waiting for something to happen. He thought about it, taking that small step back into her life.

Instead, he turned and walked down the rose-lined path to her gate. She kept a beautiful garden. He imagined it was full of color all year round.

He punched the gate open, wondering why the very thought made him so angry.

19

Carin waited outside Halo Industries next to the pearl-white Cayenne Turbo. The car was Porsche's answer to the SUV craze back when gasoline was still under two bucks a gallon. It was a muscle car for all those Peter Pans who finally grew up to raise a family. Now daddy could take his half of the soccer team from zero to sixty in just under four seconds.

Carin thought it was a hoot. Imagine, Zag de Rozières with a juiced-up version of the daddy-mobile.

Halo Industries had offices in Atlanta, Chicago, Seattle and Los Angeles. Zag, Carin knew, preferred L.A., the land of the famous and fabulous. He had a house in Malibu and another in Laurel Canyon. When he wasn't tooling around the world in his Gulfstream V, he'd be holed up here at his L.A. offices.

Carin had been waiting for almost an hour in the parking lot for him to show.

At the security booth, she'd flashed her badge and a smile and trotted out some excuse about a meeting with Donald Hertz—she'd looked him up, a middle-management drone who wouldn't raise any red flags. What she lacked in cleavage she made up for in confidence. The security guard waved her to drive on through.

Now she waited in the parking lot, knowing she'd never get inside the building. Not without alerting Zag.

Hers was an old tactic: beating the bushes to see what might come flying out.

She looked up at the sixteen-story building, eerily reminiscent of the black monolith in Kubrick's *2001: A Space Odyssey*. The sun was setting on the Halo Industries insignia, concentric circles connected by a line radiating out from the center to its base. The image reminded her of an all-seeing eye.

She glanced down at the screen of her BlackBerry and frowned. Earlier today, Erika had texted a photograph of Gia's latest painting. The attached message read: We need to talk.

Tomorrow was the autopsy on the latest vic. Erika would have a hell of a lot more questions after that.

Using the controls on the BlackBerry, Carin focused on the stones painted just above Mark Dair's head. They were a perfect depiction of the Bimini Stones.

In the early 1900s, Edgar Cayce, the "sleeping prophet," predicted that evidence verifying the existence of Atlantis would be discovered in the Bahamas in 1968. That same year, aerial photographs taken by pilots flying over the island of Bimini showed structures resembling fallen walls or a road under the waters offshore.

Since then, Bimini Road had become the subject of much speculation. Skeptics and believers alike spun the facts to support their particular point of view. But there was no denying that the slabs of rock on the seabed fit together like paving stones. Bimini Road appeared man-made.

And there was more. In 1972, a rumor surfaced concerning an obscure discovery made in Bimini that had been squirreled away by a private buyer. The expedition in the Bahamas itself had been a kind of cloak-and-dagger operation, financed by investors who'd made it their business to remain "anonymous." Divers had scoured the waters off Bimini, presumably shooting a documentary. When no film surfaced, it only fueled the rumors.

According to the scuttlebutt, the expedition uncovered stones inscribed with some sort of writing. Like Bimini Road, the stones supported the premise for an ancient civilization.

The Bahamian government immediately filed a protest with the State Department, claiming a proprietary interest. The investigation that followed had been feeble at best. It was still an open file at NISA…which is how Carin knew about the Bimini Stones.

The only reason she knew Benoit de Rozières, Zag's father, had financed the Bahamian expedition all those years ago was because she and Zag had shared a bed.

It had taken every favor she had—as well as some much-needed clout from Morgan—to get assigned as SAC, Special Agent in Charge, on this case. The stones found in the hands of the victims appeared to be tiny replicas of the Bimini Stones.

Unfortunately, Zag was a powerful man. No way could she point the finger without some solid proof.

Carin put the BlackBerry away. The man thought he was untouchable—and maybe he was. Maybe Carin was just too stubborn to admit it.

She'd spent a frustrating day searching for the smallest vulnerability. As she'd warned Morgan, it wasn't a good sign that Zag became interested in Morgan's work only after Carin managed to spirit away the Eye of Athena. She had no idea how he'd discovered her subterfuge with the FBI, but she didn't believe in coincidence when it came to Zag.

Now, she felt as if there was this time bomb ticking inside her head. *Time's up!*

In the end, she'd even called Terrence. When it came to getting the job done, Carin had no shame.

Terrence McGee had been her boss at NISA. He'd retired six months ago—or more likely, he'd been asked to resign. Another thing she wasn't proud of.

"Carin, this is crazy, even for you."

"Come on, Terrence. The kids in Zag's Halo-effect schools, they're all around the same age. Fourteen."

"So that makes the man a serial killer?"

"Zag wouldn't see it that way. The end justifies the means. Terrence, the victims—there were clear signs that they'd been injected with something. What if, instead of torture, these children suffered some sort of experimentation?"

"That's one hell of a leap."

"Each victim had a mark on the top of the hand or on the inside of the arm just below the elbow," she said. *"Marks consistent with an IV."*

"You're looking for a serial killer. Did you even profile the guy?"

"Why do you think I started investigating the great Zag de Rozières? Only, everywhere I go, I hit a wall."

"So what do you want?"

"Help me. No one can be that bulletproof."

At least, that's what she hoped.

Now, she watched as Zag stepped out the gilded doors of Halo Industries and strolled out into the parking lot. Carin crossed her arms. She knew enough about body language to recognize the instant he saw her standing next to his car.

He dressed like the celebrities whose company he so

coveted. Today it was skin-tight black leather and a shirt straight out of the Renaissance. He'd spiked his hair into a faux Mohawk. She could never be sure the true color of his hair—the only hair on his body was on his head and ever since she'd known him he'd kept that dyed an almost white-blond. He looked like a manicured bad boy. She'd heard he'd recently extended his many talents to producing a rock band.

He came to stand very close. She imagined he was trying to intimidate her. *Nice try.*

"Hello, Zag."

He had the strangest eyes. They appeared almost colorless they had so little pigment. And the pupils were always enlarged. She remembered staring into those eyes as he made love to her. To think she'd given the asshole her virginity.

"Are you following me, Goddess?"

That had been his pet name for her. Goddess. The man was nothing if not in touch with the female ego.

She stepped even closer, enjoying the tension. "You bet your ass."

"I'm flattered. It's not every day I find the FBI at my door."

"That's not what I hear. According to my sources, you're knee-deep into the alphabet."

That much she knew about Zag and Halo. Only, his government contracts were the kind that didn't show up on the books.

He leaned in, almost touching her. Carin was tall. She could have been a pole-vaulter or a supermodel. Zag's five feet eleven inches had always fit nicely against her.

He whispered, "This sounds like an extended conversation. Perhaps over dinner?"

"No thanks," she said drily. "I don't enjoy choking on my food."

He clucked his tongue. "You always did hold a grudge."

"That's me, Zag. The vindictive bitch. Speaking of which, I found something the other day that might belong to you. Guess where I found it? Clutched in the hand of a dead girl. You wouldn't know anything about that, would—"

He put his hand on her mouth, stopping the accusation. "Now, now. I'm not responsible for everything that goes bump in the night."

She yanked off his hand, fighting the urge to break that pretty nose again. She leaned in. "I know you, Zag. How you think. Do you really believe you're that untouchable?"

He smiled and whispered, "Guess what, Goddess? I *know* I am. Now, how about that dinner?"

She stepped away from the car door, allowing him access. "I believe my answer stays as always—when hell freezes over."

He shook his head. "Suit yourself."

He stepped around her, making sure he brushed up against her.

Once inside the car, he rolled down the window. "You know that old saying, Carin. You catch more flies with honey."

Watching him speed away, she could almost hear that tick, tick, tick, inside her head.

Zag burned rubber on the turn heading out of the parking lot.

Fuck.

He settled back into the leather seat, reaching for calm. But it wasn't going to happen. Not with Carin in his rearview mirror.

No one could get to him like the Goddess.

There'd been a reason he'd given her that nickname. Once upon a time, he thought he'd found his soul mate, a woman capable of reaching the heights he dreamed of scaling. Carin was beautiful, brilliant, ambitious.

Unfortunately, that's where their wills collided: their dueling ambitions. Carin had been one of the greater sacrifices he'd made for his dreams.

He punched a number into his cell phone. Evie picked up on the second ring.

"Dearest, you will never guess who I ran into."

There was a stop sign ahead. The intersection was most likely deserted at this time of day. He floored it, liking his chances.

"Special Agent Carin Barnes of the fucking FBI." He lowered his voice to a stage whisper, "I believe she suspects me of some sort of foul play. Can you imagine?"

There had been a time when he'd seen Carin as an ally, someone with the knowledge and desire to help him get to that crucial next level.

But Carin had lost faith…or maybe she just wanted to call the shots and that wasn't the way he played the game. Her stint with the FBI had sure come as quite the surprise. Fortunately enough, he'd had the money and connections to neutralize any possible threat from that direction.

And now, she thought she could take him on?

She had absolutely no idea who she was dealing with.

"By the bye," he asked, knowing Evie had met with Markie Barnes, Carin's brother, earlier that day, "how is our boy doing?"

20

Ghost boy had gone missing.

Stella felt stuck in some weird game of hide and seek. She could almost sense him waiting, biding his time until he could nail her with some horrible *gotcha!*

She'd spent another sleepless night waiting for just that. Only, it never happened.

Abracadabra. He'd disappeared.

At breakfast, she'd choked on every bite of cereal, hoping her mom didn't notice—which was kind of stupid. Mom noticed everything. Oh, sure, she might leave you alone. Wait until Stella felt comfortable talking about it. But she knew.

All morning she'd been on edge. She didn't know what was worse, that horrible presence or the fact that he was MIA.

She felt stuck, waiting for the other shoe to drop.

Until it did.

She'd been at the library at school. Every other week, her English class came here, their time to check out new books. All day, she kept looking over her shoulder, wondering when she'd find ghost boy standing there, taunting her.

When he finally appeared, it wasn't anything like what

she'd expected. He didn't jump out at her like those Halloween gags in a haunted house. This time he was almost gentle. She just looked up and there he was, seated across from her at the table.

"Stella?"

Stella flinched at the sound of her name. But it was only her English teacher hovering. Miss Nieman had been walking around, checking on her students, making sure everyone was on task. Stella had been edgy most of the day, spooking anytime she'd been caught unawares. This time wasn't any different.

"Do you feel all right, Stella?"

"Oh, yeah."

Stella smiled, but from the look on Miss Nieman's face, she could tell she was doing a pretty bad job of it.

"What are you reading?"

Stella glanced down at her book. She had absolutely no idea what it was about, only that it had a brown cover. She'd grabbed it off the book cart just before she'd sat down. She had it opened before her like a prop as her gaze canvassed the room, searching for ghost boy.

"It's for my next book report," she said dutifully.

Miss Nieman seemed satisfied enough to move on to the neighboring desk where two girls giggled behind their books, gabbing over the class hottie. Sean McKenzie might only be in eighth grade, but he was already almost six feet tall. Stella kept her gaze on the pages of her book—something on veterinary medicine. But she could still see ghost boy out of the corner of her eye.

Her mother always said a powerful gift attracted some pretty hairy spirits. That was her mother's problem. She attracted the bad ones. Like Stella's father.

It was hard to think of him like that. *My father.* She'd never even known him. He'd been in jail, accused of murdering Stella's grandmother when her mother ran away. Stella didn't know the whole story, just that her father was an archaeology student working at a dig site run by her grandmother, Estelle. He'd romanced her mom thinking he could use that connection to help him. He'd wanted her grandmother to trust him because she had the Eye of Athena. He planned to steal it.

By the time her mother figured out what was going on, it was too late. She was pregnant. And then she'd had her vision about him wanting to hurt them.

He'd almost succeeded—almost killed them both. Mom said he'd gone a little crazy. Because of the Eye. She said the crystal could drive you crazy if you didn't know what you were doing.

Well, now he was dead and he couldn't hurt them anymore. And things had gotten really good—good enough that Stella had sort of let her guard down.

Now, she worried it was happening to her. That just like her mom, her gift had attracted a bad spirit.

She looked at her hand spread out on the library table. Her fingers were shaking.

She squeezed her eyes shut. *Screw it.*

She looked up, bracing herself.

"I am not afraid," she whispered at ghost boy still sitting across the desk. "You either tell me what you want right now," she said, keeping her voice super low, "or I ask my mom how to get rid of you. Forever. No second chances."

In answer, he lay his hand, palm up, on the library table.

She frowned, staring at that milky-white skin. There was a red dot on the inside of his arm right below his elbow. She frowned, seeing that the spot was actually blood. Very slowly, a pearl of blood slipped down his skin.

She took a breath, remembering the last time she'd

taken his hand. She'd ended up having some kind of fit on the bathroom floor at Mindy's house.

But then she remembered what her mother said. This was an ancient gift—she was one of them, one of the Fegaris women.

Across the table, clear as day, ghost boy spoke for the first time.

He told her, "Don't be afraid."

And then he smiled.

It wasn't that scary smile she'd come to expect. It was more like Miss Nieman's smile. He was trying to encourage her.

His hand was still stretched out toward her on the table. Only the pinprick of blood was gone. His skin was smooth now, like there'd never been anything wrong with him.

Stella looked around. Nobody was paying the least attention, and still she hesitated.

Again, ghost boy spoke. "It's okay. I promise."

She bit her lip and nodded. She realized he was meeting her halfway. That was kind of a sign, right? She'd asked what he wanted and he was willing to talk. Progress.

The more she thought about it, the more it made sense. Maybe this was the only way he could let her know what he really needed, through his touch. He might not even know he'd hurt her in the bathroom. Maybe, like her, he didn't exactly have control of things.

Don't be afraid.

Slowly, she reached across the desk.

He didn't wait. His hand darted out. He grabbed her hand in his and squeezed her fingers tight. Suddenly, she felt as if a hundred needles were driving into her hand.

Her head jerked up. She looked at him, seeing his friendly smile was gone.

You lied. This hurts….

But the words didn't come out. Instead, she felt herself getting light-headed. She blinked rapidly, trying to keep her eyes focused.

Until everything just went black.

She stared up the chiseled stone steps. Up in the sky, there were these flying cars. She felt like she'd stepped into some strange future world, only there was also this ancient quality, like the Mayans could have built stuff here.

People were walking around her as if she were invisible. Mothers were talking to their kids. Men were deep in discussion. No one even noticed her.

She had a thought. *Maybe I'm the ghost now.*

The men and women were dressed regally. They reminded her of paintings in museums. They wore togas made of some kind of iridescent material she didn't recognize. And all of them wore these crystals around their necks. She looked down to see that she, too, had a crystal hanging from her neck. It felt like it was on fire, burning into her skin.

Suddenly, she wasn't in the futuristic Mayan world anymore. Instead, she was lying on what looked like a hospital bed with leather straps anchoring her ankles and wrists. There was an IV in her arm and a metal stand with bags and tubes hanging from it.

A man stood over the bed. He had red hair and bright blue eyes. And a syringe.

He jammed the needle into the IV line, then emptied the syringe.

"No!" she screamed.

Now she reclined in a bathtub filled with warm water. It felt nice. Only, she couldn't move. She was paralyzed.

She realized the water was on and the bathtub was slowly filling. She wanted to reach out and turn off the faucet. She tried to will her body to move, to reach out and turn off the water, but she couldn't.

Two hands came to rest on her shoulders. She couldn't see who it was—they were somewhere behind her—but they slowly pushed her under the water.

She wanted to kick her feet and flail her arms. She desperately wanted to fight. But the hands on her shoulders just kept pushing, lowering her face under the water.

I can't breathe, she thought.

I can't breathe!

"Plato? I'm impressed."

Stella opened her eyes and looked up. Miss Nieman was standing over her.

She realized she wasn't drowning. In fact, she was sitting in her seat at the library, her book still opened before her.

Only, this was clearly a different book than the one she'd had earlier. The cover was a different color. Instead of dull brown, it was dark blue with gold trim on the pages. The book had nothing to do with veterinary medicine.

Across the table, ghost boy was gone.

"Did you get lost in your book, Stella?"

Miss Nieman nodded over to where Stella's classmates were lined up, ready to check out their books.

"Get the lead out, girl," Miss Nieman said with a smile. "Time to go."

Stella nodded, again giving that awkward smile. She glanced down at her book. Had she somehow sleepwalked her way to the shelves and picked it out?

She read the heading on the page. It had something to do with dialogues written by Plato.

Dazed, she closed the book and stood. She went to stand in line with her classmates. She caught sight of Amanda whispering to Amity. Both girls were looking right at Stella. They looked away and started to giggle when she caught them staring.

She didn't care that they were talking about her. Maybe Mindy had even told them what happened at her house—she was friends with Amity.

They would think she was a freak. A weirdo. And they'd be right.

She could still remember what it felt like, that water covering her face…the terror of impending death.

She realized none of it had happened. The redheaded man with the needle, those hands pushing her under the water—none of it was real.

But it felt real.

"Your book, please."

The librarian held out her hand. Stella glanced down at the blue book, the one she didn't remember getting. The title was one word.

In bold print, the cover read *Atlantis*.

21

Seven walked in on the county coroner, Dr. Alice Tang, going over a bit of shop talk with Erika...the kind you didn't discuss in mixed company. In this case, mixed company was anyone outside of law enforcement.

It was a hazard of the job, the war stories. The problem was, soon enough, your world got smaller and smaller. Not that many people knew the head of a jumper burst on impact like a pumpkin or that the intestines flew out like one of those trick cans of snakes.

Both women stood over a stainless-steel drawer, examining the body.

"A shotgun blast to the head," Alice said. "The crime scene was painted in brain matter. Luckily we were able to put Humpty Dumpty back together again."

Seven came to stand next to Erika and stared down at the body. Half the man's face had been blown away.

"Ah. Good times," Seven said.

"Sometimes we get lucky," Alice said with a grin.

Seven wondered if Alice just pretended not to catch on to his blatant sarcasm. Like maybe the joke was on him.

Alice closed the drawer. "We folded and pieced his head and face back together and one of the guys thought he recognized him. Sure enough, we found a few teeth left in his lower jaw—with fillings." She picked up her coffee cup and shrugged. "Dental records matched him to the prime suspect in a drug ring."

"New coffee mug?" Erika asked.

Alice held a cup big enough to hold half a carafe of coffee. It was black with a big pink cat wearing black whiskers and super long lashes, one eye winking. The caption read Sex Kitten.

She grinned. "A gift from a certain someone."

At a guess, Seven would peg that certain someone as Everett, Alice's husband.

Dr. Alice Tang was in her early fifties. She wore glasses, the kind heralding back to the days when people wore glasses to see rather than to make a fashion statement. She kept her hair in a sensible page boy and stood all of five feet tall. She and her husband were both foodies. Seven wouldn't call her fat, but Alice didn't mind carrying around a few extra pounds for the sake of gastronomic delights.

Alice opened another steel drawer to show Katie Sweeny, the girl found in the marsh. She was covered with a sheet, a toe tag hanging from her foot. On that steel slab she looked positively tiny.

Her hair was dry now. Just as he'd imagined, her sun-bleached curls surrounded her head like a halo.

"I haven't received any records on the other victims from the feds, but this mark…." She turned the left hand. At the top was a perfectly round mark coming up from the index and middle finger.

"It's a puncture wound," she said. "And there's some phlebitis, most likely caused by a catheter. I believe your victim was given an IV."

"Jesus," Erika whispered under her breath.

"And another thing—the cause of death—your victim drowned, but there's lividity."

"Lividity?" Erika glanced over at Seven. Lividity was a result of gravity working on the heavier red blood cells once the heart stopped—something that didn't happen when the body was buoyed up by water.

"That's right." Alice pulled back the sheet and pointed along the right side of the body at the purple-red discoloration that marked where the blood pooled after death. The marks followed along the entire right side of the body.

"There was water in her lungs but she didn't die *in* water. Possibly, she was only partially submerged or you found the body relatively soon after disposal. Judging from the compression lividity, I'd say she was curled up on her side. I also found some trace evidence. I can't be sure until I get results back from the lab, but I'd guess carpet fibers."

"She was moved," Erika said.

"A good narrative would be in the trunk of a car. It's just a hunch, of course," said one of the most experienced coroners in the country.

"It would explain the position of the body and the fibers," Erika said.

"We'll have more answers when I hear back from the lab."

Seven tried to imagine what it must be like for Alice. Here she was waltzing from a professional hit to a serial killer targeting kids like it was just another day's work.

Maybe that's how she does it, he thought. *She just keeps moving.*

Alice stepped over to a cabinet and grabbed a file folder. "But here's what's really interesting." She flipped through several pages. "There was froth in the trachea and bronchi.

Sure enough, the water from the lungs had traces of both chloramines and chlorine."

"And me just a few credits shy of that chemistry degree," Erika said.

"Looks like you're going to have to dumb it down for my partner here, Alice," he said, earning himself a sharp jab from Erika's elbow.

"The girl's body was found in the marsh. That's brackish water—part saltwater from the ocean and part freshwater from an underground source. But the water in the victim's lungs wasn't brackish."

She leaned forward, ready to deliver. Seven felt himself tense.

"Chloramines and chlorine are typical disinfectants used in water treatment plants. Judging from these results—" Alice held up the report "—I'd say our victim drowned in good old tap water."

For Evie, fighting her brother was like playing chess with herself. It wasn't a matter of anticipating his next move. She *knew* what was coming. Theirs was more like a carefully choreographed dance rather than sparring.

She delivered a jumping spindle kick. Adam ducked and attacked with an outside snap crescent kick.

"Nice," he said.

She didn't waste her breath answering, launching herself into a roundhouse kick to his midsection with her left leg. They'd been free-sparring for almost an hour and both were dripping in sweat. They'd been trained by their father in most of the martial arts, karate, jujitsu, tae kwon do.

They wore no protective equipment; they didn't need it.

Adam counterattacked with a turning back kick that

just missed as Evie sidestepped out of range. She aimed an ax kick to his shoulder; it connected, bringing him down.

"How am I doing now?" she asked.

But even from the ground, Adam was still a threat. As if he'd planned her attack, he was already down on one knee, balanced perfectly to aim a side kick to her jaw. The blow was glancing, but gave him enough time to regain his footing. He launched into a turning sidekick to her diaphragm.

That's when it happened, a kind of stop-action effect. She saw her brother balance back to execute his next move.

Only, the image was like one of those old-fashioned flip books. There came a succession of flashes, each showing her brother coming closer.

Until she saw nothing at all.

Adam's foot connected with enough force to send her reeling backward. She hit the wall of the exercise room with a hard thud, knocking the wind out of her.

When her vision settled, Adam was standing in front of her, his hands down at his sides.

"You didn't see that," he said.

There was this touch of alarm in his voice. Evie almost smiled.

It wasn't so much that they couldn't catch the other off guard. If the sparring progressed fast enough, even Evie and Adam couldn't keep up. But never had there been this *blank*.

When she regained her footing, she attacked with an inside twisting kick to the side of the jaw quickly followed by a hammer fist to the clavicle.

With a yell of frustration, she grabbed his shoulder with her right hand and delivered a heavy upper cut to his stomach with her left.

Jab, jab, cross.

Her brother, the stronger of the two, had her pinned on the ground in an instant. He was leaning over her, breathing just as hard as Evie.

"What the hell is going on, Evie?" he asked.

Because he'd felt it, too, that moment of darkness.

Inside her mind, she felt his gentle probing. Immediately, she pushed him out of her head, blocking his mental touch.

Nothing could have shocked her brother more.

He regained his feet, staring at her. Evie sat up, too. With her hand, she wiped away the blood at the corner of her mouth.

She'd never tried it before, blocking him out. She wasn't even sure she could do it. There had never been any need to keep him from her thoughts…until now.

She smiled up at Adam and said, "Surprise."

Adam didn't respond. Instead, he turned and left the room.

But she knew what he had planned. He hadn't tried to hide his thoughts. Rather, he'd projected his next move.

"Good luck, Daddy," she said under her breath.

Nathaniel looked up when Adam burst into his office on the second floor. His son was dressed in a white T-shirt and loose drawstring cotton trousers, clothes usually worn during his martial arts exercises with his sister. He was breathing hard, his long red hair dark with sweat, his blue eyes blazing with emotion.

Nathaniel took a moment to admire his son. Adam was everything he'd hoped, fit of mind and body. If he'd had the choice, it would be Adam he would have kept close, knowing his talent had the greater potential.

But that was the problem. Adam was the stronger of his two children. Maybe too strong. Certainly, he wasn't as easily manipulated as his sister.

At the moment, he looked like a man ready to take Nathaniel on.

"What's happening to her?" he demanded.

"What do you mean?" Nathaniel asked.

"Evie. She…" Adam struggled to find the right word. "Blanked."

Nathaniel didn't react, giving nothing away.

It's begun, he thought. The separation.

Identical twins were a favorite subject for research on nature versus nurture. There were cases of orphaned twins raised in different households who still maintained startling similarities. Despite their changed circumstances, twins chose at a statistically significant frequency like spouses or identical cars…even something as simple as lipstick color could be the same.

One famous case study on twins involved a botched circumcision. Eventually, through subsequent surgeries, the injured twin was able to regain full penile function—many thought too late. He committed suicide. It was assumed the childhood trauma and subsequent suicide were connected. But when the second twin took his own life, the question arose: Bad surgery or not—were both twins genetically predisposed to commit suicide?

In the general population, many assumed there was some sort of psychic element when it came to twins. But the fact was, physiology could account for common behaviors. If your hand musculature was exactly the same, why wouldn't your handwriting look identical? If your taste buds were essentially a carbon copy, why wouldn't you prefer the same foods or restaurants?

That wasn't the case for Adam and Evie.

Brother and sister looked extraordinarily alike, the male

and female version of one person, but obviously they were not identical. And yet, the connection between them went far from that of fraternal twins.

While there were documented cases of twins creating their own language, Adam and Evie required no language at all. Neither spoke a word until the age of five. Words weren't necessary—certainly not when you could hear each other's thoughts.

With time, the situation became severe, enough that Nathaniel determined brother and sister should be separated, attempting to break a bond so strong it threatened to suffocate. He couldn't afford for his children to cut him out.

He set up two households. Adam and Evie were raised by nannies. The story was that Nathaniel traveled, a lot. He could only be with his son or daughter half his time. He kept them separated for almost a year.

With time, it became clear that separating the twins didn't have the desired effect. Quite the opposite. Their need to communicate with each other only strengthened their psychic powers, allowing each to read the other's mind at long distances.

That's when Nathaniel made an even more difficult decision. His beloved wife had given mankind a gift. He needed to make certain it wasn't wasted.

He brought his children back together again. They were homeschooled by Nathaniel—but not in the traditional manner.

There were theories that all children were born with paranormal powers; the ability to see spirits, for example, was considered quite common. Children often interacted with invisible friends or feared the monster under the bed. But at some point, society closed off those powers. Children were chastised into believing the paranormal couldn't exist. What they felt or saw just couldn't be. It was all a figment of their imaginations. The continued negative enforcement had a distinct dampening effect.

Nathaniel was well aware of these theories. In raising Adam and Evie, he'd focused on one thing and one thing only: helping his children develop their special abilities.

Some might consider his tactics cruel. There had been some experimentation with sensory deprivation and drug therapy. But Nathaniel didn't care about the opinions of others. If his children had been musical prodigies, he'd never be judged for demanding extended hours of practice.

"Your sister blanked?" Nathaniel repeated the statement as if he didn't understand. "Explain."

By now, Adam had calmed down, regaining that singular focus that so characterized his son. Nathaniel told himself to be careful.

"We were sparring," Adam said. "She…turned off. I couldn't see her next move. And neither could she."

Nathaniel took a moment. It wouldn't do to give a facile explanation. Not to Adam. "What do you think happened?"

Adam stepped forward, looming over his father. "You're pushing her too hard, Father."

Nathaniel nodded, taking a deep breath as if steadying himself. Adam must never know how hard Nathaniel had worked to bring them to this moment.

He reached out and took his son's hand in his. "Yes, I've seen it, too. Your sister is exhausted."

He knew the right tactics to use. He'd had both twins tested extensively. Adam in particular responded to human touch, perhaps because he'd been so deprived of it during his formative years.

He squeezed his son's hand. "Only, what if it's not me

doing the damage? What if it's Zag and the work he forces on Evie with those Halo-effect children?"

Adam remained silent, giving his father an enigmatic stare. It was getting more difficult to fool his son.

"Think about it, Adam. Do you really believe these are ordinary children Zag has brought together? They are most likely powerfully gifted. Who knows what battles your sister wages inside their minds only to satisfy Zag's ego?"

He released Adam's hand and turned away, feigning parental distress he didn't feel. Not that it mattered what he felt. From the time his children had been conceived, he'd known the difficult task that lay ahead. He'd used his extensive training in military intelligence—mind control, behavior modification—to perfect their abilities.

It was up to his children to finish what Celeste had started so long ago: remote view through time and space to rediscover technological marvels long lost to mankind. Adam and Evie were the answer and it was his duty to keep them on their path.

He took off his glasses and rubbed his eyes. "I've asked her to stop. Her work here is difficult enough—not to mention important. She doesn't need the additional stress of Zag's little pet projects. Perhaps you can talk some sense into her?"

For the longest time, Adam stared at his father. Nathaniel kept a neutral expression, careful to meet his son's steady gaze.

"Will you help her, Adam? Will you help Evie?"

Adam didn't respond. Instead, he turned and left.

Nathaniel watched his son disappear into the hall, knowing it was a good thing Adam couldn't read his mind.

* * *

Seven leaned back against the Crown Vic. He was standing just outside Jordan Intermediate School, home to the Jordan Jaguars. It was a quarter to three.

He was parked in the mommy lane, the coveted parking space that mandated all cars move on after a mere three-minute wait—the same lane where eager moms and dads parked a good twenty minutes before the bell rang to mark the end of the day.

He'd made some lame excuse to Erika. *I have a thing with this guy.* Erika was smart enough to not ask questions.

He spotted Stella immediately. She was smaller than most of the kids but still stood out in the crowd with those bouncing black curls.

And the attitude. The erect carriage making most of her four feet something. The gaze that cut right through as though you weren't even there. You couldn't miss it a mile away.

He could see she was a loner. He imagined that not many at the tender age of thirteen could get past that fierce expression of hers. He remembered the first time he'd been on the receiving end of that stare.

Not that he blamed her. The kid had it tough. Daughter to Gia, granddaughter to Estelle. Not to mention her homicidal biological father she'd been hiding from all her life.

As he watched, she made her way through the crowd, heading straight for him. He hadn't seen her for months, something he didn't feel great about. They'd made a connection, the two of them. When Gia vanished during the fortune-teller case, it was Seven who'd helped Stella cope. She'd worked with him to help find her mother. Unfortunately, when he'd walked away from Gia, by necessity, he'd cut Stella off, as well.

When she came close enough, he opened the passenger door.

But Stella wasn't going to make it easy. She crossed her arms and stared at him.

"What are you doing here?" she asked.

"I was just passing by. Hop in. I'll give you a ride home. Just so you know, you're getting a ride from not just any old homicide detective. I am now special liaison for the FBI."

"Whatever," she said, her tone making it clear she wasn't impressed. "Mom sent you."

"And that's a bad thing because?"

Stella rolled her eyes, the gesture saying that he was pathetic but she'd play along for now.

Once she was inside, he slammed the door shut, saying, "That's what I thought."

They drove in silence—he wasn't sure if it was out of stubbornness or awkwardness. In the end, he knew it was up to him. The kid might be an old soul, but he was the adult.

"So," he asked, "seen any ghosts lately?"

She kept her face glued to the window as if they were passing through Tuscany in Italy instead of Garden Grove. "Is that supposed to be funny?"

He turned on his blinker. "It's called an icebreaker."

"Ice officially broken. Tell Mom I'm fine."

"Tell her yourself. So why are you keeping her out of the loop? I mean, isn't this her thing—the spirit gig?"

"A lot you care."

He frowned. "I'm afraid I don't have a pithy response for that."

More silence.

He sighed. Well, he hadn't thought it was going to be easy.

Five minutes later, he pulled up in front of her house.

He turned off the engine and looked at her. She sat in the passenger seat, staring ahead.

"You think my mom and I are freaks," she said.

Of course, that's what she'd think when he'd stopped coming around.

Only, the story was a hell of a lot more complicated.

Not that he could tell Stella. *You, see, when I shot your father—you know, the insane guy who tried to kill your mother—I realized that maybe your mom's gift was the real deal. But that would mean she'd known all along what was going to happen through her vision thing. So it follows that she probably used me...which sort of sucks as a basis for a deep and meaningful relationship.*

Try to soft sell that one.

He turned Stella to face him. "Your mother and I had a fight—the normal kind, where a woman and a man disagree. Only, the stuff we clashed over was pretty fundamental. But it had nothing to do with you." And here he threw in the requisite little white lie. "And it was certainly not to distance myself from your mother's gift. Remember me? The homicide detective? I deal with some pretty dark stuff myself. A little hocus pocus here and there?" He shook his head. "Not going to get under my skin."

She kept that fierce look aimed right at him, trying to gauge what to believe. But he was a cop and had a serious leg up on Stella when it came to the psych-out.

"Talk to your mom," he said. "Whether you believe it or not, she was put on this earth to guide you through it. So suck up all that teenage angst and tell her what's going on." He put his hand on hers and gave it a squeeze, trying to take the sting out of his words. "You're all she has, Stella. And trust me when I tell you that, whatever is going on, your mother has already imagined twice as worse."

He could see Stella was having a hard time keeping it together, that she was trying not to cry in front of him.

"You'll talk to her?"

She nodded her head. "Yeah."

He leaned over and opened the door. "Good. Oh, and let's make this a regular thing. Only, next time, we'll go for ice cream. You a chocolate or vanilla girl?"

She frowned, like it was a trick question. "Pistachio."

It was his turn to roll his eyes. "Figures."

22

Theodore Fields hustled down the halls of the Institute. He was what Martha had termed "in a lather." Theodore would use something stronger to describe his current state. Murderous rage came to mind.

What had that bitch Martha thought his reaction would be? She'd attacked his very character, bringing up MK-ULTRA, the CIA's mind-control experiments initiated in the 1950s. The project had been universally vilified in Congress and the press for the CIA's use of extreme measures in keeping up with how U.S. prisoners of war had been interrogated by China, Korea and the Soviet Union. Their methods included sensory deprivation, electric shock, chemical treatment and possibly psychosurgery.

And she'd accused *him* of being involved? Of condoning such work?

Of course, he knew what she was trying to do: bring emotion into the discussion. But the fact was, Theodore wouldn't have wasted his time on that kind of mind-control silliness.

But then she'd brought up the government's secret program with radiation, alluding to his rumored involvement.

Those allegations were never more than a blatant attempt by a rival to discredit me, Martha, and you know it!

He hadn't meant to pop off like that, giving the kind of reaction that made him look guilty.

To make things worse, he'd actually walked out on the latest meeting of Morgan's beloved Brain fucking Trust. He'd looked around the table, searching for support. But there they were, staring at him like they believed every blessed word of her accusation.

Well, fuck them. And fuck whoever in the government had leaked his name. His participation in those experiments was supposed to have been special access/need-to-know only.

Theodore pulled at his bow tie. He noticed lately that his clothes were getting tighter. Evie was a hell of a cook. He'd gained weight, which wouldn't help his blood pressure. He figured that right about now, it was through the roof.

He still couldn't believe it. Morgan had chosen that prick, Zag, to work with his mystery artifact, the Eye of Athena.

Normally, Theodore couldn't give a flying fuck. Some magic rock that supposedly focused psychic powers like a lens? Jesus, it was about as relevant as Zag's theories on Atlantis being the first source of dark matter. Pure science fiction.

But he didn't have that luxury anymore.

Again, he clawed at his bow tie.

What am I gonna tell Evie?

The fact was, a woman like Evie wouldn't step into Theodore's bed without an agenda. She came with a price, one he'd led her to believe he could pay.

He remembered when he'd first met her. She'd been brought to the Institute to work with several of the residents, part of an experimental program to study how to communicate with the autistic. Some mumbo-jumbo she called "psychic therapy." He knew she did similar work at Zag's Halo-effect schools.

When Evie heard about Morgan's claim to have the Eye of Athena, she'd come to him. Theodore Fields. Not Zag.

Evie Slade was a work of art. She was beautiful beyond compare *and* she had a brain. She could keep up with Theodore on topics ranging from Renaissance art to String theory. And she was a gourmet cook. Last night, she'd shown up on his door with a bag of groceries. She'd fed him these amazing seared scallops accompanied by a lovely white Pomerol while they both lay naked in bed.

She was any man's dream come true. No, she was better than that. She was *Theodore's* dream come true, and he had *much* higher standards.

And now that prick, Zag, would ruin this, too?

Last night, he'd practically had a heart attack during what was some incredibly rigorous sex. Evie was very athletic—not to mention extremely flexible. Thank God for his little blue pills.

He'd been lying in the bed, spent, Evie still straddling him. He was having trouble catching his breath; he'd figured his pulse would probably clock in well over a hundred.

That's when she'd leaned over him, pressing her exquisite breasts against his chest, her long red hair draping over his shoulders.

She'd said, "I heard Zag will be working with the Eye."

She reached between them, caressing his balls with one hand, using those incredible muscles of hers to somehow stimulate him back to life. Jesus, if they made love again, it just might be the end of him.

"You know how Zag is," she whispered next to his ear.

"He'll never share. Not without some…special compensation."

Which meant she'd move on, leaving his bed for Zag's.

She'd made it clear from the beginning what she wanted. She'd thought Theodore would have access to that fucking stone. Evie thought she was psychic. To her, Morgan's silly rock was like the Holy Grail.

He didn't blame her. He understood ambition. Okay, maybe he couldn't take the psychic stuff seriously, but she did and that's all that mattered.

Hell, he'd been more than eager to pay the price. It didn't take his IQ to figure out a woman like Evie wouldn't have sex with his fat ass if there wasn't a payoff.

The mistake he'd made was in stringing her along. He knew the minute she had her hands on the rock, she would be long gone. His position in the Brain Trust and his relationship with Morgan were his only leverage.

So he'd stalled, giving Zag just the opening the bastard needed.

And now, she'd started to press a little.

"Come on, baby," she'd whispered last night. "Give me what I want. I will make it worth your while."

He'd spent the last few days kissing Morgan's ass, playing the game. Each and every time he'd had to bite his lips not to blurt out that Morgan and his crystal were the only things standing between Theodore and some serious tail.

And now he had to learn from Evie that Zag had been given permission to work with the Eye?

No way. No fucking way. If Morgan didn't give Theodore a shot at the crystal, then he'd find another way to make Evie happy.

He wasn't about to lose her.

He'd won the Nobel Prize, for Christ's sake. How difficult could it be to get access to the damn crystal?

What he needed, he decided, heading toward the parking lot, was an excuse just to see the damn thing. Once he had Morgan's confidence, he'd figure out a way to exploit it.

He'd get the crystal and the girl.

Damn straight he would.

Adam waited at the perimeter of the parking lot. He'd been trained by his father in the art of reconnaissance. He'd downloaded the schematics for the compound. He knew exactly where to stand so he had the best view but could remain out of range of the security cameras.

He was staring at the back entrance to the Institute for the Dynamic Studies of Parapsychology and the Brain, cell phone in hand. The ocean breeze whipped a lock of hair across his face. He pushed it away and hit the send button on his cell.

Adam understood he was irritated, a unique condition for him. It wasn't often that he was ignored, particularly by his sister. But here she was, ignoring his calls.

The whole thing was starting to set off some alarm bells. That sudden instant of separation during their sparring and Evie's subsequent attempt to block him out of her mind—he didn't know what to think.

His father blamed Zag. That he was pushing Evie too hard. Adam wasn't so sure.

It wasn't the first time Adam had waited for his sister. She might be the elder by two minutes, but he was certainly the more responsible.

He'd taken a great risk coming here. Anyone who saw them together would see an immediate resemblance. Not that he had a choice. Time was running out for Polly.

Holding the cell phone at his side, he could still hear his sister's voice-mail message piping through the speaker. He punched End.

His sister's Saab convertible waited in her parking space just under the floodlights in the parking lot. The car was new, a gift from Zag.

He pressed redial.

There'd been a time when something like this wouldn't have been possible. They were Adam and Evie—all that was left of the great Celeste Slade, Remote Viewer A-001. Like many twins, they could finish each other's sentences. And more.

Inside his head, he could talk to Evie, and she to him.

But here he was, trying to connect with his sister using a damn cell phone.

He heard her voice-mail message and punched End.

He itched to dial again. Better yet, he imagined himself storming the doors of the Institute, searching for her.

She was his twin, his better half.

There'd been other men in Evie's life. She didn't like to be alone. Neither did Adam. She liked powerful men. Usually, that meant physical strength, but not always.

He hadn't always approved of her choices. But Zag seemed to be an improvement. Adam suspected his sister was troubled and here was someone who actually made her happy.

After talking to his father, he wasn't so sure.

He frowned and redialed then cut off the call before her voice mail could pick up.

He closed his eyes and took a deep breath. He knew several meditation exercises. He could drop his heart rate at a phenomenal rate. But not tonight.

She pushed me right out of her head.

The thought was like a mental burr.

When he opened his eyes, he concentrated on the back entrance, almost willing his sister to walk through.

The door burst open. But it wasn't his sister who marched out onto the asphalt of the parking lot.

The woman was tall and slim. She wore a dark suit and carried a briefcase.

She was blond and very pretty, the kind of woman who could catch any man's eye—then bully him into walking away with just a hard stare.

But it wasn't her beauty that had him mesmerized.

Suddenly, she stopped. She whipped around and stared right at him.

He knew she couldn't see him. Where he was standing, the parking lot's floodlights would be in her eyes, making him invisible.

And still, she just stood there, staring in his direction.

He didn't move, didn't breathe. She had these amazing lights dancing around her. He was very familiar with the significance of that aura, as well as its rarity.

You're the Finder, Adam; Evie is the Destroyer.

She switched her briefcase to her left hand. He watched as she pushed aside the edge of her jacket with her right.

She was wearing a gun holster.

Only now, she was looking around the parking lot. He realized she'd *sensed* his presence. But she had no idea he was watching her just a few yards away.

He wasn't sure why—maybe it was something as silly as Evie blowing him off. Whatever the reason, he stepped out of the shadows and into the light, walking right for her.

Seeing him, she pivoted on one foot to face him. It was an experienced move. She'd obviously had training. Still, she didn't pull out the gun. In fact, she did a pretty good job of hiding the fact that she had a holster there.

Adam had never had a problem with women—quite the opposite. But here was trouble.

When he reached her, she asked, "Can I help you?"

"I hope so," he said. He scratched his chin and looked around. "I'm…well, I'm lost. I drove down from Santa Barbara to visit my baby sister. She's a freshman here at UCSD. I guess I didn't feel like staying around for the Thursday night kegger."

He flashed a disarming smile, complete with dimples. From the moment she'd stepped into the light, he'd recognized her. Carin Barnes.

There was a chance that she would make the connection between him and Evie. At over six feet, with red hair and piercing blue eyes, they didn't exactly blend. Only, he knew Carin had met Evie only once. Since then, his sister had dodged Carin's calls for a meeting to discuss her brother, Markie.

More importantly, he knew that when Carin met his sister, Evie had projected the image of Estelle Fegaris. Looking at Evie, Carin had remembered vividly the connection her brother had made with the powerful psychic, someone she trusted. Evie had used the maneuver to distract Carin.

It was one of their abilities, to project images that would cause strong emotional responses.

Again, he smiled, strangely enjoying what was starting to feel like an adrenaline rush. *Interesting.*

"I thought I would just get in the car and tool around," he told her, "but this place is kind of screwy. I mean, there are all these freeway exits going in weird directions."

His father had trained him that it was important to be

engaging. If you had a good enough story, people let down their guard.

He shoved his hands in the pockets of his jacket, playing the part of nervous suitor. "You wouldn't know a good place to grab a bite to eat around here?"

As lines went, it wasn't his best. Which was the point. He didn't want to come off as smooth. He wanted to project the image of the clumsy asshole asking her out—something he imagined had come her way a time or two.

She cocked her head, looking at him like a bird. She had gray eyes and a beautiful mouth. Her boy-cut blond hair only accented her heart-shaped face, making her look fey and feminine.

"You shouldn't be here," she said.

"Yeah," he said, laughing. "That much I figured out by the Fort Knox effect," he said, gesturing toward the compound.

She took a step back, but dropped her hand from her hip. She switched her briefcase to her right.

"Take the 5 freeway north, back to Mission Bay," she said. "It's a tourist area. You'll probably find something there."

She turned to walk away. At the last minute, he put his hand on her arm.

A sudden heat crept up his fingers as they touched. From the widening of her eyes, he could see that she'd felt it, too.

She drew back, staring up at him.

"You wouldn't want to join me?" he asked. "I mean, for dinner. Or maybe even a drink?" He laughed. "Hey, I'd settle for coffee. Otherwise I'm back at party central watching my kid sister down Jell-O shooters. Come on, you've got to save a guy from that."

But she was already backing away. "I have to go," she said.

As he waited there under the floodlights, watching her get into her rental, the cell phone in his hand chimed.

He flipped the phone open. He didn't need to look at the LCD screen to know who it was.

"It's about time, Evie."

23

Erika stared at the flowers, an artistic arrangement of daffodils, white tulips and some pretty purple flower she didn't recognize. They'd been delivered just minutes ago by a middle-aged Asian man. She was still standing in the kitchen in shock.

The attached card read Happy Anniversary!!

Two words—two exclamation points.

"Wow, Greg," she said to herself. "Now that is some *tight* writing Mr. Journalist." She dropped the card on the counter next to the flowers. "Really, the man has a gift."

Six months since she'd given him a drawer and some closet space and Greg was celebrating an anniversary? *Jesus.*

She reached into some hidden recess of her cupboard and actually found a vase. She had to marvel at his optimism. And tenacity.

Of course, Greg's resolve was exactly what had earned him that right hook from her partner, Seven, when Greg had broken the story on Gia, exposing her as the psychic involved in the fortune-teller murders…headlines that eventually led the woman's ex to find her, then attempt to kill her.

She set the flowers on the kitchen table and poured herself a glass of wine.

"Well, crap."

She felt just as out of place as those flowers on her kitchen table.

Men didn't send Erika flowers. They bought her drinks and fucked her, then ran along home, just the way she liked it.

But here was Greg, celebrating six months with two exclamation points.

The weird part? She wasn't about to show him the door, which could only mean that major heartache must ensue. Who it brought down first was anyone's guess.

With a sigh, she reached into her bag and pulled out the file Sherlock had sent over in response to Erika's telephone call.

"You'll never guess what the autopsy showed on Katie Sweeny. Oh, wait, maybe you can. Maybe it's exactly what you found during the two other autopsies?"

Now, she had reports on both Mark Dair and Megan Tobin. Just like Katie, the cause of death had been drowning. In all three cases, there'd been lividity present—extremely unusual in drowning cases. Despite the fact that the victims had been found near large bodies of water, it was tap water the coroner found in their lungs.

All three had marks consistent with an IV. Erika didn't have the toxicology results back on Katie, but there'd definitely been a chemical substance used to subdue the other victims.

Sherlock, of course, had a perfectly logical explanation for keeping Erika and Seven in the dark. She hadn't wanted to influence their findings. She needed fresh eyes on the investigation. That's why she'd brought Erika and Seven in as special liaisons in the first place.

"Fresh eyes, my ass," Erika said.

Because Erika had a different theory on why Sherlock had called her bright and early on the morning they'd found Katie Sweeny's body. Gia Moon and her painting practically proved the point.

She flipped through the file, making a mental note to go over the toxicology with Alice. Jesus, she really did need a degree in chemistry to understand the shit this freak had used on his victims.

Twenty minutes later, she closed the files and put away her notes. She picked up the wineglass and finished her drink.

She stood and made her way to the fridge, filling the glass again, then turned back to stare at the flowers front and center on the table.

She couldn't stop thinking about those kids. They'd been all of fourteen years old. Each had been lured away by what was most likely a romantic interest.

"Apparently, love kills," she said out loud.

She thought about her notes, the private ones she kept in a special notebook meant for her eyes only. Special Agent Carin Barnes worked for NISA, the National Institute for Strategic Artifacts. She'd known all along that Gia, a woman with whom Barnes had significant history, would get involved. And Erika was supposed to believe they weren't in cahoots?

There was something about those stones in the kids' hands that Sherlock didn't want her to know. Shit, it might even be tied back to that artifact, the Eye of Athena.

But Erika wasn't about to share her suspicions with her partner. Unfortunately, she'd cried wolf before when it came to Gia. When the superpsychic had turned up with all that information on the fortune-teller murders, to Erika, it could mean only one thing: special knowledge that pointed to guilt.

As things turned out, Gia Moon wasn't the killer. She hadn't even known him or any of the victims.

But she had been connected to the case. Through the artifact, the Eye of Athena. And even though the damn thing turned out to be a fake, it was also her connection to Barnes.

Erika felt suddenly overwhelmed. She didn't want to believe in weird shit like psychic art or visions or artifacts that went bump in the night. Give her an old-fashioned shooting any day, the kind with ballistics and fingerprints and even the occasional DNA.

She walked back to the table. She leaned forward and smelled one of the mystery purple flowers.

And just maybe, she didn't want to believe in love.

"Oh, Greg. What am I going to do with you, baby?"

So serious…so fast.

She heard the key turn in the door. For one foolish second, she could feel her heart do this funny skip. Her stomach followed along, doing the roller-coaster dip into one of those free falls.

Greg had accused her of having a fear of intimacy.

Oh, yeah. This was fear all right.

She put down the wineglass and reached out to break off one of the tulips from the bouquet. She'd told him tulips were her favorite flower.

She could hear him call her name. When that didn't work, he did his, "Lucy, I'm home" shtick in a thick Cuban accent. She didn't answer.

By the time he found her in the bedroom, she was completely naked, wearing only a single tulip in her hair.

He stood in the doorway. "Looks like I should send flowers more often."

"I had a shitty day," she told him.

He unbuttoned his shirt as he walked toward her.

He said, "Don't worry. It's about to get a whole lot better."

Carin stared at the stones contained in their marked evidence bags. There were three in all, one for each victim.

She'd spaced them out on the desk in the hotel room. Eenie, meenie, minie....

The stones weren't big. They were small enough to fit inside the victims' hands. Each had just a few lines etched on the surface.

The markings weren't deep. The lab determined whoever made them had used the tip of a sturdy knife, probably a pocket knife.

She picked up the Polaroids of Gia's painting, couriered to her courtesy of the Westminster PD, and flipped through them.

Throwing down the photos, she grabbed the small key to access the room's minibar.

She took out the full bottle of chardonnay and opened it, pouring the wine into one of the coffee mugs the hotel provided.

Mug in hand, she stared back at the desk where the evidence bags waited, stretched out across the blotter. Each contained what was surely a miniature of the Bimini Stones.

Not that she could prove it. Hell, she couldn't even prove Zag *had* the stones.

She drank the wine, thinking she should just walk away from the case. This wasn't why she'd joined the FBI. She had the crystal, for God's sake.

Carin took another drink from the mug.

She'd brought her brother to the Institute, hoping for a

miracle. She'd thought that, with the crystal and Morgan's resources, Markie had a chance.

Only, now, she had all these balls in the air. She couldn't even keep track of her own brother's therapy. She'd made several attempts to meet with his therapist, but apparently Dr. Slade was one busy gal.

"I hear ya," Carin said out loud.

It was the story of her life. She hadn't followed up with Markie's therapist because she was too busy trying to catch a serial killer. And while she took solace in her brother's interaction with Dr. Slade—how the image of them together seemed to morph into Estelle holding Markie the day he spoke his only words—she still felt uneasy about her brother's lack of progress.

Then there was the situation with Zag. Morgan was right, she couldn't ignore her history with the man—but not for the reasons Morgan thought. Carin might be the only person alive who knew about Zag's connection to those damn stones…and how easily a man like Zag would justify experimenting on children.

She felt torn in so many directions.

Time to walk away.

Like most hotel rooms, there was a mirror that showed her reflection from head to toe.

In that mirror, Carin Barnes did not see a woman who walked away from things.

Her desire to keep with it, to work the problem and never say die, had always been this double-edged sword. It was perfectly clear she should stop. Let someone else bring the bastard to justice. She had too much skin in the game.

But she couldn't. The unfortunate truth was that Zag was her responsibility.

When she'd seen the etched stone found in the hand of the first victim, she'd assumed that son of bitch Zag was involved. With the realization came a strange elation. Finally, *finally,* she would bring him down.

That's why she'd contacted Erika. She and her partner were her gateway to Gia.

Carin took another sip of wine. She spread out the photographs of Gia's painting.

She picked one up. In the painting, a grisly version of Mark Dair stood holding a fishing pole with an empty birdcage hanging from the end. In a clear blue sky above his head floated five stones just like the ones found with the victims.

So far, they only had three victims. Were there two others waiting for some psycho to shove a stone in their dead hands?

"Fuck."

She poured more wine.

She didn't drink often. She knew it was a trap of the job—booze to sleep, coffee to wake up. Next, it's over-the-counter drugs, then something stronger. The whole thing was a slippery slope.

Halfway through the second drink, she lay down on the king-size bed and thought about the man in the parking lot.

It was pretty damn cocky, him walking out of the shadows to ask her out. She'd been fairly certain he'd been watching her. She'd felt his eyes on her—that's why she'd unsnapped the holster on her gun.

The case *was* getting to her. Standing under the floodlights in the parking lot, she imagined the guy was the kind of man who could charm a poor girl into running off with him.

She reached up and rubbed her arm where he'd touched her. She felt it again, that heat rising up her skin.

There was a knock at the door. Carin stood and walked to the door. Room service.

The waiter wheeled in the dinner tray. Cheeseburger and French fries. He smiled and thanked her profusely when she handed him a ten-dollar tip.

She removed the cover off the plate and grabbed a French fry.

At least she'd made somebody's day.

24

The brunette at the back of the Greyhound bus stared out the window. She wore sunglasses like some movie star hiding her identity.

She could have been an actress, she was that good-looking.

Despite the long hours, she hadn't slept, drinking cup after cup of coffee. At every stop, she would cover her head with the hoodie of her jacket. The matching sweat pants had the Juicy trademark branded across the ass. The expensive travel clothes had been a present from her husband. She'd packed only a suitcase small enough to be stored in the overhead compartment of the bus. She paid for everything in cash.

The trip from Indiana had been long. More than once, some guy had come to sit in the seat next to her, trying to chat her up. She'd shut them down, fast.

If Peter found her with a guy, he'd kill her for sure.

She stared out the window and sighed. Maybe that's what she deserved.

Oh, Jack.

She couldn't imagine that her baby would ever forgive her. But that didn't matter now. She had to find him; she had to make sure he was okay.

Every Tuesday, Sandra went for a manicure and a pedicure at her sister's salon. Lisa had wanted to open her own place for years, but it wasn't until Peter came along as an investor that she'd had the money.

Peter liked to help. He liked being needed.

For her part, Sandra took care of herself. She knew Peter liked her to look just so. Those trips to the salon were just the kind of thing Peter didn't mind paying for.

She and Jack had a system. Tuesday at 10:00 a.m., Jack called the salon. For the last six months, Sandra would talk to her baby every Tuesday, making sure that he was okay.

But two Tuesdays in a row now, she didn't get a call. And that worried her plenty.

She scrunched down farther into the padded seat of the Greyhound. It wasn't that long ago that she'd thought Peter was her Prince Charming, taking her from a life of rags to riches. Only, in Sandra's life, the rags were some awful years whoring.

At first, Peter had made her happy. Especially because he'd taken such an interest in Jack. Finally, her boy had a father figure.

She wasn't sure when she figured out what was going on between Peter and Jack.

Sandra brushed back her tears. She'd been crying a lot lately. As if that was any help.

When she'd sent Jack away, she'd made excuses. She had to be smart about the whole thing. If she stayed with Peter, she could still send Jack money. It wasn't a lot, but it was something—enough to keep him off the streets. And Peter treated her like a queen, not to mention that he'd helped her sister with the salon. He'd bought the property and was leasing it to Lisa dirt cheap.

But the truth was, Sandra hadn't wanted to go back to

her life before Peter. Quickies in the alley or bringing a different man home every night, making excuses to Jack about her "dates."

So she'd convinced herself that it would be okay. She'd help Jack get away. He might be young, but he was smart—and really good-looking.

She told Peter he'd run off to become a movie star. Peter hadn't even been mad. He'd almost seemed relieved. And he'd stayed with her.

It was a nice little fairy tale…for a while, anyway.

Then would come Tuesday mornings.

She'd always known those stories Jack told her couldn't be true. *I have a talent agent, Mom… Today I auditioned for a national commercial. Can you imagine? That's* beaucoup *bucks if I land the part. Soon it's going to be me sending you money, not the other way around.*

But his stories sounded all too familiar: a fantasy life that made the nightmare of living on the streets bearable.

Her baby was just shy of his fifteenth birthday. He had no address and always called from a pay phone using one of those calling cards. She'd done a little research, realizing how stupid she'd been. The money she sent couldn't keep a dog alive in Southern California, much less an adolescent boy.

When he didn't call Tuesday, she'd thought the worst. *He's dead!*

At first, a couple of bottles of wine got her through the panic. *Just wait, he'll call next week.* But soon, the pain of not knowing became unbearable.

And then another Tuesday came and went without a call.

She hadn't told Peter she was leaving. He wouldn't understand. She was his, bought and paid for.

So she'd packed her bag and the money she'd squirreled away for a rainy day. The minute his Lexus left the driveway, she called for a taxi.

Now, she wore her sunglasses and kept her hoodie low over her face. Each and every stop, she worried Peter would be boarding the bus, taking her home.

But she didn't care. She wasn't even afraid anymore. What she wanted most was to find Jack, to hold him in her arms.

She told herself a mother would know if her child was dead.

Only, she wasn't sure.

So instead, she stared out the window at the passing landscape and sipped from the cardboard coffee cup.

I'm coming to get you, Jack. She closed her eyes and tried to make her thoughts reach him somehow. *I'm coming.*

25

Adam sat facing his sister, their chairs so close, their legs almost touched. For brother and sister, this was a familiar configuration, one used to promote a synthesis of their powers.

Adam placed his hands on Evie's knees. She in turn covered his hands with hers. To anyone watching, they looked like a piece of art.

Neither spoke. They remained unmoving, their eyes closed, their breathing slow and rhythmic, trancelike.

They were seated in what could pass for a hospital room in an exclusive sanitarium. Flowered wallpaper and antique furnishings almost disguised the hospital equipment. There came a soft beeping from the monitor bedside.

Twenty minutes into the session, Evie spoke, breaking the silence.

"Don't worry so much."

These were the only words she said out loud, but it was far from the only communication between them.

Now brother and sister stood. Hand in hand, they walked over to the hospital bed where the boy, Jack, lay strapped to the bed.

There were risks. So far, none of the children had lasted through more than three sessions. This would be Jack's second, and already there were ominous signs. But their father had taught them that theirs was a mission worthy of great sacrifice.

Jack fought his bonds as they approached. He was talking nonstop. Of course, nothing he said made sense—another bad sign.

Adam stood on the left side of the bed, Evie on the right. Over the body, they held hands. Each placed their free hand on Jack.

The minute they touched him, he quieted down.

"It's too soon," Adam said.

"Stop fussing," Evie answered.

Adam frowned, looking down at Jack. He didn't quite understand his feelings toward these children. When he found them, all he could see was their potential. It surrounded them in a glorious light. But in this hospital bed, as his sister probed their minds, he could see that light dimming.

Darling brother. Evie was inside his head now. *You're forgetting the greater good.*

That gentle caress of his sister inside his mind, it was almost a relief. He depended on that closeness. The possibility of losing her, a possibility that became all too real when she'd so violently blocked him out as they'd sparred, was something he found difficult to bear.

The greater good.

It was what they'd always been taught. The only thing they'd ever known to be absolute. The reason why their mother had sacrificed her life. Their work would one day save the world.

For that reason alone, they had no choice.

He asked, "Ready?"

Evie smiled and squeezed his hand. "Set and go."

* * *

Seven thought it a touch ironic that Martini Blues was actually decorated in red. Still, he had to admit the décor of the lounge—deep burgundy leather booths and black drapes covering red walls—gave the place just the right bluesy ambience. He thought there was probably a science to the interior-decoration thing.

He was just starting in on his second martini—they called it the Ultimate—listening to Chico's Bail Bonds doing their rendition of Aretha Franklin's "Chain of Fools," when a woman slid in next to him in the booth.

"Imagine running into you here," Beth said.

Chico's Bail Bonds finished the set. Seven clapped as the band bowed and put down their instruments, ready for a break.

"Have I become predictable in my dotage?" he asked.

She signaled the waitress over and ordered a Diet Coke with a twist of lime. "Looks like that vocabulary builder you bought is working out."

He shrugged. "Erika is still beating the crap out of me. Hell, I'm pretty sure I knew the word *dotage* before we started on Battle Vocab. Did you know you can bet on the Spelling Bee?"

"That sounds wrong on so many levels."

"True." He leaned back in the booth. "So let me guess. You tried the House of Brews first, *then* came here."

"Don't sound offended. One man's predictable is another woman's reliable."

"That's me," he said. "Mr. Reliable."

"Speaking of, that was nice, what you said to Nick." She thanked the waitress and took a sip of the Coke from the straw. "He says he wants to go with you next week when you visit Ricky."

After he'd dropped off Stella, he'd had a long talk with his nephew. Seeing how much Stella was struggling hurt. Only, she wasn't exactly his responsibility. That wasn't the case with Nick.

He took a drink of the martini. "Let's hope taking him to see his father is a good thing."

They both knew Ricky had been acting erratically, talking about getting a law degree and representing himself on appeal. It wasn't exactly unexpected. A man didn't go from pillar of the community to murderer in one fell swoop without some serious mental issues.

He wondered if his brother hadn't been acting erratically for years. Maybe, he'd just been a hell of a lot better at hiding it.

Beth sighed. "He needs to see him. He's his father, Seven."

"Ain't that the hell of it?" Seven popped one of the two olives that came with the Ultimate into his mouth and chewed.

"Do you really know a girl whose father was a murderer?"

He gave her a look. "I am a homicide detective, Beth. It comes with the territory. It's a shame, but criminals can procreate, just like the rest of us."

"Yes, but you made it sound as if you had a personal relationship with her."

He'd told Nick a little about Stella, keeping some of the details vague.

"I wanted Nick to know that he wasn't some freak because his father was in jail for killing a man. I thought it might help if he understood he wasn't alone. The fact is, we can't pick our family. Of course, that's just talk. But to know someone just about your age is going through the same thing, that it can happen to anyone, I thought it could help."

"Well, it did—help that is. So, since no good deed goes unpunished, I'll pry. What's going on with you? I've left you three messages."

He smiled. "So much for reliable."

But he knew what she meant. Apparently, he was starting to show some cracks himself.

"I have this theme going in my head. Days that really suck." He ate the last olive. "I realize I've managed to string together quite a few lately."

Next week would be the twins' birthday. He knew that because Laurin, his ex, and he had finally taken the high road. Now that she was happily remarried with two darling children, she thought they should keep in touch. See, it had been kind of tough on Laurin, hearing about Ricky on the news and all, *then* contacting Seven under those circumstances. Awkward.

No shit.

Seven's little record of days that really sucked made a man think—made him wonder if it wasn't time to hang up the badge and look into a sunnier career choice. Like maybe interior design or cake decorating.

"You know, Beth. I can still remember when all I thought about was becoming a homicide detective." He shook his head, marveling. "Imagine, I actually scrounged up a little ambition." He frowned. "I thought what I did mattered."

She put her hand on his. "It *does* matter." And when he didn't respond, she said, "Hey. Listen to me. Ricky has destroyed so many things by his act of cowardice. He took Scott's life—he devastated the man's family. Then there's what he did to us, to me and Nick. To his brother and parents." She squeezed his hand tight. "Don't let him destroy your career, too, okay?"

He shook his head. "This isn't about Ricky."

She turned his face to look at her. "Isn't it?"

She was right, of course. Ricky was a big part of his struggles with his career the last year. Seven felt distracted, vulnerable in a way he'd never felt before. He was making mistakes. Never in a million years would he have slept with a possible witness in a case. Then Gia comes along and he goes for it, breaking all the rules.

Before coming here to drink his dinner, he'd given her a call. He'd started with a little chitchat, asking about how Stella was doing. Then came the awkward segue.

Hey. I'm sorry I didn't come inside when I dropped her off—

I know. A bad day.

Again with the mind-reading.

He'd said it half-humorously, but the fact remained he feared just that. He wasn't sure how much he bought into her gift, but he had to admit it freaked him out a little.

Into that silence, Gia had launched her own little bomb.

Seven, do you want to come over for dinner tonight?

Jesus. Had he ever.

Look, Gia, I'm not psychic, but I happen to know a few things myself. Like the fact that no good can come of us alone together at your place.

That's your opinion.

She'd hung up, not waiting for a response.

He'd told Stella he wasn't afraid of her mother's gift because he was a big bad homicide detective. Even to Gia, he hadn't admitted the whole truth, letting her assume that he couldn't trust her not to lie to him again.

But it was more than that. It *was* her gift. The idea of

living with someone who could see the future, read your mind. Loving a woman who'd admitted she attracted "dark spirits." How was he supposed to protect her from that? Jesus, he'd barely got off the shot before that maniac ex of hers had almost killed her.

Only he was so fucking lonely—missing her 24/7—that he wondered why he'd ever pulled away in the first place. Living this half life seemed like a pretty high price to pay for his fucking ordinary life.

In the booth, he turned to Beth, thinking about all the things that went along with making him want to throw in the towel. How it wasn't all about his brother. But sure, that's when things had started going south.

He told her, "It's complicated."

She put the Coke down. "Isn't everything?"

She grabbed his arm and turned it so she could read his wristwatch. He still wore one, even though Erika had informed him a wristwatch without bling was totally out. These days, everyone had a cell phone to give them the time of day.

"Come on." She scooted out of the booth. "I got a sitter, which means you're taking me to dinner."

"Duke's on the pier?" he asked stepping out of the booth with her.

She looped her arm through his. "See? Reliable." She patted his hand. "It's a good thing."

26

Terrence sat at the dinner table, staring at his wife's pot roast. Raquel made a mean pot roast. He remembered his sister, Virginia, asking for the recipe, no small compliment given Ginny's own culinary prowess. Raquel had just smiled and instructed Ginny the trick was not to over-handle the meat. Terrence, he always figured it was the layer of ketchup Raquel slathered across the top.

His wife put down her fork. "What's wrong?"

"Nothing," he said, reaching for his wineglass.

"Nothing?"

He looked at the handsome woman seated across the table. His wife was Brazilian and spoke with an exotic accent no one could ever nail down. She was a tiny thing, well under five feet, maybe a hundred pounds soaking wet. She wore a white linen blouse and jeans and very little makeup, but she could still make his heart race. Unlike Terrence, she barely had any gray in her shoulder-length chestnut hair—her only vanity, she always said. She was four years older than his sixty, but could still leave him in the dust on their runs together.

Everyone said they were the consummate odd couple. A petite Latina and a tall, stately black man. It wasn't a first marriage for either, but it was the one that stuck.

He sighed, knowing it was useless to hide anything from his wife. Not only was Raquel the current chair of psychology at the college where she worked, they were also coming up on twenty-seven years of marriage.

She picked up her fork, shaking her head.

"Carin," she said with the finality of someone who knew him all too well. "That girl."

Of course, he'd told his wife about Carin's call.

Raquel always said he'd get this special look whenever he was bothered about something. Well, he'd been bothered plenty ever since he'd been politely asked to step down from NISA almost ten months ago. The head of the FBI had thanked him for his thirty-five years of service and made it clear it might be a perfect time to think about retiring.

Carin—who he strongly believed factored into the decision for him to step down—was a strong reminder of all that.

"She needs a favor," he said. "A big one."

"Hmm."

Now it was Terrence's turn to ask, "What?"

"Carin, asking a favor? I find that a bit ironic."

Because Raquel shared his belief that Carin had been part and parcel of the decision to kick him out as head of the NISA. Only, from Raquel's point of view, that wasn't necessarily a bad thing.

The truth was, his life *had* improved since he'd left the job. Currently, he was enjoying the fine art of fly-fishing, as well as spending time with his new grandchild—all of which he would have missed in the day-to-day maelstrom that had been his life in government office. His wife claimed that if she looked up *workaholic* in the dictionary, there'd be Terrence, grinning back at her.

Not that his current satisfaction with life excused what he'd come to believe was Carin's betrayal.

"How many times has that girl called you since they asked, ever so politely, for you to retire?"

He couldn't help but smile. "I believe, darling, this would be the first."

"Humph. In my professional opinion, all that avoidance could very well be the result of a guilty conscience."

"Or a busy schedule, Raquel."

"If you say so."

Carin had been in charge of the last major project he'd headed at NISA. When the mission imploded, Terrence could blame no one but himself. He'd always known it was a little too convenient that Carin, a closet acolyte of Estelle Fegaris, would discover the Eye, the very artifact that cost Fegaris her life.

When the crystal Carin delivered turned out to be a lovely fake, he'd always suspected she wasn't telling him the whole story.

The entire mission had been a disaster. Terrence didn't have a lot of fans in the Bureau…which was how he'd landed in that basement office as head of NISA in the first place. It hadn't taken much to get the powers-that-be to ask him to step down.

"You're going to help her, of course," his wife said with her usual authority.

"Now why would you say that?"

"Because you're going to want to enjoy that beautiful pot roast, and until you call her to give her the information she wants—which, my dearest husband, knowing you as I do, you have already procured for Carin—that meat will taste like sawdust in your mouth."

And when he just stared at her, she picked up her wine-glass and raised a brow.

"Oh, take that silly expression off your face, Terrence. I can read you like a book, despite all that fancy FBI training. Now, is it dangerous, what she's asking you to do?"

"It's risky. I could piss off some pretty powerful people—the kind who don't forgive or forget." His eyes met hers. "But three children are dead."

"Well, then," she said. "What are you waiting for? Three children are dead and one of your best agents needs your help. Call her."

"When I said these people didn't forgive and forget, I wasn't worried about my pension plan."

She sighed and pressed his hand on the table. "How many years did you work for the FBI? I trust you to be careful. Now, you think about those babies, Terrence."

But he was already pulling away from the table, heading for the phone.

"And hurry," she said, picking up the pot roast and heading for the oven. "Or the only place you're going to see this pot roast is in a sandwich tomorrow."

Stella stared out the window of the bus. There was a good public transportation system here with the Orange County Transit Authority, the OCTA. You could go just about anywhere by bus. Like today, she'd hopped on after school. Now she was heading east on route 076. Beside her sat ghost boy.

She had no idea why ghost boy wanted her on this particular bus; she just knew she was tired of waiting for the bad stuff to happen. When he'd guided her on board, she hadn't hesitated. It was like ripping off the bandage in one quick motion. Just dive in and get it over with.

That's what she'd decided to do last night. *Just get the job done.* And despite that little pep talk from Seven, whatever she had to do, she planned to do it alone.

Last night, she'd talked to her mother, just like Seven had asked her to do. Only, that hadn't worked out so well.

Immediately, Mom got all weird, popping off a bunch of questions. It was like she needed to know every little detail.

Stella could tell her mom was worried, like maybe what was happening to Stella with ghost boy was *über* strange—even in her mom's world—which really freaked Stella out. Especially when her mom kept trying to reassure her that everything was going to be okay.

And then Seven had called, and things got even stranger. Stella could see that her mother was really hurt by whatever he'd said to her.

Here the guy had picked Stella up after school, giving her a bunch of bullshit about caring about her and her mom—making Stella believe him.

Only last night, seeing her mother just standing over the sink with the phone in her hand, it didn't seem like he was telling the truth.

The next thing she knew, Stella was shutting down, telling her mother that she hadn't seen ghost boy for days and she thought everything would be okay. Her mom was overreacting. This was no big deal.

Stella glanced over at ghost boy, thinking she'd done the right thing, keeping her mom out of it. Heck, she was even starting to get used to him now that he'd stopped with the stupid scary stuff. Today, he looked pretty normal, just another kid around her age. Sure, maybe he could use some help in the wardrobe department—who tucked their shirt into their shorts?—but otherwise he was okay for a dead kid.

Besides, it wasn't all bad, him hanging around. Sometimes, she got a little lonely.

It wasn't that she didn't have friends. It was just that her life wasn't exactly an open book. Oh, her mother tried to give them a normal life, but Stella had always known they had secrets.

She stared out at the passing landscape. He hadn't spoken a word since the library. She wasn't really sure how the thing worked—this was her first spirit—so she didn't make anything of his silence. Besides, he'd managed to communicate just fine without using words.

Like today. In English class, Stella had been writing her in-class essay when suddenly it was like someone took over the pencil or her hand or something, because she couldn't control what she was writing. Just when she was going to really freak out, the sensation stopped. On the paper, in a strange handwriting she didn't recognize, there was a name: Shipley Nature Center.

She'd had to start her essay over. Probably, it would cost her a whole grade, though it was strange that she even cared. Like grades mattered anymore when you saw dead people.

When ghost boy showed up after school, she'd known to follow him to the bus stop. She had the paper with the address wadded up in her hand. Three transfers later, she was still following him.

Now ghost boy stood and walked out into the aisle of the bus. He walked through the people standing there like they were butter. He stopped at the exit and looked back at her.

She picked up her backpack, guessing this would be her stop.

It was bit of a trek, but they ended up where they were supposed to.

The Shipley Nature Center was just off a busy street.

The traffic was pretty loud as she jogged down into the park from the road. Once inside, ghost boy guided them off the paved walkway into a forest of trees. She had to push back the shrubbery it was so dense.

They came to a chain-link fence topped with several rows of barbed wire. On the other side was one of the flood channels. There hadn't been much rain; the channel was pretty dry except for a few pools of stagnant water. There was a lot of trash alongside branches and vines. She even saw a rusted hub cap.

There was a sign: Trespassing Forbidden By Law. Just the same, someone had cut the fence and pulled back the chain-link. That's where ghost boy headed.

Stella squirreled through the opening and continued down the embankment. It was all dirt here, but across the channel, enormous rocks covered the opposite side. The rocks led up to a cinderblock wall where the backyards of the neighboring track abutted the flood channel. Stella walked along the red clay earth, following ghost boy until he came to a dead stop.

It wasn't like her mother's painting. Not one bit. Here there were no pretty flowers or blue skies, just a girl facedown in standing water made red by the clay.

She dropped her backpack and rushed down, almost falling into the drainage ditch herself. She wasn't sure what she would do when she got there, but she had to do something. Why else would he bring her here?

Suddenly, she felt a pain. It started in her head, like someone had taken an ice pick and shoved it in both her eyes. The pain radiated down her face to her spine. She fell to her knees. She grabbed her head, the pain almost unbearable. This wasn't anything like the other times.

She tried to catch her breath. But water filled her nose

and lungs. She realized she must have fallen into the drainage ditch. She was drowning.

Only, she wasn't in the ditch. She was in a bathtub, held underwater by hands on her shoulders. She could hear someone humming what sounded like a lullaby. She was kicking and fighting, trying to get that weight off her.

Just as suddenly as it came, the vision stopped.

She sat up and crawled on her knees up the side of the embankment. She kept coughing, trying to clear her lungs of water.

When she could breathe again, she looked up, realizing she *hadn't* fallen into the drainage ditch, after all. She was nowhere near that stagnant water.

Ghost boy turned, looking over to where she'd just seen the girl's body.

The girl was gone.

"No," she said.

Stella stood and ran down the incline into the drainage ditch. She ran into the stagnant water, turning in a complete circle, searching.

But there wasn't anyone there. No girl. No body.

Back up on the embankment, she heard her cell phone go off.

She crawled out of the water, her heart hammering in her chest. She dropped down beside her backpack and pulled out her phone. She'd missed the call, but she could see it was "home" calling.

She flipped open her phone and tried to catch her breath. Pushing Redial, she waited as her worried mother picked up.

She said, "I'm sorry. I should have called. I had some stuff to do after school. I'll be home soon. I promise."

She was careful to hang up before her mother could ask any more questions.

27

Carin tried to relax on the plane. It was a long flight, a good five hours. Sitting in first class—God knows she had enough frequent-flyer miles for the upgrade—she reclined in her seat to an almost horizontal position. Not that she'd thought she'd actually get any sleep.

The last two hours, she'd been trying to work, inputting notes into her BlackBerry. Information on the Atlantis Project.

Good old Terrence.

Two hours after he'd called, she'd been on a jet heading to North Carolina. That's where Terrence and Raquel now lived in a bucolic suburb. There wouldn't be anything suspicious about their meeting. After all, she was the special agent in charge on a key case. Why wouldn't she seek the advice of an old mentor?

They'd met at his house. He'd poured her a cup of coffee—Terrence was keen on his coffee—and slapped down the file.

"It's called the Atlantis Project," he'd told her.

Ignoring the coffee, Carin flipped through the pages in the file folder, reading as fast as she could.

"The program was an offshoot of Star Gate," he said as she read ahead. "Based on the finding of one remote viewer, a psychic given the number A-001. A woman."

"A remote-viewing program? That's not exactly revolutionary."

Remote viewing was a protocol often used in paranormal research. The viewer would gather information—sensory impressions, as well as nonsensorial information. Sometimes it was merely a sense of just "knowing," a kind of psychic dowsing. The remote viewer had the ability to perceive places, persons, even actions far outside the normal range of the five senses.

The target could be anything—the mountains on Jupiter, a buried body, a terrorist-cell meeting in a cave in Afghanistan.

There were over a hundred peer-reviewed articles published on remote viewing, not to mention several dozen books. The broadcast channels, as well as several cable channels, couldn't get enough on it, conducting over a hundred live-to-video experiments.

Carin kept reading through the file. She was familiar enough with the psi power to know remote viewing wasn't hindered by time or space. One of the best known remote viewers, Joseph McMoneagle, had written predictions as far as three hundred years into the future.

Terrence put down his coffee cup. "It's what Remote Viewer A-001 saw that made things interesting. I assume with your background you're familiar with the concept of dark matter?"

"Of course. It's matter of unknown composition that can't be directly observed. It helps reconcile the big bang model, the idea that the universe developed during an enormous explosion and continues to expand. Along with dark energy, it causes the expansion to accelerate. Dark matter and dark energy make up for the missing-mass problem."

Terrence took the file from her and flipped through the pages. He pointed out a paragraph highlighted in yellow.

"See there. I'm told that's cutting-edge stuff involving dark matter. Only this analysis was done by a woman with a high school education in the 1970s claiming to remote view the lost city of Atlantis."

Now, on the plane home, Carin carried a copy of the transcripts from Remote Viewer A-001. She kept going over the highlighted sections in disbelief.

There it was in black-and-white. The theory of dark matter presented in complex equations consistent with results published only in the last decade—theories transcribed from observations made by a woman claiming to remote view through time to the lost city of Atlantis.

"They've resurrected the Atlantis Project," Terrence had told her when he'd handed over the files. "It's a black project, of course, but my sources say Halo Industries is the prime contractor. Now, I don't know how that can help you with these murders—I don't see a connection—but you asked me to dig up dirt on Zag de Rozières and this is what I found."

On the plane, Carin settled back into her chair, the file still opened on the tray table in front of her. She closed her eyes and tried for a few minutes not to think, to let her mind go blank.

She worked for an unconventional branch of the FBI, what was jokingly known as the X-files. Her work with Estelle Fegaris had opened her mind to possibilities she still didn't understand. But this Atlantis Project, it was well beyond anything she'd ever imagined.

She knew Zag de Rozières was a ruthless man, capable of justifying any means to an end. Now she had him linked to a bizarre remote-viewing project. It was just the kind of psychic ability Zag claimed to enhance at his Halo-effect schools.

In the cabin, the soothing voice of a flight attendant asked everyone to bring their chairs into an upright position and buckle up. Carin put away the file and settled in for their landing into LAX. The minute the captain gave the go-ahead, she turned on her cell phone.

She had voice mail. She always had voice mail.

She listened quietly, taking notes—until the third message.

It was from Erika in Huntington Beach.

They'd found another victim.

28

Seven stared down at the ditch and the beehive of activity surrounding the body. He was standing in the flood channel just outside the Shipley Nature Center. Crime-scene techs were placing orange cones and snapping pictures. Watching them work, he discovered an emotion he'd been missing the last year. Rage.

On the way over from the station in Westminster, Erika had gone over the toxicology report on the victim found in the Bolsa Chica, Katie Sweeny.

"It took a while, but I finally got Alice to use words understandable to someone without a doctorate." She was seated in the passenger seat and flipped through the report. It was one of the few times his partner had let him drive. "Here are the highlights. All three victims were drugged with a chemical substance similar to thujone."

"Wow." He been driving on the 22 and exited on Goldenwest. "And here I thought you said I wouldn't need a Ph.D. Thujone?"

"It's a substance found in absinthe."

He lined up with the traffic in the turn lane. "Absinthe? I thought that was illegal."

The little he knew about absinthe was the result of his ex-wife's fascination with historical novels. A highly alcoholic drink made with wormwood, it was often called the Green Fairy, a reference to the liquor's color, as well as its purported hallucinatory effect.

"According to Alice, the gourmet coroner," Erika said, "there's been a bit of a revival. And hell, you can get just about anything on the Internet."

He was heading south on Goldenwest. "So talk to me about this thujone."

She flipped through her notes. "Apparently alpha-thujone blocks brain receptors for gamma-aminobutyrid acid, that's GABA, a natural inhibitor of nerve impulses. Alice said the victims were given a juiced-up version. The result would be a clearheaded inebriation. It's supposed to have some kind of conscious-shifting effect."

"Are we talking sodium pentothal?" he asked, referring to a substance often used as a kind of truth serum.

"More like LSD. Looks like our whack job is heavily into mind-altering drugs. And there's more. The chemical composition of the water found in the victims' lungs? It's identical for all three victims. Alice thinks they were drowned in the same zip code."

Half an hour later, Seven couldn't get that toxicology report out of his head. He was staring down at yet another crime scene, imagining this young victim, bound and drugged like Katie and the others.

Just last night with Beth at the club, he'd been thinking about walking away. The job was getting to him—he wasn't up to his game. He thought he'd lost his cop mojo.

At the moment, nothing could be further from the truth.

Ever since he'd gotten the call on the newest victim, those doubts had started to burn away. The toxicology report only fueled the fire. And now, looking down at that poor girl facedown in the flood channel, left there like so much trash, all he felt was hot, white anger. Rage against the prick who thought he could get away with this kind of carnage.

Walk away?

Fuck that.

He removed his sunglasses and made his way down to the victim again. He'd been examining the perimeter, looking for evidence—a cigarette butt, a piece of torn clothing, skin or blood if the perp had brushed up against the heavy vegetation, anything that might help identify the bastard who did this. Erika was kneeling over the body beside Special Agent Barnes.

"The same ligature marks," Barnes said, pointing with the tip of her pen. "And the IV mark here." She pointed to the inside of the arm.

"Did you find another stone?" Seven asked.

Barnes held up the evidence bag. "Just like the others."

Seven took the bag and examined the design, some curved lines etched into the smooth surface.

He stared at Barnes. Feeling that lost mojo of his kick into high gear, he suddenly shoved the evidence bag in her face.

"You've seen this before, right?"

He was looking right at her when he asked the question. All along he'd suspected she was hiding something.

Her gaze met his. For the first time since he'd met Special Agent Barnes of the fucking FBI, she flinched.

Gotcha.

He put his sunglasses back on. "Well, Special Agent Barnes," he said, handing her back the evidence bag. "When you feel like you need your *special liaisons* to do real police work instead of acting like some nice window dressing, you'll let us know."

He glanced over at Erika. She gave him the nod. Both partners turned and headed back up the embankment.

"Wait," Barnes called after them.

But Seven kept on walking.

"Just wait, dammit."

Both partners continued on, ignoring Barnes.

"Wow, Seven," Erika said. "You just pissed off the FBI."

"Glory be."

Barnes caught up with them just before they hit the fence.

"Okay," she said. "Full disclosure."

"I very much doubt that," Seven said, "but I'll settle for what the damn stones mean—and don't give me any need-to-know FBI crap. We all know those stones are artifacts, so stop blowing smoke up my ass and explain."

"You're wrong," Barnes said. "The stones are not themselves the artifacts. They're crudely made replicas. Have you ever heard of the Bimini Road?"

"As in the road to Atlantis, Bimini Road?" Erika asked. "*That* Bimini?" And when Seven gave her a confused look, she took off her sunglasses and rolled her eyes. "I keep telling you to watch the Discovery Channel."

"Yes. *That* Bimini," Barnes said. She turned to look at Seven. "Just off the shore of North Bimini in the Bahamas, there's a series of rectangular stones laid out in two almost-perfect rows. The formation lies less than fifteen feet under water. Some think it's what's left of the lost city of Atlantis."

Erika stepped forward. "How is that connected to these stones?"

"Once the road was discovered, there was an expedition launched—privately financed—to discover possible artifacts related to Atlantis. It was pretty much a cloak-and-dagger operation, but eventually someone leaked information on stones found with what looked like some ancient form of writing."

Here Barnes stopped. Seven gave it a beat, bracing himself for what might come next.

"I may have seen one of the stones," she said. "It was…some time ago. But I remember. This—" she held up the evidence bag "—looks very reminiscent of what I was told was one of the Bimini Stones."

"And?" Seven prompted, his rejuvenated mojo telling him there would be more.

"And, I've connected the stones to Zag de Rozières."

"De Rozières?" Seven said. "Now that name I know."

"You and half the known world," Erika piped in. "Jesus Christ, Sherlock. Are you saying what I think you're saying? You think Zag de Rozières—billionaire Zag de Rozières, the man from Atlantis—is good for these murders?"

"The man from Atlantis?" Seven asked. "What am I missing?"

Erika turned back to Seven. "Seriously, start watching the Discovery Channel. Zag de Rozières," she explained, "as well as his whole clan, has been linked to the Lost City of Atlantis. As in rumors that he may be a descendant."

Seven looked from Barnes to Erika. "If the guy thinks he's from Atlantis, I think we just found our whack job."

But Erika shook her head. "It's not that easy. Atlantis is like the guy's shtick, part of the smoke and mirrors that's put him at the top of a billion-dollar industry into the paranormal." She turned back to Barnes. "Come on. De Rozières wouldn't leave a clue like this."

"Unless he wants to get caught," Seven said.

"Or it makes him feel powerful," Barnes said. "He's daring us to figure it out."

"Baiting us," Erika finished.

"Wait a minute," Seven said sharply. "This guy's into the paranormal, right?"

"He's the king," Erika answered. "He has this company, Halo Industries. Let's say you want to check out one of your employees for that big promotion using handwriting analysis or numerology, or maybe you really want to roll the dice and do a little corporate espionage using remote viewing? He's your guy."

"Katie Sweeny thought she was psychic," Seven said, turning to Barnes. "Do we know anything about the other victims? If they claimed to have any psychic abilities?"

But Barnes wasn't listening. She was standing frozen, staring back out over the crime scene.

"What is it?" Erika asked, following the agent's gaze down the flood channel.

Seven frowned. The perspective here was different. They were standing up, above the body, staring down at the crime scene.

Up on the rocks on the other side of the flood channel, at the foot of the cinderblock wall, someone had placed a bouquet of daffodils.

"Erika," he said, "Do you still have that photo of Gia's painting on your cell?"

But Sherlock beat them to it. "Here," Barnes said, handing them the BlackBerry, now with a photo of Gia's painting on the screen.

Erika came in close, looking down at the small screen. The boy with the fishing pole was standing on a nondescript road with a ditch of murky water in the background. At the water's edge, syringes like darts on a dartboard stuck out of the ground in the shape of a crime-scene chalk outline. As they watched, Barnes took back the BlackBerry and deftly zeroed in on the image of the syringes.

"The body," Erika said, looking back at the flood channel.

"It's in the same position as the outline made by the needles."

"And the daffodils," Seven said. "Look at the daffodils."

They were the only flowers in the painting, a tuft of daffodils sticking up gaily from the ground.

"Wait a minute." Erika frowned. "I count five stones in the painting." She looked up at Seven then Barnes. "We've found four victims."

Agent Barnes pocketed the BlackBerry. "You two ready to do some real police work?"

Erika looked at Seven. They both knew where she'd be headed.

The next stop, Gia's.

It was human nature to be drawn to death. Perhaps it was morbid curiosity—or the fact that one too many television shows and video games made the horror of a car crash or a hit-and-run commonplace. On the freeway, it was called rubbernecking.

Crime scenes were no different.

Across the street from the Shipley Nature Center, a significant crowd had gathered.

Among them, a tall, handsome redhead focused the lens of his camera, snapping photographs.

The woman at the center of the frame was a tall willowy blonde sternly dressed in a black jacket and slacks.

She seemed very much in charge. He liked that about her. When he'd first seen her in the parking lot, she'd quietly reached for her gun holster. There hadn't been the least bit of panic in the move. Rather, it had been a practiced gesture. Like now. She was instructing those around her.

He snapped another photograph. With the telephoto lens, he could see the color of her eyes.

Almost as if she could sense him there, she turned, appearing to look straight at him through the lens. But he knew better. He was a good hundred feet from where she was standing. He'd made sure to blend in perfectly with the milling crowd.

She was a beautiful woman. He'd noticed that about her right off. But that wasn't what interested him.

He snapped another photo. The camera could capture her beauty. The rest, only he could see.

Unlike the people standing around him, he hadn't come to see a dead girl. He hadn't been drawn here by the cops swarming to keep the crowd at bay.

Eventually, he lowered his camera and stepped away. He'd parked several blocks down the road.

Poor Polly, he thought.

How many times had Adam thought just that, while staring at her struggling against the leather straps holding her in the hospital bed?

He put the digital camera on the passenger seat and got into the black Prius.

She'd always been stuck in that same fantasy—an escape from some tropical island.

He started the engine, checked his rearview mirror and turned into traffic, wondering when Jack's fantasies would come to an end.

29

Gia had been expecting them.

That wasn't how her gift usually worked. Normally, she would dream or experience a vision, guided by a photograph or a memento belonging to a lost loved one. There'd been a few times when she'd painted, trancelike, finishing the canvas without the least awareness.

But sometimes—in situations involving strong emotions—she just knew things…which was often the case with Seven. She had her own theories about why, none of them good.

So when the doorbell rang, she knew exactly who would be standing at the door and why.

"You found another victim," she said.

Seven stood on the threshold next to his partner. Right behind them was Carin Barnes.

Not one to hesitate, Erika stepped forward. "We have a few questions, Ms. Moon, if you don't mind?"

Gia caught a quick glance between Carin and Seven.

She opened the door wider. "You'll want to examine the painting again, now that you've found the girl."

She didn't often throw that kind of knowledge in people's faces. That had been her mother's tactic. Estelle's life work had been to make the world understand people like her and Gia. To that end, she hadn't minded shoving the paranormal in front of the establishment, daring the scientific community to stop marginalizing those with psychic abilities.

Gia couldn't worry about the world at large. Her focus was Stella.

She followed the three into the garage studio. Carin marched right up to the canvas, examining the outline near the water's edge.

"The body was actually in the ditch," she said, seeming to talk to herself.

"But it was in the exact same position," Seven pointed out. "Almost posed."

Carin turned to look at Gia. "How did you know the victim was a girl?"

Gia shook her head. "It was just a feeling I had when I painted it. Then again this morning. I was here, staring at the painting, and I knew you'd found her."

Gia turned to Seven. Right away, she noticed a change in him. That sadness that usually surrounded him like a shroud—an emotion she'd come to associate with the tragedy of his brother—she couldn't see it. What she felt from him now was like a fire burning, heating the very space around him. A near-uncontrollable rage. She knew he was having trouble keeping his emotions in check as he stared at the painting.

"These flowers," Carin said, pointing out the daffodils growing in a tuft near the outline of the body. "They were set out like a bouquet several feet away on the other side of the ditch."

"A gesture of condolence?" Seven suggested.

"The killer could have put them there," Erika said. "Like flowers on a grave."

Carin shook her head. "I don't know. The body was dumped in one of the flood channels. Not exactly prime real estate."

"Unless you want her to travel out to sea," Gia said. "Were any other victims placed in a way that they would end up in a large body of water?"

"Yes," Seven answered. "Katie Sweeny. Her body was dumped in the Bolsa Chica. At first, we thought the tide dragged her into the marsh, but the body was never fully submerged. The killer could have put her there hoping the tide would take her *out* to sea. Only, we found the body first."

"But why not just dump them in the ocean in the first place?" Erika asked.

Gia frowned, looking at the boy in the painting, his decomposed skin and mangled clothes, the curious birdcage at the end of the fishing line. "Maybe it's the journey that counts."

Carin turned, her unblinking gray eyes focused on Gia. "What do you know about the stones?"

Gia frowned. "Whoever made those stones was very sad."

"Is this it?" Seven asked. "Is the painting finished?"

She shook her head. "I can't answer that."

"Shocker," Erika said, her voice harsh and unforgiving. She turned to Carin. "We're wasting our time here." And when Carin didn't respond, she added, "Come on, Sherlock. We need to do better than this."

Carin stepped back from the painting. She turned to Gia. "Four children are dead. All the same age—fourteen. There's also a possibility that one, Katie Sweeny, claimed to have psychic powers."

Gia nodded. "Adolescence is a time of great change.

Many psychics first get in touch with their gifts in their early teens. Were the other children psychic, as well?"

"I interviewed the families extensively. If those kids did have any psi powers, real or imagined, they did a good job of hiding it."

"Gia," Seven said, "you painted five stones."

Immediately, she understood the new sense of alarm radiating from the group. "There'll be a fifth victim."

"No," Carin said. "That's not happening."

There was a harsh quality to her voice, emotion that the agent didn't normally allow to show. But that's all it was— show, bravado. The reality was they had very little control over what happened next. Carin abruptly turned to Gia. "You'll call me if you think of anything else?"

"Of course," Gia said.

Gia walked back into the house, ready to show them out. But once inside, Seven lagged behind. When Erika turned around with a questioning look, he told his partner, "Why don't you get a ride with Barnes. I'll meet up with you later."

Carin was already down the walk, but Erika hesistated. She glanced over at Gia. Her laser stare could have melted Gia into a puddle on the ground.

"Seven, I'm not your keeper, but I am your partner so I'm going to say it anyway. This isn't a good idea."

"That's your opinion," Seven said, echoing the words Gia had said to him just the other night over the phone.

It was Seven who shut the door on Erika.

Seven turned, watching Gia in silence. She could feel her breath coming fast, an effect that wasn't necessarily unpleasant.

"About the other night—"

"I understood," she said, cutting him off.

"Yeah, okay. But I don't."

That's what she hated about Seven. He could open up fearlessly, show everything most men would hide.

And now there was this energy radiating from him. It felt like something wild and on the edge of control. The rage coming from him, it was all mixed up—a complex ball of emotions in which she played a role along with his brother and the murders.

She shook her head. "What if you're right? What if this isn't a good idea?"

She wasn't talking about the case or her daughter. She was talking about them.

He seemed to focus just above her head, thinking about it.

He shoved his hand through his short brown curls. Those beautiful hazel eyes focused on hers.

"Yeah. Okay. It's crazy," he said. "Only, I can't stop thinking about you."

She could feel her breath catch. She'd been angry and devastated the other night. On top of which, her discussion with Stella had gone all wrong. But most of all, she thought Seven was right. She'd betrayed his trust—why should he ever trust her again?

"I know you have a difficult job, Seven. You've seen some horrible things. Please don't confuse our connection in this case for feelings for me."

He looked away and sighed. He shook his head as he stepped around her, reaching for the door.

Before he left, he told her, "Now that one? That one you got all wrong."

Stella raced to her room. She shut her bedroom door slowly, careful not to make too much noise. She threw herself on the bed.

She'd been spying, listening in on the cross-examination of her mother in her studio by the cops.

That's the way it always was; no one ever believed her mom's gift. How many times had Stella seen her mother treated like a weirdo, interrogated in some damn inquisition?

They'd found the girl. The body she'd seen in the ditch. They found her right there in that stagnant water, just like Stella had imagined her.

She could feel her heart racing in her chest. She wanted to hide here, pretend it would all go away.

A part of her knew she should tell her mother what had happened to her, but she felt trapped into silence. What was happening to her felt painful and private.

The realization came: She didn't want to share this with her mother. She didn't want to finally cross that line. To be one of them. A Fegaris woman. The person who gets cross-examined at every step. The one nobody ever believes.

When she opened her eyes, ghost boy sat at the foot of the bed.

Behind him, written on the vanity mirror were two words: *Don't tell.*

Stella slipped out of bed and walked over to the mirror. He had taken a pink highlighter from her backpack and written the words on the glass.

She turned to look at him. She licked her lips, almost afraid to ask. "Why? Why can't I tell?"

Suddenly, vividly, an image came to her head. She saw her mother lying on the polished concrete floor of her garage studio. A paintbrush rested in her hand. Her eyes were wide open.

She was clearly dead.

"No." The denial came out as a harsh whisper.

Instantly, the vision dissolved.

Ghost boy remained sitting on the bed, watching her.

Stella dropped onto the vanity stool, her breath coming hard and fast from fear.

"Are you trying to tell me my mother will die if I tell her what's happening?"

But he didn't answer. Since the library, he'd retreated into his cone of silence. It was up to her, and her alone, to make sense of his actions.

She couldn't say how long she sat there, thinking. Finally, she turned to face the mirror.

Don't tell.

With the palm of her hand, she erased the words off the glass.

30

Carin took the next exit. She'd been driving for two hours. She was on her way to visit the new center for advanced learning established by Halo Industries, one of Zag's Halo-effect schools.

She wondered if she'd lost her mind, taking Zag up on his invitation.

The request had been one of several messages she'd received when she'd returned from North Carolina. She would have blown him off but for the fact that she was now in possession of secret government documents involving Zag. She thought the timing of his request inauspicious. Her visit today was like the old adage: Keep your friends close and your enemies closer.

The architecture of the school made the building appear like the giant bow of a ship stretching out over the grounds below. Windows lined the side like enormous portholes. The structure was the work of a famous Dutch architect and had landed on the cover of several architectural magazines. Nothing but the best for Zag's brave new world.

Carin was met at the entrance by none other than the school's principal, Ms. Candie Pinkerton. With her smile and erect posture, the brunette was head-to-toe Prada perfection. Apparently, alternative education paid well.

Ms. Pinkerton gave Carin the full-court press as they toured the facility. Not all the children taught in the Halo-effect system were necessarily psychic but they were all "special." The curriculum here allowed each and every one to thrive as an individual. No ho-hum textbooks or memorization—forget the three Rs—classes centered on expanding the mind's potential.

Zag's Halo-effect kids showed many of the same attributes of the more familiar Indigo Children. They had uncommon intuition; they might even exhibit telepathic powers or telekinesis. They might come off as detached and, according to Zag, could be misdiagnosed as suffering from attention deficit disorder or even autism.

To Zag, these were magical children with more advanced brains. They exhibited extremely high IQs or special savantlike talents. They were, he claimed, the next step in human evolution.

Carin thought it went deeper than that. Zag's father had financed a mystery expedition to the Bahamas. For all intents and purposes, he'd stolen the Bimini Stones. Zag continued to fuel rumors about his ancestry, the possibility that he'd descended from refugees who'd escaped the destruction of Atlantis. Of course, it was a beautiful publicity ploy for a man who made his living off those who believed in the paranormal.

But Carin knew Zag intimately. And she wondered, these Halo-effect children, had Zag found a way to winnow out others like him? Did he believe these kids were descended from Atlantis?

"Do you know that, on average, we use less than five percent of our brain?" Ms. Pinkerton asked, throwing around the kind of numbers any idiot could look up on the Internet. "Einstein dedicated his brain to science—literally.

After his death, they weighed his brain and found it was actually smaller than the average male's. It's possible that he accessed greater portions of his brain and that's what made him a genius."

"So it's not the size that counts? It's what you do with it?" Carin countered.

The woman turned a prim shade of crimson. "Right this way, please."

They ended the tour in a kind of observation room. Carin could see into what looked like a small classroom through a two-way mirror. At the moment, the room had only a teacher and one student, a blond girl with pigtails and denim overalls who looked about eight. On the desk in front of the girl were several crystals of different shapes and colors.

"You're teaching the kids about crystals?" she asked.

"Since when do you have a problem with crystals?"

The response came from Zag as he swaggered into the room. Today, he wore leopard-print jeans that fit him like tights, tucked into Doc Martens boots. His white-blond hair was shorn close at the sides, accenting his fauxhawk hairstyle. The jacket he wore had enough buckles to mimic a strait-jacket.

"Last time I checked," he said, "you dedicated your life to a crystal. Or have you moved on from all that?"

Carin refrained from comment as he thanked the principal for her help. The words came out like a distinct dismissal.

After Ms. Pinkerton made her hasty exit, Zag gestured toward the glass and the room beyond. "What do you think?"

"An observation room? How very Joseph Mengele of you."

He clucked his tongue in disapproval. Zag leaned toward the glass. "This isn't just a teaching facility. We are here to gather evidence of the paranormal. The feedback helps to focus future instruction. Parents who bring their children here know that."

"And probably signed the waiver forms in triplicate."

"We have a lengthy waiting list."

"Of parents willing to pay to believe that their kid is somehow better than anybody else's, imbued with special powers?" She crossed her arms, looking at the girl sorting the crystals. "I can't imagine."

"How very tiresome to see that you've joined the rank and file." But his eyes were still on the child beyond the glass. "I remember a time when you, too, were willing to bend the rules."

"Did you really ask me here to try and convince me that what you're doing is anything more than blatant exploitation?"

He turned to look at her. "I wanted to talk to you about something quite different, actually."

He smiled, making her wait for it. When his eyes met hers their color appeared the palest shade of green. "I thought we might talk about the Atlantis Project."

She felt herself stiffen. "Wow. You must have that squad of psychics working overtime."

"I didn't need anything quite so dramatic to find out what your little trip yielded."

"Oh, right. It's about knowing all the right people—and their price, I imagine."

He took a step closer to her. "I shouldn't even be talking about a black project, but I wanted to make sure you didn't waste your time following any false leads. These children you've found. I had nothing to do with that, understand?"

Once again, Zag had managed to ambush her. And he wasn't near done.

Under his jacket, he was wearing a loose-fitting shirt. He'd left several of the top buttons undone. It was an easy thing for him to pull the shirt to one side, exposing the area right over his heart.

There was a tattoo, a design they'd created together when they'd been in love: their initials artistically entwined.

"I wanted to help," he told her softly. "For old time's sake."

"I wonder, Zag, when you were a kid, how many wings did you pull off butterflies just to see them squirm?" She looked back through the two-way mirror at the little girl seated at the desk. "Poor little butterflies."

She turned to leave, but Zag grabbed her arm.

Without a second thought, she turned and twisted his arm up behind his back. She was standing behind him, her other arm was now locked around his neck. Zag was fast— and strong—but she'd had years planning for this moment.

"Get fucked, Zag," she whispered in his ear. "We're not on the same side anymore. Maybe we never were."

She pushed him away and quit the room.

That fucking tattoo, she thought, racing down the halls for the exit to the parking lot.

Unfortunately, she had the exact same image tattooed on her skin. Only, hers wasn't over her heart.

When she reached the rental, a black RAV4, there was a note on the windshield.

It wasn't a flyer but a folded piece of lined paper. She pulled out a handkerchief and removed the paper. She opened it, careful not to leave any prints.

The message was short: *Don't trust him.*

She glanced around, but there was no one there to account for the note. She placed it carefully in her bag.

"Fool me once," she said to herself, starting the car, "shame on you. Fool me twice and you can put a fucking gun to my head."

31

The woman seated next to Seven's desk was a tiny thing, the kind of woman you wanted to offer a sandwich to. She had dark hair and enormous cornflower-blue eyes. She fiddled with an unlit cigarette in her hand.

She held the cigarette up in apology. "I'm trying to quit."

Seven could imagine. Her kid was missing. Not exactly *primo* time for big changes in her life.

"I started with the police in Hollywood—he was going to be a big movie star, you see." She bit her lip. "He's a good-looking boy, my Jack." She gave Seven a tired smile. "Last time we talked, he was auditioning for this commercial. It sounded so exciting."

Sandra Blake was a handsome woman. But right now, those puffy red eyes said she hadn't had a lot of sleep.

"But then I read the stories about those kids they found. They were all fourteen. That's how old Jack is." Here, her lips trembled as she fought against her fears. "At the Hollywood police station, they didn't think much about it. I mean, what are the chances, right? But I had to come."

"When was the last time you heard from Jack?"

The question came from Erika, who was standing next to Seven. Her gentle tone extinguished any possibility of accusation.

"Almost two weeks ago. Every Tuesday he calls. It's this system we have. I go to my sister's salon and he calls me." Sandra looked up at Erika, her eyes filling with tears. "Jesus, I really fucked up, didn't I? He's just a baby. What kind of mother am I?"

She shook her head, biting her lip to keep the tears at bay. When she could talk again, she explained. "I'm not making excuses. But you see, things weren't so good at home. And I thought he could make it here. That he was smart and beautiful and someone would see that and help him. You read about it all the time, how these kids get to be movie stars because someone sees them in a coffee shop or walking down the street. And I sent money. Every month, I sent money."

She choked on the words. Seven tried to imagine what kind of denial would allow her to believe her son's claims of stardom.

"Stupid." She hit her fist on her thigh. "So stupid."

Erika pulled up a chair and put a calming hand on the woman's. A lot of people only saw one side to his tough-as-nails partner. But he knew she'd have just the right touch for this situation.

"Do you have a photograph of Jack?"

The woman nodded, and dug out a dog-eared wallet-size photo—the kind they took the first day of school.

"You're right," Erika said. "He's really good-looking."

Jack Blake had moved out at the age of fourteen, taking a bus out west to, as his mother put it, become a star. But Seven had been on this job for too many years not to see there was more to the story.

No one just "sent off" their baby boy, as Sandra kept referring to Jack.

Seven figured it was a case of abuse. A pretty bad one,

judging from the way Sandra Blake shirked away any time he got close.

There was that look about her. Her eyes shied away from his, seeking Erika's. Her small body hunched over, as if it didn't deserve the space it took up in the chair.

A couple times, when he'd reached across the desk, she'd stiffened, almost as if she were bracing for a blow.

"He left six months ago?" Seven asked, going over his notes.

"But we talked once a week," she said, her voice getting stronger. "Every Tuesday, every single Tuesday, he called me at my sister's salon. Ten in the morning. Tuesday."

Erika glanced over the woman's head, meeting Seven's gaze. Of course, she'd caught on to the scenario. Either Sandra Blake didn't have a phone, or she was afraid to use her home phone or cell to contact her son.

When they'd asked about the boy's father, Sandra Blake told them, "He was never in the picture."

But somebody was. Some man had put that look of fear in Sandra's eyes—probably the same man responsible for her baby boy hopping a bus to Los Angeles.

"When he didn't call that first time, I worried," she said, concentrating. "That wasn't like Jack. I snuck out every day, going to the salon. Ten in the morning—every day for a week. I thought maybe something happened to make him miss the call. He'd know to call at the same time some other day."

Sandra looked up at Erika. Seven noticed she'd crushed the cigarette between her fingers.

"The second Tuesday he didn't call, I knew something happened to him. So I came out. I started with the police in Hollywood, because that's where he was supposed to be. They knew him. I guess he'd been—"

She shut her eyes. She swallowed hard, taking a minute. But the tears came just the same.

"—the police said he'd been picked up for turning tricks. They put him in some kind of group home, but he ran away."

"It happens," Seven said, handing her the Kleenex box.

A fourteen-year-old living on the streets turning to prostitution? It sure as hell happened.

She took the tissue and wiped away at her tears, angry. "I gave him money when he left. Every little bit I could put away, I gave him. I sent him money whenever I could. I thought it was enough. Stupid, right?" She shook her head and tossed the broken cigarette into the trash. "I thought he'd be better off leaving."

Seven tried to imagine what kind of home life Jack had if pulling tricks at fourteen made him better off.

"Then I read about those girls. I mean, they were fourteen, just like my baby boy. I couldn't help thinking, what if someone took him? This guy who killed those girls?"

"The chances are, he's just run away again," Erika said, stepping in. "But now that he's in the system, we'll find him. It's good that you came."

But the look Erika gave Seven said it all. A fourteen-year-old was missing. He'd been missing for two weeks.

Given what they knew about the other two victims, those facts alone alarmed.

"Those kids—the girls they found," she said. "In the paper, it said they drowned. But it wasn't an accident."

She kept her eyes on Erika, occasionally throwing a glance at Seven.

"The police, they suspected foul play," Sandra Blake continued. "That's how they wrote it in the paper. Foul play."

"It's part of an ongoing investigation," Seven said, keeping it vague.

She gave it a minute. This time when she spoke, she met both their gazes. "Let me tell you something, Detectives. I haven't had an easy life. I've done a lot of things I'm not proud of. And I've got an imagination. In my life, foul play? Well, that's just not so good, you know?"

Erika put a reassuring hand on her shoulder. "We will find your son, Ms. Blake."

She grabbed Erika's hand, holding it tight. "You find my Jack. And I *swear* I will never let anything bad happen to him again. Okay? Never."

Seven stepped in. "I know you're afraid, Sandra, but I assure you, this is what we do, Detective Cabral and I. We help find kids just like Jack." He held up the photograph of Jack. "We will coordinate with LAPD. Any information we get, we will contact you immediately. Detective Cabral and I will see to it personally."

She nodded, again biting her lip. "All right." She stood and walked toward the door. "But would it be okay if I call you? Just to check every once in a while?"

Erika gave her card to the woman and smiled. "I'll be expecting your call. Every day."

Both partners stood, watching the poor woman exit. When Sandra Blake left, Seven turned to Erika.

"What does that Latino voodoo of yours think?"

Because he trusted his partner's instincts. It might not be Gia and her psychic gifts, but Erika's sixth sense could be downright uncanny at times.

"You mean Santeria. Cubans don't practice voodoo." Erika pursed her lips. "But my gut says it's not good."

"Ditto," Seven answered, looking back at the photo of Jack Blake smiling up at him.

* * *

That gut feeling kept eating away at Seven well into an afternoon of phone calls and coordinating with the crime unit covering Hollywood and Vine. Eventually, he pocketed Jack's photo, thinking he'd go out and maybe show it around. Westminster was just within a few miles of several beach communities. Hollywood wasn't the only place young kids ended up selling sex for a hot meal or a place to stay.

He didn't get far. Just as he pushed the door open to the parking lot, a woman stepped out from the shadows.

It was Sandra Blake.

"I've been standing out here for hours," she said in a quiet husky voice. "Telling myself—Sandy, you are one stupid bitch. The police? Come on. What are they gonna do for your baby?"

Seven could imagine what experience had taught Sandra Blake about the police. *I haven't had an easy life. I've done a lot of things I'm not proud of.*

She wore tight jeans and a V-neck T-shirt that left very little to the imagination. Whoever did the implants, even his brother, the plastic surgeon, would have given a thumbs-up.

Her high-heeled sandals showed off her pedicure. Someone had painted flowers, complete with a rhinestone at the center, on each big toe.

"I told myself—waiting like this? I'm just wasting my time. I should be out *looking* for Jack. That's what I want to do, Detective. Just run around like some silly chicken with her head cut off, screaming his name up and down the streets."

She stepped in closer. Looking up at Seven, she said, "I ask myself, how did I let it happen? How did I ever think this could work out? Why didn't I—" she choked on the words "—why didn't I just cut that fucker's dick off?"

Seven felt a cold knot in his stomach, getting the picture. "You sent him away because he was being abused."

And she'd been too afraid of the abuser to protect her son.

She wiped away her tears. She looked up at him, mascara running, those big blue eyes daring him to judge her. "I've never had money. Peter? Gawd. He has so much. I'm not making excuses, but Jack and I had a house. I could stay with him. There were no more men."

She shook her head. She took out a cigarette and a lighter. "Fuck it." She was about to light up, when she hesitated. "Do you mind?"

He shook his head.

She lit up and inhaled the smoke deep into her lungs. She looked away. This time, when she spoke, her voice was strong and clear.

"I thought Peter wanted me." She gave Seven a hard look. "It turns out, what he really wanted was my son."

The photograph of Jack in his shirt pocket felt like a coal burning through the cotton, branding his skin beneath.

This was just the kind of thing Gia did. Someone showed her a photograph or a memento and she could paint an image or get some message from her spirit guide.

The whole thing was crazy, of course. It didn't matter how many times Gia pulled a rabbit out of a hat, what she did wasn't police work—evidence that a D.A. could present in court.

Only, looking into Sandra Blake's face, he knew that's not what she needed. She just wanted her boy safe.

"Anything," she said, reading his hesitation. "Any little thing you might know. I can take it. I can. Please, tell me."

That's the way it always was with the victim's family, that desperation for some sort of answer. He'd felt it himself, only he'd been coming from the other side of the equation.

Please, God. Don't let it be true. Don't let Ricky be a killer.

He asked, "Do you believe in the spirit world, Sandra?" And when she looked surprised, he added, "Or psychics? Are you familiar with that sort of thing?"

She frowned. "I had an aunt who could read tea leaves. Everyone said she was real good at it."

But he could see her putting it together, hope beginning to put a light in those sad, blue eyes.

"And I've seen that show on television," she said. "That one with the medium who helps the police? Do you know someone like that? Could you take me to her?"

"I can't promise it will help."

She nodded. "You're worried I'll be disappointed or hear something bad."

For the first time, he saw her face clear of any weakness. Instead, she looked determined, a woman ready to fight.

She threw the cigarette out and crushed it under her heel.

She held up her chin, looking straight up at him. "Don't worry about me, Detective. I'm stronger than I look."

32

It was a horrible thing to know that your child might be dead. That's the kind of knowledge Gia saw in Sandra Blake's face.

"I'm not sure what you need for this to work," the boy's mother said in a nervous voice. "Ask me anything. I can tell you his birthday, his favorite color."

They were seated in the living room, Sandra on the serape-striped chair across from Gia; Seven, in the love seat.

Sandra began digging through her purse at her feet. "Or maybe I have something of his with me."

"This will do fine," Gia said, holding up the school photo of Jack, the woman's son.

"Just a picture?"

She sounded disappointed. Gia understood. Sandra Blake wanted something to do; she *needed* to be useful. Handing over a photograph couldn't even begin to fill that hole of fear growing inside her.

And her fears didn't stop there. She needed someone to believe in. Not a quack or a fake. Sandra Blake desperately wanted a real-life miracle.

"It's different for other people," Gia said gently. "For me, a picture is best."

The woman nodded. "When will you know something?"

Gia sighed, because she already knew.

"Ms. Blake—"

"Sandy, please."

"Sandy. I paint, that's how my gift works. I'll have something soon, I promise."

She nodded, but Gia could see she was barely holding it together.

"Gia knows what she's doing," Seven said. "As far as anyone can know about these things. She's helped the police before, on another case."

Gia knew what he was doing, stepping in to reassure the bereaved, the bewildered, the ones left behind to worry about the victims. He would have a lot of experience at it.

She reached across the coffee table and took the woman's small hand in hers. "Would you like anything, Sandy? Tea, perhaps?"

She shook her head. "I better go. I thought maybe I could go back out tonight, talk to some of the kids out there."

Seven stood, as well, but Sandy held up a hand, staving him off. "If it's okay with you, Detective, I think those kids might talk to me better than a cop."

Just then, the door opened. Stella walked inside, dropping her backpack at the door.

"Hi," she said, looking around.

Sandra Blake turned, her gaze fixed on Stella. "This is your daughter?"

Stella came to stand next to her mother. Gia put a comforting arm around her, suspecting she knew what Stella was seeing.

"Stella, say hello to Ms. Blake."

"Sandy," she corrected again. She gave another tired

smile. "I recognized her from the pictures." She gestured to the photos decorating the room.

Sandy came to stand in front of Stella. She was small enough that she didn't need to bend down to look her in the eyes. She stroked Stella's hair. "You're fourteen, aren't you?"

Gia saw her daughter's unflinching gaze on Sandy Blake. "Thirteen. Just a couple of months ago."

"A year younger than my Jack," she said. "Well, he's almost fifteen. His birthday's next month."

Sandy Blake stepped away reluctantly, shouldering her heavy purse. "Detective, you'll call?"

Seven nodded. "The minute I hear anything. I'll show you out."

"Are you okay?" Gia asked, seeing that frozen look on her daughter's face.

Stella nodded. "Sure." But before her mother could question her further, she added, "I ate at Mindy's. I have a lot of homework."

Gia watched her daughter step carefully around the chair where Sandy had been seated. She picked up her backpack from the door and headed down the hall to her room.

When Seven came back, he immediately knew something was wrong.

"You know something?" he asked.

She pointed to a puddle of water next to where Sandra Blake was seated.

Seven followed her gaze, confused. "What?"

Gia sighed. Of course, he wouldn't see it.

She went to the kitchen and returned with a paper towel. She dropped it on the floor. Immediately, water soaked through the paper.

Seven stared at the paper towel now soaked with water. "That's a neat trick."

Only he knew it wasn't a trick.

"This boy, Jack? I think he's the spirit attached to Stella."

Seven crouched down next to the chair. "Because of the water?"

She nodded. "And because Stella saw the puddle. She was very careful to walk around it."

He stood, getting what she left unsaid. "But she didn't say anything."

Gia looked to the hallway beyond where her daughter had disappeared. "Not a word."

Stella sat on her bed, her knees tucked up under her chin. When she'd walked into the house, that sad woman had been seated in the big chair. Ghost boy had been standing right next to her.

They didn't look anything alike. And still she knew the sad woman had to be his mother.

Now ghost boy stood at the foot of her bed, waiting.

"It's you, isn't it?" she asked. "You're not dead. You're just lost."

He didn't answer. She'd given up on him ever talking to her again. He'd always been a quiet spirit, more inclined to communicate through his actions rather than his voice.

"Your mother was here. She looks pretty messed up about you being gone."

She stood and turned to face him. All this time, he'd been following her around, trying to tell her something. Now, finally, she thought she understood.

"You'll show me how to help you?"

He got off the bed and walked toward her. He stopped

when they were less than two feet apart and held out his hand.

After all he had done, it seemed that the final choice would be hers.

She hesitated. She knew what would happen if she touched him.

But she also remembered that poor woman and how badly she wanted her Jack to come home.

"Okay," she said, reaching for his hand.

33

Erika jammed her key in the door of her condo, mentally and physically exhausted. It felt as if she and Seven had combed the entire O.C. looking for Jack Blake, searching out parks and beaches where runaways and homeless tended to hang out before they got rousted by the cops.

They'd come up with nothing. So had the detectives in L.A.

As usual, Special Agent Barnes was MIA. You'd think the crime scene was "out of town" since that's where Sherlock spent half her time.

It was a long, frustrating day and Erika had been looking forward to putting her feet up and opening that bottle of Langtry Meritage Greg promised would blow her mind.

That's what she wanted. Great booze and a warm body to cuddle with.

What she found was Greg pilfering through the file she'd left on the kitchen table, a file containing her personal notes on the case.

She could feel her heart pounding in her chest. "Searching for your next byline?"

He closed the file in his hand, but he couldn't erase the look of guilt on his face.

She shook her head. *The last thing I need.*

But she'd known all along this would blow up in her face. No good could come of falling for a reporter with Greg's hyper ambition.

She said, "Fuck you."

"You're wrong."

"*I'm* wrong?" She threw her keys on the table. "I'm not the one sneaking through *your* private shit."

She headed for the bedroom. Greg quickly followed. He found her digging his clothes out of the lone drawer she'd granted him, dumping socks, boxers and T-shirts on the bed.

"Okay," he said. "That was a shitty thing I did." He grabbed the next load out of her hands and threw them to the floor. "I should never have read through your notes. But the file was just there on the table. Look, I didn't go into reporting because I don't have a healthy curiosity."

"Not to mention bloated ambition."

She couldn't believe how angry she was. It was almost as if all the emotions of the day were catching up to her right here, channeled at the man standing before her.

She kicked the clothes on the floor. "Damn it. I knew this was never going to work."

"Never work? Don't you think that's a bit of an over-reaction?" He grabbed her shoulders to steady her, but she yanked his hands away.

"I'm a cop, Greg. You're a reporter. I'm not the source for your Pulitzer."

He took a step back, his eyes wide behind his glasses. "Wait a minute. Was this some kind of test?" he asked. "You leave out the file on a hot story and see if I take the bait?"

She was pissed enough to lie. "Yeah, and you failed."

She waited for him to pick up his clothes and start packing. That's what she'd do—give up, give in.

But not Greg. He took a minute, looking away as if he were thinking over his next move.

He said, "You're just scared, sweetie."

"Scared? You bet your ass I'm scared." She stepped into him pushing him hard in the chest. "If you print anything from that file, it's my ass."

"I would *never* do that."

"You couldn't stop yourself."

He looked at her in disbelief. "You really believe that, don't you? I always thought when you said stuff like that, you were just kidding around, egging me to say I love you and would never hurt you."

I love you. He'd never said those words before. Neither of them had.

He cupped her face in his hands. She couldn't stand it that there were tears in her eyes. That he could see them.

He said, "I love you, Erika."

"Sure you do. That's why you were reading that file. Out of love for me."

"Okay, so I made a mistake. So we need…rules."

She shook her head in disbelief, again pushing him away. "Rules? It's fucking common sense!"

"Well, maybe I don't *have* common sense, not when it comes to this sort of thing. I can't help it. I like to *know. Mea culpa.* But I would never betray you by using the information." He pushed his fingers through his hair. "Jesus, Erika. Every day I wake up next to you and I think how the hell did I get so lucky? And every night I think you're coming home to tell me it's over. But I don't care. I hold my breath until I get past that first kiss and think, not today."

She hadn't moved. She stood frozen before him, his clothes at her feet.

"I have some serious skin in this game," he said, stepping in, his hands closing around her arms. "Don't push me away. Not yet. Please, babe. Give me another day."

She closed her eyes, hearing him say it again: *I love you.* Three words she'd never thought she'd hear from anyone.

He tried to kiss her, but she pushed him away. He kept at it, kissing her until finally she stopped fighting, allowing those kisses. She realized she wasn't ready to let go. She didn't want to come home to an empty house, not when her days were filled with death. She wanted this—whatever *this* was. It didn't need to last forever. It's like he said: just one more day.

She grabbed his belt and began unbuckling it.

"I swear to you," he said, kissing her mouth, her chin, her eyes. "It will never happen again." He spoke between kisses, taking off her jacket. That was one thing about Greg, he could multitask. "But maybe, in the future, you should hide stuff. You know, just so that I don't fuck up—"

"Greg?" She cupped his face in her hands. "Shut the fuck up."

Kissing him, she pushed him back on the bed.

Erika watched Greg serve her chow mein with chopsticks. They were seated at the kitchen table. Greg was wearing those Hanes boxer briefs she'd bought him when she'd moved him out of his tidy whites. She was wearing only his shirt.

"Jesus, you make that shirt look hot," he said before biting into an egg roll. "In fact, I'm never wearing it again. I'm going to hang it up like a piece of art."

"Not here you're not," she said.

She thought to herself, *He has nice hands.* She'd always loved his hands.

They'd opened the bottle of Meritage, which was every bit as divine as he'd promised.

"You had a bad day," he said, refilling her glass.

"Yeah."

She left it at that, not wanting to fill in the blanks. But here was Greg, Mr. Curious.

"Come on," he said. "We're off the record. Total cone of silence. Hey." He touched her cheek. "I know the sex is good—but you need to be able to talk to me, too. Okay?"

She put down the glass. "How about admitting the sex is amazing. That you've never, *ever* had it this good—"

"Oh, shit. Did I forget to say it?"

"—Sex so good, you'd pass on even the Pulitzer, given the chance."

"Of course, I would," he said, suddenly deadly serious. "I told you, Erika. I love you."

She sat back in her chair. *Crap.*

"I didn't say it to hear it back," he told her. "Oh, what the hell. My big mouth has gotten me into plenty of trouble before, so I'll ask." He met her gaze. "Did you ever tell Seven you loved him?"

She felt the question like a punch to her solar plexus. "Why would you ask that?"

He gave her a wan smile. "It's a gift. Fatal curiosity."

She shook her head. "No. I have never said those words to any man. Now," she said. "You tell me. Which is better?"

His gaze met hers. "I think I'll get back to you on that."

She reached over and put her hand on his. "He's my partner."

He brought her hand up to his lips and kissed the inside of her wrist. "I know. And I get that. The whole life-in-your-hands, watching-your-back thing. But maybe you could trust me a little, too?"

She thought about it, trusting someone. What that would mean. Her father had left her mother when Erika and her brother were just kids. He'd abandoned them and moved to Costa Rica where he'd married Consuelo and started a bright, shiny new family that included two young sons. Only now, the bastard lived here, in Santa Ana, just a stone's throw away from Erika.

Her father made the whole trust thing kind of rough.

But then, so did finding a fourteen-year-old in a ditch.

She got up and walked over to where she'd put away her file, the one he'd been reading earlier. She took it back to the table and dropped it in front of him.

"What if the local law enforcement suspects the FBI is holding back critical information?" she asked.

She didn't know why that look of relief on his face made her so happy.

"Well, here's the thing," he said, pushing the file aside. He grabbed the bottle of Meritage and topped up both their glasses. "I have a photographic memory, so I don't need to read your notes again."

She sat down, pleasantly surprised to discover something she didn't know about Greg…enjoying the possibility that he'd been holding back.

He winked. "I know. I'm a man of mystery. What you need, babe, is leverage. And I think I found it for you." And when her smile grew even wider, he added with his own grin, "Is my stock going up?"

"Maybe," she said, excited despite herself.

"In your notes, you mention the Eye of Athena. That's the crystal they found during the fortune-teller murders. My research shows that the FBI discovered the crystal was a fake. A damn fine one, but a fake just the same."

"That's right."

"And there's a connection between Special Agent Barnes and the Eye," he said.

"Again, correct."

"So, in my business, those are the kinds of connections that start raising a red flag."

"Meaning?"

"David Gospel put together a collection of mystic artifacts, one that included the Eye. Every single piece in his collection was deemed authentic—the guy had money to burn, right? He sacrificed everything he had to get his hands on the Eye—even his life."

"Okay."

"Okay? That's all you got?" He popped the last bite of spring roll into his mouth. "You don't think it's kind of strange? Everything in his collection is authentic *except* the Eye? Think, babe, who delivered the artifact to the FBI?"

Her mouth dropped open. "Special fucking Agent Barnes."

"Who, as you pointed out in your very detailed notes, has a special connection to that particular artifact."

"Fuck," she said under her breath. "She traded it out. She kept the real thing."

She'd known there was something wrong all along. She just hadn't been able to put her finger on exactly what. She'd suspected only that Gia and Barnes were in on it together.

"But what do I do with this?" she asked, completely blown away by Greg's revelations.

Greg gave her a smile. "Give me a minute."

He picked up his cell phone and punched in a number. She'd never seen Greg at work. Watching him call his sources while he finished off dinner, she understood why the guy could get under a woman's skin. There was a power to him, a confidence. And persistence. One call led to another, and then another.

When he finally finished, she just stared at him, mystified.

"What?" he asked. And when she still sat there, staring, he added, "It's called *investigative* reporting."

"Really?" she said. "And what if I hadn't asked for your help?"

He gave her a kiss on her forehead and picked up his wineglass. "Maybe that's the moral of the story. You never know what you're missing until you ask."

34

Gia put down the brush and regarded her newest canvas.

She'd painted a house, an old Victorian. The structure was two stories high with a turret rising yet another story. There was a wraparound porch with elaborate spindles and brackets and several projecting bay windows. The roof had patterned shingles and finials at the roof's crests.

It reminded Gia of the haunted mansion at Disneyland. She understood it was haunted, but not in the conventional sense. There was a very dark energy living in that house.

"How long have you been standing there?" she asked without turning around.

Seven stepped into the studio. "You're the psychic. Why don't you tell me?"

She grabbed a towel off the chair and wiped her hands. He came to stand behind her, examining the painting over her shoulder.

"I couldn't sleep," he said. "And, of course, there's my magic cop powers that told me what you were up to."

She turned to look up at him. She felt an instant ache in her stomach. Regret, no doubt. A lot of it.

"Magic cop powers?"

He shrugged. "What we in the business call following my gut. You told Sandra Blake you'd have something soon.

I figured *soon* for you would be the moment she walked out the door. By the way, I knocked—softly. I didn't want to wake Stella. And keeping the door unlocked? Not a good idea."

"The things I worry about aren't held back by doors, Seven."

"Then get a dog. A big one. Is that where Jack is?" he asked, pointing at the house.

The house, painted in black and white, was hidden in the shadow of oak trees.

"Yes." She looked at the painting in frustration. "But there's nothing distinctive about the home other than that it's a Victorian. It could be anywhere."

"What about these?" he asked.

He pointed out several signs painted into the scenery. They reminded him of election time, when every piece of real estate was plastered with some campaign slogan. The lawn in particular was covered with placards stapled to posts, making it look like a graveyard. There were more signs nailed on the front door, peeking through the windows.

Each read the same thing: Keep Out!

She shook her head. "It's some kind of symbol or metaphor. At this point, it's not very helpful. But I do know one thing—" she looked up at Seven, meeting his gaze "—Jack is alive."

"A prisoner in this house?"

"I can't be sure." She gestured in frustration at the painting. "I wish there was more."

"It's something." He stepped back, taking a photo of the painting with his cell phone before pocketing it. "I'll get an image of this printed up. We can start searching through some of the local Victorians. You never know, we could get lucky."

But she frowned, still trying to find more in the image.

"Hey," he said, reaching out to place a comforting hand on her shoulder.

The instant he touched her, a spark of electricity shocked him.

He pulled away, staring at his hand as if suddenly it was something alien. He looked down at Gia.

"I'm sorry," she said.

He frowned. "Why?"

"Why am I sorry or why does it happen?" she asked.

"For fuck's sake, Gia. It's static electricity, nothing special."

She gathered up her brushes and stepped over to the sink built into the wall of her garage studio. She dumped the brushes there. She could still feel that energy beaming from him. But she didn't need any special abilities to know he was a man on the verge. She could hear it in his voice, could see the tension in his face.

A part of her wanted to take on that heat. She was feeling a little tense herself. A boy was missing, her daughter was involved. She felt vulnerable and utterly alone.

She told herself it wasn't a new emotion. God knows she'd faced worse. Taking a breath, she reached for the water faucet.

Seven grabbed her by the shoulders and turned her around. His hazel eyes looked like a kaleidoscope of gold and green, there was so much emotion in them.

"See," he said, holding up his hands and giving her a hard smile. "Nothing."

He was referring to the fact that, this time, there had been no startling shock of electricity when they'd touched.

She didn't know why she did it—or maybe she did. A

long day, bad news, the frustration of wanting answers where there were none.

Or maybe it was just the look in his eyes, daring her.

She stepped forward and stood on her tiptoes. She didn't touch him with her hands. Instead, she gave him a light kiss on the mouth.

Even before their lips touched, the shock came fast and sharp, connecting them.

She stepped back. She could see she'd caught him off guard. But he wasn't about to be outdone.

He scooped her body into his, his gaze locking on hers. He lowered his mouth slowly, giving her time to stop him.

She didn't. Instead, she stepped into the kiss, pressing herself against him.

She knew it would be like this, as if no time had passed. She'd only been with two men in her life. With Thomas, she'd been so young. Naive and vulnerable. What she felt with Seven was nothing like that.

He helped her pull off her T-shirt and unbutton her jeans as she unbuckled his belt. When they were naked, they lay down on the floor. She remembered everything about him, his smell, the shape of his shoulders, how his hands felt against her skin.

They would have made love right there on the polished cement of the studio, ten months of separation suddenly feeling like ten days, but Seven pulled away, breaking their frantic kisses.

He was lying over her, balanced on his arms. She could feel his heart beating against her skin.

"I don't know what I'm doing," he said, that same hot energy in his voice.

"Letting go," she said.

She realized it was true. That heat, the frantic edge—

he'd been keeping himself in check too long. Keeping it together for his sister-in-law and nephew, trying to deal with his own emotions over his brother.

All that loss and confusion. She was part of it.

She threaded her fingers through his hair. "I am so sorry for what I did," she whispered. "I was so scared. I knew Thomas would find us. All those years of hiding, and there you were. Someone who made me feel safe—"

He covered her mouth with his hand. He shook his head.

After a while, he stood. He held his hand out; she took it. He helped her to her feet, scooped her up into his arms and cradled her against him.

He asked, "What are my chances of making it to a bed before your daughter catches you naked in my arms?"

She nestled her face into his shoulder. "I would never bet against Stella."

He gave her a quick kiss. "Is that a no?"

No, don't do this.

No, don't stop.

She didn't look at him. Her face still buried in his neck, she whispered, "No."

He headed for the door leading back into the house and the guest bedroom, accepting the ambiguity.

35

Nathaniel sat on the upholstered chair across from Evie, the formation reminiscent of how she communicated with her brother. He'd seen it often enough, how their knees practically touched, they'd sit so close holding hands.

Nathaniel wasn't psychic. That had never been his role. He was the facilitator.

"You understand that you're special, Evie," he told her. "Much more than your brother can ever hope to be. Because Adam is weak."

Evie looked away. She never liked the comparison. She didn't want to hear about any lack in her brother. But Nathaniel knew. From the time they were little, he'd always known who would be willing to see this to the end.

It was part of the reason he'd needed to break the bond between them. Adam might sacrifice himself, but he would never allow his sister to do the same. Adam would always put Evie's safety over any mission. It was a weakness Nathaniel couldn't allow.

"I've seen the changes in him—how much he worries for the hosts. He sees them as children, innocent. I taught you not to do that, Evie."

"They're the host," she repeated. "Without them, nothing changes."

"That's right. The government used your mother as a host. But like Adam, they lost their nerve. They would have buried the great gifts your mother brought to the world. That's why we ran away, she and I."

"To finish the journey."

"Now it's our time to finish. Always remember, Evie, why she brought you and your brother into the world, giving up her own life."

"To bring the world the truth."

"And now Adam hesitates? When we are so close?"

"It's up to me," she said, repeating the words he'd taught her.

He turned her face back toward his. "You are the Destroyer, Evie. The more powerful."

He'd given her the name of the Hindu goddess, Kali the Destroyer. They each had their role in this journey—to search through time and space and reach that place where Celeste had discovered her secrets, secrets the government was too fearful to seek out.

He brushed her hair from her face. "To the strongest goes the most difficult task."

"Adam is weak," she repeated softly.

"You must do this for him."

"I am the Destroyer," she said.

He took her face in his hands and kissed her forehead.

He could see her glance up at the portrait over the fireplace. She was the image of her mother.

Her face still cupped in his hands, he smiled at her. "Now, are you ready?"

Adam stood next to the hospital bed. At the foot were two chairs, one facing the other. They were preparing for another session with Jack.

His father had always said three was a powerful number. Adam thought he might be right. After all, they always lost the host after the third session.

Jack appeared to be sleeping, but Adam knew he was in a drug-induced trance. He'd been given a specific cocktail through his IV to produce just this state.

He looked pale. Weak.

Adam's gift was to find people like Jack. He could see their life force as a halo of light surrounding the body. The drugs helped the host reach a state of mind that allowed Evie, with his help, to use them as a vehicle for remote viewing.

At the moment, the light surrounding this host had dimmed to a nearly imperceptible glow. The boy, Jack, was dying. He wouldn't make it past another session.

And Evie was on her way.

He could still sense her presence even at a distance, but just like Jack's life force, their connection seemed muted.

He'd been noticing the subtle changes for months now. He'd attributed the difference between them to her relationship with Zag. He thought perhaps his sister was in love.

It made sense that their bond would suffer. His sister had connected with another. The growing separation between them was anguishing, but acceptable.

Zag made her happy. Adam wanted his sister happy.

But now his father posited quite a different rationale. He believed that Zag was taking advantage of his sister's gifts, using her up.

What his father said made sense. During his sparring with Evie, that blank she'd hit in her mind, it had nothing to do with any kind of romantic relationship.

That's why Adam would seek out Carin Barnes, why he would help her to bring down Zag de Rozières.

Adam's life had always been a well-orchestrated plan. When his father had told him about Zag's influence on his sister, Adam had read between the lines: Get Zag out of the picture.

And so he'd contacted Carin. He had plans for her.

Only, sitting here waiting for Evie to arrive, he had the feeling his sister's problem might not be all about Zag.

When Evie walked into the room, he said firmly, "Not today. He won't make it."

He could feel her anger, but he experienced the emotion as muted.

She came to stand next to him. "We are running out of time. If he doesn't make it, someone else will. That's how we do this, Adam."

"Not today," he insisted just the same.

"It's been two days—"

"So it will have to be three."

His sister reached out mentally. Instinctively, he raised a block.

It was a repeat of their sparring match. Only now, it was Adam shutting her out.

She took a step back. "What are you doing?"

"Why act so surprised?" he asked, referring to his mental push. "I learned it from you."

He headed for the door. He wasn't as good at it; he hadn't been subtle, not like Evie. When she wanted to keep secrets, she could turn her thoughts into smoke, so insubstantial they dissolved into nothing with his touch.

Adam didn't care that she'd experienced the block. That had been pretty much the point.

"Adam," she said before he could leave the room. "We're so close."

"So Father keeps saying. All I see is children dying,"

he told her. "I'm sorry, my love, but if you want to kill him, you'll have to do it yourself."

He walked out, wondering what else his sister would learn to do without him.

36

The instant Stella touched the ghost boy's hand, she dropped to her knees. She thought she'd been ready. She'd done all this before; she knew what was coming. Even before they touched, she'd braced herself. *It will hurt and then it will be over.*

And still, the pain just kept coming. She felt an electric charge that set her every nerve on fire.

"It's too much," she told him, doubling over in pain. "I can't."

But he didn't let go. Instead, he fell to his knees before her. Slowly he raised his free hand, the motion labored, as if his arm were too heavy to lift. He dropped his hand on her shoulder.

A tremendous force pressed down on her heart with that touch. The weight of it squeezed the air out of her lungs. She couldn't catch her breath.

"Stop." The word was barely a whisper. "Please, stop. You're killing me."

She knew he wouldn't. Somewhere, beyond the pain, she knew it wasn't ghost boy in charge anymore.

The woman had long red hair and very blue eyes. Stella could feel the way she reached inside Jack's head, a hot poker searing a path. She consumed his every thought, depleted his will. And still, she wanted more.

Jack. What do you see, Jack?

Stella was back in that strange city. There were pyramids that looked like something in her history textbooks on the Mayans or the Incas. People wearing robes seemed to float above the ground as they walked past her. A crystal swung from the neck of every man, woman and child.

Suddenly, she was back in her bedroom with ghost boy still holding her. He glanced over at her backpack on the floor. A book came flying out and slid across the floorboards. It was the library book, the one she'd checked out on the city of Atlantis.

The book flipped open to a particular page about the sleeping prophet, Edgar Cayce. Only, she didn't need to read the words. They were there, inside her head.

The firestone generates energy…its preparation is in the hands of the initiates…invisible rays act on the aircraft and pleasure crafts…rays emanate from the stone at the power station…the Sons of Belial destroy…

Now she found herself in an old-fashioned room furnished with antiques, only there was a hospital bed with some medical equipment, too.

Keep with me, Jack! Just a little longer.

The redhead, the woman she'd seen before, sat on the edge of the hospital bed. She was holding a boy in her arms, rocking him against herself. Stella couldn't see his face. Even as she tried to focus, the room grew dimmer.

The boy stiffened in the woman's arms. Stella felt a new wave of pain shock her body.

She's going to kill him, she thought. *She's going to kill Jack.*

Adam waited at the hotel entrance. He was dressed in dark slacks and a dress shirt. The clothes might be understated, but the man was not. The silk shirt only accentuated the musculature of his arms and abs. The red hair alone, sweeping in layers to brush his wide shoulders, attracted the eyes of passersby, as did his chiseled features and electric-blue eyes.

A woman, a confident brunette in her forties wearing a strappy dress and sandals, stopped to ask if he had a light. He was happy to oblige with her cigarette, but no, dinner was out of the question. He was otherwise engaged.

After leaving his sister, he'd come here. He hadn't let his father in on his plans, but Adam knew he'd approve. Adam might not be willing to satisfy Evie and his father's desire for a third session with Jack, but he could still be useful here.

He watched Carin Barnes step out of her rental and hand the valet her key. She was dressed in black slacks and jacket with a white shirt—FBI clothes that fit her well without being provocative. She had her head down as she shouldered a large satchel and stepped away from the RAV4.

Adam stepped out of the shadows and walked up behind her. Before she could stop him, he looped her arm over his and guided her toward the front entrance of the hotel.

When she reached for her weapon, he dropped her arm and took her gun hand in his. He threaded their fingers together and begun to swing their hands between them like two kids.

"Gotta love a lady who's armed, Agent Barnes." Women had always told him he had a disarming smile. "But I only want to buy you a drink."

"Well, well," she said, "if it isn't the loving brother from Santa Barbara visiting his coed baby sister. Looks like you figured out the freeway system if you found your way here."

He made sure to guide her into the hotel. "You'd be amazed what I figured out, Carin."

Just as he planned, her expression changed from suspicion to curiosity.

"You know," she said, "it really was a lousy cover story, though the kegger bit was a nice touch. You've been following me. So, who the hell are you?" she asked.

Once they stepped inside, he released her hand and stepped back, giving her some space.

"It's public and crowded," he said, gesturing at the hotel lobby. "And if you want the information I have—and trust me, Carin, you do—you'll let me buy you that drink."

Again, he took her hand. He lifted it to his lips and pressed a kiss to the inside of her palm. He gave her a long, lingering look that wasn't meant to be erotic.

He said, "You really should be flattered, all this trouble I went to."

"You're right. Some women would find it exciting to have a handsome man stalking them. Then there's me. I just think it's kind of creepy."

He dropped her hand, giving her the option of walking away. But he knew she wouldn't. They'd made a connection. It was the sort of thing that came easily to him, the Finder.

She watched him for a moment. She had short blond hair cut in a boyish style that made her gray eyes look large and luminous. Unexpectedly, he felt heat rise up through the fingers of the hand that had held hers.

Interesting, he thought.

She pointed behind him. "I believe the bar is that way."

He took her bag, ever the gentleman. She didn't bother to argue, just stepped ahead to lead the way.

It was late afternoon; early enough that the restaurant was almost empty. Carin hiked up to the bar and motioned the bartender over.

"You have five minutes," she told him before ordering a Perrier.

"The lady will have a Macallan," Adam corrected. "With a splash of water."

Carin nodded her acceptance to the bartender. Adam rewarded her with another dimpled smile.

"Make it two," he told the man, never taking his eyes off Carin.

"I hope you know that's a twenty-five dollar drink here," she said.

"Not a problem," he told her.

"So, is this the time in our relationship when you ask, what's my sign?"

"Leo," he responded without thinking.

"Wow," she said, picking up the drink the bartender placed before her. "You know my drink and my sign. Do you have a complete dossier?"

"Maybe I just read your mind. You know about that sort of thing, don't you, Carin?"

She took a nice long pull of the Scotch before putting the glass down. "Nice try, but that one was a little lame considering you found me outside Morgan's Institute. Psychic powers are a bit of a specialty there."

He took a drink from his own glass and savored the whiskey opened up by the water. Nice. She had good taste.

Adam liked sex. He liked feeling close to someone. Most of his life had been dedicated to something greater than his own happiness. But finding someone to sleep with for a night had never been a problem.

He realized he wanted to have sex with Carin Barnes. He also knew it would never happen.

"How about this," he said. "You've been thinking about

me a lot lately. Oh, sure, there's the sexual attraction, but there's more to it. Some niggling suspicion at the back of your mind that I look familiar, but you can't place me. And you, Carin, don't like loose ends."

She toasted him with her glass. "Better, but still a little on the talk-show psychic side."

"You should smile more often," he said, brushing a finger across her chin. "It's nice."

She grabbed his hand and placed it on the bar. "As scintillating as this conversation is, you've used up three of your five minutes."

He gave a shake of his head. "Usually, I have a more positive effect on a woman. The stones. The ones you found in the victims' hands. They're a puzzle. You like puzzles, don't you, Carin?"

He stood and reached for his wallet. Carin grabbed his arm and reached for her gun.

He placed a hand on her shoulder and focused.

Instantly, she went limp.

He caught her in his arms and laid her gently on the bar's counter so that her elbow pillowed her head.

When the barkeep glanced over, Adam said, "Looks like she can't hold her liquor. Will you call a bellman, please? I'd take her to her room myself, but—" he flashed that same disarming smile "—we don't really know each other that well. It might be awkward."

He dropped a hundred-dollar bill on the counter, knowing the money would answer any other questions.

When Stella came to, ghost boy was looming over her. She sat up, disoriented. Her head was on fire with the disturbing images. That weird city, the lady with the red hair…and Jack in the hospital bed.

"She's killing you, isn't she? And she's using some sort of weird Vulcan mind meld to do it."

Over the last week, she'd learned a few things about the psychic world. When she first figured out her mother wasn't your average mom, she'd done a little reading, but not a lot. The whole thing just sort of freaked her out. But since ghost boy had shown up on the scene, she'd done research on the whole attached-spirit thing. How sometimes, if someone didn't "move on," his or her spirit could latch on to a host, sometimes making that person feel sick or mentally ill.

But the stuff that she'd seen in her vision just now, she had no idea what that was about.

"You're in a room in some old house," she told ghost boy. "That woman is keeping you prisoner there. She's the one killing the kids, isn't she? Only, she's not trying to kill anyone. She's trying to find this weird place." She picked up the book he'd sent flying across the room. "She thinks it's the lost city of Atlantis, the place Plato wrote about, that sunk into the ocean. She uses your mind somehow to search for it. The dying, it's a side effect. She's killed four. Now she's doing the same thing to you."

He watched her silently, not uttering a word.

"Why don't you talk?" She threw the book back on the floor, suddenly angry. The whole week had been such a mess. She didn't want to have any part of it. But here she was, Jack's only hope. "I mean, come on. You talked in the library. You want me to help? Then say something!"

But she knew it didn't work that way. He had his reasons for staying silent.

She sighed, hurt and confused. She kept seeing Jack's mother with her sad blue eyes. The longing in her voice when she'd talked about "my Jack."

"I…I don't think you have a lot of time," she whispered.

He watched her, those big gray eyes on hers.

"Okay," she said, coming to a decision. She gathered herself up, coming to her feet. "My mom, she knows a lot more about this kind of thing. She can help."

Instantly, her vision was filled with the image of her mother lying dead in her studio.

"No!" she told him. "I don't believe you. I think you're just trying to scare me so I won't tell her about you. But I'm just a kid, Jack," she said, for the first time using his name. "I can't do this by myself."

His expression remained unchanged; still, she sensed a difference in him.

"Jack?"

She realized his image was getting dimmer.

"Jack? What are you doing?"

He was disappearing right before her eyes.

"All right, all right," she said, giving in. "I get it. It's me or nothing." She stepped closer, trying to act as if she wasn't afraid. "I won't tell anyone. I swear."

He became solid again.

She remembered all the things her mother had been telling her about the Fegaris women. Stella told herself this was what she was born to do. Help spirits like ghost boy. She was a Fegaris, just like her mother.

Only, Jack wasn't a ghost. Not yet.

"I can help you, Jack. But you have to show me how. Maybe if you led me to where she's keeping you. Can you do that, Jack?"

She didn't know what else to do. Once she found him, then she could call the cops.

They'd be safe then, both of them.

It was a decent plan, she told herself. Unfortunately, it was the only plan she had.

37

Carin sat in her hotel room. She'd taken a shower and was on the king-size bed wearing cut-off sweat pants and a T-shirt.

Three ibuprofen hadn't made a dent in the headache that bastard had given her.

Jesus, she didn't even know his name.

She'd been trained in the art of combat. She knew how to incapacitate a man, even one that towered over her own near six feet. But what that guy did, it was like nothing she'd ever learned at the academy. She'd been out cold in an instant.

On the bed in front of her, she'd lined up the four evidence bags. Each contained a rock etched with a design.

He'd known about the stones found in the victims' hands—which meant he was somehow connected to the murders. And now, he'd vanished.

Shit.

She scrubbed her face with her hands. There'd been something about him, that disarming smile. And more. He projected the idea that here was a man who would work to find out everything about her, down to the smallest detail.

To use you.

"What's wrong with me?" she said.

But why lie? It was more than his good looks that captivated. She couldn't remember a time when a man had made her heart race.

Zag and a possible killer. "Atta girl, Carin," she said. "You can really pick them."

She told herself he'd caught her off guard. Until today, he wasn't even a suspect, just a guy lost in the labyrinth that was Mission Bay and the larger San Diego area, looking for a good place to eat, maybe even some company.

Carin took a breath. Not that it mattered, the how or why of what happened at the bar—even if she'd fallen for some stupid sexual tension—not if it yielded results.

She stared back at the stones, visible through the clear plastic bags. He'd said it was a puzzle. The last two hours, she'd been sitting here, placing the rocks in different formations.

You like puzzles, don't you, Carin?

"I freaking hate puzzles."

What Carin liked was to be in control, something that appeared unlikely in this case.

She frowned. She'd been positioning the evidence bags around to make the etched markings form a recognizable image. Only, she couldn't see how that was possible. The stones were round and smooth. There were no edges to fit together. Most of the markings didn't even reach the end of the stones but rather were centered on the flat surface.

You like puzzles, don't you, Carin?

"Two fucking hours and I've got nothing but a headache."

Even as she said the words out loud, the idea came. Maybe that was the problem. She wasn't *doing* anything.

She licked her lips and began repositioning the stones on the bed like a street performer moving pieces in a shell game. She wasn't quite sure why she did it. Maybe because she was getting the feeling that someone was playing games with her—or maybe because what *she* needed was to lose control and stop staring at the stones and hoping to find something that probably wasn't even there.

She closed her eyes, shifting the stones on the bed faster and faster. She didn't claim to have one ounce of psychic ability, but she knew a hell of a lot about psychic artifacts. She'd dedicated the last twelve years of her life to the study of how they worked. One thing she'd learned working with Estelle and Morgan—even during her time with NISA—was that psychic objects were drawn to energy.

Maybe she lacked any kind of psi powers, but she was a scientist. Motion was kinetic energy.

What the hell. Sometimes the simple things worked best.

She had no idea how long she sat there moving the stones, eyes closed, but suddenly, the stones beneath the plastic began to *feel* warm. She kept at it, moving the evidence bags faster until suddenly, it actually hurt to touch them. They were hot as coals.

She jerked her hands away and opened her eyes.

She expected to find the evidence bags melted, that's how hot the stones had felt. She peeked at her fingertips, but neither the bags nor her fingers were damaged in any way.

The stones now lay in a pattern on the bed cover. If she thought of it as a grid, one stone was at the very top and to the right of the grid. The next two stones lay in the middle just to the left of the top one. The final stone lay below those two, only lined up vertically with the top stone.

She stood and stepped away from the bed, trying to get

a different perspective. If this was an image—a puzzle—then there were several pieces still missing.

"Okay, so how do I fill in the blanks?" she asked herself.

She walked around the bed. She wondered if this might be like one of those puzzles where you had to keep your eyes unfocused in order to see the hidden image.

She kept walking, staring at the stones in their evidence bags, turning to pace back in the opposite direction—until she saw it.

"Fuck me."

She grabbed the notepad off the desk. She ripped out several sheets, then tore those papers into even smaller pieces—sections about the same size as the stones. On each piece, she drew lines and curves. When she was done, she placed the torn pieces of paper among the stones, arranging them on the grid to fill in the blanks.

She took a step back, trying to catch her breath.

There on the bed was what appeared to be a series of concentric circles connected by two lines radiating out from the center. Even though the picture looked disjointed, made from four stones and ripped sheets of paper, she recognized the familiar design.

She was staring at the logo for Halo Industries.

It was late at night, and still there was plenty of traffic heading south on the 405.

The cars whizzed past as Gia stumbled along the side of the road. A few drivers lay on their horns to discourage her encroachment, the sound dropping in pitch in a Doppler effect.

Gia walked on. She was barefoot and wearing pajamas.

She had no idea what she was doing here on the freeway in the middle of the night.

Ahead, a blue Chevy truck pulled off the freeway and onto the soft shoulder. The engine was running and the brake lights were on; clearly the truck had stopped for her. The night was cold, and yet she hesitated.

The passenger side door opened. A girl stepped out of the truck.

"Stella?" Gia asked.

But her daughter didn't respond. Instead, she got back into the truck and shut the door.

Gia started running. The truck ahead was pulling away, picking up speed.

"Stella!"

"Gia! Come on, honey. Wake up!"

She woke suddenly, sucking in air. Seven was there. Immediately, she fell into his arms.

"It's okay," he said. "I'm here. It's just a dream."

Only, they both knew her dreams were never so simple.

She threw back the covers. She was naked and grabbed her robe, the image of her daughter getting into that truck too real to ignore. She shouldered on the robe as she headed down the hall and through the front room.

The last few nights, Stella had returned to sleeping in her room alone. Gia had taken the move as a good sign: Her daughter wasn't afraid anymore. Now she wasn't so sure.

Stella's door was closed. Gia knocked softly, then harder. She didn't wait much longer before she opened the door.

The bed lay empty, the sheets undisturbed.

Seven raced in behind her, having managed to put on his trousers. He grabbed her before her legs crumpled beneath her. If he hadn't been there, she would have fallen to the floor.

On the vanity mirror, Stella had written a message: *Don't worry. I'll be okay.*

Gia stared at the mirror and whispered, "She's gone."

38

Stella stuck out her thumb and readjusted the strap of her backpack, hoping she knew what she was doing.

It's not like ghost boy had drawn a map or anything. He was still deep into the silent treatment. But she'd managed.

It was a little like playing a game of Hot and Cold where someone says "hot" the closer you get to finding a hidden object. Ghost boy's image—or Jack, as she had started to call him—grew more distinct whenever she made the right choice.

Right now, she was standing at the entrance to the 405 heading south, Jack right beside her.

Stella sighed. She would have taken a bus or a cab. She had some money she'd been saving. But the hot-hot-cold approach didn't work that way.

Already, several cars had pulled over to offer a ride. But Jack would just stand there, getting dimmer if she walked toward the car or talked to the driver.

Cold, she figured.

Now, a truck had pulled over, a blue Ford Chevy. Jack immediately walked toward it. She noticed it had San Diego plates.

Hot.

She jogged over to speak with the driver through the

passenger-side window. He looked like he was in his mid-twenties and was wearing the white uniform and hat that house painters wore. He was heading home to San Diego and was happy to give her a lift.

By the time she tossed her backpack onto the bed of the pickup, Jack was already there waiting.

Soon enough, the wind tossed her hair over her face as the truck sped south on the freeway. Stella took off the hairband she'd looped on her wrist earlier and used it to pull back her black curls.

She'd left a note written on her vanity mirror telling her mom not to worry. Not that she believed such a message would be much of a comfort. Her mother would be hysterical. Stella had never done anything like this before.

She'd been hiding a lot of things from Mom lately. She wondered about that a little. Why couldn't Jack trust anyone but her?

He was still seated next to her, watching the passing landscape. He looked so…normal. After a while, she felt herself falling asleep. She sat up, changing positions. She didn't want to miss anything.

An hour and a half later, Jack turned to look at her.

Suddenly, he vanished.

Stella turned and knocked on the cab's window. The driver gave her the thumbs-up and took the next exit.

The driver took her to the nearest gas station. He was really nice. Even though he was young, he looked kind of worried. He actually gave her the riot act about hitchhiking, asking if she wanted to use his cell phone to call someone.

She'd told him she was sixteen.

She held up her own cell phone and said all the right things. Her parents had recently split up; she was having a hard time with it. But she knew running away wouldn't solve anything. She was heading to her older sister's house. Once she got there, she'd call her mom.

She watched the guy drive off. She frowned. She hadn't known she was such a good liar.

"Jack?"

Suddenly, he was there, standing beside her. He started walking away. When she didn't follow immediately, he stopped and looked back, then kept on going.

"Okay, okay," she said, following.

She knew where she was, of course. She came here most weekends. She could just make out the towers of her grandfather's Institute.

She had no idea what it meant. Why had Jack brought her here? In her vision, there'd been a room full of antique furniture and a hospital bed. There was nothing like that at the Institute. Besides, no way her grandfather would hold someone prisoner.

But there was Jack, walking ahead. As usual, he gave her little choice but to follow.

It wasn't until after Carin had dressed and called up her rental car from the valet's desk that she started thinking about the redhead.

That's how she thought of him, *the redhead.* She didn't know his name—not that she'd have believed any name he gave. He was tall, extremely attractive and slightly familiar.

It was the latter fact that bothered her most.

He'd said it himself at the bar: *You've been thinking about me a lot lately…some niggling suspicion at the back of your mind that I look familiar, but you can't place me.*

She'd lost a good half hour doing mental gymnastics,

trying to figure it out. Normally, her next step would be to talk to Morgan; at this point, the redhead's knowledge of the Institute was her best clue. But was Morgan too enmeshed in Zag's camp?

In the end, she knew she had to keep her faith in Morgan. She'd entrusted him with her brother. If she was wrong about Morgan—if she'd made a mistake judging his character—the sooner she learned the truth, the better.

She'd called him at home. When his machine came on, she tried his cell. Morgan lived near the Institute. Sometimes he stayed late into the night working, even bunking down in one of the dormitories set up for staff and clients. Tonight, he was working in his office. She told him to sit tight until she could get there.

When she reached the Institute in San Diego, she parked her car in the back lot. She was just getting out of the RAV4 when she caught sight of a woman slipping inside the back entrance.

It was Evie Slade, Markie's therapist.

She felt a sharp pain like an ice pick go through her head. She dropped back onto the driver's seat, clutching her head.

She didn't know how long she sat there, holding her head, waiting for the pain to stop. But when she did, there was no sign of Evie Slade. She couldn't even be sure it was her.

Which was odd. Carin had trained in Quantico. She'd been first in her class. Her years in science had honed her acute powers of observation. She'd met the woman only once, but still, she should be able to recall her image.

And she couldn't. Every time she tried she saw only Estelle Fegaris holding her brother, Markie, in her arms just as she had twelve years ago.

"What the hell?"

She sat back inside the RAV4 and shut the door. She concentrated, trying to quiet her mind. She kept her breathing deep and even. The pain came again, but this time, she pushed it aside, focusing only on her breathing.

This type of meditation hadn't been part of her training for the FBI. It was Estelle who had taught her how to calm her mind. She'd told Carin the exercise was crucial if she wanted to communicate with her brother someday. Ever since, Carin had spent at least twenty minutes a day meditating, honing her skill at shutting out the noise in her head, quieting her mind just as Estelle had taught her to do.

She took her time, again focusing only on her breath. When she felt she could, when the pain seemed conquered, she slowly probed her head for one image in particular: Evie Slade.

Suddenly myriad pictures flashed through her head like shuffling cards. Evie Slade introducing herself in Markie's classroom. Evie holding Carin's brother, connecting with him in a way that Carin had seen only once before. Mystery redheaded man in this same parking lot asking for directions.

Carin opened her eyes wide.

"They're twins."

Those were her last words before the pain crashed down on her, no longer held at bay by her meditation. She felt herself falling forward, her head landing against the steering wheel.

For the second time that day, Carin Barnes blacked out.

39

Evie leaned back into the shadows.

Fucking asshole was late.

"Figures," she said, checking her cell phone for the third time.

From the beginning, Theodore Fields had struck her as the type to get cold feet. Weak.

Evie didn't like weakness. She could almost hear her father's warning about Adam. *He's weak....*

Adam hadn't wanted to go through with the final session. *If you want to kill him...*

When had that mattered? Of course they died. They *all* died.

Their own mother had died. It was all part of the sacrifice required for greatness. The hope was to make those deaths mean something. If they stopped now, it was all for nothing.

But here was Adam, mewling his weakness, pushing *her* away, making it clear that he knew *she'd* been keeping secrets.

Well, her brother had no idea.

Their father had been right all along. Adam wouldn't stay the course.

But she would.

She heard a rustling and stood. She had excellent hearing. But it wouldn't take much to hear Theodore's lumbering approach.

"Evie?"

Dr. Theodore Fields waddled toward her. He was wearing a black trench coat—no doubt, his idea of the appropriate attire for a break-in. He was already wiping the sweat from his balding head.

"This is insane," he told her.

"But so exciting," she said with a smile as she wrapped her arms around his neck.

Fields was part of the all-important Brain Trust. His ID card had a higher clearance than Evie's, allowing entry into almost every part of the compound. She'd hoped to do better with Theodore—she'd wanted the crystal. But she could see now that would never happen. Zag had his itchy hands on it, and if there was one thing she knew about her lover, he didn't share.

Which meant it was time for plan B.

No, Fields wouldn't get her access to the Eye. But she'd settle for his key card and his fingerprint.

Adam was right. She had been keeping secrets.

"Come on, Theodore," she said sweetly, stepping backward with her arms still around him, guiding him back toward the door. "Why are you so worried?" She bit his ear and whispered, "Are you afraid someone might see us together?"

"Of course I'm afraid we'll be seen. We're here to steal the damn crystal, for God's sake."

She could hear his heart hammering practically out of his skin. Jesus. The man was a heart attack waiting to happen.

"Shouldn't we get going?" he said, staring around.

"This is one of the dormitories, Evie. I hope you don't think the crystal is anywhere near here."

She had told him she knew the location of the Eye of Athena. All she needed was for him to show up with his access card. The man had a big enough ego to actually believe he'd been given that kind of clearance.

Evie had no idea of the crystal's location. She imagined a vault in some secret chamber in the Institute's sub-basement—if Zag hadn't already stolen it. But that's not why she wanted Theodore here or needed his key card.

She held his face in her hands. She was tall enough that she had to lean down to kiss him.

"Now, Theodore. I need you to do something for me, okay?"

"What?" he asked, trying to kiss her back even as she pulled away.

"This."

She put her hand on his shoulder. Immediately, his body went limp. She caught him in her arms and laid him on the ground. She searched through his pockets and found his key card. She dragged his considerable girth the rest of the way to the door.

Once she had him leaning up against the wall next to the security lock, she slid his card through the lock, then immediately placed his thumb on the print pad. The light on the lock blinked green. Quickly, she jammed the large rock she'd found earlier between the door and the jamb, keeping it from closing.

He hadn't even questioned her choice of meeting at the Institute's dormitories until just now. So much for the man's big giant brain. Apparently, it didn't come along with any common sense.

She tied his hands and legs with the silly suspenders he

wore, then she jammed the bow tie into his mouth and strapped it into place with the cloth belt from his trench coat.

She would have killed him. What she did tonight made it impossible for her to continue here at the Institute. But her father thought Fields might be useful in the future. Blackmail was a powerful weapon against a man like Fields.

She dragged him behind some shrubbery. She had no fear that Theodore would point a finger at her. Again, all the man had left was his reputation and she had enough incriminating evidence to destroy him. Tying him up would give him the perfect excuse.

He came up behind me—I couldn't see who it was.

She could depend on Theodore to be self-serving.

"Sweet dreams, Theodore," she said, blowing him a kiss.

She was dressed in black slacks and turtleneck, and wore a scarf to disguise her hair. She kept her head down as she entered the dormitory where Markie Barnes had a room.

It had been easy to hack into the surveillance system. She knew the route used by the security guards and the location of every camera. Even if she was discovered, her presence could be easily explained.

You're going to kill him....

She could still hear her brother's voice. He'd said it like an accusation. Suddenly, Adam was afraid of getting his hands dirty?

She'd tried enabling the host without her brother—to no avail. The boy, Jack, wasn't strong enough. She was beginning to believe none of them would ever be.

Well, if Adam didn't want to play, Evie would just have to find a way to make things happen without him.

What she needed was to become the host. Isn't that what her mother had done? Traveled with only the guidance of her father through time and space?

What she needed was Markie.

At the Institute, she hadn't been able to fully complete their connection. Too many prying eyes—too many weaklings like her brother to stop her from taking risks. Back at the mansion, she'd have him all to herself.

The challenge would be to convince Markie to leave his dormitory room. She'd worked hard to earn his trust, but she'd always felt that slight resistance. It was just enough to stop her from fulfilling her goal with Markie—using him and his quiet mind to allow her to see what her mother had seen.

No, she couldn't rely on Markie's cooperation. She pressed her hand to her pocket where she carried a syringe filled with a sedative.

"I'm coming, Markie. Get ready, my love."

Half an hour after that mind bomb someone planted inside her head left her unconscious, Carin burst into Morgan's office.

He was sitting at his desk. He rose now, alarmed by the sight of her. "Jesus, Carin. What happened to you? You said you were on your way—"

"Markie's therapist, the redhead, Dr. Slade," she said, almost out of breath from running there. "Who is she?"

The look on Morgan's face said it all. *He has something to hide.*

"The redhead! Dr. Slade. Who is she?" she repeated, raising her voice.

Morgan held up a calming hand. "She's someone I know and trust."

"Why?" she asked, coming to lean over his desk. "Why do you trust her?"

There was something there, something Morgan didn't want to tell her.

"Jesus Christ, Morgan." She could barely catch her breath. "What have you done?"

"Your brother is a twenty-three-year-old man, Carin. Don't you think it's time to take a few risks?"

She felt as if her heart would burst right out of her chest. "What kind of risks?"

"Evie Slade is a psychic. She worked for Zag de Rozières at his Halo-effect schools. You might hold the past against him, but Zag only wants to help you. She's the best there is," he assured her. "Zag made sure your brother had the best. That's what I wanted for you and Markie. But I knew if I told you about Dr. Slade's connection to Zag, you'd never accept her."

Carin backed away from the desk. She shook her head in disbelief.

Morgan wouldn't know. He'd been just as much a pawn as Carin.

That's why the man at the bar had inside information on the victims. Through his sister and her connection to Zag.

Evie Slade worked for Zag. And now, a man who bore a striking resemblance to her, who could very well be her twin, had just fingered Zag as the murderer.

What had started as a strange night was now downright weird.

Stella found herself crawling through the air-conditioning system, following a bobbing light that reminded her of a big firefly. The Institute had the kind of suped-up security used in places like this, but Stella had a key card courtesy of her grandfather. Only, her key card hadn't opened any of the dormitory doors.

So now she was following her guide—Jack, in the form of a ball of light—through a maze of aluminum tunnels, dragging her body along on her elbows, sliding her backpack behind her.

When the light finally stopped, she could feel her heart go into overdrive. There, just ahead, was a vent.

She watched as the ball of light passed right on through.

Stella came in closer. She tried to peer through the vent to the room below, but all she saw was that damn ball of light. It was floating, doing this funny figure eight in the air almost as if it were waiting for her to make the next move. The only thing she could think was that somehow here was Jack, or at least the next step to finding him.

She turned in the tight quarters. Using her feet, she pushed out the vent screen. She heard it clatter to the ground. She held her breath, waiting for lights or sirens or shouting.

The room remained dark and quiet.

She turned and peered into the room. All she saw was the ball of light still weaving in its eerie figure eight.

"In for a penny," she said to herself.

She grabbed her backpack and lowered herself into the room. Her toes didn't quite touch, but she didn't think it was too far a drop. She let go.

She hit the floor harder than she'd expected and felt her legs giving way. She gave herself a couple of seconds, then stood. She let her eyes adjust to the darkness, then looked around the room—and froze.

There was someone sleeping in the bed.

Could this be one of Jack's captors? she thought.

She fumbled through her backpack and found several pens but discarded them for the compass she used in geometry. If she opened it wide enough, it had a sharp metal end that could cause some serious damage. She took it out, holding it like a weapon. She reached for the light switch and turned it on.

The man sat up in bed and turned toward her. He didn't seem the least alarmed to find her standing there. He had dark blond hair and gray eyes and looked like he was somewhere in his twenties, except he was wearing pajamas with penguins on them. They looked like the kind of thing a kid might wear.

And there was ghost boy, standing next to the bed.

"Tell me where he is," she demanded in a shaking voice. "Take me to Jack."

The man carefully pulled back the bed covers and stood. Stella held out the compass menacingly.

"Tell me!"

Whether it was the compass needle in her hand or something else, the man stopped. Jack stood right next to him, looking at her with almost the exact same expression as the man.

"You should leave," the man said quite plainly. "You're in danger."

40

Stella kept the compass in her hand. It was metal and damn sharp, but the guy was pretty big. She wasn't going to do a lot of damage, not with the compass. The best she could hope was to surprise him enough to run away if she had to.

"Why? Why am I in danger? Do you know Jack?" she asked, trying to sound forceful. "Come on! You know *something*. Tell me!"

The man didn't answer her.

Great. Another one with the silent act.

She looked around the room. It was your typical dorm room. There was a desk with a chair and an armchair and a bed. On the desk she could see a wooden puzzle, the kind they used sometimes in IQ tests at school. Next to it was a box of crayons.

She stared back at the man, confused. She knew the dormitories were for staff or visiting faculty. Some of the subjects who volunteered also stayed here, but she'd never thought they were dangerous.

"Wh-where's Jack?" she asked, losing some of her nerve.

"You're in danger here. Leave now."

Despite his dire warning, his expression had changed very little.

She didn't know what to make of him. Jack stayed right

there, standing next to the guy. She'd come here because of Jack, following his lead, only it looked like a dead end.

"Look," she said, trying a different tactic. "I'm trying to help this kid. His name is Jack. And he's in a lot of trouble. Like, someone might kill him if I don't find him really soon." She tried to remember the woman's name, Jack's mother. "Jack Blake. He's about my age, but he's kind of tall for a kid. I think you're supposed to know him. Or maybe help me find him?"

She caught a slight movement; the man's head turned. He looked right down at Jack there next to him.

She dropped the compass in shock. "You see him, don't you?"

In the same precise voice, the man repeated, "Leave now."

Beside him, Jack vanished.

"Jack?"

She backed away, suddenly afraid. She'd done something wrong—she'd misunderstood a clue. She backed up against the door. She fumbled for the knob, keeping her eyes on the guy, wishing now she hadn't dropped the compass. But when she turned the knob, it didn't open.

It was locked from the outside.

She felt a sudden chill. Whoever this was, this man wearing kid's pajamas, he was dangerous enough to get locked in for the night.

She heard a noise. She recognized it immediately—the same sound all the doors made at the Institute whenever a key card slid through the lock.

Someone was coming.

Slowly, the door behind her began to open.

Gia could barely catch her breath. She knew what Seven was doing, trying to help her reconstruct her dream.

"She was in a truck," she said. "A pickup. It was on the freeway."

But the dream remained a blur. Her thoughts kept racing. She couldn't focus. All she could think about was her daughter. That Stella was missing.

Don't worry. I'll be okay.

Stella had written the message on the vanity mirror with a dry marker, trying to somehow alleviate what she knew would be her mother's fears. But Gia read beyond the words, interpreting a darker message.

The spirit was back. And he was leading her daughter somewhere—most likely into danger, given what she knew of Jack's circumstances.

"I was driving her away with all my questions," she'd told Seven. "I could see how she just shut down every time. Then, when she started sleeping alone in her room, I thought she had control of it—while I couldn't get a hold of my own fears for her. I thought we had more time."

But time had just run out.

Seven had already called in the Amber Alert. Every highway patrol and beat cop out there would be looking for Stella.

But Gia knew it would do no good. What was happening to her daughter wasn't about a kidnapping. It was about the spirit of a boy whose life was in danger. He wouldn't care who he sacrificed.

"Okay, we both know it's not a coincidence that you see your daughter hitchhiking in a dream and wake up to find her gone." They were seated at the bistro table in the kitchen. Seven had brought his chair around so that they faced each other.

"Take a breath," he urged. "You'll remember. You just need to quiet your mind. Any little detail can help."

But it all seemed a blur of fear. "I can't do this," she said, looking up at him.

He cupped her face in his hands. "Yes, you can. You have never doubted your spirit gift or guide or whatever you call it. Now, close your eyes."

She did what he asked, putting herself in his hands, at the moment trusting his instincts.

"Take deep breaths. That's good. Don't even try to remember. Keep your mind a perfect blank and breathe."

She listened to his voice, blanking out any other sounds.

"Imagine that beautiful blank space in your head is one of your canvases. You reach for a brush and dip it into the paint."

She kept breathing, trying to channel that calm in his voice.

"Now, look at the tip of the brush," he told her. "What is the color of the paint?"

"Blue."

"Okay, good. Now, go ahead and paint. Don't look at what you're doing until you're done." He gave it a minute. "What do you see?"

"A truck," she said. "A blue Chevy."

"Now, put that Chevy on the freeway. Can you see any signs? An exit or speed limit?"

Suddenly, she saw it. The freeway shield with the number 405.

"405, she's on the 405." And then, looking back at the truck on the canvas of her mind, she added, "The plates. The truck has San Diego plates."

Right then, Seven's cell phone rang. He cursed softly at the interruption, but, under the circumstances, they both knew he had to answer. He did so immediately.

Gia watched his face, but he gave nothing away.

When he slapped the phone shut, he said, "That was Erika. She just heard about the Amber alert. She's been doing a little snooping around on her own. Did you know your father was taking care of Markie Barnes?"

"Yes. At the Institute—" again, the vision of that license plate flashed in her head "—in San Diego." She stood, staring up at Seven. "If Stella were ever in any trouble—something she didn't want to tell me—she'd get in touch with Morgan."

He opened his phone again. "I'll call Barnes, you call Morgan."

Carin opened the door and rushed inside. She wasn't sure what she thought she'd find, racing here to her brother's room—she wasn't even sure why she thought he was in any danger. According to Morgan, Evie Slade had been his therapist for months.

So why this pounding in her chest? Was it the visit from a man who could be Evie's twin, or even seeing the woman at the Institute so late at night? Whatever the reason, she just knew she needed to find Markie *now,* needed the relief of seeing him asleep in his bed.

What she found was her brother standing in his pajamas, completely awake, the lights on.

She ran over to him, practically tripping on something on the floor. She wrapped her arms around him, holding him. Markie was considerably taller than Carin. It felt good, seeing him here, safe and sound.

"You're okay, Markie. You're going to be fine."

Strapped to the side of her belt, her BlackBerry sounded. She brushed the hair from her brother's face and sat him down on the bed.

"I'm sorry I just barged in like that. I hope I didn't scare you, okay?"

She didn't expect her brother to answer. She hadn't heard her brother's voice in twelve years. No one had.

The BlackBerry kept ringing.

Giving her brother a reassuring smile, she pulled out the BlackBerry. When she saw who was calling, she told Markie, "A minute, okay? Barnes," she barked into the phone.

The call was from Detective Seven Bushard.

Carin listened as he filled her in. There was an Amber Alert. Stella Moon was missing. Gia thought she might be heading down to her grandfather's in San Diego…which brought up the matter of her own brother's residence there. Some might consider it a little suspicious that Markie was under the care of one of the therapists employed by Zag, the very man she just fingered for the murder of four. How had she failed to mention that little gem, he wondered?

But Carin was barely listening. She was staring at the floor in Markie's room. There, right where she'd tripped on it when she ran into the room, was a backpack.

As Detective Bushard continued his tirade, something about Erika knowing "what she'd done," Carin opened the backpack and searched through it. She found a Mickey Mouse wallet in one of the inside pockets.

Even before she pulled out the student ID, she knew what she'd see.

Stella Moon's smiling face.

41

Stella ran down the hall. She was a rollercoaster off its tracks. She didn't even feel her feet hit the floor.

She had no idea who the woman was, the one who'd opened the door and burst inside, flying past her. She hadn't waited around to find out if she was friend or foe. She had no idea why Jack had disappeared like that, but she didn't take it as a good sign.

She turned the corner, heading for the nearest exit, running so fast that she tripped over her own feet.

She should have fallen facefirst; she'd braced herself for just that. Then, out of nowhere, a set of arms seemed to be there, catching her.

The arms belonged to a woman. She was dressed all in black. She was wearing a scarf around her head, but a wisp of hair had escaped. It was a memorable deep red.

Even as her fingers tightened around Stella's arms, she recognized her as the woman in her vision, the one hurting Jack.

The woman smiled, showing even white teeth.

Before Stella knew what was happening, the woman twisted her around and locked Stella under her arm. Her free hand slapped across Stella's mouth.

Stella felt the stab of a syringe.

The woman leaned down and whispered, "Hello, darling. Where are you going in such haste?"

Gia sat in Morgan's office. Her father paced from one end of the spacious room to the other. She knew exactly how he felt. He managed to project his emotions quite clearly. Guilt. Despair.

The Institute was now a designated crime scene. Police and FBI roamed the grounds, investigating what was clearly some kind of malfeasance, given the discovery of Dr. Fields bound and gagged and Stella's backpack.

There was no sign of Stella.

In Morgan's office, a different sort of investigation was taking place.

Zag de Rozières sat on the low-slung leather couch. Looming over him, her arm pulling her jacket from her hip to expose her weapon, stood Special Agent Carin Barnes. If that wasn't intimidating enough, Seven hovered at the man's right.

"Am I being accused of a crime?"

Zag was also dressed all in black, the leather jacket and pants embossed in panels to look like snakeskin. The outfit said he'd been pulled away from an evening out, but his near-colorless eyes gave nothing away.

"Should I have counsel present?" he asked.

Seven sat down on the couch beside Zag, flashing a smile that could cut steel. The two men couldn't be more opposite. Seven was the taller of the two, with the body of a middleweight fighter and a look in his eyes that said he wouldn't mind going a few rounds with Zag. With his legs casually crossed, Zag had a more sinewy strength. He wore his eyeliner smudged Goth style and his white-blond hair immaculately gelled into a fauxhawk, the perfect image of a man used to flashing a smile for the stalkerazzi.

Seven put his arm across the back of the couch, managing to make the gesture menacing. "Now why would you need an attorney, de Rozières? We're all friends, right? You're part of—what do you call it, Morgan? A Brain Trust? Maybe we just want some input from a big important man such as yourself. Unless, of course, you have something to hide?"

"Zag has plenty to hide." It was Carin's turn to play the badass FBI agent. "Here's the thing, Zag. There were stones found with each one of those murdered kids. Perfect replicas of the Bimini Stones—you know about those, don't you?"

The man looked up at Carin. In his gaze there appeared to be a hint of something. Remorse? "I believe you know the answer to that, dear heart."

"That's right," she said, steamrolling over any possible emotion. "Whoever etched those marking into the stones made them *look* just like the artifacts. Only, you couldn't stop there. No, you wanted to be *clever.* So you made the stones fit together like a puzzle forming your company's insignia." She leaned in close. "What was it, Zag? Your way of giving us the finger?"

Gia sat in one of two wingback chairs across from Zag, her legs curled beneath her. She'd been watching him carefully during his interrogation, close enough that she'd caught a hint of something when he'd first responded to Carin. Now, the only thing she saw in those kohl-rimmed eyes was amusement.

"I assure you, Agent Barnes," he said, looking more pleased than concerned. "I would never be such an idiot. I'm a little insulted that you would even think it possible."

"Sometimes, people like you," Seven said, "they leave

clues. You didn't really want to hurt those kids. And now you *want* us to stop you."

Again, the man seemed completely unfazed. "Morgan, this is a waste of time. I have no knowledge about your granddaughter's disappearance or the murder of those children."

Morgan took three quick steps toward Zag. Immediately, Gia stood and blocked his way.

"Father," she said. "Sit down."

Morgan waited for a frozen moment, torn between listening to Gia and strangling the truth out of Zag.

Gia turned and looked calmly at Zag. She said, "You're lying."

His amused expression didn't change. "About which part?"

"You son of a bitch."

But again, Gia held up a hand, shutting down Seven's attack. "He didn't kill those children—and he didn't take Stella."

Carin didn't change her menacing pose over Zag. "Are you sure, Gia?"

"She's my daughter, Carin. Of course I'm sure."

She kept her gaze on Zag, trying to block out the energy from everyone else in the room. She thought she sensed something behind that cocky smile of his. *Fear?*

"Everyone, please leave the room," she said.

She didn't bother to listen to the chorus of protests. She remained completely focused on Zag.

"If you don't leave now," she said quietly. "I won't be able to help my daughter."

She said it with quiet authority, and still, they hesitated.

"Morgan," she said, knowing her father would understand. "I need to do this alone."

She waited, standing there as he ushered everyone out into the hall, Seven being the last to leave. As soon as the door shut, she walked over and sat down next to Zag on the couch. He had the eyes of a chameleon. They would change with his mood or the color of his clothes. At the moment, they appeared the palest shade of silver, the same color as his hair.

She cocked her head. "You're hiding something— something that makes you *very* afraid."

He didn't respond, but the smile on his face had turned into an ironic twist.

"Do you know what frightens you, Zag?" she asked. "Because I do. The thing that scares you to your core is the possibility that you could be wrong." She waited a beat. "It scares me, as well. It frightens me that your mistake may have cost those poor children their lives. That it may cost my daughter hers."

The smile disappeared, but his gaze never wavered. He lifted his hands and started clapping.

"Very good, Gia," he said. "But then, you are the daughter of Estelle Fegaris. She was one of the best, you know. I had the pleasure of meeting her once. I'm afraid I didn't make a good impression."

"I can't imagine."

"I'll tell you the same thing I said to your mother—you should be working for me. You're wasted on those poor souls you try to help with your paintings."

"Tell me what you know," she said.

He sighed, for the first time, looking away. "Possibly not enough."

42

Stella woke up in stages, slowly surfacing past the fog in her head. She was sitting in a chair that seemed to be circling and rocking like a top losing its momentum until it settled into place.

A bleary light suffused the room. She realized it came from a fireplace. There were also light fixtures attached to the walls like torches. She blinked, having trouble focusing.

She remembered a sharp sting—remembered that she'd thought it might be a needle.

Just like in my dream.

The realization that she'd been drugged brought a rush of adrenaline. Her blurred vision settled into two identical images.

It took her a moment to understand: Not identical—a man and a woman.

They looked alike. Twins.

"Are you the granddaughter of Estelle Fegaris?"

The question came from a male voice somewhere behind her. She tried to turn to look at him, but found she couldn't move. Her hand was stuck somehow.

She looked down. Someone had used plastic ties to anchor her wrists to the arms of the chair.

"Are you the granddaughter of Estelle Fegaris?" the voice repeated.

"Of course she is," said the woman. "Didn't I tell you she was?"

It was the redhead from her dream, the woman who drowned those kids.

The redhead stepped forward. She knelt down in front of Stella. She was tall enough that, even kneeling, she towered over Stella.

"I saw you," she said, smiling. She wore only mascara and a bright red lipstick; her beauty didn't require anything more. "You visit Morgan on weekends. He sends his chauffeur. Sometimes even the company helicopter. Grandpa likes to impress," she said, with an expression in her bright blue eyes that made her look hungry with anticipation. "Oh, he's very proud of you." She reached up and stroked Stella's hands. "He has pictures of you all over his desk."

The redheaded man, the twin, grabbed the woman's arm and pulled her to her feet. "Stop it, Evie."

"Why?" she asked. She put her arms around her twin, hugging him. The brother was tall, way taller than Evie.

She had even white teeth and a beautiful smile. "Trust me, Adam. You don't have to be careful with her. Can't you feel it? She's so strong."

Adam and Evie.

"You look like her. Like Estelle Fegaris." This time, the man stepped from behind her chair into the light. He wasn't tall like the other two—he barely reached Adam's shoulder. He looked old, older even than Morgan.

"If they're Adam and Eve, who are you?" Stella asked. "God?"

Evie laughed, delighted. "See? What did I tell you?"

Adam pushed his sister away and came forward. He crouched down in front of Stella. When his gaze met hers, she felt strange, almost light-headed.

He stood. "Maybe too strong."

"Nonsense." Evie turned back to God. "Nathaniel, she's exactly what we need."

God—Nathaniel—came to stand next to Evie. The twins, they were beautiful, like two angels with red hair. But this guy, he looked like a gnome. He had dark hair and milky-blue eyes framed by bushy eyebrows.

"Estelle Fegaris was a powerful psychic, the only one ever to manage the crystal." He glanced over at Adam. "What do you see?"

Once again, she felt the man's clear blue gaze on her.

"This is a mistake," Adam said.

Evie playfully punched her twin in the arm. She knelt down in front of Stella's chair again and covered Stella's hands with hers.

"You couldn't be more wrong," she said. "This is an opportunity." There was an almost scary reverence to her voice. "We can start over. She's better than the others. Perhaps even better than Markie." Where Evie touched her, Stella's hands started to feel warm. "Maybe even better than the crystal itself."

"I'm here to save Jack," Stella cried out, desperate for the woman to let go.

But Evie's fingers wrapped around hers, heating up. "Not to mention, Father, that—as they say—my cover is blown. Zag and Morgan, they won't be fooled again."

Evie squeezed Stella's fingers. The fire in her hands crept up to Stella's shoulders. It burned into her lungs.

I can't breathe!

She felt herself arch up, almost out of the chair. But Evie and the ties on her wrists kept her tethered there.

The last thing she heard was Evie whispering, "You, my darling, are more than enough."

43

For the first time in her life, Carin Barnes felt out of control. She wanted to kill him; she wanted to pull the trigger and shoot her 9 mm straight into the bastard's black heart.

Zag, you piece of shit.

They were still in Morgan's office, no closer to finding Stella Moon. To complicate matters, not only did Zag continue to proclaim his innocence, he'd somehow managed to convince Gia, the girl's mother, of it.

Now, he wanted Gia to use the crystal, the Eye of Athena, on Markie, Carin's brother.

"Do you want to waste time cross-examining me or save the girl?" Zag asked.

"What I want," Carin said, "appears to be irrelevant." Not since Carin had made the colossal mistake of stepping out to give Zag one-on-one time with Gia.

Zag looked over at Morgan. "She could do it. She could reach Markie. Her mother did."

"What the hell is he talking about?" Seven asked.

Zag hadn't actually brought up the crystal. Only he, Morgan and Carin knew what he meant when he suggested a session between Gia and Markie.

The lying snake had managed to manipulate Gia,

frighten her into taking any risk for her daughter's life. Now, Carin had to decide if he was doing the same to her, if he was manipulating them all.

"Carin," Zag said, "Markie was the last to see her."

"Morgan? What's he asking Gia to do?" Seven asked, pressing for answers.

"It could work," Zag said, his voice gaining strength. "There are kids at the Halo schools just like Markie. But none of them had his experience." He turned to look at Morgan. "Estelle, she changed him—changed his condition, putting him on a different level. Evie saw that much in her sessions with him. That's why she insisted on working with him."

"It's a terrible risk," Morgan said. But in his gaze, Carin saw the beginnings of acceptance.

"Gia could use the Eye," Zag said, for the first time mentioning the crystal by name. "She could reach Markie, find out what happened in that room."

Seven stepped forward, realizing what was going on. He grabbed Carin by the arm and turned her around. "Jesus Christ. Erika said you stole it. I didn't believe her."

Carin didn't try to break away. She'd always known this day would come. Somehow, it didn't surprise her that Erika Cabral was the one to uncover her secrets.

"When she called tonight," Seven continued, "she told me you changed out the artifact for a fake and kept the real one. She said you used the Eye as collateral, so that Morgan would help your brother."

Zag looked at Carin and smiled. "Oops," he said.

But they didn't have time for recriminations. "That's right," she said. "I changed out the real artifact. This is where it belongs—at the Institute, with Morgan."

Seven released Carin. He turned to Gia. "Did you know?"

But she was shaking her head, just as surprised as Seven.

"Don't you get it?" Carin asked. "The FBI would have buried the thing in some lab, never to be seen again. Morgan had a chance to use it to help people."

"People like your brother?" Seven asked.

"I don't know if Evie or anyone else took your daughter," Zag said, interrupting. "But here's what I do know. Stella was in that room with Markie. Whatever else happened, the information is trapped in Markie's head."

Zag walked over to Gia and placed his hands on her shoulders. There was fire in those eyes. "Use the crystal. Your mother would have."

Seven pushed Zag aside. He took Gia in his arms, forcing her to look at only him. "Listen very carefully to me, sweetheart. You said it yourself—that thing is cursed or haunted. It drives people insane. Remember Thomas? He tried to kill you. The mother of his only child."

"Thomas wasn't Gia," Zag said. "She's the daughter of Estelle Fegaris."

"Please, baby," Seven urged. "Don't do it. We can find her. Let me work the case. Look at the evidence."

But even as he argued, he knew it was futile. Gia could see in his eyes how much he hated what she had to do.

Gia took his hands in both of hers. "It's Stella," she said. "It's my daughter, Seven."

After a moment, she turned to look at her father. "How do we start?"

44

Stella was back in front of the beautiful temple. Space cars hovered overhead like a flock of sparrows. The cobbled stones looked like they were made of molten metal.

Just like before, people floated around her in gowns made from some iridescent material she didn't recognize. They wore crystals around their necks. No one acknowledged her presence. She was a ghost.

The crowd slowly parted. Standing there, waiting for her was a woman.

Evie.

She was dressed all in white. A shimmering light emanated from around her as she held out her hand.

Stella moved toward Evie, her feet floating above the strange metallic stones.

She realized she was in that place Evie went to when she'd done that weird Vulcan mind meld with Jack. Before, Stella had seen it through Jack's eyes. Now, everything looked brighter, sharper.

"I knew you were the one." Stella heard Evie's words inside her head. "You're so strong."

Stella didn't feel strong. She felt as if her head was stuffed with cotton and her body tingled. She was under some sort of spell, trapped in the mind of a madwoman.

"I tried so hard with the others," Evie said, continuing to talk inside Stella's head. "But they always gave up. I could feel them slipping away, weak as rice paper in my hands."

Evie never lost her smile. There was no reason for her to speak out loud. Anything she wanted to convey was coming in loud and clear.

"You have no idea how many years—how many lives— it has taken to get here."

Stella realized Evie thought they were in Atlantis, the city in the library book. Stella told herself that wasn't possible. She was still sitting in that chair in the old-fashioned room. This thing that Evie did with her mind, it was just that—something she did with her mind.

Stella told herself to move, to get away. There was nothing holding her here.

Move!

But she couldn't. Instead, she just floated there in front of Evie.

Before, when Evie had seized her hands, Stella had felt hot. On fire. But now she felt frozen stiff with paralyzing cold.

"Markie was Zag's idea. He had these theories. His Atlantis Project, he called it. But you—" Evie stroked her face "—You're the real deal."

She's going to make me do something, Stella thought. *Something awful.*

"Don't be afraid." Evie held out her hand again. "You're on a righteous path. We'll go there now. Together."

45

It wasn't the first time Seven had watched Gia risk everything. In fact, it was starting to feel like a bad habit, standing on the sidelines of her life, waiting for things to go bump in the night.

"This is a mistake," he said.

Special Agent Barnes didn't bat a lash. She kept her attention focused strictly on Morgan as he handed Gia, his only child, the Eye of Athena. For Morgan and Barnes, this was just another day in their paranormal world.

Seven, too, had seen the artifact before…unfortunately, that had been at the scene of a multiple homicide.

The crystal was half the size of his fist and was wrapped in what looked like a ball of gold wires. Supposedly, depending on the light, the stone itself could appear a deep blue or the crimson-red of blood. At the moment, it was a dull, dark blue. In Seven's opinion, it didn't look all that special. Hard to believe it had any special powers. Where were all the bells and whistles?

At least, that's what he told himself as he watched Gia focus on the damn thing as if it were a Magic 8-Ball about to reveal the fate of mankind.

To Gia, who did believe, it just might.

She was seated in a chair across from Markie Barnes,

a twenty-three-year-old autistic man. Markie remained stoic on his bed, allowing Carin, his older sister, to hold his hand as everyone watched and waited.

Ironically, the last time Seven had witnessed a similar scenario, it had been Stella, Gia's daughter, trying to find her mother. Back then, Seven had helped Stella access "the power" within. She'd come up with the address where her father had been holding a gun to her mother's head. At the time, he hadn't questioned the why or how of it. He'd been too busy trying to save Gia's life.

But this was different. Here, he was out of the loop. Powerless. He could only stand by and watch Gia cup the crystal in her hands, waiting for some power he'd begun to believe she truly possessed to kick in. Worried what it might do to her.

He knew the Eye's bloody history.

And still, he could do nothing. It didn't feel good; it didn't feel right. He didn't want to be safe when Gia was sitting right in front of him rolling the dice.

Maybe that was the problem, he thought. Why had it taken him ten months to end up back at her door? Not because she'd lied or betrayed him. He had to face the possibility that what kept him away was fear, pure and simple.

He didn't understand her world. He wanted to laugh and say it was all bullshit. Instead, here he was watching her with his heart in his throat.

As if somehow connecting to that fear, Gia suddenly tensed in her chair. Before anyone even noticed the change in her, Seven was at her side, ready to rip the crystal out of her hand.

He didn't get the chance.

She dropped to her knees in front of Markie, the crystal still tight in her grip, glowing with an eerie blue light.

She threw her head back and screamed.

As soon as Gia held the crystal in her hands, she thought about her mother.

She didn't need the Eye as a reminder. She had a very important one in her life: Stella, her mother's namesake. She was the vision of her grandmother.

All her life, Estelle had spoken of the crystal as if it were a family heirloom. She believed the crystal was the key to paranormal abilities. If the Eye could enhance the Sibyl's power to foretell the future during the time of Apollo, surely it could guide the average man or woman to find the psychic within.

That had been her mother's goal: to make what was feared—what was unique—commonplace. Magic available to every man would no longer be magic.

There was only one problem. Thus far, anyone who had touched the crystal lost their mind.

Except Estelle.

Now, Gia held the Eye clutched in her hands, feeling its energy wrap around her heart and expand her mind.

Suddenly, the room was gone. The only thing she saw was Markie.

She didn't see him on a physical realm—this wasn't a room with a floor and ceiling and chairs.

Markie appeared the same as he had in his room, a man wearing children's pajamas with vacant eyes and dark blond hair. And yet, the experience felt extremely *physical.* As if it were an easy thing to take a step forward and hold his hand.

There was a part of Gia that experienced a different

reality. In a small corner of her mind, she fell to her knees and screamed in agony.

But here she felt no pain. In this dimension, she held Markie's hand without consequence. She could peer into his eyes and see what he had seen.

Stella.

There she was. Her daughter.

Stella was standing in front of Markie, screaming at him, demanding that he help her to find Jack.

Gia found herself asking the same.

"Where's Jack?"

It was a simple enough question. But there was nothing simple about Markie's condition. Even as she asked the question, his eyes rolled back into his head, showing only the whites.

It happened too quickly, that wall between what she did here, in this dimension, and what was going on in Markie's room fell away. The pain she'd pushed to that corner of her consciousness became all too real. It swept over her, bringing with it a blanket of darkness.

The last thing she remembered was the crystal in her hand glowing a vibrant cerulean-blue.

Seven reached for Gia. Before he could touch her, Barnes pushed him out of the way.

"Look at her hand," she said.

Gia lay prone on the floor, but her right hand was stretched out across the carpet. The fingers appeared crimped around an invisible pen. Her wrist moved as if she were writing something.

Carin walked over to the desk at the far corner of the room. She searched through the drawers until she found several pieces of construction paper. There was also a box of crayons. She slipped out the black crayon and, taking Gia's hand, wrapped her fingers around it.

Gently, she lifted Gia's hand and placed the construction paper on the floor beneath it. She stepped back and watched as Gia's fingers continued to move.

Eventually, the scrawled markings began to form words: *Keep out, keep out, keep out.*

When the words crept off the page, Carin slipped a new sheet of construction paper on the floor. Gia kept writing the same warning.

Keep out.

Seven stepped forward, transfixed. He knelt down beside Gia, watching as she continued to write.

It didn't make sense—not in his world. And still, here was Gia in this trance.

He pulled out his cell phone and brought up the photograph of Gia's last painting, the one of the old Victorian house. He showed it to Carin.

In the painting, the signs posted on the lawn and in the windows and doors were clearly visible. Each and every one said the same thing.

Keep out.

Seven heard someone swear behind him. He turned to see Zag standing there.

"What is it?" Seven walked over to Zag. He practically shoved the phone in the man's face, repeating, "What do you see?"

Zag took the phone from Seven, gripped by the image on the screen.

"The detective asked a question," Carin prompted.

His eyes still on the painting, Zag said quite clearly, "I know where they are."

46

Stella was in front of what looked like an enormous blue obelisk. She was floating just off the ground, close enough to the stone to see her face reflected on the glass surface. Only, as she peered closer, her image became fragmented, as if she were staring into an enormous crystal.

The firestone generates energy...its preparation is in the hands of the initiates...invisible rays act on the aircraft and pleasure crafts...rays emanate from the stone at the power station...the Sons of Belial destroy...

She'd heard those very words before. They came from that Atlantis book, the section about Edgar Cayce, the sleeping prophet. It was the same passage Jack had showed her.

She realized she was inside the temple she'd seen before. There were strange inscriptions written all over the walls. The enormous crystal before her had to be the firestone Cayce talked about during one of his psychic predictions. According to Cayce, the crystal allowed the people of Atlantis to do fantastic things. Only, the people began to abuse the crystal. Eventually, it led to their destruction.

But not before a few refuges escaped. Atlantean society was divided into two political factions—the Sons of the

Law of One and the Sons of Belial. According to Cayce, the former were the good guys.

Evie, she thought. *She thinks she's a descendant of Atlantis.*

Stella felt dizzy with the thought. She told herself none of this was real. She was trapped in some weird mind game with a powerful psychic. She couldn't allow herself to fall into Evie's dementia. That's how the others had died. Evie used them up like so much fuel.

But there was Evie, standing at the temple door.

"Look inside the crystal, Stella. There you'll see the secrets of the universe."

The firestone had been erected in the middle of the temple. The building itself was oval and had a stone dome. Stella imagined the dome would open, giving access to the stars like an observatory.

"Is that what you made the others do, Evie? Look into the crystal?"

"I told you, they were weak. Only you and Markie ever brought me this far, and Markie, never inside the temple. The others got lost in a different past, stuck in time in their minds. They went insane, reliving their own worst nightmares."

Stella heard Evie's words like a strange echo inside her head. She realized she already knew what had happened to Evie's victims—she knew about this place, too…knew about the firestone and how it was used to control all matter in the universe, even dark matter. And she knew these things not because of some passage in a book. That's the secret Evie wanted.

We're connected, she thought. *I'm in her head just as much as she's in mine.*

With the realization came a strange sense of duality. Everything Evie did, she did. Whatever Evie felt, she felt. She knew even before she heard Evie's voice inside her head what to do next.

She felt lighter than air. It was exhilarating, watching her fractured image on the crystal's surface as she rose higher and higher.

I want this just as much as she does.

"That's it." Evie waited below, encouraging her.

That's what Evie had said to Jack in Stella's vision, urging him forward to find just this very place. But Evie was right, the others couldn't come here. They went crazy, lost in some thread in a different past. The elation Evie felt was Stella's. She shared in her joy.

At last!

Stella remained floating before the crystal. Its energy seemed to reach inside her chest, filling her heart. She could feel it pumping blood through her veins with a force that exhilarated like a drug. She was atomic.

"Focus on the crystal, Stella."

She looked into the crystal. In each facet, she could see a million futures and just as many pasts.

She realized this is what she'd been brought here to do, what she alone could accomplish. Travel here, see this. A miracle of time strung together like pearls.

This is Evie's fantasy. Not yours!

And still, she raised her hand and stretched her palm toward the crystal.

As her hand neared, her heart heated up. *No! Too much!*

"Don't give up on me now," Evie said inside her head.

And then it happened. Reflected back in the crystal was another Stella, one willing to lose all control.

She felt lit up. She was energy itself.

She turned away from the obelisk. She wasn't scared anymore. She knew there was nothing Evie could do to her.

She reached her hand toward Evie.

Evie flew across the temple. Her back slammed into the stone wall. She fell in a crumpled heap to the floor.

Evie.

It wasn't Stella speaking, but she heard the voice inside her head in the same manner that Evie heard. She knew the woman was standing behind her, but that didn't matter. She was in Evie's mind. She saw her just as Evie did; she knew who she was.

She had red hair, just like her daughter. And like Stella, she was pure energy.

Evie pushed herself up into a sitting position. Her eyes were wide in disbelief. In a small, questioning voice, she spoke out loud for the first time.

"Mom?"

The woman—or more like the energy of her—filled every inch of the chamber. Evie reached out with her hand, trying somehow to make contact.

Suddenly, Evie, too, floated up, her feet hovering inches off the stone floor. Again Stella felt that eerie duality—she and Evie were one and the same.

Evie, your father has lost his way….

Stella wasn't sure how the woman appeared—or even if she was just a fantasy, a memory Stella plucked from Evie's head. The story she told, too, could very well be a truth Evie had hidden even from herself. It was a tale of love lost and the consequences of that loss. How a dream became a nightmare. In his quest to make his wife's death meaningful, Evie's father had treated his children as expendable then trained them to do the same to others.

This isn't what I want, Evie. It was never what I wanted.

"But it has to be," Evie said, her voice shaking. "Father said I am the Destroyer. He said I was the strong one—the one you would count on to see things through. And I have, Mother. I'm here."

A part of Stella knew she was experiencing the event as Evie would experience it. There was no truth or lies. There was only perspective. The only person who could stop Evie was her mother, whether the energy of the woman was real or a fantasy didn't matter.

There's only one thing I want, Evie. I want you to stop Nathaniel.

Just as quickly as it arrived, the woman's energy dissipated. Only Evie and Stella remained in the temple with the firestone.

They were standing several feet apart in the shadow of the crystal. Evie towered over Stella. She no longer wore white. The clothes she wore now were the same she'd had on in the old-fashioned room—dark pants and turtleneck.

Evie stared into the empty space between them, her eyes blazing not with hope, but with rage.

"I am the Destroyer," Evie said.

The thought seemed locked in the woman's head. Only now, it held a completely different meaning. Hers was no longer the role of a warrior using her gift to help mankind into some kind of evolutionary ascension. It was empty and cold—an end and not a beginning.

It was death, only that.

Stella held her hand out, knowing what she needed to do as Evie lowered her gaze and focused on Stella.

I am the Destroyer.

For the first time, Stella spoke out loud. "Not today."

Stella woke with a sudden start. She was back in the old-fashioned room, still tied to the chair.

Evie lay sprawled out on the floor. Her twin, Adam,

knelt over her. He was staring at Stella, his expression saying it all: Whatever just happened, Stella was responsible.

His attention soon returned to Evie as his sister moaned in his arms. Slowly, she sat up, her brother helping to steady her. But the instant she saw her father, she pushed her brother aside as she stood.

She walked straight toward her father, her hand raised before her. Immediately, he was lifted off his feet. His body crashed against the flowery wallpaper and crumbled to the floor.

"Liar!"

Evie kept coming, following him around the room, raising her hand over and over. Each time, Nathaniel slammed against furniture, the wall, the floor.

"You said I was special. How special am I now, Daddy?"

She raised her hand again—this time, Adam grabbed her from behind and swung her around.

"Did you hear?" she said, screaming the words. "I am special! Not you, Adam. Me! I'm the special one."

Over Adam's shoulder, she saw Stella. It was almost as if the sight of her settled Evie.

She pushed her brother aside and walked slowly toward Stella.

She knelt down before the chair. Stella no longer felt any connection between them. She had no idea what Evie was thinking as she reached into her pocket.

In her hand, she held a pocket knife. She cut off the plastic ties anchoring Stella's wrists to the arms of the chair.

"*You* know I'm special, don't you, Stella? You know what he did, how he made sure that we, the children of

Celeste, would finish her vision. That's what we were taught, you see. There was a plan so great my mother gave her life for it."

The bindings dropped to the ground. She had Stella by her wrist.

The look in her eyes…

"No!" Stella yelled as Evie yanked her to her feet and dragged Stella to the door.

"But I was the special one. I was the one with the courage to follow through to the end of her vision. Not my brother. Only me," Evie said.

Stella grabbed for a chair, the leg of a table, anything to anchor her. But Evie was too strong.

"Adam, his gift is different," Evie continued. "He's the Finder, only that. He's the weak one, isn't that what you told me, Daddy? Only, what you really meant was he couldn't be manipulated by the idea that he was oh so very special. Not like me."

She dragged Stella to her feet and pushed her out of the room. Adam watched, doing nothing.

Stella caught a glimpse of Nathaniel. He, too, watched quietly.

Evie continued down a long hallway, forcing Stella along with her. Adam kept pace behind his sister.

"Help me," Stella cried out to him. "Please."

"They were suffering," Evie continued, talking over Stella's pleas. "I made them suffer. I made them insane. I was the one who could do that because I was strong. And a strong person takes responsibility. It was left to me to stop the suffering."

Evie hauled Stella into a bathroom. Stella grabbed the door, holding on for all she was worth. Evie peeled her fingers off the doorknob. Stella clung to the doorjamb.

She knew this bathroom. She recognized it from her vision. She knew what happened here.

This is where they come to die!

"Please, make her stop! Help me," she screamed again and again.

But Adam did nothing, watching stoically from the bathroom door.

Evie grabbed Stella around her waist and carried her to the bathtub. She dropped her there, pushing her against the porcelain.

"Zag never knew. He thought I was part of his great experiment. His Atlantis Project. He thought *he* was using *me.* But we were using each other."

Stella hit her head on the side of the tub, seeing stars, almost blacking out. Evie pressed her palm to Stella's chest, pinning her there with one hand as she used the other to turn on the water.

"This is where I drowned them. I put the stones in their hands. He wouldn't want them to suffer, that's what Daddy told me. That was his reason: Do it for Zag."

The water was rising now, reaching her shoulders. Stella clawed at Evie's arms, trying to dislodge that pressure on her chest, flailing with her feet, then digging in her heels to try and get some sort of leverage.

"But I knew what he really wanted. He wanted Zag destroyed. And I am the Destroyer. He wanted the bodies found. He wanted the stones brought together. I watched Nathaniel carve each and every one."

She held Stella down in the bathtub. The water kept rising. She was struggling to keep her mouth and nose above it, taking deep, halting breaths.

"All those children, my brother found them. We gave them drugs—we entered their minds. They suffered so much. Only here, their suffering came to an end. Here, they found peace."

The water was now slowly covering her face. She took two last breaths of air.

Evie smiled almost lovingly at her. "Don't worry. I won't let you suffer."

47

Seven jumped down from the helicopter onto the helipad. He waited for Gia to do the same and guided her out from under the blades.

Erika had spearheaded the efforts on the ground as they'd flown in from San Diego. SWAT was already in place at the address Zag had given, an old Victorian nestled in the older district of Costa Mesa. Seven didn't take it as a good sign that Erika was waiting for them, standing next to a black Escalade.

The look of concentration on her face didn't make him feel better. Neither did the news she had to deliver.

Erika glanced at Seven before focusing on Gia. "It's not good," she said.

Stella fought for her life, trapped beneath the water. She could feel herself getting light-headed; it was getting harder and harder to hold her breath. She felt herself losing her grip on Evie's wrists.

She knew what it felt like to drown: terror followed by a sense of surrender. She'd done it before, right here in this bathtub, in her vision. She'd felt that poor girl slowly let go of her life. Stella couldn't do that. Even though she knew she was no match for Evie's strength, she wouldn't give up.

She reached out, screaming inside her head: *Help me!*

At that moment, the weight on her chest suddenly lifted. Stella sat straight up in the tub and sucked in a lungful of air.

Adam stood over the bathtub. He had his sister locked in his arms. He said only one word.

"Run."

"The house is booby-trapped," Erika said, driving pedal to the metal with the siren blasting. "It's leased to one Nathaniel Slade. We don't know who the hell he is—all the information on the lease is bogus."

"He's military intelligence and he has a lot of imagination," Zag said from the backseat.

Erika glanced up at the rearview mirror. Beside her, Carin asked, "He was part of the Atlantis Project?"

Zag nodded. "The facilitator for Remote Viewer A-001. Nathaniel disappeared with Celeste, but my sources say they married. They had twins, a boy and a girl. Celeste died during childbirth. Something that might not have happened if they'd had proper medical care. But they were in hiding."

"Evie Slade," Carin said, making the connection between her and the mystery man who'd been following her. "Psychic twins?"

"Yes. And extremely powerful."

"So you hunted them down for your renewed Atlantis Project? You recruited them," Carin pressed.

"Only Evie. I knew Adam would be a harder case."

"And Nathaniel Slade?"

"Didn't even try. That's not his real name, by the way. It's an identity he assumed after he staged his death. The man's completely unstable. He believes there's some sort of government cover-up to stop the world from accessing

the secrets of Atlantis where we as a people would…
evolve, or something like that. I had a look at his record—
the usual control issues growing up, really took to the re-
gimented military frame of mind. And the training—he
excelled at every task. The more out there, the better. From
military intelligence, he was recruited to the government's
remote viewing program in the 1970s."

"Well, ain't that a pretty picture," Erika said under her
breath.

"Nathaniel believed his wife could remote view to the
lost city of Atlantis," Zag continued, "but he wanted
control. Look up paranoid and that's our guy. Then there's
the whole 'I killed my wife because I let her have my
twins in the woods.' He wanted her death to mean something. When I took up the program, I figured the less
contact with him, the better."

"You might have mentioned a little of this before we
sent out the SWAT team," Erika said angrily. "We have four
men in the hospital now."

Gia was sitting in the backseat next to Seven. She
gripped his hand with the realization.

All those signs on the lawn: Keep out.

"My painting," she said, "the signs posted all over the
property, in the windows, on the doors. The whole place
is a trap."

Adam grabbed his sister and shook her. "Stop it, Evie.
This isn't what you want, more blood on our hands."

"*Our* hands?" she laughed. "You're the Finder, remember? Light to my dark. Which one did you kill?"

"We killed them all. We entered their minds, together."

But Evie wasn't listening. "The girl, the granddaughter of Estelle Fegaris, she took me there, to Atlantis. She

touched the crystal. And then, suddenly, *she* was inside *my* head. There, in that realm, *she* was in control."

Adam took in the information, showing nothing of his surprise.

Suddenly, Evie stopped struggling. She leaned into her brother, allowing him to hold her. She rested her head against his shoulder and whispered, "She showed me our mother."

Adam kept stroking his sister's back. He'd come to a few realizations himself these past days about his father and his great plan. He didn't need to hear the agony in his sister's voice to understand what she'd discovered.

Suddenly, Evie dug her fingers into his shoulders. She pulled back, looking up at him, her eyes growing wide with realization.

"You're right, Adam," she said slowly, deliberately. "This isn't what I want."

She twisted free of his grip and ran for the door. Adam cursed softly and ran after her.

He caught up with Evie in Nathaniel's study. She stood in front of their father, her hand raised palm forward. The force of her will had him two feet off the ground and up against the wall.

The fire burning in the fireplace seemed supercharged. Adam realized Nathaniel had been burning documents.

He looked over at his sister. "Evie?"

She kept her gaze steady on Nathaniel. "I'm here, Father. I'm just as you trained me to be. Only, today, I am your destroyer."

48

Stella raced down the hall, running for her life. She saw the stairs ahead and made for them. She took them two at a time.

She was almost to the front door when she saw him. Ghost boy, blocking her way.

"No," she said. "I've done enough. I can't help you anymore. Not like this."

She was crying, looking at that door desperately, her only avenue to escape. All she could think about was getting out. The door, it was just a few feet away. The man, Adam, he'd told her to run.

Only ghost boy was no longer blocking the way. She turned to find him behind her. There, on the opposite side of the room, were a second set of stairs leading to a different part of the house.

"I know what you want." She could barely get the words out. She was pushing that fear down her throat, keeping the tears from coming. "You want me to save you, Jack. But I can't. I'm too scared."

She knew Jack was here. This was the house where she'd seen him. That room filled with antiques and hospital equipment, it was probably just up those stairs.

If she left him here, he would die.

Just like the others.

And still, she took two steps toward the door.

Jack again appeared in front of her, blocking the way to the door. Just as quickly, he vanished.

Slowly, Stella turned. Jack was standing at the stairwell again.

Stella heard shouts coming from the opposite side of the house. Evie screaming at her brother.

She had only seconds to make her decision.

"Okay," she said, choking on her fear as she ran to follow Jack.

Gia stood across the street from the Victorian. Police cruisers surrounded the house. So far, they hadn't been able to get in contact with anyone inside.

SWAT had discovered pressure mines littering both the back and front lawns. Despite protective armor, ball bearings and nails had torn up their feet and legs, even punching past some of the protective vests. The side door had been even more lethal, a shotgun rigged so that the trigger went off when the door opened. Luckily, the agent had taken most the hit in the vest, but he was still in the hospital.

Now SWAT and police alike had backed off until they could more fully assess the situation.

In the meantime, her daughter was trapped inside.

Gia waited across the street, her arms hugging her sides. The last year had been a difficult one for her daughter. Finding out about her past…dealing with what she'd come to call the Fegaris Curse.

The last few weeks, Gia had found herself giving all those tired speeches her own mother had delivered years ago. Gia remembered she'd paid about as much attention to her mother as Stella had to Gia.

But there were other things Estelle hadn't told her.

Tonight, Gia had held the Eye of Athena in her hand. She had reached inside and tapped its powers.

Her mother had always claimed the Eye was her legacy. That she and others of her family were true descendants of Gaia's Sibyl.

Your talent is wasted on those paintings.

That's what Zag had said earlier.

Her mother had a different take on it.

You're scared. I understand. But darling, one day you'll get past your fear. Something will happen to trigger the next step. Whenever that happens, I know you, Gina. You'll be ready.

Gina Fegaris. The name she'd been born with.

But now she was Gia Moon. And at long last, she was ready.

Gia started walking, crossing the street. Seven caught up to her, grabbing her arm, stopping her.

"No way," he said. "That's not happening, Gia."

He was a cop, a good one. He knew her enough to know her intentions.

"You are not going in there like some charge of the light brigade," he said.

But she was looking only at the house. "I painted it. It's there, in my mind, inside and out."

Every placard, every sign. She knew the location of each and every one.

She turned to look up at Seven. "I can do this."

Seven stared at her. "Jesus."

He glanced back at the phalanx of police, FBI and SWAT. The air was filled with the music of police radios and officers conferring.

"You're not going anywhere near that house if they

have any say in it. Come on," he said, taking her hand. "We'll need to get in around the back."

But Gia dug in her heels. Looking up at him, she said, "I can't protect you, Seven."

"Who the hell asked you to?" he answered, again walking her down the street.

Evie kept her father pinned to the wall. For now, his feet touched the floor. She had her arm jammed against his Adam's apple.

"Look at the fireplace," she told Adam. "He's burning everything. All our plans—our hopes and dreams. You gave us those dreams, Daddy. Our purpose, you called it. And now you're destroying everything? Like it never happened?"

"It's the exit plan," Nathaniel said, lowering his voice, that familiar gleam of energy coming to his eyes. "We leave here and start over somewhere else. It's what your mother would want us to do."

Evie shoved her arm harder, cutting off most of his air. "Did you hear that, Adam? Mommy would want us to go away and start over. You find the host and I kill them."

"Evie, not like this," Adam said, knowing exactly where this was headed.

"Those papers are nothing." Nathaniel tried to push her off, but his strength was no match for hers. "Our purpose isn't in that fireplace."

"Of course! How could I forget the mantra of the Slade clan—our purpose. The big plan. Did you know Father told me I couldn't trust you, Adam?" Evie asked, her gaze still on Nathaniel. "Was that part of our purpose? To pit me against my brother? Manipulate me into pushing him out of my head and letting you inside. Because you're the only one who could ever matter? Do you know what you did to me?"

"I made you stronger!" Nathaniel said, raising his voice to match hers. "Everything I did made you that much stronger. I had to pull you away from Adam. Your brother might have sacrificed himself," Nathaniel said. "But he would never have let you do the same. He would have stopped you from using the full extent of your powers."

"And making the same sacrifice as our mother? Isn't that how you always put it? Make her sacrifice mean something? Only, now I wonder if that was ever what she really wanted, to die and leave her children. I wonder if it wasn't what you wanted that killed her."

"How can you say that? She was everything to me!"

"Like I am now, Daddy?"

Adam came to stand beside his sister. "Let him go, Evie."

"I can't," she said, her gaze never leaving her father's. "He's in my head—he tells me what to do." She kept focused on Nathaniel. "I didn't want to hurt those children. He made me believe it was my fate—the reason Mother gave us life."

Nathaniel managed to get loose. He pointed to the portrait of Celeste. "Everything your mother ever did was for this moment! You, Evie, the strong one—the special one. Only you could go where Celeste went. And you did it. You found her."

A strange intensity came to Evie's gaze as she focused on her father. "That's right, Daddy. I did find her."

She raised her hand again.

"Evie, no!" Adam yelled.

Nathaniel rose inches from the ground. Like a ragdoll, he was thrown across the room.

Evie raised her hand again. "Mommy sends her love."

49

Gia knew the crystal had changed her.

It wasn't magic. Her mother had taught her that much. All her life Estelle had fought for a kind of legitimacy. If the world could study abilities like those in the Fegaris family—if science didn't cut them off in fear of appearing backward—what marvels could they discover?

Those were the powers Gia searched for now as she walked across Nathaniel Slade's minefield of a lawn.

Seven had taken her around the street to the back alley. With his help, they'd scaled a few fences to end up in the yard next to the Victorian. The police had done a good job of evacuating the area; there were no dogs or neighbors to impede their progress.

Seven was right, if she'd just walked across the street, she would never have made it past the police barricade. Now, slipping over the neighbor's fence in the dark, she took a breath and focused within. She began stepping across the grass toward the back of the Victorian.

Behind her, Seven carefully stepped in the exact spot Gia vacated in what appeared as a bizarre game of Twister.

"You know, most people worry about getting a little dog crap on their shoe doing this sort of thing in the dead of night, not having some shrapnel blow off their foot."

Gia barely heard him. She was focused on the painting in her head, visualizing the position of the Keep Out signs staked into the ground. It didn't seem to matter that she hadn't actually painted this section of the yard, they were still there inside her head, a three-dimensional mental map.

She felt Seven slip his hand into hers. She stopped and turned her head. She could just make out his eyes.

"I figure if we get blown up," he said, "I want to be holding your hand when it happens."

"Now you're the budding romantic?"

"I know. My timing sucks."

She stared back at the house. "I see it, the painting. All those signs on the lawn—"

"Represent the location of a mine," he said, finishing the sentence. "Yeah. I kind of figured that out."

She squeezed his hand. "Then follow very carefully," she said, taking the next step.

Stella stared at the door as ghost boy, Jack, walked on through. She followed without question this time, wanting to make this happen as quickly as possible. *In for a penny...*

She had climbed up two flights of stairs. This part of the house was like a little turret. The stairs led to the one door.

She opened the door and walked into the familiar room. It was decorated with antiques, just like the rest of the house. Only, here, in the dead center of the room, was a hospital bed surrounded by medical equipment.

Stella walked slowly toward the bed, her footsteps timed to the beep-beep-beep of some machine. How many times had she imagined this moment? She'd done everything he'd asked—she'd taken every risk. And now, she was finally here.

The boy in the bed appeared to be asleep. He had a blanket neatly tucked under his arms and his wrists were bound in leather cuffs.

He had black hair—just like Stella.

Black hair?

Ghost boy wasn't around. But she knew just by the hair color this boy wasn't Jack. She had no idea who he was.

The boy's eyes fluttered open. They were this really unique cornflower-blue.

Stella inhaled a quick breath, recognizing the color. She'd seen it before. The blue eyes of that poor sad woman. The one who had come to the house.

He looks just like his mother, she thought.

The boy was clearly drugged. Still, he managed a whispered plea.

"Help me."

Erika was the first one to notice that Seven and Gia had broken rank.

"What the hell?"

The words were barely audible. But Sherlock was standing next to Erika and not much got past Special Agent Barnes.

She followed Erika's gaze to where, ten feet away, Seven and Gia had been standing just minutes ago, heads bowed together in conversation.

"Crap."

Agent Barnes did not keep her voice down. Nor did she stay frozen in place like Erika. She checked her gun and jogged across the street to the Victorian.

Erika immediately followed. The woman might be an artifact-stealing liar, but then what girl didn't have a few secrets? Nor was Erika a big fan of the feds. The only thing that mattered to her was the fact that Sherlock wasn't going to let Gia's girl die.

Once they reached the edge of the property, Sherlock flashed her badge, getting them past the police barricade. She pulled out a flashlight and shone a steady beam of light on the lawn wet with dew. Zag came to a stop behind her.

She looked at Erika.

"Around back," Erika said, knowing Seven wouldn't have come this way, not without some fancy FBI badge to impress the gatekeepers.

They headed for the neighbor's yard, Carin leading the way. She opened the gate and stepped through the side of the house to the back pad. Standing on the patio, Carin shone the flashlight on the pristine lawn.

There, on the wet grass, were clear marks where someone—possibly two someones—had hopscotched across the yard, leaving a trail from the alley entrance to the block wall shared with the Victorian next door.

"Okay, then," Erika said, heading there.

Erika found a lawn chair. She pushed it up against the cinderblock wall. She held her hand back for the flashlight. Carin complied.

Again, the dew-laden grass told the story. Footprints marked the steps to a complicated dance meant to avoid any pressure mines. The footsteps ended at what looked like the entrance to a crawl space. The wood door was open.

Erika looked back at Carin. "This is it. This is the way they came." She flashed the light on the tracks leading to the house. "By the looks of it, they made it inside without a single kaboom."

Right then, Zag came jogging into the yard. Erika tried to figure out how the hell he got past the police barricade.

Not that it mattered. Erika knew Sherlock would give him the heave-ho.

Only, it didn't exactly go down that way. Sherlock ignored the twerp. Instead, the very agile FBI agent stepped back, away from the six-foot block wall, and took a running start. She had no trouble scaling the damn thing, leaving Erika standing on her patio chair. But then, Sherlock had a good six inches on Erika.

Erika watched as the woman dropped onto the exact same spot where the disturbed grass showed someone else had recently found refuge.

Erika pulled herself up on the wall, no longer worried about the excess baggage of Zag de Rozières.

50

"Jack?"

It scared Stella to say the name out loud. She was here to save ghost boy, right? She didn't know who this kid was strapped in the hospital bed. He couldn't be Jack. He just couldn't.

But there it was. That instant look of recognition on his face when she called out his name.

"Please," he croaked.

She was still breathing hard from running up the stairs. But now, she sensed her labored breath came from fear. She stood frozen with indecision.

The boy's eyes closed. His head lolled to the side, as if even the effort of holding her gaze had depleted him. He exhaled a deep sigh.

That sound—she recognized it for what it was. The sound of defeat.

He wasn't planning on leaving this room alive.

She turned, her gaze scanning over the room. *Something sharp.* She'd need something to cut through those leather cuffs.

She started searching through drawers and cabinets, expecting any second now to have Evie burst into the room and drag her back into that bathroom.

The best she came up with was a letter opener.

She began sawing away at the strap, but the leather was thick and securely attached to the hospital bed. She turned the letter opener in her hand and began to punch through the leather using the point.

In the bed, the boy she now believed was Jack stared at her listlessly.

Minutes later, she hadn't made a dent in the leather.

She dropped to her knees, crying. She leaned against the frame of the bed, one hand clutching the sheets, the other still holding the letter opener. She had no idea what she was doing. This boy's life depended on her and she couldn't deal. Couldn't figure out the next step.

Suddenly, she felt a hand on hers. She looked up, seeing that Jack had reached as far as the leather cuff would allow him to take her hand.

He said, "Don't…cry."

She knelt there stunned, looking at him. She had an idea of what this boy had been through, pretty much anybody's definition of hell on earth. And he was comforting her?

Stella jumped to her feet and brushed away her tears. She looked for something to use as leverage.

There, in the corner. A mop.

She threaded the plastic handle of the mop through the cuff she'd been punching at with the letter opener. Taking the handle, she braced her foot against the bed and pulled.

She could feel the mop handle bending in her hand.

Please!

Suddenly, the cuff gave way, breaking where she'd managed to make some headway on the leather with the opener.

She fell to her knees, the tears coming from a completely different emotion now.

She didn't waste any time. She grabbed the letter opener and began punching into the second cuff.

Only, she hadn't done much damage before she heard what sounded like footsteps just outside the door. She looked up.

As she watched, the doorknob slowly turned.

Carin stared down at the entrance to the crawl space. The door was made of painted plywood, three feet by three feet. There was a simple latch that someone had already opened—most likely Gia. The door remained ajar.

"And there go our breadcrumbs," Erika said behind her. She was referring to the dew marks they'd followed to the door, avoiding the pressure mines on the lawn. "What do you think?" she asked.

Carin pulled out her 9 mm and took the flashlight from Erika. "I think we watch our step."

She crouched down low and flashed the light inside the crawl space. The area was fairly large, spanning about a tenth of the footprint of the house. There was about four feet of headroom. In the far corner, she saw what looked like stairs—probably leading to a root cellar or a more formal basement.

She flashed the light on the dirt floor. Here, too, she could see tracks. Only, there were too many to determine what path Gia and Seven might have taken.

Carefully, she stepped inside, crouching down low to avoid the ventilation ducts, water pipes and creative electrical wiring that sometimes plagued old houses. To the right of the entry, there was a pile of old bricks, probably left over from some renovation project.

She heard Erika and Zag follow her inside. She stopped,

giving them all a chance to catch their breath. What they were doing was extremely dangerous. Any wrong step and—

And there it was. A distinctive click.

She'd heard it before. The first time had been during her training at Quantico.

When the pin is pulled from a hand grenade, it's never like in the movies. No one grabs it with their teeth before lobbing the grenade. Every grenade has a safety. You pull the pin and the safety goes off. Once the safety is off, you have five seconds.

Carin had been taught to always hold the safety down with her thumb before she pulled the pin. That way, the grenade had a complete five seconds to reach its target before going off.

Unless it was set off by a trip wire.

"Run!" she screamed.

As the door burst open, Stella ran to the head of the bed. She held the letter opener in both hands like a weapon.

Seven stood in the door. He had his revolver pointed straight at her.

"She's here," he said, holstering his gun.

But Gia hadn't waited for the all clear. She was already halfway across the room.

Stella dropped the letter opener. She could feel her legs grow weak with relief. She ran into her mother's waiting arms. Gia kissed her face, her hair.

"Are you all right?" she asked.

Stella nodded, holding tight to her mother. "I can't believe you're here. I can't believe you came."

Her mother just kept kissing her. "I'm here baby. Oh, Jesus. I thought I'd lost you. Oh, and before I forget? You're grounded. Possibly until your eighteenth birthday."

She almost laughed, but then she remembered. Stella pushed her away and turned to look at the bed where Seven now stood, checking the boy's pulse.

"Mom," she said. "It's Jack."

Five seconds can be a long time. If you counted slowly in your head—one one-thousand, two one-thousand—five seconds actually seemed like a fairly substantial length of time.

When you're running to avoid flying shrapnel? Not so much.

Carin made for the stairs. She knew Erika and Zag were close behind. The ceiling was low, about four feet. Then there were the pipes, heating ducts and wires to avoid. The stairs were a good thirty feet ahead.

Four one-thousand.

Halfway up the plank wood steps, the ceiling rose, allowing for more headroom and greater speed. Carin yanked open the door at the top of the steps.

Five one-thousand.

The percussion blow of the grenade propelled all three past the door. Carin felt herself flying until her body slammed into a wall. A plume of dust and debris billowed through the opening where the door now hung half-off its hinges.

Next to her, Carin heard Erika groan.

"You okay?" she asked, checking her gun. She'd managed to holster it during their frantic climb out of the crawl space. The flashlight had fallen out of her hand. Miraculously, it was still on. A beam of light cut through the still-settling dust.

"Yeah," Erika replied. "How about you?"

"Got the wind knocked of me." She stood slowly, letting

her eyes adjust to the darkness. She walked over and picked up the flashlight. She shone it around what appeared to be a finished basement.

That's when she saw Zag, lying facedown on the wooden floor.

"Shit."

She hurried to him and carefully turned him over. She wasn't sure why it made her heart skip with relief when she heard him groan in pain. How many times had she wanted the bastard dead?

But here she was, helping him to sit up. Erika was there, too, propping Zag up against her.

Carin used the flashlight to find an alternative light source. There. A bare bulb hanging from the middle of the ceiling.

Seeing it, as well, Erika stood. She walked over and pulled the chain. The room filled with a weak glow.

"Help me take him over to that desk," Carin said.

The two women dragged Zag over to a big green metal desk, the kind used in government offices. They helped him sit up and leaned him back against the side of the desk.

"You took some shrapnel to the shoulder," Carin said. She started taking his jacket off. The motion brought a sharp intake of breath from Zag.

His eyes looked glassy with pain when they met Carin's. He smiled and said, "You suck."

She ignored him, and focused on the job of taking off the thick leather jacket. "It looks like this jacket saved your ass."

He closed his eyes for an instant. "I live for fashion."

His shirt followed next. She held the flashlight directly at the wound at the back of his shoulder, seeing that a bullet-size piece had lodged inside.

Erika was already ripping pieces of his shirt to use for bandaging. Zag looked up at her. "Ouch. That's an eight-hundred dollar Dolce & Gabbana shirt."

"Really?" Erika said, still cutting the shirt into strips. "You obviously haven't heard of outlet shopping."

When Erika handed the strips to Carin, her gaze settled on the tattoo on Zag's chest.

Zag's breathing was fast and shallow with pain. His eyes on Carin, he said, "Like my ink? It's mine and Carin's initials intertwined. We designed it together." He frowned, as if trying to remember. "I think there was a lot of tequila involved. Carin has one just like it. Want to tell the detective where it is, honey?"

Carin pressed a little too hard with the makeshift bandage, getting the satisfaction of seeing him wince.

But Zag wasn't done. He looked up at Erika. "What do think, Detective?"

"I think," Erika said, "that Barnes has shitty taste in men. I'll go watch the door. See if we have company coming."

But before she turned away, Zag grabbed her leg. He was staring down at the floor, frowning. This time, the expression had nothing to do with pain.

He reached behind him, slipping something out from beneath him. It was a pair of handcuffs. Someone had attached one end to the leg of the metal desk.

"Fuck," Erika said.

"Listen to me, Zag," Carin said, finishing the bandage. "Do you have a weapon?"

"Don't leave me here," he said. "I can make it."

"Bullshit." She pulled up her pant leg where she retrieved a second gun. She handed it to Zag.

"I told you," he said, suddenly angry. "I can make it."

"We'll come back as soon as we can."

"Fuck," he said under his breath. "All right. Just go find the girl and her mother and get them out of here."

Carin shifted the light ahead. Erika now waited at the top of another set of steps, these most likely leading into the main house. Again, whoever had been here first had left the door ajar.

Erika met her gaze. She nodded, giving Carin the all clear.

Carin ran up the stairs. Erika allowed her to pass, giving Carin the lead. Carin opened the door wider. Ahead was an empty hallway. She stepped onto the carpet runner and moved on.

She put the flashlight away, moving forward along the dimly lit corridor, her gun drawn. Just as she passed what appeared to be a laundry room, she heard shouting ahead.

People arguing?

She sensed Erika behind her and glanced back.

Gun in hand, Erika gave another quick nod.

Carin moved toward the landing of the stairwell ahead. The stairs came to a split. One set of steps heading down; the other, up.

The voices were clearly coming from the floor above.

When she reached the landing, Carin pressed back against the wall. She focused, slowing her breath.

In one fluid motion, she swung around the corner, her back to the wall, arms extended and weapon trained down the steps.

There was no one there.

She slowly made her way up the stairs, careful to make as little noise as possible. In an orchestrated dance, Erika followed behind, covering her back.

In this section of the house, the corridor on the second floor led to a set of double doors. The voices grew louder.

When she reached the doors, she and Erika took opposite sides.

Carin gave the signal and kicked in the doors. Both women burst into the room.

The tableau before her might have confounded other law enforcement. But this was what Carin Barnes was all about. The impossible. Science fiction.

An older man, possibly in his late sixties—Carin assumed it was Nathaniel Slade—floated above the ground. Dr. Evie Slade stood a mere foot away, her palm facing the man as if shooting out some kind of force field to keep him suspended there. The redheaded man, the one who had ambushed her at her hotel, stood at the woman's side.

Carin focused on the woman, knowing that Erika would train her gun on the man standing beside Dr. Slade.

But even as Carin attempted to keep her focus on Evie, the man turned and walked toward her.

She fired at his feet.

"Stop where you are!" she yelled.

Erika changed targets, her aim visibly shifting to the woman as if she and Carin had been partners for years.

The man raised his hands in the air, his blue eyes unreadable as he watched Carin.

"Evie, listen to me," he said. "It's done."

"This time, I say when it's done, Adam. Not him."

Evie Slade shifted her hands. The floating man dropped to the ground. As if he bounced off the floor, his body lifted again and slammed against the wall.

The man called Adam dropped his hands and grabbed his twin. Carin realized that, like everything else, his easy surrender had been a ruse. He wasn't afraid of Carin or her gun.

This is about Evie. He thought I could stop her.

"Evie!"

The shout came from Zag as he stepped inside the room. He'd managed to get his good arm through the black jacket. The other sleeve hung empty at his side, the leather jacket perched over his hurt shoulder.

His presence had the desired effect. Evie Slade forgot her prey, her attention now fixed on Zag. Nathaniel Slade remained prone on the floor.

"You should be honored," she said. "You were part of his grand plan. He wanted me to ruin you." She cocked her head, the motion almost birdlike. "What did you want?"

Zag kept walking toward her fearlessly. Carin didn't know who to aim her gun on. She glanced at Erika, seeing the same concern. Too many targets.

Who's the real enemy?

"Get back, Zag," Carin warned.

But he ignored her, his attention only for Evie. "You. I've always wanted just you. Your power, your beauty. I still want you."

Evie Slade pushed away her brother. She stood to her full height.

Evie smiled brilliantly. "Guess what, my darling?" she told him. "I wanted more."

Evie again raised her hand. This time, Nathaniel Slade remained lying on the ground, his only move, to clutch his chest.

Adam said, "She'll kill him."

The statement was a cold observation. He made no move to stop her. Instead, he addressed Carin. "By now, you know the house is booby-trapped. There are several explosive charges set on a timer. Once the perimeter was breached, it triggered the timer. I estimate you have fifteen minutes to get out before the whole house blows up."

On the ground, Nathaniel flopped around like a fish ready for gutting.

Carin didn't know why or how she knew, but she was absolutely certain about her next words.

"You're lying," she said, her gun still on Adam.

"You're here for the girl. She's at the other side of the house, up the spiral staircase to the turret room. The boy you're looking for is there, as well. I highly recommend that Zag and your fellow officer here help them."

"Jesus," Zag said.

Adam kept his gaze on Carin. "You can stay here with me and decide if I'm telling the truth. But why sacrifice the children?"

"Carin," Erika said. "My gut says you're right. He's lying."

But they all knew they couldn't take the chance.

"Go," Carin said.

Erika looked like she might argue. But as soon as Zag ran for the door, she followed him out.

"Make her stop what she's doing," Carin said, her gun still on Adam.

"Drop the gun and I will," he said.

Instead, Carin turned and aimed for Evie's leg.

At that exact moment, Evie turned, her palm now stretched out toward Carin. The gun flew out of her grasp and skidded across the floor, landing right at Evie's feet.

Before Carin could stop her, Evie picked up the gun and fired.

51

Seven looked at the plastic bag hanging by the bedside. "It's a saline drip." He followed the plastic tubing until he reached where the catheter had been inserted on the peripheral artery on Jack's hand. "My guess is they kept the drip and injected the drugs through this line."

He turned and looked through the metal drawers of the medical equipment until he found gauze and medical tape. He pulled the catheter out, then quickly bandaged the hand.

"Is he going to be okay?" Stella asked in a quivering voice.

"Not if we don't get him out of here."

Taking the mop, Seven snapped off the final cuff. He picked up the boy and carried him in his arms. Jack wrapped his arms around Seven's neck.

"I suggest a quick exit," Seven said.

"Make that superquick."

The comment came from Erika as she slipped inside the room with Zag de Rozières at her heels.

"The place is supposed to blow in approximately fifteen minutes," she told them. "It's the approximate part that has me a little edgy."

"Supposed to?" Seven said, catching his partner's uncertainty.

"The news came at a very convenient time for the guy who delivered it."

"But he was right about Stella and the boy being here," Zag pointed out. "He didn't lie about that."

"Unless he's tricking us into making a mistake? Running out and actually triggering one of the booby traps?" Erika countered.

Seven turned to Gia. She didn't hesitate.

"We leave the way we came in," she said. "And we leave now."

Nathaniel Slade lay dead at his daughter's feet, shot through the heart.

Carin raced forward, anticipating the next round.

But Evie wasn't concerned with Carin. Instead, she turned and aimed her pistol at her brother, Adam.

Carin pushed her aside just as she fired.

The two women fought over the gun. With a roundhouse kick, Carin dislodged the weapon. The gun flew out of Evie's hand. Evie punched Carin in the stomach with her palm. Carin doubled over.

When she could breathe again, Carin saw that Evie again stood holding the gun. Her blue eyes looked lit up from inside. Slowly she raised the 9 mm.

And put it in her mouth.

But Adam was already there. He grabbed her arm. Brother and sister fought over the weapon.

"I would have killed you, Adam!" Evie screamed. "I would have! I kill everything. Let me die!"

Adam swung Evie around and seized the gun. He was standing behind his sister, holding her around the waist. He had the 9 mm trained on Carin.

Evie was kicking and screaming, the motions hardly the

deadly moves of before but rather weak and childlike. She repeated over and over, "Let me die."

The gun still on Carin, Adam backed away, bringing his sister along with him.

"You've been hit," she said, seeing the blood blossom at the shoulder of the white shirt he was wearing.

"It won't slow me down."

But Carin kept pace, walking toward him. "You're not going to shoot me."

He fired. She could swear she felt the bullet whiz past her ear.

"I wouldn't be so sure," he said.

He kept backing away, but not toward the double doors. Carin stayed with him, passing a desk piled with folders and papers until she'd backed him and his sister up against the wall.

He waited there, cornered between the fireplace and the wall. He said, "I shouldn't have hurt those children."

"But you did. And you'll pay the price."

"Of course, I will. But not the way you think," he told her.

"You sure enjoy the whole man-of-mystery routine, don't you?"

"One last piece of advice— Don't trust Zag."

"*You* left me that note?" she asked, realizing that, even then, he'd been following her. "Trying to keep the focus on Zag and away from you and Evie?"

"That doesn't make it any less true."

"Your sister," she said. "You didn't know she killed those kids, did you?"

"I knew. We killed them together. We gave them drugs; we used up their brains. They became trapped in some horrible loop, living their worst nightmare over and over. She just wanted to stop their suffering."

His shoulder was bleeding heavily now, the brilliant red soaking into the cloth of his sleeve. His sister no longer fought him. She was like a ragdoll in his arms as she murmured her pleas for death.

"You have a beautiful aura, Carin," he said. "I hardly ever see an aura like that."

"It's not my aura you're going to see if you don't drop that gun," she told him, hoping to hell she was right. "Any minute now, this place is going to be filled with cops."

For the first time, his cool expression changed. She thought she saw a glimmer of emotion. Regret. "I'm going to miss you, Carin."

Suddenly, he turned his head and focused on something behind her. Out of nowhere, a maelstrom of papers flew at her. She realized they must have come from the desk behind her. The pages swirled around her like some weird vortex.

When her vision cleared, she saw the wall behind Adam and his sister give way. A small door appeared.

He said, "You were right, Carin. I lied about the explosive device—but not about Zag."

Brother and sister vanished behind the door.

Carin raced forward, but she didn't reach the door in time. The panel slid back in place with a *snap-click*.

She searched the wall for a switch he might have pulled, or a pressure point he could have used to activate the door, but couldn't find a damn thing. She had no idea how he'd opened the wall door. There'd been too many pages obscuring her view.

She punched the wall in frustration.

Behind her, Erika burst into the room with her gun drawn.

"They're gone," Carin said, walking over to Nathaniel Slade.

"Should I call medical?" Erika asked as Carin checked for a pulse.

Carin shook her head. "He's dead."

"The bomb?" Erika asked. Seeing Carin's expression, she rolled her eyes. "I knew he was lying."

"About so many things," Carin said, already heading toward the double doors and the stairs beyond.

52

Carin stood outside the Victorian as the coroner rolled out the body of Nathaniel Slade.

She hadn't found any trace of Adam or his sister.

Across the yard, Zag de Rozières appeared, looking dapper in black leather with his arm in a sling. He was talking to the slew of reporters as if they were his own personal paparazzi, ready to pitch his version of the truth to anyone willing to print it.

"Disgusting, isn't it?" Erika said. "I bet the damn stock goes through the roof after he puts his spin on tonight. You can't buy publicity like this. Hey, maybe we should go buy a few thousand dollars worth? Not like a cop can be accused of insider trading."

"Maybe," Carin said.

Erika clucked her tongue. "Don't take it so hard, Sherlock. Every once in a while, the bad guys get away."

Carin kept her eyes on Zag. "And rub our noses in it."

"That's about the size of it. But if you ever get anything on the guy…"

"Don't worry, Detective. You'll be my first call."

"I'd like that. Very much. You need a ride?"

Carin turned to look at Erika.

Erika winked. "I know, I know. Why so warm and

fuzzy? Here you are, hypothetically, this lying sack of shit who possibly stole the Eye. You see, my partner and I had a little talk. The thing is, last we heard the artifact they found at the murder scene wasn't even real. It wouldn't really make sense to have more people dying because of it, don't you think?"

Carin felt an enormous sense of relief. At the same time, it felt odd. The life she'd chosen didn't exactly make room for friendship. She didn't know what to make of Detective Erika Cabral.

Erika patted her hand. "Lighten up, will you? Haven't you heard? Scrunching up your forehead like that gives you wrinkles."

Carin actually smiled. "Thanks, Detective. I owe you."

"Don't I know it. Now, what about that ride?"

Carin shook her head. She turned back to stare at Zag. "I have unfinished business here."

Erika followed her gaze. "So where exactly is the tattoo?"

"On my ass," Carin answered.

Erika nodded. "Hope someday you get the chance to kick his. Ass, that is."

"It might just be my life's ambition."

Carin walked toward Zag. She could feel the frustration of the day bubbling up with each step.

She started walking faster.

Reaching Zag, she turned him around by digging her fingers hard into his bad shoulder. To the indiscriminate eye, the gesture might pass muster as something other than an assault.

Under the lights set up by reporters, Zag turned a nice shade of white. "Fuck, Carin," he said under his breath.

"A word," she said.

He nodded, following her out of earshot.

"What the hell are you doing?" she asked with a nod toward his waiting press. "Holding a press conference for Halo Industries?"

"I'm protecting my reputation, if that's what you mean. Don't worry, Carin. I was discreet."

She came in close, whispering furiously, "You listen to me, you prick. You got away with something here. And I don't care if it costs me my career, I will get to the bottom of it and I will expose you."

"Carin," he answered. "What could you possibly accuse me of doing? You heard Dr. Slade. Her father was trying to destroy me. She killed those children. She put those stones in their hands. She framed me."

But she was shaking her head. "There's something else."

"Really, Carin, you wound me."

"You bet your ass, Zag. Any chance I get."

He took a few slow steps back. He turned and walked away, but not before she got a good long look at that cat-who-ate-the-canary smile.

Sandra Blake walked alongside the gurney where her son was now strapped in. That nice detective, Erika Cabral, had sent over a patrol car to get her. They'd used the siren and everything.

"They say you're going to be just fine. They're going to take you to the hospital and make you better."

She had his hand clutched in hers. She kept picking it up and kissing his knuckles.

She wanted to tell him how stupid she'd been. How she'd called and pressed charges against Peter, just like the detective told her to do. But this wasn't about her anymore and her excuses. It was about Jack. All about her baby boy.

She watched as the paramedics put the gurney into the truck. One of them was nice enough to help her inside where she sat down next to Jack.

She picked up his hand again. She wondered if she'd ever be able to let go of it.

She had so much to tell him, but what good would it do him to hear a bunch of promises? Time enough later to tell him about how that nice detective had a friend who ran a shelter for battered women. That they had counseling and stuff there.

But staring down at her son, she couldn't hold back the tears. Or the apologies. He looked so weak.

"I hate myself for what I did to you," she whispered.

She wasn't sure he'd even heard her, his eyes were closed and he looked like maybe he was too weak to even try and open them.

"Don't," he said.

"What, honey?" she said, brushing back her tears and leaning down close to listen to him.

"Don't…hate…yourself."

She bit her lip. "I don't know if I can stop. What I did, it's unforgivable."

He opened his eyes. *Like looking into a mirror,* she thought. Her beautiful boy.

She was still holding his hand. She thought he tightened his grip just a little.

"If you can stop hating yourself," he said, "then, some day, I can, too."

"Can what, honey? You don't have to forgive, honest."

But he shook his head. "I can stop hating myself for the things I did."

"Oh, no, baby. You're just a child. An innocent victim."

But again, he shook his head. "No. Not a victim. Never

again, okay, Mom? Neither of us will ever let anyone make us victims again."

She dropped her head on his chest, his words just opening something inside her. The realization came.

"You're right, baby," she said softly. "You're so right."

Stella stood with her mother's arms around her. Someone had given her a blanket. Funny, she hadn't even known she was shaking. Shock, that's what the paramedic had called it.

She was looking over at the boy, Jack. They were wheeling him into the back of an ambulance, his mother right there at his side. She was brushing back his hair, smiling at him as tears rolled down her face. Stella couldn't hear what his mother was saying, but even from back here, she could see the lady looked pretty damn happy. So did Jack.

"What is it, sweetie?"

She looked up at her mother. Mom would want to know every little thing. Stella sighed. She might even tell her this time.

Only, she had to figure it out first.

She watched the ambulance drive away.

"Mom?"

"Yes, baby?"

"Tomorrow, will you take me back to the Institute?"

She felt her mother tense. "Why?"

Stella kept her eyes on the ambulance as it disappeared into the night. "There's someone there I gotta see."

Zag walked toward his car, whistling under his breath, keys in hand. He kept savoring that image of Carin in defeat.

It had taken everything he had to just stand there while she berated him. Poor thing, it was almost comical, her distress. If he hadn't thought it would cost him his balls, he would have finished that tête-à-tête by sweeping her up in his good arm and kissing her.

Sometimes he thought that's what the two of them needed to get the past behind them. A nice long session of lovemaking. A blast from the past, as it were.

Well, if there was one thing Zag had, it was patience.

He almost laughed out loud at the idea of him and Carin together again. He'd need a hell of a lot of patience for that to happen.

When hell freezes over...

Carin aside, it was the end to a very good day.

It hadn't started that way. For a while there, things had looked pretty bleak. He couldn't believe how badly he'd miscalculated, how close he'd come to that precipice with Evie.

Well, no risk, no gain.

He did feel badly about the children. He felt somewhat responsible, though he put the majority of fault squarely on that psycho, Nathaniel. The families left behind would never know, their children had been casualties of war—a war Zag was one step closer to winning.

He pressed the button on the remote control in his pocket and heard the Cayenne Turbo chirp as the locks opened. He made a mental note to make a sizable contribution to the families of the lost children. Anonymously, of course.

He was opening the car door, ready to step up into the SUV when he felt the gun barrel press against his back.

"Hello, Adam," he said. "I was expecting you. Not particularly at this time or in this fashion," he added. He turned around fearlessly. "You have Evie with you, of course," he said calmly. "Why don't you put her inside the car?"

Adam towered over Zag. He kept the gun aimed squarely at Zag's chest. "So you can finish the job you and my father started?"

"I see things differently," Zag said.

"Don't you always?"

"You and I both know Nathaniel had his own agenda. He wanted Celeste's death to be meaningful. He wanted a legacy. Only you and your sister could give him that. You and the children you killed. I didn't put your sister on that path."

"No, but what happened to her—to her mind. That, you very much had a part in."

"I disagree," Zag said, pressing his point. "Your sister came to me, Adam, not the other way around. Nor was I standing next to her when she used those children." Zag snapped his fingers as if remembering something. "But I believe you were?"

"You stood next to her when she used the children you paraded into your schools."

Zag chose his words very carefully. "Evie has never hurt a child under my care."

"But what did it do to her? What did it cost Evie to get inside their minds?"

"So let me pay my penance." He stepped in closer, ignoring the gun. "I can help her."

"Take the final steps to becoming a monster?"

"No," Zag said emphatically. "Unfortunately, Adam, you and I both know she has already become that—your father made sure of it. We also know I am your sister's only hope right now. Only Halo Industries has the resources to help someone like her."

"And the price?" When Zag hesitated, Adam demanded, "Oh, come on, Zag. Surely you and I are beyond all this? What do you want? Nothing to say? How about

I tell you, then. How long did it take you to find us, Zag? The son and daughter of Celeste, Remote Viewer A-001 of the Atlantis Project?"

Zag smiled. "A very long time."

Two years, to be exact, Zag thought. That's when he'd finally been given the information he'd needed on the project.

It wasn't a particularly lucrative contract for Halo Industries—an ancient government program thought to be long dead but for the efforts of a few devotees. But money wasn't what Zag was after.

He wanted Adam and Evie, the children of Celeste, one of the few known remote viewers to reach Atlantis.

"So," Adam said, "I ask again. What's your price?"

"You," Zag answered. "And your sister, once we mend her. You both come to work for me."

Adam watched Zag. There was an almost frightening intensity to the man. Zag had always thought Evie the greater prize, but he wondered now if he'd underestimated Adam. If they all had.

Adam stepped aside. He gestured to the shadows where Evie waited propped against a tree. Even from a distance, her eyes looked vacant.

Zag opened the car door. "Put her inside."

53

He didn't have the penguin pajamas on, but he still looked a little dorky. He was a grown man who dressed and acted like a kid.

His room, too, was decorated for someone much younger. Someone who didn't shave like this guy surely did. She wondered how that worked, a kid trapped in a man's body.

She knew his name now. Markie. Markie Barnes.

Everyone was standing around—Mom, Morgan, Markie's sister, the FBI agent, and Seven. She didn't exactly know what the big deal was, but at least they were giving her a little space.

She looked at Markie's dark blond hair and gray eyes.

"It was you. You're ghost boy," she said. "Only, when you came to me, you made yourself look like you were Jack's age."

He seemed to think about that, but didn't respond. She looked around the room again. *A child's room.*

"So, what's the matter with you?" she asked.

He shrugged. "I don't know."

"Okay," she said, understanding that he really didn't. The man seated on the bed saw himself as a kid and didn't know there was anything bad about that.

"So why me?" she asked.

"I see you here all the time. You visit Morgan. And I could tell you were…different."

She nodded. Of course, he would. Because *he* was different.

"How did you know about Jack and those kids?"

"Dr. Slade. Evie. She would sleep inside my head sometimes."

She nodded, getting it. "And you would take a look around in hers while she was at it."

He thought about it. "Something like that."

It was kind of what happened when Evie had taken over Stella's mind. That's when Stella had realized all that stuff about Evie's mom. She'd known that was the only way to stop Evie, by reminding her of the kind of person her mother really was. That she'd never condone what Evie was doing.

"How old are you?" she asked.

He shrugged again. "I'm not sure. Old I guess. Old like you. I'm tired. Can we talk more later?"

"Sure," she said, standing.

She turned around. Everyone was staring at her like something was wrong. She looked back at Markie still sitting on the bed.

She said, "He's tired."

She looked over at Agent Barnes, Markie's big sister. She was crying.

"What's wrong?" she asked, looking at her mother for guidance.

"Stella, you were talking to Markie."

"Yeah. He was ghost boy, the spirit I kept seeing. Only…" Even as she talked about it, she was trying to figure it all out. "He's not actually a spirit. And he didn't look like that when he came to me, either." She frowned. "I think he believes he's, like, my age."

When she'd woken from that nightmare, the one where the kid was handcuffed in a basement and some guy rammed a syringe into his neck, she'd woken to find ghost boy in her room. She'd been so shook up, she'd assumed they were the same person. They appeared the same age; they were the same height and build.

Her mother took her hand. "Do you know what astral projection is, sweetie?"

She shook her head. She had no idea.

"Markie can travel places without his body. Maybe when he does that, he appears as he sees himself, not as we see him."

Stella nodded. "That makes a kind of sense, I guess."

Her mother held her face up to hers. "You know that Markie is autistic?"

"Well, he was never very talkative, even as a spirit." She was still watching him. Agent Barnes had come over to the bed and was sitting next to him. She was holding him, kissing his face and hair like he was the most wonderful person in the world. The sight of her doing that made Stella smile.

"I guess he snapped out of it," she said.

That must be why Agent Barnes was crying now. Tears of joy.

"Stella?"

Stella knew what her mother was about to say was really important because she looked pretty damn serious. She braced herself. "Yeah?"

"Just now, with Markie? You were the only one talking."

"What do you mean?"

"Markie never answered you, sweetie. Or at least, you're the only one we could hear speaking."

"Oh," she said, a bit startled.

She frowned. It had been a heck of a ride, this whole ghost-boy thing. Really scary. But in the end, it turned out okay. She thought maybe she was starting to understand some of the stuff her mother had been telling her about the Fegaris thing.

She watched Markie as Agent Barnes continued to fuss over him and smiled.

Stella walked back to the bed. She sat down next to Markie and held out her hand.

Without hesitation, Markie took it.

Agent Barnes was crying full on now. It looked kind of weird because she was dressed like some hard-ass FBI chick, gun holster and all, but here she was crying buckets over her kid brother.

"I can hear him," she told Agent Barnes, knowing it would be most important to her. Stella squeezed Markie's hand, letting him know everything was going to be okay. "I can hear him just fine."

From the author of *Trust Me*

BRENDA NOVAK

Who was the real killer?

Romain lost his reason for living when his daughter was kidnapped and murdered. He used a cop's gun to mete out his own justice and spent years in prison. Once he was freed, he learned that he might have killed the wrong man.

And now Jasmine, a psychological profiler, believes the same man kidnapped her sister, Kimberly, sixteen years ago.

What happens next?

Jasmine knows Romain can help her...if he chooses. But searching for the man who irrevocably changed both their lives means they have to rise to a killer's challenge....

"Brenda Novak writes nonstop suspense at its very best."
—*New York Times* bestselling author Carla Neggers

MIRA®

*Available the first week of July 2008
wherever books are sold!*

www.MIRABooks.com

MBN2460

From the author of *The Tunnels*

MICHELLE GAGNON

On the trail of a serial killer, the path splits in two...

FBI special agent Kelly Jones has worked on many disturbing cases in her career, but nothing like this. A mass grave site unearthed puts Kelly at the head of an investigation that crosses the line—from wealthy vacationers to poor transients, from a serial killer to a copycat nemesis.

Assisted by law enforcement from both states and a forensic anthropologist, Kelly searches for the killers. But as darkness falls, another victim is taken. Kelly must race to save him before he joins the rest...in the boneyard.

"Boneyard is pure reading pleasure—
creepy, terrifying and utterly believable."
—*New York Times* bestselling author
Douglas Preston

*Available the first week of July 2008
wherever books are sold!*

MIRA®

www.MIRABooks.com

MMG2539

A new Barbara Holloway legal thriller
by bestselling author

KATE WILHELM

Who knew that being a Good Samaritan would lead
Barbara Holloway to face her biggest challenge ever:
being named prime suspect in a high-profile kidnapping?

When a terrified young boy seeks Barbara's help for his badly
battered mother, then disappears, the boy's family accuses
her of aiding and abetting his disappearance.

Barbara delves into the mystery of the missing child.
But troubling obstacles continue to thwart her every
move—including the justice system that employs her
and the false identities of those around her. Yet none
of these things will compare with the shocking
murder scene that awaits her....

**Available the first
week of July 2008,
wherever books are sold!**

A
Wrongful
Death

"Wilhelm claims a leading place in the
ranks of trial suspense writers."
—*Publishers Weekly*

MIRA®

www.MIRABooks.com

MKW2567

MIRA®

A sexy sequel by

STEPHANIE BOND

Two-for-one trouble!

With fugitive parents, a brother dodging loan sharks, a hunky cop who's made her outlaw family his business, a buff body mover looking to make a move on her, and her ex-fiancé back in the picture, Carlotta Wren thought her life couldn't get any more complicated. And then... she's placed under suspicion for murder!

"What a great book! I'm really glad my wife made me read it."
—Stephanie's husband

BODY MOVERS:
2 BODIES
FOR THE PRICE OF 1

Available the first week of July 2008 wherever books are sold!

www.MIRABooks.com

MSB2606

REQUEST YOUR
FREE BOOKS!

2 FREE NOVELS
FROM THE ROMANCE/SUSPENSE
COLLECTION PLUS 2 FREE GIFTS!

YES! Please send me 2 FREE novels from the Romance/Suspense Collection and my 2 FREE gifts (gifts are worth about $10). After receiving them, if I don't wish to receive any more books, I can return the shipping statement marked "cancel." If I don't cancel, I will receive 4 brand-new novels every month and be billed just $5.49 per book in the U.S. or $5.99 per book in Canada, plus 25¢ shipping and handling per book plus applicable taxes, if any*. That's a savings of at least 20% off the cover price! I understand that accepting the 2 free books and gifts places me under no obligation to buy anything. I can always return a shipment and cancel at any time. Even if I never buy another book from the Reader Service, the two free books and gifts are mine to keep forever.

185 MDN EF5Y 385 MDN EF6C

Name _____ (PLEASE PRINT)

Address _____ Apt. #

City _____ State/Prov. _____ Zip/Postal Code

Signature (if under 18, a parent or guardian must sign)

Mail to **The Reader Service:**
IN U.S.A.: P.O. Box 1867, Buffalo, NY 14240-1867
IN CANADA: P.O. Box 609, Fort Erie, Ontario L2A 5X3

Not valid to current subscribers to the Romance Collection,
the Suspense Collection or the Romance/Suspense Collection.

Want to try two free books from another line?
Call 1-800-873-8635 or visit www.morefreebooks.com.

* Terms and prices subject to change without notice. N.Y. residents add applicable sales tax. Canadian residents will be charged applicable provincial taxes and GST. Offer not valid in Quebec. This offer is limited to one order per household. All orders subject to approval. Credit or debit balances in a customer's account(s) may be offset by any other outstanding balance owed by or to the customer. Please allow 4 to 6 weeks for delivery. Offer available while quantities last.

Your Privacy: Harlequin is committed to protecting your privacy. Our Privacy Policy is available online at www.eHarlequin.com or upon request from the Reader Service. From time to time we make our lists of customers available to reputable third parties who may have a product or service of interest to you. If you would prefer we not share your name and address, please check here. ☐

BOB08R

CAMERON CRUISE

32408 THE COLLECTOR   ___ $6.99 U.S.   ___ $8.50 CAN.

(limited quantities available)

TOTAL AMOUNT $ _____
POSTAGE & HANDLING $ _____
($1.00 FOR 1 BOOK, 50¢ for each additional)
APPLICABLE TAXES* $ _____
TOTAL PAYABLE $ _____

(check or money order—please do not send cash)

To order, complete this form and send it, along with a check or money order for the total above, payable to MIRA Books, to: **In the U.S.:** 3010 Walden Avenue, P.O. Box 9077, Buffalo, NY 14269-9077; **In Canada:** P.O. Box 636, Fort Erie, Ontario, L2A 5X3.

Name: _____
Address: _____ City: _____
State/Prov.: _____ Zip/Postal Code: _____
Account Number (if applicable): _____

075 CSAS

*New York residents remit applicable sales taxes.
*Canadian residents remit applicable GST and provincial taxes.

MIRA®

www.MIRABooks.com   MCC0708BL